The Memphis struggle continues . . .

Welcome back to Memphis, where when the sun goes down, shit pops off. The three major female gangs ruling the gritty Mid-South are the **Queen Gs**—who keep it hood for the **Black Gangster Disciples.** The **Flowers**—who rule with the **Vice Lords.** And the **Crippettes**—mistresses of the **Grape Street Crips**.

Rules are: There are no damn rules. Survive the game the best way you know how. If you want to be king, show no remorse. Memphis's divas are as hard and ruthless as the men they hold down. Your biggest mistake is to get in their way.

Also by De'nesha Diamond

The Diva Series
Hustlin' Divas
Street Divas
Gangsta Divas
Boss Divas
King Divas

Anthologies
Heartbreaker (with Erick S. Gray and Nichelle Walker)
Heist (with Kiki Swinson)
Heist 2 (with Kiki Swinson)
A Gangster and a Gentleman (with Kiki Swinson)
Fistful of Benjamins (with Kiki Swinson)

Published by Kensington Publishing Corp.

Queen Divas

DE'NESHA DIAMOND

WITHDRAWN

Dafina
Books

KENSINGTON PUBLISHING CORP.
www.kensingtonbooks.com

DAFINA BOOKS are published by

Kensington Publishing Corp.
119 West 40th Street
New York, NY 10018

All Kensington titles, imprints, and distributed lines are available at special quantity discounts for bulk purchases for sales promotion, premiums, fund-raising, and educational or institutional use.

Special book excerpts or customized printings can also be created to fit specific needs. For details, write or phone the office of the Kensington Sales Manager: Kensington Publishing Corp., 119 West 40th Street, New York, NY 10018. Attn. Sales Department. Phone: 1-800-221-2647.

DAFINA and the Dafina logo Reg. U.S. Pat. & TM Off.

ISBN-13: 978-0-7582-9259-9
ISBN-10: 0-7582-9259-7
First Kensington Trade Paperback Printing: April 2016

eISBN-13: 978-0-7582-9260-5
eISBN-10: 0-7582-9260-0
First Kensington Electronic Edition: April 2016

10 9 8 7 6 5 4 3

Printed in the United States of America

Acknowledgments

This has been quite the adventure. I want to thank everyone who has supported me through a very trying time in my life to complete this series. To Granny, who inspires and watches me from up above. My sister Channon Kennedy—you're the best. My beautiful niece, Courtney—I love you. My number one fan, Evette Porter, and my favorite cousin in the whole wide world, Josephine Johnson—thanks for the laughs and the support.

To my patient editor Selena James and tell-it-like-it-is agent Marc Gerald, many thanks.

And to the fans who loved the series from day one. Thanks so much.

Best of Love,
De'nesha

Cast of Characters

Ta'Shara Murphy was once a straight-A student with dreams of getting the hell out of Memphis, but she took a detour from her dreams when she fell in love with Raymond "Profit" Lewis, the younger brother of Fat Ace. Ta'Shara has now moved to Ruby Cove and become Profit's official woman and a Vice Lord Flower. New trouble came when she stumbled across Profit kissing one of the deadliest chicks in the game: Lucifer. Ta'Shara then moved in with her new best friend Mackenzie "Mack" Grimes. There she learned the truth about her old best friend Essence's death and killed Qiana Barrett *and* LeShelle. It was still not enough to save her and Profit.

Willow "Lucifer" Washington is Fat Ace's right hand and as deadly as they come. Her latest vendetta has been against a small clique within the Grape Street Crippettes and the group's leader, Shariffa Rodgers. Her girls were responsible for killing Lucifer's brother, Juvon "Bishop" Washington. Lucifer systematically killed each member of Shariffa's crew despite her growing pregnant belly—until the night Shariffa decided to stop being the prey to become the hunter.

Captain Hydeya Hawkins is the new Memphis police captain unraveling the secrets and corruption of her predecessor. With King Isaac released from prison, it's a matter of time before her secret of being the infamous gangster's daughter reaches the chief of police's ears. But with the recent death of her husband, Drake, and a forced administrative leave, she's unprepared for one more shocker that slips out of Momma Peaches's Bible.

Mackenzie "Mack" Grimes is a Vice Lord Flower who, along with her sidekick Romil, befriended Ta'Shara Murphy once she became a full-fledged Flower. Seeing her girl Ta'Shara try to leave the Vice Lords' prince Profit, Mack breaks her own rules about staying out of people's business to put her nose directly where it doesn't belong in order to get them back together.

Chief Yvette Brown is the police chief, who's riding Captain Hawkins to solve the gang war violence without causing waves within the Memphis political system. She may have slept her way to the top and is currently the mistress of a top political official, but it doesn't mean that she doesn't care about fixing her city. The question remains: at what cost?

Lucille Washington is the widow of Darcell "Dough Man" Washington, the ex-mistress of the deceased super-cop Captain Melvin Johnson, and mother to Juvon "Bishop" Washington (deceased) and Willow "Lucifer" Washington.

Officer Wendi Hendrix is a beat cop currently having an affair with Lieutenant John Fowler. She was also a part of ex-captain Johnson's criminal ring. Recently the Vice Lord's head chief, Fat Ace, reached out to Fowler to restart their illegal gun trade. She is thrilled. The extra money will help her financially support her ailing mother. The only problem is that Lieutenant Fowler is no Captain Johnson. His inexperience leading this criminal endeavor could get them killed or locked up.

Cleopatra "Cleo" Blackmon is the older sister of Essence, Ta'Shara's deceased best friend. She and her boyfriend Kalief are trying to launch her in the music business. Things go left when she signs Diesel Carver as her new manager. Not only that, she now suspects her new manager of being responsible for his aunt Peaches's murder, orchestrating the shooting at her burial, and covering his butt by framing the Vice Lords to take the fall.

Nefertiti is Diesel's right hand chick and business manager, and is always down for whatever; that includes putting up with his wandering eyes when it comes to other women. As the streets of Memphis are set to explode, Titi finds herself smack in the middle of it all with a secret of her own.

Massacre

1

Mack

I've been in the game a long time as a Vice Lord Flower and I've seen my share of some fuckery, but I have to admit, even if it's just to myself, that nothing has prepared me for the shit that has gone down tonight. My girls Romil and Dime had joined forces to help the newest member of our crew, Ta'Shara Murphy, get her whacked-out sister, LeShelle, off of her back.

Why the fuck not? The bitch has spent the past year tryna murk Ta'Shara first, so it was the least that we could do. Actually, the order was: LeShelle ordered Ta'Shara gang raped for dating the brother of an enemy to her man. Ta'Shara attacked LeShelle with a pair of knitting needles at the mental hospital that her rape landed her in. LeShelle escaped police custody at the hospital to kill Ta'Shara's foster parents as revenge. And then the two were engaged in a contest to see who would do what next.

Romil, Dime and I agreed to help. Of course it was only after we were drawn into killing two from our set: Qiana Barrett and GG.

I'm still not trying to think about that shit too much. Their murders happened so fast, it's still hard to wrap my brain around it. There was something about Qiana making a deal with LeShelle.

First of all, LeShelle Murphy was the head bitch in charge of the Queen Gs, the female gang that holds down the Gangster Disciples and also the sworn enemies of our gang, the Vice Lord Flowers.

Qiana had no business making *any* deal with that crazy bitch so she got what she deserved. The deal was for LeShelle to kill Essence in return for Qiana killing her man's baby momma. But Qiana did more than kill a pregnant bitch; she sliced the girl's baby out and brought him over to Ruby Cove to raise—like a dumb ass.

So of course LeShelle Murphy cried foul and was threatening Qiana's life if she didn't return the baby.

The webs we weave when we practice to deceive.

After Qiana's confession, Ta'Shara attacked Qiana with a bottle of Johnnie Walker and then pushed the girl into a table loaded with candles, or maybe she tripped. I forget which. All I know is that the girl ran out of my living room looking like a human torch before she keeled over in my backyard. By the time I got the water hose working, the chick was dead.

GG, who'd brought Qiana's ass over to my crib for help with her LeShelle situation, then turned in a rage toward Ta'Shara, but she never made it back into the house before Dime put two slugs in the girl.

Dime claimed it was payback for Ta'Shara saving her life when a store owner went all jihad on them a few weeks back.

Regardless, this left my ass with two dead bodies in my house that we had to get rid of. Now, I'm not normally down for plugging our own, *but* Qiana did confess to killing a fellow Vice Lord Flower, Tyneisha, while doing a job for, of all people, LeShelle—so maybe there's a case to be made that the bitch deserved what she got. I don't know. Street politics can get tricky sometimes.

There was also one other piece of valuable information that Qiana gave before Ta'Shara lit her ass, and that was the exact place she was supposed to meet up with LeShelle. Knowing when and where to find that bitch was like hitting the lottery.

Still, when we rolled up into Hack's Crossing, the shit didn't go down like I thought it would. We had to play out a whole cat-and-mouse thing and take out two other Queen G bitches before we were able to snatch LeShelle. Ta'Shara's ass went straight psycho on our asses. She didn't kill her sister like a normal gangster bitch. She drew the shit out and tortured LeShelle while she was hogtied to a chair out in a warehouse building. Ta'Shara interrogated LeShelle and blasted holes into the girl each time the bitch said something that she didn't like. Ta'Shara ordered us to bring her boy Profit to the party because he needed to see the shit, too, since LeShelle had pumped a whole clip into his ass about a year back.

Profit wasn't the only thing that Ta'Shara wanted brought back to the warehouse. She wanted a can of gasoline. I thought she'd use it *after* she killed the girl. I never dreamed that she would light her ass up *while* LeShelle was still alive. The next few minutes were like something out of a horror movie. Ta'Shara doused LeShelle's helpless ass with the gasoline and tossed a match like she was unwanted trash.

LeShelle's screams are fucking with my ass. It was different from the way Qiana raced out of here. It's hard to describe it. The sound curdled my blood. I doubt that I'll ever forget that shit or the triumphant look on Ta'Shara's face.

There was no love lost between the sisters.

We dropped Ta'Shara off at Profit's crib alone. While he got rid of the human barbeque, Romil, Dime, and myself are holed up at my place, marinating our livers and snorting lines of this bomb-ass coke.

After my third line, I *still* can't get that bitch's screams out of my head.

"You gonna get that?" Dime asks, lifting up her big head from the arm of my couch.

"Uh?"

"Your phone. Don't you hear it ringing?"

"My phone?" I look around, slow to see my phone on the table next to the last line of coke. "Shit." I fumble with the screen and answer the call before it goes to voicemail.

"Yeah?"

"Wake your ass up," Ta'Shara says. "Come and get me."

"Where you at?"

"Where do you think?"

Fuck. She's really going to leave Profit. "You sure?"

"I called you, didn't I?"

Aww. Shit. I look around for where I last placed my car keys.

"What the fuck?" Ta'Shara snaps.

"What?"

"Not you," she says, sounding distracted. "Hey, Mack. Let me call you back."

Click.

"You still want me to come and get you?"

Silence.

"Hello? Ta'Shara, are you still there?"

No answer.

When I still don't hear anything, I pull the phone from my ear and see that the call has been disconnected. "Well, shit."

"Who was that?" Romil asks, slurring her words.

"Ta'Shara." I toss the phone aside and lower my head back against my favorite La-Z-Boy.

"*Now* what does she want?"

"A ride. Looks like she and Profit are really gonna call it quits."

"Shit. She's a damn fool," Romil says, shaking her head. "Hell, if I was a few years younger, my ass would give her a fucking run for her money."

I laugh. "You and me both."

Dime stands when her fantasy boo, Trey Songz, plays on the radio. The fact that her ass is off beat doesn't faze her in the least. "So, are you going to run over there and get her or what?"

The fact that Ruby Cove is less than five minutes away is a plus right now. "I guess. You girls rolling with me?"

Romil moans like she's reluctant to un-ass her chair. "Do we have to? I mean. Damn. How many favors can a bitch ask for in one night?"

"You ain't gotta go—but somebody should make sure that my ass don't fall asleep behind the wheel."

"I'll roll with you," Dime says, rolling her hips and snapping her fingers. I don't know whether she's trying to get tonight's wild episode out of her mind or if she's celebrating a couple of good kills tonight.

I'm more concerned about the changes I've witnessed in Ta'Shara. When we met her ass, she was like a scared rabbit about to take on some Queen Gs on lockdown in the county jail. Now she's dropping bodies like she was born into the life. I don't know why that shit bothers me—but it does. Deep down, I want to see *somebody* make it out of the game—alive. Ta'Shara doesn't belong in the life, but like it's been since the beginning of time, the streets change muthafuckas. There is no getting out.

"Well?" Dime stops dancing.

"Well, what?"

"Are we gonna ride through and pick T up?"

"Shit." My ass forgot just that damn quick. I push up out of my seat, dropping my phone and car keys on the floor.

Romil and Dime laugh. I flash them the bird before bending over to pick the items up. I'm far from being steady on my feet as I head to the door.

Dime asks, "Are you sure that your ass can even fucking drive?"

"I got this," I boast, struggling to put the key into the ignition.

"I'll drive," Dime declares, snatching the keys out of my hands and then shoving me.

"Fine. Fine. Fuck it. You drive." We have a big laugh as we exchange seats and then cruise toward Ruby Cove.

2

Lucifer

"**P**ush. Push," *Dr. Modi coaches from between my legs.*

Déjà vu. I'm once again submerged in pain as I push and grind to get his baby out of me, but no matter how much I grunt, curse, or scream, he refuses to budge. In fact it feels like he's spinning and clawing to stay in the womb.

"It's okay, Willow. You got this."

I look over. It's Bishop again—the left side of his head still missing. I grab his hand. "No. I can't do this. If he comes out, he'll die. You gotta help me."

Bishop smiles. "Don't be silly. Everything is going to be fine. I'll take good care of your baby."

What the hell is he talking about? He's dead. I release his hand and try to shove him away. "No. No. I don't want you taking care of my baby," I pant. More pain seizes me and I wonder if I'm going to survive this nightmare. "Awwwwww. Mason! Where is Mason?" I don't understand why he isn't here.

Tears splash down my face as I fight not to push, but my body has a mind of its own and the contractions are never ending. "No. Please. I don't want this. Make it stop!"

Bishops laughs. "It's a little too late for that."

"Push. Push. Push," Dr. Modi shouts.

"Aaaaargh. Shut the fuck up, you piece of shit muthafucka!" I growl at the smiling doctor between my legs. I hate his fucking face.

"Here comes the head," Dr. Modi cheers. "Push!"

"Aaaaargh! I swear to God, after I deliver this baby, I'm going to fuckin' kill you!"

The doctor keeps smiling. "Push!"

Sweat pours down my face and burns my eyes. I can't see a mutha-fuckin' thing. And I'm alone. I'm so fuckin' alone. This isn't how this is supposed to be. Mason is supposed to be here. Why would he leave me all alone?

"Don't worry." Another voice joins this madness. "I'm here."

I look to my left and am stunned by the face approaching the bed. "Dad?"

He smiles and lights up the room. "Hello, Willow."

Seeing him somehow cuts my pain in half. It's been so long and he looks exactly the same as the last time I saw him—right down to the bloody rose on his chest where he'd been shot. "Daddy, my baby. You got to help me save my baby."

"Shhh. Calm down. I know you got a lot on your plate, but you can't worry about that right now. You need to wake up."

"Can't worry? B-but he's going to die."

*"You **have** to wake up."*

"What?" I can't process what he's saying.

"There's somebody in the house—and they've come to kill you."

My eyes pop open in the semidarkness and catch the gleam of a steel blade as it makes a sweeping arc down onto the bed. Instinct kicks in. I roll to the other side of the bed instead of reaching for the gun tucked underneath the pillow.

The knife slices into the pillow-top mattress with a muted *thump*, ripping through the material.

I keep rolling and crash over the left side of the bed. The gravitational pull is cruel and I hit the hardwood floor with alarming force, belly first. Pain shoots through every part of my body. I struggle to block it out as my hand flails for the other piece in the nightstand, but my movements aren't as quick as normal.

"Grrrrrrrrrr!" My attacker leaps over the bed and grabs a fistful of my hair and tries to yank it out of my scalp.

Another bolt of pain rips through me while cartoon stars spin behind my eyes. Before I can get that shit to stop, my head is mashed into the wall. I make a big dent in that muthafucka because I taste bits of plaster. Balling my fist, I strike out and sock this bitch dead in her pussy—my first clue that my attacker is indeed a woman.

She grunts, but the punch has less effect than if my attacker had been the opposite sex. It's enough for her to release her hold on my head for a millisecond, and I'm able to sweep my arm out and hit those knees.

She drops like a stone.

I spring up on this bitch, but I lose a second when something warm rushes down my inner thigh. A punch hits me square in my jaw, knocking my ass to the left, where I trip over the foot of the bed.

More cartoon stars. *This bitch is pissing me off.*

My attacker launches toward me again. I block her first two blows, keeping my elbows together, like Bishop taught me. When I come out from behind an arm shield, I wail on this bitch like a heavyweight champion. In no time, I pin her to the floor, my fist as bloody as my thighs.

She whimpers.

While I got this bitch under the moonlight spilling through the window, I snatch the wool mask from her head. When her hair stops tumbling out, I'm shocked. *Shariffa?*

This bitch ain't this muthafuckin' bold. But there's not a damn thing wrong with my eyes.

Enraged, I wrap my hands around Shariffa's neck and squeeze with everything I got. "You stupid bitch!" My arms tremble as my grip tightens.

"ACK. GACK." She chokes, clawing at my hands.

"That's right. Let me hear death rattle around in your chest. When you're gone, I'm going to take my fucking time peeling and slicing your ass from your head to your toes."

"ACK. GAAACK."

"There's not going to be anything left of your treacherous ass. I'm going to make damn sure of that shit."

"ACK. GAAAACK!"

This bitch is seconds away from passing from this world to the other when an ungodly pain shoots up from my abdomen and straight to my brain.

"Aaaaaargh!" The scream is out of my throat before I have a chance to stop it. Then it happens again and I pitch over and hit the floor, gripping my belly.

I'm only mildly aware of Shariffa coughing and wheezing next to me.

Pull it together. Pull it together. But I can't. *The baby!*

Shariffa scrambles for the knife.

Somehow I swing out an arm and grab her ankle. She trips with a loud *thump!*

Desperate, Shariffa kicks me with her free leg. My head. My neck—and then a firm kick straight to my belly.

"Aaaaaaargh!" *This dirty bitch.* But she's going to win this battle. The knife glistens in the moonlight before it makes its second swinging arc straight toward my baby.

BAM!

The bedroom door is kicked open.

Shariffa jumps.

POW! POW! POW!

She is lifted into the air as the bullets slam into her, and then she collapses into a bloody heap beside me.

"Lucifer!" Ta'Shara rushes into the room and drops down beside me. "Lucifer, are you all right?"

I want to answer her, but instead I tumble into darkness.

3

Ta'Shara

Oh *shit.* I stare down at Lucifer and at the carnage around her
moonlit bedroom with a gun still clutched in my hands. Lucifer
is barely recognizable with her long black hair matted on both
sides of her head. Her pink satin nightgown is ripped and
bloody. Her gigantic pregnant belly protrudes straight up and
is splattered with bits of brain from the crazy bitch I dumped
three bullets into when I stormed in here. I didn't even have
time to think before pulling the trigger. I reacted . . . again. I've
been a Vice Lord Flower for just a couple of months and I've
already dropped my third body.

Fuck. It was all by chance that I even saw the bitch creeping around outside of the house. If I weren't in the middle of
leaving my man, Profit, again, I wouldn't have seen shit.

It's bad enough that hours ago I finally put an end to my
evil-ass sister, LeShelle. I'd dumped at least a dozen slugs into
her before dousing her ass in gasoline and lighting her up.
Given that the fire was the exact same way LeShelle killed my
best friend, Essence, and then my foster parents, Tracee and
Reggie Douglas, it was a fitting ending for the crazy bitch
masquerading as my sister.

And now this shit. Can't I catch a break?

After a full minute, my mind remains blank on what the hell I'm supposed to do next—but I have to do *something*.

Is she breathing? Kneeling beside Lucifer, I place two fingers against her neck to check for a pulse.

I can't find one.

Oh God, no.

I check again, frantically sliding my fingers along the groove between her neck and her collarbone. Between my own hammering heartbeats, I detect a slight thumping against the pads of my fingers. I almost pass out in relief. Then I remember that Lucifer and I aren't exactly on the best of terms. Once upon a time, I actually looked up to the deadliest gangsta diva in Memphis's mean streets, but that was *before* I'd caught her kissing my man. Now, I don't care too much for her. *So why in the hell did I save her?*

Lucifer's stomach moves. I inch back and nearly trip over the brainless girl behind me. *Fuck.* With horror and fascination, I watch as Lucifer's belly rolls and drops lower. *Is the baby trying to get out?*

Lucifer emits a low, winding moan that makes the hairs on my arms and the back of my neck stand straight up. As she comes to, she clutches at her moving belly. In no time at all, her moans deepen into a low guttural roar. Glancing down between her legs, I note the vibrant red blood on her thighs glowing in the moonlight.

My heart leaps up into my throat and I'm paralyzed with fear. I've been through a lot of shit in my seventeen years on this earth, but this shit right here is *waaay* out of my fucking league. I don't know shit about delivering babies, not to mention one whose mother looks like she's on the edge of death herself.

Lucifer stops roaring and starts sucking vast amounts of air through her teeth. When she finally manages to lift her fevered gaze toward me, her face is blanketed with fear and pain. "H-help me."

I blink. I'm willing to bet everything I own that Lucifer has never asked for help from another bitch a single day in her life. It's gotta be tearing her up inside that she must ask me, of all people, right now. Taking a step back, the memory of Profit locking his lips against hers flashes inside my head. It reminds me of the long knife of betrayal still buried in the center of my back.

Lucifer said that *he* kissed *her*.

Profit said it was a mistake.

The shit still hurts like a muthafucka—and it is the reason my ass was leaving.

"Please," Lucifer adds. "H-help."

I want to tell her that I've already helped her ass once tonight—this other shit she might need to get someone else. I take another step back. However, watching the baby inch its way even lower, my conscience makes it clear that there is no way I could leave her like this. *Push all the bad shit aside and do what you gotta do.*

"Okay. Tell me what you want me to do," I say, sweating.

"Maybe you should boil some water or something."

"For what?" My confusion annoys her.

"I don't know. Isn't that what they always say on TV when a woman goes into labor? They always ask for towels and boiling water."

"Oh." *And then what?* "So . . . you want me to boil some water?"

"Yes . . . no . . . I mean, I don't know." At the next bolt of pain that flashes across her face, Lucifer bears down and growls through it. After an eternity, she relaxes and pants as if she's finished running a marathon.

Lucifer looks up. "Whatever you do, please don't just stand there like a statue."

"Okay. Okay." I force myself to breathe, but my nerves are far from calm. "Lucifer, hang on. Don't you think about dying on me," I tell her and then look around the room again.

The phone. I race to hit the bedroom's light switch so I can search around for a landline. The horrific scene in the room is even worse under the harsh bedroom lights. Blood paints almost everything in the room: the walls, the floor, and even the bedsheets.

"Aaaargh!" Lucifer's deepening growl sounds demonic.

I search around like a deer caught in headlights. "Where the fuck is the phone?" I glance back at Lucifer to see whether she can help me out.

Sweat pours down her face. It's all she can do to suck in quick sips of air and remain conscious.

Hell. I don't even know what the fuck I did with my cell phone, probably dropped it somewhere outside when I rushed into the house. *There's got to be a phone downstairs.* "Lucifer, I'll be right back," I shout. I race out of the room and take the stairs two at a time. At the bottom of the staircase, I find a portable unit sitting in its base on an end table by the sofa. I snatch it up and punch in 9-1-1.

As soon as the operator comes on the line, I blurt, "I need an ambulance. I have a pregnant woman unconscious and bleeding out."

"Calm down, miss. Can you tell me your name?"

"Yes. It's Ta'Shara Murphy. Please. Hurry. Someone broke in here and tried to kill her. I shot the intruder but—"

"Miss, please. Slow down. Help is on the way. Did you say that you shot someone?"

"Yes. Damn it! Hurry! She's lost a lot of blood." Vaguely, I'm aware of something rumbling outside. Sounds like a couple of foot soldiers cruising down Ruby Cove in their loud-ass hoopties. It's still possible help. I head toward the window.

"The police and ambulance are on the way, ma'am," the operator says, "but I need to get a little more information from you."

I nod and reach to peek through the venetian blinds.

"SIX POPPIN', FIVE DROPPIN'," voices shout from

outside. A second later, bullets fly into the house. Before I can think or move away from the window, I'm lifted off my feet and thrown back. Pain sears through me as the onslaught continues and the house turns into a war zone.

As I collapse on the floor, my legs twist beneath me.

"Fuck you, you dirty muthafuckas!" another ominous voice shouts from outside.

Six poppin'. The Gangster Disciples? How in the hell did they make it onto Ruby Cove?

The war between the Vice Lords and Gangster Disciples stretches so far back that no one living or locked down remembers how the shit got started in the first place. For the longest time, my ass never wanted to get involved in this street shit, but I was dragged in, kicking and screaming, when my sister, LeShelle, became the wifey of Python, chief of the Gangster Disciples. By her locking down that ugly, reptile-looking muthafucka, people viewed me as Gangster Disciple property, too. Everything went left when I met and fell in love with Profit—who happened to be the younger brother to the chief of the Vice Lords.

When I refused to give Profit up, LeShelle and a group of her GD minions kidnapped Profit and me on our prom night. LeShelle stood there and watched as those dirty muthafuckas took turns raping me. After that, she put seventeen bullets in Profit and left him for dead. I ended up in a mental hospital, where they kept me stoned out of my mind for months. When Profit pulled through and my foster parents managed my release, LeShelle and I were right back at it.

Then she murdered the Douglases.

It was a matter of time before LeShelle and I went head-to-head. When it happened, LeShelle didn't think I had the balls to take her out—but she didn't know just how far she had pushed me.

The bitch is gone, but the Vice Lord and Gangster Disciple's war continues.

"Ta'Shara! What the fuck is going on down there?" Lucifer shouts.

I lay gasping on the floor. My shock delays the pain, but only briefly. Before I know it, the entire right side of my body feels as if it's on fire. I watch as my own blood bloom across my white T-shirt. When a bullet grazes my left temple, I realize that I don't have time to work the shit out inside my head. I have to get out of the damn way.

Rat-a-tat-tat-tat
Rat-a-tat-tat-tat

I pull in a deep breath, but the shit makes the pain worse. Bullets zip and ping around my head. Then one sears into my back.

"Ta'Shara! Are you still down there?" Lucifer shouts.

The world spins. Nothing is real any more. I don't have enough energy to shout back. Alarm bells goes off when I realize I can't feel my legs. Still, I drag my body across the floor—away from the living room's front window. Stabbed at least a million times by broken glass and splintered wood, I struggle to remain focused. I certainly don't want to die here—not like this.

Profit's face flashes before my eyes. Not the slim pretty boy I met that one fateful day at the mall, but the handsome, chiseled, and virile Vice Lord soldier who broke my heart. An hour ago, I couldn't imagine *ever* forgiving him for kissing Lucifer. Now I wish that he would rush through the front door and save the day.

Rat-a-tat-tat-tat
Rat-a-tat-tat-tat

From the corner of my eye, I spot the phone and the gun that was knocked out of my hands, several feet away from me. The idea of crawling to it exhausts me. But I have to do something.

Rat-a-tat-tat-tat
Rat-a-tat-tat-tat

A wave of tears soothes my burning eyes, but I manage to make it halfway across the living room when the gunfire stops.

I take the lull in ricocheting bullets to collapse in a pool of my own blood. However, it's the pain that I can't get away from. I wish that I could crawl out of my skin.

Clunk! Clunk!

My head snatches up at the noise coming from the top floor. *Lucifer.*

How in the hell did I forget about her—and the baby?

Rat-a-tat-tat-tat

Rat-a-tat-tat-tat

Panting and sweating like a pig, I pull myself up into sitting position. Despite that success, the room won't stop spinning.

The baby.

It's the idea of an innocent life hanging in the balance that prevents me from drowning in self-pity right now. Never mind that the child picked the wrong night to come into this dangerous world. Then again, when is a safe time?

Rat-a-tat-tat-tat

Rat-a-tat-tat-tat

Are those muthafuckas getting closer? I swear someone is shooting right near the front door.

Bam! The front door explodes open. Booted feet race inside the house.

Rat-a-tat-tat-tat

Rat-a-tat-tat-tat

An explosion of more firepower does a number on my eardrums, but I only have a couple of seconds to decide on a play. Both the gun and the phone are still out of reach. *But I can't move my legs.* Within seconds of them rushing into the living room, I figure my best option is to play dead. Since I'm already in a pool of my own blood. Quickly, I flop back down onto the floor and close my eyes. Through the mesh of my lashes, I recognize the first man through the door.

Python. The six-foot-five giant storms inside, cloaked in all black except for the blue flag hanging from his back pocket. He looks like he's just been spat out of hell. His muscular arms are boulders and are tatted with so much ink that you can't make head or tail of what they all are. Black as sin and ugly as shit, LeShelle really knew how to pick them. Behind him rush in three other men—all equally terrifying.

I hold my breath and pray.

The world shifts into slow motion. Though I'm trying my best to lie still, I fear one of these thugs will fire off another bullet to make sure that I'm dead.

"Who is that bitch?" a voice asks.

There's a long pause in which my lungs begs for air.

"If I'm not mistaken, it sort of looks like LeShelle's sister, Ta'Shara," Python answers, standing over me. With his black Timberlands, he nudges my leg to see if I respond. I stay in character like an Oscar-winning actress.

Rat-a-tat-tat-tat
Rat-a-tat-tat-tat

The bullets from outside again.

It takes everything I have not to flinch or open my eyes to check out what the fuck is going on.

"Hurry up! These bumblebee niggas are coming out the woodwork!"

Another explosion of gunfire erupts. It feels like my eardrums are bleeding inside of my head.

"Everybody split up and search this bitch. I know that muthafucka got to be around here someplace!"

Who the fuck is that? The voice isn't familiar, but he's definitely an older dude. *But why is he giving orders instead of Python?*

Rat-a-tat-tat-tat
Rat-a-tat-tat-tat

"Hurry!"

Everyone peels off. Heavy footsteps rush up the stairs. Seconds later, more gunfire.

Bam! Bam! Bam!

Lucifer! I steal a small sip of air and risk opening my eyes.

Rat-a-tat-tat-tat

What the hell is going on up there?

"Yo! What the fuck?" Python thunders from above.

Rat-a-tat-tat-tat

Rat-a-tat-tat-tat

"Move your ass!" the OG barks as he takes on the VL soldiers closing in on the house.

"We got a situation up here," Python roars back.

"Handle it!" The older gangster continues blasting at the Vice Lords.

My heart drops as I steal another sip of air. There's not much I can do for Lucifer . . . but pray.

4

Lucifer

"SIX POPPIN', FIVE DROPPIN'."

Rat-a-tat-tat-tat

Rat-a-tat-tat-tat

"What the fuck?" The Gangster Disciples. How in the hell did they get past security on Ruby Cove? Then I remember: My man, Mason, likely took the bulk of our soldiers with him to meet our new arms dealer, Fowler. After the ambush of our last distributer, the Angels of Mercy motorcycle club, Mason wouldn't risk walking into another trap. Only problem is that our enemies caught wind of the light security and decided to strike.

Panic, an emotion I'm not accustomed to, seizes me. I'm not in any condition to go into battle. I've never needed Mason more than right now. Hell, I've never needed *anyone* more than I do right now. What if I really have to deliver this baby alone—next to this dead bitch?

Damn it. I knew shit was going to pop off when the news broke about King Isaac, the ex-chief of the Gangster Disciples, returning home from prison. While he was serving his dime bid, his stepson-slash-nephew, Python, became the head nigga with the Gangster Disciples. The recent revelations of Python and Mason actually being biological brothers has changed nothing, especially since they are now operating under the mis-understanding that Mason killed Python's beloved Aunt Peaches.

Rat-a-tat-tat-tat

The windows behind me explode and shards of broken glass rain over me. Belatedly, I cover my head and press my body against the floor.

My baby shifts and a bolt of pain shoots through my body. My attention snaps toward the door. "Ta'Shara! What the fuck is going on down there?" I lie still and strain my ears to listen for the teenager's response, but there's none. "Ta'Shara! Are you still down there?"

Rat-a-tat-tat-tat.

I can't hear shit.

Now what? I look around, but there's nothing here but this dead bitch who got me in this weakened condition in the first place. My anger renewed, I scoot over a couple of inches so I can shoot out a foot and kick Shariffa one last time in the head. However, my toes bend at contact with her mushy dome. *Did I just break my shit?* My irrational anger has me wishing that I could shoot the bitch again myself.

Where the fuck did she even get the balls to roll up in my crib to try and take me out? Surely after I chopped up most of her small crew of Crippettes, she should've known better.

Shariffa and her purple-flagging minions were responsible for my brother Bishop's death. Before that, they were a con-stant thorn in the Vice Lords' side while we raged our street war with the Gangster Disciples. The Crippettes took the op-portunity to knock over a number of the Vice Lords' chop-and trap-houses. Our lack of response to those small attacks gave these Kool-Aid bitches a big enough set of balls to hit Da Club, one of the Vice Lords' main establishments. Bishop, along with his poker partners in the back of the club, ended up being smack-dab in the middle of their hit and got their heads blown off.

I smirk at Shariffa's brainless body. *Karma is a bitch.*

"Aargh!" I clutch at my moving belly. *I'm not ready. Please, God. I'm not ready.*

My body's response to that move is to hit me with a one-two punch that literally snatches my breath away. The pain is never ending. After all the battles that I've been through in these streets, it's the thought of actually delivering a baby that terrifies me.

Tears splash down my face. Within seconds they're like a river that I don't even attempt to stop. Crying is not my thing, but I'm at a loss at what else to do.

Rat-a-tat-tat-tat

Rat-a-tat-tat-tat

Mason Junior delivers a fierce kick to my kidneys. To further embarrass myself, I piss on the floor. "I don't fucking believe this shit." To my surprise, a strong part of me wants to submit, lie here and accept whatever my fate might be. Caring about what happens takes up too much energy. That shit is so fucking tempting . . . until I hear the front door of the house kicked in.

Bam!

I spring upwards using some reserve of strength that I didn't even know I had. I take another glance around for a weapon. I know that there is a gun tucked underneath one of the bed pillows—but there's no way I can get to it. There's another one in the nightstand and two more in the chest of drawers—but I can't reach any of those either.

"This can't be happening," I say, stressing as I attempt to pull myself together. I push aside the fact that my baby is splitting me in half and force myself to figure a way out of this fucked-up situation.

The only weapon that's even close is Shariffa's Browning knife—and I learned a long time ago to never bring a knife to a gunfight.

Think. Think. Think.

That's hard to do when terror overtakes you like a tsunami and then drowns out logical and strategic thinking.

My gaze falls back onto Shariffa, and I have a sudden thought: There's not a gangster bitch walking Memphis's mean streets who doesn't strap on more than one weapon, especially when she's going into battle.

Inspired, I struggle to inch my pain-riddled body across my bedroom floor. As I reach her, male voices travel up the stairs.

Hurry. Hurry. Hurry.

I roll Shariffa onto her back, ignore that she's missing half of her face, and pat her ass down. I grope under her titties, slide my hands down her waist and over her hips. I find what I'm looking for strapped around her left calf: a .38—fully loaded.

Heavy footsteps rush up the staircase.

I unclick the safety. With the weapon in my hand, my panic shuts down and the blood in my veins turn ice-cold. Within seconds, Python's reptilian ass materializes and I squeeze the trigger.

Bam! Bam! Bam!

Python's reflexes are fast as fuck. He dives out of the way and then returns fire, his semiautomatic spraying bullets in my direction.

I drop back, trying to duck. All but one bullet misses me. More pain shoots up my arm as the .38 flies out of my hand. Once I'm disarmed, Python takes another tentative step into my bloody bedroom.

His gaze zooms to the body lying next to me. Recognition slams into him.

"Yo! What the fuck?" he thunders.

I can only imagine what must be running through his mind at seeing one of his ex-wifeys sprawled across my floor with half of her head missing. Despite the damage to my hand, I throw my pain-riddled body toward the gun that had flown out of it.

Rat-a-tat-tat-tat

Rat-a-tat-tat-tat

Bullets slam into the floorboard in front of me and I am repelled backwards a second before I'm nailed by another bullet in the center of my hand.

"Aaagh!"

"Ah. Ah. Ah," Python warns before inching farther into the room. This time his weapon and his attention are trained on me. "Where's your nigga at?" he growls.

"Don't you mean your brother?" I challenge.

Rage flares in Python's black eyes while his square jaw hardens like cement. "That ugly shit-stain ain't nobody to me but one of the walking dead," he sneers. "And I'm going to fix that shit soon enough. Now where the fuck is he?"

"Fuck you," I hiss, and thrust up my chin. "I ain't telling you shit."

"Move your ass!" a man barks from downstairs.

"We got a situation up here," Python roars back.

"Handle it!" the man shouts.

Watching Python erase the small distance between us, I quickly put together the identity of the man who's barking orders. *King Isaac.* No way my ass is getting out of this shit alive.

Python places the barrel of his weapon against my forehead. "Are you seriously going to make me ask your ass the question a third time?"

I press my head forward, ignoring the way the barrel digs into my skull. "Fuck. You. Do I need to tell *you* that a third time?" Our gazes lock in a showdown. Surely this muthafucka don't think my ass is going to beg him to spare my life. I knew what the fuck this life was about when I joined the Vice Lords. And I've put down plenty of begging niggas in my lifetime to know that the shit ain't cute nor does it help the situation.

Python blinks and then sweeps his black gaze across my belly where my unborn child visibly wiggles beneath my nightshirt.

"Python! We got to roll," King Isaac shouts up the stairs. "We can't hold these cockroaches off much longer."

Someone else rushes up the staircase. "Whoa," a miscellaneous nigga gasps when he reaches my bedroom door. I'm sure he's assuming that Python put down Shariffa.

"Boss, we really gotta go! Their reinforcements are descending fast."

If Python hears his boy, he gives no indication. His horrific features remain a hard, unchangeable mask of contempt.

"C'mon. Let's get this shit over with," I snap, pressing my head even harder into the barrel. "Shoot me." The pain ricocheting up my body has me thinking, for a moment, that a bullet would be a welcome reprieve. Hell. Anything would be better than the torture that my unborn child is putting me through.

Python lowers his weapon. "Grab her," he tells his man.

His boy and I look at Python, confused.

"What?" the soldier asks.

Python steps back as disgust reflects in his face. "You heard me. We're taking her with us."

His man rushes forward.

"Fuck you. I'm not going anywhere with you." I slap his soldier's grabbing hands away from me.

"Just snatch her up," Python snaps. When his man is unable to get ahold of me, Python steps forward again, leans down and crashes his fist across my jaw.

My head rockets backwards as an explosion of cartoon stars spin like a carousel behind my eyes. I'm aware of being jerked up and tossed over a muscled shoulder. The pain in my body accelerates and every muscle, tendon, and even atom seizes with mind-altering cramps.

I black out—but only for a moment. When I come to, the broad back that I'm staring down at has reached the bottom of my staircase.

Rat-a-tat-tat-tat

Rat-a-tat-tat-tat

"We're going to have to make a run for it," King Isaac shouts.

I turn my head in the direction of his voice, but it's not the infamous gangster that catches my attention. There, in a pool of blood in the entrance of the living room, lies a motionless Ta'Shara. *Shit.*

"Let's go!"

My kidnapper takes off running from the house.

Rat-a-tat-tat-tat

Rat-a-tat-tat-tat

Bullets fly all around us, a few whispering by my head as I kick and pound on Python's back. It's no use. Before I know it, I'm slung into the backseat of an SUV. Thoughts of further rebellion are shut down when I spring to attack, only to be elbowed so hard across the face that I reel backwards. My head connects with the side window, knocking me out cold.

5

Mack

Gunfire has a way of jolting muthafuckas out of a high and slamming them back to reality. Shit happens so quick that the world tilts on its axis. This shit isn't one or two shots from random niggas, popping off some bullshit. The gunfire that we hear as we approach Ruby Cove is long, sustained, rapid fire.

"What the fuck?" Dime asks a second before bullets puncture the windshield. Her foot comes off the accelerator and her hands off the steering wheel to shield her face.

I lunge for the wheel before we run up onto a curb. "What the fuck, Dime?" I shout, pissed at her inability to protect our lives. Though I've grabbed the wheel, we still go up on a curb. Thank God I'm able to get us off it before we smack head-on into a utility pole.

"Sorry. Sorry!" she shouts, taking back control of the wheel.

"You got it?" I double-check, not sure whether I'm ready to trust her ass again.

"Yeah. Yeah. I got it."

Rat-a-tat-tat-tat

Rat-a-tat-tat-tat

More lead slams into my ride. The passenger-side window

explodes into a million pieces while the hood pops up and blocks our line of vision.

"Shit!" Dime slams on the brakes without checking to see if anyone is driving behind us. At the sound of another set of brakes squealing in protest, I twist in my seat in time to see a black Lincoln plow into us.

Crash.

Flying backward, I bang into the dashboard. The car horn blares a second time when Dime's head smacks into the center of the steering wheel. When she lifts it, there's a visible dent in the center of her forehead.

"Shit, Mack. Are you all right?"

Romil cries out. I'd forgotten that she was passed out in the back. She's no longer lying on the seat but crumpled on the floorboard, unable to distinguish which way is up. Still, the gunfire continues. My shock wears off and I push away from the dashboard and then dive head first between Dime's legs so that I can search the floorboards under the driver's seat for a weapon. When I climb back up with my Glock in hand, I click off the safety and scan the perimeter.

"SIX POPPIN', FIVE DROPPIN'," the unmistakable war cry rings out.

No these niggas ain't. The Gangster Disciples laying assault on our muthafuckin' territory? What the fuck? I can't remember these muthafuckas ever being this goddamn bold.

My mind flies to our murking LeShelle's ass tonight. Have the Gangster Disciples found out about the shit that fast? Is this a revenge assault? Had Profit gotten caught dumping the body? My mind reaches for any scenario that would make some sense of this shit. At the end of the day, the whys don't matter. The only thing to do now is to stand our ground and fight back.

The driver's-side window shatters and Dime's head explodes like a watermelon. Brain and blood splatters everywhere and for a few seconds I'm in shock again.

Romil climbs up from off the floor, notices Dime's body slumped over the wheel, and screams.

Rat-a-tat-tat-tat

Rat-a-tat-tat-tat

"Shut the fuck up," I shout, pushing Dime's body away from me so that I can have access to return fire.

Pow! Pow! Pow! I aim for any damn thing moving. I don't give a shit.

Romil shuts up and dives back onto the floorboard. It was probably best, since she doesn't have a weapon. A gangster bitch no-no.

The car behind us is also filled with Vice Lords, and they exit their vehicle and engage in the firefight as well. I can tell that we're on the losing side. We're outmanned and out-gunned. There are too many of these muthafuckas blasting and too many of us dropping dead on the street.

This shit can't be happening. I fire my last round at one GD soldier with a big head and miss. *Fuck.* I scramble around in vain for another clip. In my mind's eye I can see it lying on the coffee table next to the mirror with the last line of cocaine. Our asses are sitting ducks out here. There ain't shit that we can do about it.

"What now?" Romil asks.

"The fuck if I know." More bullets slam into the side of my vehicle. By some miracle, our asses weren't hit.

"They got Lucifer!" somebody shouts.

What? I cast my gaze to Lucifer's crib and I catch those muthafuckas slinging her ass into the backseat of one of the SUVs. "Is that who I think it is?" I don't know why I asked—there's no mistaking Python.

"The fuck?" My heart, which was already beating double time, goes harder. This does have something to do with LeShelle. Python is kidnapping our head bitch in retaliation.

Fuck. Fuck. Fuck. We have to do something, but what? The

only thing we can do is watch these dirty muthafuckas peel out while spraying bullets in every direction. "Duck."

I hit the floor. I avoid looking in Dime's brainless direction as more bullets hit the car. The rancid scent of burning rubber fills my nostrils. When I glance up again, I see the red glow of the SUV's taillights. I scramble out of the car. Out on the street I look around, amazed at the sheer destruction. There are piles of bodies lying everywhere.

"Can you fucking believe this shit?" Romil asks, awed.

I shake my head in dismay. I even entertain the notion that this is all a bad dream and I'm still back at the crib, trippin' on some bad coke. In the distance, the wails of police sirens pierce the night.

"You think those muthafuckas got Fat Ace?" Romil asks.

I have no idea, but start jogging toward Lucifer's crib to check. Her front door is still wide open, but it's not Fat Ace we see when we rush inside.

"Oh my God. Ta'Shara!"

6

Wendi

"I have a bad feeling about this." I check my watch again. "They're late."

My police lieutenant and on-the-down-low white boyfriend, John Fowler, looks around the perimeter of this old abandoned factory for any sign of the people who are supposed to be meeting our small crew of six tonight. If he's worried, he doesn't show it. Then again, he's a master at remaining cool under pressure.

I am nervous as shit.

This is the first time that we're doing a deal like this on our own. In the past, Captain Melvin Johnson ran the illegal arms shipments. He had all the street connections and knew the military arms dealers personally. Not only that, but he knew and controlled this city with an iron fist. Well, for a while anyway. The past two years, things have spun out of control, but the money is what keeps drawing us back. Good damn money. The kind of money that makes pinning on these tin badges and putting up with shitty police paychecks tolerable.

Now Captain Johnson is six feet under, and all of us who worked with him miss the extra cash. Before Johnson was placed in the ground, police chief Yvette Brown promoted

Hydeya Hawkins to take his place. Hawkins is cool, but she's a pit bull with a bug up her ass about cops following the law. Instead of closing Johnson's case after finding his murderer dead, she kept snooping until she discovered the millions of dollars the ex-captain had foolishly stashed throughout his house.

Hawkins freaked everyone out when she remained determined to get to the bottom of the source of Johnson's money My ass included. I kept expecting that any day she would put all the pieces of the puzzle together and slap handcuffs on all of us.

Thank God Captain Hawkins's husband was recently killed and Chief Brown forced her onto administrative leave. We all can breathe again. When the Vice Lords reached out to Fowler, we were excited to get back to business and stack more paper.

"What time is it now?" I ask.

"It's midnight."

Fowler pulls out a pack of cigarettes. It's the first time he has shown concern about these people being late. "I thought that you quit."

"I have."

He plants one cigarette between his lips and pushes in the truck's lighter. While he waits for it to heat up, he looks at his cell phone as if to double-check if it is working.

The lighter pops and he reaches down to place it against the tip of the cigarette.

"Maybe something came up," I suggest. "How much longer do you want to give them?" I can tell by the way he pulls a deep breath that my questions are getting on his nerves, but I can't help it. I get chatty when I'm nervous. When Fowler doesn't bother to answer my question, I press my lips together, determined to keep them closed. Another five minutes pass and my mouth unglues itself. "Maybe they—"

"Goddamn it, Wendi! I don't fucking know! All right? Now can you please shut the fuck up? I can't think!"

"All right! Fine! Fuck!" I shrink back into my seat with my jaw clamped tight.

Fowler takes one look at me and exhales a long puff of smoke. "I'm sorry," he says. "I didn't mean to snap."

I refuse to look at him.

Fowler leans across the truck and then drapes his arm around my shoulder. "Forgive me?" he asks.

Since my anger is the only thing that has softened him toward me, I hold on to it for a while longer. But then he takes my chin between his fingers and forces me to look at him.

"I'm sorry," he insists.

I melt. "It's fine," I whisper back.

A pair of headlights sweeps across us and we shift back into business mode.

"It's them," Fowler says. A smile hooks his lips.

Four black SUVs roll to a stop directly in front of us. The fact that they leave their headlights on bright is a dick move, but I know that neither of us will say anything about it.

We sit, looking like deer caught in headlights while waiting to see who'll make the first move.

Finally the Vice Lords shut off their lights, but no one makes a move to get out of their vehicles.

I glance over at John, but hold in a question for fear he'll snap again.

Another minute passes. I shift around in my seat. *Are we going to do this shit or not?*

John's patience must've reached its breaking point, too, because he hasn't said or signaled anything to me before exiting the vehicle. I stay planted in my seat with hope in my heart that everything will go as planned.

Once John is out in the open, the driver's-side door of the vehicle in front of us opens.

Here we go. I make the sign of the cross and pray for the best.

I was part of a number of these deliveries when Captain Johnson ran the operation. I recognize the large, muscular frame of the notorious Vice Lord leader, Fat Ace. But there is also something different. Has he lost weight? Are those burns all over his face? I lean forward to get a better look. It's hard, given that it's past midnight and it's dark as hell in this lot.

John and Fat Ace greet each other with a shoulder bump and handshake. Their words are nothing but a low mumble, and I find myself dying to know what is being said, but until John gives the signal, I don't make a move.

After two minutes stretch my sanity to the limits, Fat Ace turns and signals to another person in his SUV. The passenger door opens and a tall, younger man steps out of the vehicle carrying a black duffel bag.

"Um. How are you doing?" I say in my internal Wendy Williams voice. My gaze sweeps over the guy a couple of times with more than mild interest. Sure. I have a few years on the kid, but I wouldn't mind teaching the young buck a thing or two in the bedroom.

The duffel bag is dropped onto the hood of our truck and then unzipped in order for John to take a look inside. He grabs a couple of stacks and then flips through the crisp hundred-dollar bills for a quick check. Satisfied that the money is all there, he zips up the bag, does another unnecessary handshake, and then turns back toward the truck with the money.

John gives me the nod and I bolt out of the truck and hurry to the back. More car doors open and a crowd of Vice Lords and a few of our guys hop out of their vehicles and en-circle me as I unlock the back of our white unmarked truck. Once I get my trembling fingers to unlock and roll up the metal door, I step aside for the men to hop into the back and inspect the various crates upon crates of military-grade weapons.

An animated John hops into the back, too, and he proceeds

to give a tutorial about the latest and greatest weapons and ammunition he's secured from our supplier. He's like a kid in a candy shop.

I, however, am still a nervous wreck while I stand next to the kid. I may be mistaken, but he doesn't seem interested in the whole deal. I catch him looking off at nothing a few times.

Suddenly, phones go off all around. One by one, the Vice Lords scoop out their cells and look down at the screens. Some tap each other on the shoulder and point to whatever message they're reading.

Something is up.

A knot forms in the pit of my stomach and rolls around. I glance up at John, who's busy going on about the firepower of a weapon. I struggle to think of a way to catch his attention, but his gaze never once swings in my direction.

I cough.

Nothing.

More phones buzz.

I cough again.

Still nothing.

When my coughing and hacking sounds like consumption, the young blood to my right reaches over and pats me on the back.

"You cool?" he asks.

Before I can answer, his phone trills. "Hold on a sec." He scoops his phone out of his pants pocket. After a quick glance at the screen, his golden complexion pales even in this dim light.

I glance up into the back of the truck to see that John has ended his spiel. He notices that he no longer has a captive audience.

"Bruh." The young man next to me waves Fat Ace over.

Fat Ace hops out of the truck.

Something is definitely going down. I step back, not sure what to expect or what to do if these thugs flip the script and start blasting. Heaven knows that we've handed them a huge shipment of weapons to pull it off. Neither John nor I have a real connection to these men like Captain Johnson had, which means no loyalty. And in the streets, loyalty means everything.

Fat Ace huddles with his crew.

"Guys, are we good?" John asks, smiling, but I can tell that the alarm bells are going off for him, too. He keeps his hands wrapped around a weapon that he was showcasing in case he has to do a Rambo in order to get us out of here.

My hand inches toward the weapon inside of my jacket as well.

"We have to go," Fat Ace announces. He turns to John. "Everything looks good. We'll take it. Can you deliver another shipment—say in two weeks?"

I relax.

John's face explodes with a smile. We're back in business.

"Two weeks. Sure. We can handle that order," John boasts.

"Great. Keys," Fat Ace says, holding out his hand.

John is lost. "Excuse me?"

"The keys—to the truck. We don't have time to unload. Something has come up that we have to handle. It'll be a lot easier for my guys to take the truck."

John shoots me a look, but I'm not sure what the hell he expects me to say or do in this situation.

"If it's that important to you, I'll make sure that you get it back. Swing by our funeral home in a couple of days and you can pick it up there."

"Yeah. Well. All right," John says, thinking that we'll double back with our guys to Memphis.

With no further reason to protest, John jumps out from the back of the truck and says, "Give them the keys."

I toss them over and Fat Ace catches them with one hand.

"She's all yours." John grabs the bag of money and moves back while the men lock up the back of the truck.

Fat Ace offers his hand a final time. "It's nice doing business with you guys again."

"Same here."

We step back, feeling all kinds of vulnerable as we watch men climb into the truck and others roll the metal door back down, locking them inside.

"Tombstone," Fat Ace calls, and another large man rushes forward.

Fat Ace whispers something in his ear and hands over the keys. I can only assume that he's telling the guy where to take the shipment.

"You got it, boss man," Tombstone says and takes off to climb in behind the truck's steering wheel.

"The rest of you, head home!"

The Vice Lords scramble, and in less than a minute they are jetting out of the abandoned factory's parking lot.

Once they're gone, John and I turn to each other and let out a loud whoop as we jump into each other's arms.

"Yeah! Fuck yeah! We're back in business," John shouts.

We congratulate the rest of our team.

"We did it. We did it," is all I can say. My slice of the pie will help ease the financial money pit that I've fallen into since Captain Johnson fell out of the picture. I can stop worrying about having to find another nursing home to take care of my mother, and I can finally start paying the mountain of medical bills she's accumulated.

"Oh shit," John swears.

"What?" I'm fearful that he's about to snatch away our moment of victory with bad news.

"My cell phone," he says. "I left my cell phone on the seat of the truck."

"It's okay. You can just get it when you go pick up the truck later in the week," I tell him.

"No. You don' understand. It wasn't a burner. I'm talking about my work phone."

"Oh shit."

7

Yvette

The bedroom phone rings.

My eyes pop open before the first trill stops. I don't answer because my first reaction is to groan and fear what undoubtedly will be bad news. The temptation to bury my head beneath the pillows overwhelms me.

"Aren't you going to get that?" James's grumpy voice croaks from the other side of the bed.

That settles it. I have to answer it now. Sighing, I answer the call. "This better be good," I warn.

Behind me, James's cell phone chirps. If both of our phones are ringing, it's definitely not good news.

My deputy chief's rushed voice comes onto the line. "Sorry, Chief, but you might want to come down here. We're going to make the national news tonight—again."

My grip on the phone tightens. "What happened?" James and I ask our callers at the same time. We turn to look at each other and then sit up.

Deputy Chief Collins hesitates before delivering the bad news. "It's another massacre, Chief, like the one at the Royal Knights biker club a couple of months ago."

"Oh shit." I fling the covers back and perch on the edge of

the bed. The massacre at the Royal Knights Motorcycle Club was a level of carnage unlike anything most at the department had ever seen before. Forty-three dead bodies—*white* bodies. The fucking city went nuts. Black bodies can stack as high as the pyramids in Egypt and the citizens will whine and moan. But *white* bodies are a whole 'nother story. That's when everybody's jobs are on the line.

"Where?" James and I ask our callers. We glance back at each other again.

"Ruby Cove. Shooters damn near took out the whole block," the deputy chief reports. "The media is already all over it."

"Jesus." I squeeze the bridge of my nose and count to ten. "All right. I'm coming down. Has anyone paged Lieutenant Fowler?"

"I've called and texted, but he hasn't responded."

Shit. I slap a palm against my forehead and count to ten. Behind me, James hops out of bed while promising his caller that he's on his way downtown. My heart drops. This has been the first night in eons that we managed to synchronize our schedules. Of course, our romantic dinner consisted of a couple slices of pizza before a full ten minutes of passionate but intense lovemaking. Exhaustion hit and we rolled over and fell asleep. *Now duty calls again.*

"Chief? Are you still there?" Collins inquires.

"Yeah. Um. Hit Fowler up again and, um, I'm on my way over." I sigh, shaking my head.

"You got it, Chief."

After disconnecting the call, I return the phone to its port and then glance up to see James's fine, muscled, naked ass cheeks rush to the adjoining bathroom.

"The last one in the shower is a rotten egg," he teases.

I push up a tired smile, but it takes a few more seconds to gather my energy to actually leave my perch. This job is really wearing me down—or I'm just wearing too many hats. Something has to give—and soon. "It'll get better after the election,"

I promise myself. By the time I make it to the shower, James is lathered up and hogging all the water to rinse off.

"Hey! Didn't your mother teach you how to share?" I ask.

"Mmm. I don't remember." He laughs at his own joke before shifting to the side so that a single stream of water can hit me. By the time I'm halfway lathered up, James hops out of the shower.

"Come on, slowpoke. We got to get going," he sings.

Why and how is he always this damn chipper when he wakes? I'm always mad at the world until at least my second cup of coffee—lately my third cup.

"Yvette!"

"I'm coming. I'm coming." I lather and rinse twice more before shutting off the cooling water. Ten minutes after that, I'm dressed in plain clothes and heading out my front door— but as I race to my car, James is waving and climbing into the backseat of his city-issued town car.

I wave back—to him and his driver, Miles, and then climb behind the wheel myself. "Duty calls," I mumble under my breath and then pull out of the driveway. Twenty-two-and-a-half minutes later, I arrive on the scene near Ruby Cove. To my horror the place looks more like the set of a zombie movie. Multicolored lights from the various emergency responders' vehicles illuminate the night while dead bodies litter the ground. There are also crying babies, wailing mothers, and bloodied survivors crowded around.

It's going to be a long night.

Unable to actually pull onto Ruby Cove, I end up parking right behind a small team of news vans on an adjoining street.

The second I roll up, an eagle-eyed reporter recognizes me.

"Chief Brown! Chief Brown," the reporter shouts, wrangling the attention of colleagues.

Showtime. I draw a deep breath and climb from behind the wheel. By the time I shut my door, I'm completely surrounded by reporters from the big three news stations.

"Excuse me. Let me through, please," I say with my game face firmly in place.

They shout questions but because they choose to shout different ones at the same time, they sound like Charlie Brown's marble-mouthed teacher. I can't make out what they're saying. Finally, an officer rushes to my aid and uses his body to shield me from their cameras. Once I'm inside the perimeter of the crime scene, the reporters are blocked off. That doesn't stop them from shouting their questions at my back.

"Where's Deputy Chief Collins?" I ask.

"He's up at the address 4550. It's . . ." The officer struggles for the right words. "Well, I'll let you see for yourself."

That bad. I pull another deep breath and then maneuver around a forensic team snapping pictures of bodies. "What is our body count?"

He sighs. "I'm not sure that we have a final number yet. Can I check around and get back to you?"

"Do that."

"Yes, Chief. Right away." The officer peels away as I keep marching forward. As I near the house marked 4550, Deputy Chief Collins steps out, shaking his lowered head. *Another bad sign.*

Collins spots me and swipes the despair from his face and places his police cap onto his head. "Chief Brown, I'm glad you made it out here so fast."

We clasp hands for an official handshake before he launches into his assessment of the situation. At the mention of a survivor inside, I turn away from the conversation and walk into the house. I find her in the living room, still lying in a pool of blood—but with a surrounding team of EMTs stabilizing her.

"Is she talking?" I ask, hovering.

"A little," one EMT answers.

The young girl's lashes flutter open and for a second our eyes connect—but I can't discern what she's thinking. If I was to guess, she's someone who has seen a lot in her young life. They all have on this side of town.

"Have any of my guys talked to her?"

"I did." An officer cuts into our conversation from across the room.

I turn my attention toward the eager cop as he rushes forward. "Well? What did she say?"

"Sorry, Chief, but not much. She claims that she doesn't know who leveled the attack."

"Of course not." I don't bother hiding my disappointment. Same shit, different day.

"But we believe that she was one of the first ones to place a call to 9-1-1. They are cuing up a copy for the department right now."

"Anything else?"

My bluntness erases the hopeful eagerness from his face.

"Uh—no, Chief."

I step back and allow the EMTs to do their jobs.

Disappointed, I turn my attention back to the young girl. This time, she refuses to look at me. *She knows who did this.* I take several deep breaths to lower my blood pressure and then scan the destruction lying all around. "Any other home hit like this one?"

"No, Chief. Other than the bodies lying outside, this is the only house that was attacked."

"So that makes this house the target," I conclude. "So the next question is why."

The eager cop speaks up again. "You might want to take a look upstairs."

My heart drops and my exhaustion deepens. "More bodies?"

Everyone in the room pauses, making me dread the answer.

"Just one. And . . . it's pretty gruesome," the young cop answers, then turns his attention to the young girl with the EMTs.

"According to dispatch, our survivor claimed to be the one who shot her—*before* the entire house was attacked."

"Before?"

"That's what dispatch said regarding the 9-1-1 call. The girl now claims that she doesn't remember placing the call."

My gaze sweeps over the girl's face again and she's still avoiding my gaze. *Another lie.* "Where's Lieutenant Fowler?" I glance around, expecting to see him.

"He still hasn't answered any of our calls or texts," Collins says in a lower voice, like everyone isn't already listening to our conversation. "I even sent a squad car over to his place to drag him out of bed. He never answered the door."

Fuck. My blood pressure shoots up and my temples hammer against my skull. *Where in the hell is he?*

"So what do you want to do?" Collins asks, then stares me dead in my face while he waits for an answer. I know one thing: I'm *not* going to be the only one dragged in front of the news cameras on this one. "Call her."

"Chief?"

"Call Captain Hawkins. At least we know that she *always* answers her damn phone."

8

Lucifer

Pain.

Every inch of my body is racked with pain, but I'm a big fucking girl and I'm determined to take this shit if I have to. Better that than to let these grimy bastards get the best of me. Around me, the men bark at each other. With this strange ringing in my ear, it's difficult to tell whether they are angry or excited. By the seat's gentle but steady rocking, I can tell that I'm still in an SUV. Slowly, I peek from underneath my long lashes and zoom in on Python's hard profile.

"I still say that you should've put a cap in the bitch's head," King Isaac says from the front seat. "That nigga Fat Ace is going to come after us regardless. We don't need her to ensure that shit."

Python grumbles and then cuts a look in my direction.

Anger sweeps through me like a brush fire, but I have self-discipline if I have nothing else. I remain still and keep my breathing even. I want them to believe that I'm still out cold, so I can assess this situation.

"What? Don't tell me that your ass has gotten soft since I've been on lockdown."

"It ain't nothing like that, Isaac." Python's gaze cuts away from me to glare up into the front seat.

"No? Then what's it like?"

Python's jawline stiffens, and when Isaac presses him for an answer, he barks out, "Fuck, man. Every nigga gotta have a fuckin' code—a fuckin' line that even they won't cross. For me that's murkin' innocent babies."

Isaac lets that confession hang between them in the car for about a full minute before responding. "Then we should've left the bitch back there. We left a hell of a calling card, blasting his turf for him to come gunning."

"Yeah. Yeah. Hindsight is always twenty-twenty. We got her now. We're just going to have to make the best of a bad situation."

King Isaac's rumbling laugh fills the whole vehicle. "What's this *we* shit? If that girl gets ready to burst, don't think my ass is playing doctor or midwife with your ass."

"Hopefully her nigga will come gunning for her before any of that shit happens." Python's black gaze slithers back to me. "But as a backup, I'll have LeShelle and some of her girls sit on her."

King Isaac tsks and shakes his head. "Are you sure that your woman can handle her? From what I've heard, Lucifer is as dangerous as her man."

Python snickers and then boasts, "Clearly you don't know much about LeShelle. She's just as bad as they come, too. She can more than handle this one."

I lower my eyelids and roll my eyes to the back of my head. This muthafucka must be trippin' if he thinks LeShelle is anywhere near my league. However, before I continue my Oscar-worthy performance in the corner of this seat, I'm hit with another mind-blowing contraction. Screaming, I clutch at my rolling belly.

Python and Isaac jump.

The driver does, too, swerving out of his car lane. A series of car horns blare and the SUV is quickly jerked back into the right lane. "What the fuck?"

Still screaming with my lungs burning, warm fluid gushes out between my thighs.

Python jumps again. "AHHHH SHIT!"

"What? What is it?" Isaac looks over his right shoulder to check shit out for himself.

"Her water broke." Python scrambles out of the way.

"What? You fuckin' shitting me," Isaac groans, twisting around again for another look.

Automatically, I spread my legs east and west before bearing down to push this baby out.

"Awww. Fuck. Stop that shit! Stop it," Python shouts.

Is this nigga serious? I'd love to stop this horror show, but this situation is out of my control. My baby is determined to make his grand entrance tonight and there ain't shit that anybody can do about it.

The contractions wane for a few seconds and I steal several sips of air. All too soon, I'm hit with another, equally body-splitting contraction that has me pushing as if my life depends on it.

"We got to pull over or something," Python shouts.

"It ain't too fucking late to just put a bullet in the girl's head," Isaac tells him. "At least that will cut out all that damn hollering that she's doing."

"I'm serious, man. Pull over!"

The vehicle lunges.

"And then do what?" Isaac thunders. "Do you know how to deliver a fucking baby?"

Python's eyes triple in size—but he doesn't have a solution.

I growl at them through my teeth, "You muthafuckas make a goddamn decision. This baby is coming whether we want him to or not."

Python's and my glares clash.

"Maybe we should pull over and toss her ass out on the side of the road. She can spit that baby out by her damn self."

Python bites his bottom lip as he chews the situation over.

Isaac gets antsy with my wailing behind him. "Whatcha want to do, Terrell? Say the word and I'll pull the fuck over."

Python scopes out our surroundings. "We ain't going to make it back to the crib," he deduces. "And we sure as hell can't take her to a hospital."

While they argue, my gaze falls on the weapon that's casually lying on Python's lap. He, meanwhile, keeps closing his eyes and pinching the bridge of his nose, trying to get a thought to rise from his ass.

"If you can't do it, I can," Isaac says.

With no time to spare I lunge for Python's weapon. Before he can react, it's in my hands. He goes to wrestle it back when I fire.

The window behind him explodes and Python reels back.

"Holy shit!" Isaac twists around in his seat, gun at the ready, but I'm already aiming for the back of the driver's head and don't think twice before pulling the trigger.

Isaac and I fire at the same time. He missed.

I don't.

Pow!

The driver's head explodes. The SUV careens all over the road.

Isaac dives for the wheel.

Python lunges again. Before anyone knows it, we're airborne. When we land, it's roof first, and then we tumble around like clothes inside a dryer.

By the time the chaos stops, there's not a soul stirring.

9

Hydeya

Shotgun Row

Sitting on the cold floor in a spare room in Maybelline Carver-Goodson's old shotgun house, I'm having trouble understanding the words I'm reading. "I have a brother?" My grip on the letter I'm holding tightens. I shake my head because that Jack Daniel's I downed before storming over here to Shotgun Row to give Isaac a piece of my mind is still fucking with me—so I read the letter again:

> *Mason,*
> *I don't know where to begin. The reason I sat down to write this letter is because I fear that tomorrow when we meet I'll be too overcome with emotion to get out everything that I want to say. But I want you to know that you are loved and you have been sorely missed. Not just by me, but by your brother Terrell as well. Of course most people in the streets know him as Python. It is some cruel twist of fate that the two of you have grown up as enemies in rival gangs. Hopefully, tomorrow will be a new beginning for the Carver family. There's been so much pain and hurt already that I have to believe that a change is coming.*

Barbara, the woman who's raised you all these years, and I have sat down and exchanged information on what happened to you so long ago. Your real mother, Alice, had her demons. A few of them, I'll admit, may have been my doing. She wasn't perfect and she was unable to kick her drug habit on her own. I don't know what happened in that apartment—or why Barbara found you where she did. But what I can tell you is that we did everything that we could to find you. When the days turned into weeks and then months, we believed the worst.

That was a mistake.

We should have never stopped looking. Maybe if we hadn't, this family could've been spared a lot of the pain that we've endured.

I've been told that you've known who you truly are for a long time. I can't imagine what you must think of us. The scenarios of what happened and how it happened must be endless in your mind. I hope that I'll be calm enough to answer all your questions tomorrow. That's if you agree to show up. If not, I'll give this letter to Barbara to give you. Maybe you'll change your mind.

I can't give you your mother back. She's not here to answer any questions or defend anything. But I can give you the name of your father. He's still alive. And I'm married to him: Isaac Goodson. You know him as King Isaac.

With all my love,
Your Aunt Maybelline

It doesn't matter how many times I read this damn thing, the words aren't computing. The fact that my father has another child shouldn't be all that shocking. Men put babies on women all the time—and according to my mother, Isaac was a bona fide sex addict. There's a likelihood that he has a dozen kids running around from here to Chicago, for all we know.

Mason Carver is my brother. Ain't that about a bitch?

I lower the letter and take a deep breath. It's amazing how shock can clear the mind. This shit is the last thing I need to deal with right now. I'm dealing with the loss of my husband, Drake. Days ago, he was gunned down at, of all places, Maybelline Carver's funeral. The shooting was just another chapter in the long, endless street war between the Gangster Disciples and the Vice Lords.

Maybelline, or rather Momma Peaches, as she was known in her community *and* every police precinct in the city, was an icon with the Gangster Disciples. A lot of it had to do with her being married to my father, the ex-chief of the deadly gang. *Ex-chief.* I roll my eyes. Why the fuck am I pretending to believe his lies?

I climb up from the floor of this cold spare room and place Maybelline's Bible back onto the nightstand. The letter I slide into my pocket before heading toward the door. Not until after I try to turn the knob do I remember that Isaac locked my ass in here. When I arrived here I caught my fresh-out-the-joint father in the house full of Gangster Disciples and crates of military-grade weapons. *Out of the game, my ass.*

I should hardly be surprised that Isaac lied to my face about his ass turning over a new leaf and staying out of Memphis's growing gang wars. Of course, those promises were *before* his wife, Maybelline Carver aka Momma Peaches, was murdered in the Power of Prayer Baptist Church.

Without Momma Peaches around, there's no reason for the old chief to stay on the right side of the law. Well, other than me—Captain Hydeya Hawkins of the Memphis Gang Unit. Unfortunately or fortunately, I've been placed on temporary—or indefinite—leave. Their excuse is to force me to grieve my husband's death.

I don't need to grieve. I need to work.

But my working on *certain* cases is the last thing the department wants. My predecessor, Captain Melvin Johnson, a long-heralded supercop in the city, was as dirty as they come before Johnson and his wife were slaughtered by none other than Momma Peaches' younger sister, Alice.

Johnson was another dirty dog with a tribe of children who clearly had no idea of their being related, because two of them, his cop daughter Melanie and his son with Alice, Terrell Carver, were fucking, and had even produced a child, Christopher.

Melanie Johnson's murder is what landed Terrell aka Python on the FBI's Most Wanted list. That is until he was believed to have been killed on the Old Memphis Bridge. Him and his supposed brother, Mason. At least the blood work back from the lab says that they're brothers. Maybelline's letter from beyond the grave is further proof of that. And that wasn't all. The amount of money and weapons found on Johnson's property raised all kinds of red flags with me. With the rest of the department? Crickets.

Seriously. *Crickets.*

Even when a copy of a surveillance video, found at Captain Johnson's home, captured his daughter assassinating her partner, Officer O'Malley. *Crickets.*

My ex-partner and now rival for my job, Lieutenant John Fowler, explained the higher-ups' decision to shut my investigation down as self-preservation. Captain Johnson had been a *hero* to the city for so long, there are simply too many powerful people who'd hitched their political careers to his wagon. Taking him down postmortem wasn't going to do anybody any good.

Fowler is right. He's right about a lot of things.

But the case keeps fucking with me. Whenever you find one dirty cop, he's attached to a whole network.

I twist the locked doorknob again and then rattle the door. "Hey, let me out of here!" My father left, but I'm sure that he's left a soldier or two to babysit this locked door. "Hey! I know someone is out there! Let me out!" I pound on the door until my hand aches—then I give it a good kick out of frustration. "Fuck you then!" Spinning away from the door, I eye the lone window where the moon's full beam is slicing through the venetian blinds. In no time at all, I get the sucker unlatched, knock out the screen, and then climb out.

A dog barks from the next-door neighbor's backyard, but I flash the mean-looking Doberman the bird before racing to my car parked out front on the curb. However, to my surprise, the steering wheel is missing. "The fuck?" Frustrated, I rake my hands through my hair, ripping out a couple of strands. I'm a cop, standing on the wrong side of town without any sort of backup.

Still, I climb into the car, lean over to the passenger side to reach beneath the seat for my spare Glock. Chief Brown may have taken my badge and service weapon, but I'm like a ghetto Girl Scout: always prepared. Hell, I wasn't always on the right side of the law. In my young and wild days, I followed my father into the Gangster Disciples. I'm a Queen G by way of South Chicago. I've robbed, stolen, and I'm even responsible for a couple of cold cases in what they now call Chiraq. If that wasn't enough, my stint in Afghanistan and years on the police force have taught me a thing or two about expecting the unexpected.

I eyeball Maybelline's place again, knowing that I only have one play. No way a taxi is gonna risk rolling over here for a pickup. Before I climb back out of the car, my cell phone rings from the car's charger. My mind pulls a blank, wondering who could be calling me. Frowning, I grab the phone and get the shock of my life when I read Deputy Chief Collins's name on my screen.

What in the hell does he want?

After I suck in a deep breath and pray that I'm as sober as I think I am, I swipe the screen to answer the call before it's transferred to voicemail. "Hello, Collins. What can I do for you?"

"Thank God." Collins exhales.

"Is there a problem?"

"Other than I can't find Lieutenant Fowler anywhere? Yes.

I'm going to need you to report to 4550 Ruby Cove. We have another gang mess on our hands. There are bodies every-where."

Silence.

"Captain Hawkins, are you still there?"

"Uh, yeah. I'm here." I look around, wondering how the fuck I'm going to make it over to Ruby Cove.

"How soon can I expect you?" he asks.

"Mmm. I thought that I was on administrative leave . . . ?"

He sighs. "Can you get here or not?"

"I'm on my way," I tell him with a smug smile exploding across my face. However, when I disconnect the call and stare back down at where my steering wheel used to be, the smile melts off of my face. *Shit.*

Taking another glance at Maybelline's place, I climb out of the car with my piece hanging by my side. As I jog up to the front porch, a neighbor steps out onto hers and watches me like a hawk. I ignore her nosy ass and bogart into the house like my ass pays the mortgage.

Two big mountain-looking OGs pop up off the couch, raising sawed-off shotguns, ready to blow my ass to kingdom come.

"Police," I announce, lifting my own weapon. It wasn't necessary because as soon as they see my face, recognition reg-isters before they glance back toward the locked bedroom door.

"All right. Now which one of you has my steering wheel? I have a job I have to get to."

10

Ta'Shara

I can't feel my legs.

"Everything is all right. We're going to take good care of you," a paramedic with compassionate brown eyes tells me before a smile quivers at the corners of his lips.

I attempt to smile back, but the plastic mask around my mouth is too tight—so are the straps that are tying me to the gurney. Around me there's a circus of activity by the cops, paramedics, and the Tennessee Bureau of Investigation

"Have you seen the upstairs bedroom?" one cop asks another.

"Yeah, man. The place looks like a slaughterhouse."

I close my eyes, but it doesn't stop my tears from welling up and sliding out from the corners. Now that military-style shelling has stopped and the immediate danger has passed, I'm overwhelmed by every emotion in the book. Looking back, the entire night seems so surreal. The shooting at the park, the confrontation with LeShelle, my shooting the crazy bitch upstairs, my being shot downstairs by Python, and the Gangster Disciples' surprise attack. It's a wonder that I haven't cracked up yet.

As the paramedic maneuvers the gurney around a corner, we slam into said corner and more pain washes over me.

"Oops. Sorry about that, ma'am." The man with the smiling brown eyes hovers over me again.

I close my eyes, worried that they'll also drop me in a minute. Soon after the paramedics arrived, I grew drowsy to the point I can barely keep my eyes open. But I fight off the drug-like drowsiness with everything I have. Given my condition, I'm terrified to close my eyes. *What if I don't wake up?*

Once again, Profit surfaces in my mind. The thought of never seeing him again feels as if it's ripping my heart in half. I *have* to see him again. I don't know the words that I'll say, but I'm sure that they will come to me. *He* fucked up. *I* fucked up. There's got to be a way to put the past behind us and move on. Tears roll down my face at a surprising clip. A few of the tears are for my and Profit's situation, the rest are for Lucifer and her unborn baby. Despite hating the woman for the last couple of weeks, I feel that I could've done more to save her—even though I don't know exactly what.

As I'm carried out the front door, I ignore all the curious stares from the men and women in uniform. I'm the freak who survived. Other bodies, no doubt Vice Lord soldiers, are zipped in black bags while police chalk the area where they fell. A small gust of wind dries my tears as I'm carried past the yellow crime tape and the crowd of neighbors rubbernecking to see what's going on.

"Let me through. Let me through, goddamn it!"

Profit! My heart leaps up into my chest.

"I said, let me through!" The crowd parts as I'm lifted into the back of an ambulance.

The moment my gaze lands on Profit, emotions tumble through me and more tears roll down my face.

"Ta'Shara, baby. Are you okay?" He stretches out one powerful arm and stops the gurney from being lifted any farther into the ambulance.

"Sir. I'm going to have to ask you to step back," another paramedic, older and a bit of a redneck, says.

Profit doesn't even spare him a look. "Don't worry, baby. I'm coming with you." He proceeds to climb into the ambulance.

"I'm sorry, sir, but we can't allow that. You're more than welcome to follow us to Baptist Memorial, but you can't ride with her in the back."

"Fuck you. That's my girl you got up there!"

The redneck's face flushes at the obscenity. "Like I said. You can either follow us to the hospital or you can meet her there." He boldly moves to block Profit from climbing into the back of the truck.

Veins bulge and pulse along Profit's neck and jawline. "You need to step out of my way, old man," Profit warns with head tilted and hands balled at his sides, as if ready to strike.

Then another voice catches my attention while those two get ready to square off.

"Ta'Shara! Ta'Shara!"

Mason.

Instantly the crowd parts as our leader, cloaked head to toe in black, approaches the ambulance as well.

The older paramedic who is arguing with Profit takes one look at Mason with his purple and black burn scars and backs up.

"Where's Willow?" Mason demands, storming up into the truck and kneeling beside me. "Tell me. Where is she?"

I have trouble meeting his one good eye. The other, a gross, milky-white eye, he keeps covered with a patch. "They're saying that she's not in the house. Where is she?"

My tears return and blur his face. Even as he pulls the mask away from my mouth, it's still difficult to get words past the lump in my throat.

"Sir. Sir. I'm going to have to ask you to leave." The redneck finds his voice, mainly because he has pulled a cop for backup.

"Ta'Shara, please. Tell me something. Where are Willow and my son?"

"Sir!"

"Th-they . . . took her," I croak. My lips tremble as I force out my next words. "I'm sorry—but there were too many of them."

Mason's mangled face resembles a demonic deity. "*Who* took her?" His grip on my arm tightens. "I need for you to tell me who."

I hesitate. I don't know why. Wait. Yes, I do. My next words will plunge Memphis's streets into something that's more than a war—a crusade.

"Was it the Gangster Disciples or the Grape Street Crips?" *The Crips?*

"That was Lynch's main bitch, Shariffa, they pulled from upstairs. Is that nigga Lynch behind this shit?"

"Shariffa?" The name is familiar, but my crash course into the gang life is a bit spotty and I can't place where I know Shariffa's name.

"Sir! We need for you to step out of the vehicle." This is coming from a cop this time.

Mason doesn't pay him any more attention than the last dude.

An irritated Profit butts in. "Give him a minute to ask her a few questions."

"*You* stay out of this," the cop says, tapping Profit's chest with his baton.

Now pissed, Profit swipes that shit away and chest bumps the officer. "How in the hell are you going to tell me to stay out of it when this is *my* woman? Who the fuck is you?"

"Whoa. Whoa. Whoa." Two more cops approach the back of the ambulance. "What seems to be the problem over here?"

"Ta'Shara," Mason says, snatching my attention back. "Tell me now. Who did this? The GD or the Crips?"

"Both."

His face twists. "What?"

"The girl broke in first," I whisper. "Python and his people showed up later."

"Python." Angry veins pop all over Mason's face. "Are you sure?"

"Positive," I tell him. "They took Lucifer while I think she was going into early labor."

Rage works a number on Mason's face and his grip on my arm causes me to flinch.

"I'm going to fucking kill him," he vows.

When I flinch again, Mason releases my arm and then races out of the back of the truck with revenge written all over his face.

The angry cops and paramedics are left to stare after him when he pulls Profit along with him.

My heart drops back down into my gut again. "Wait." I don't want Profit to leave.

The redneck paramedic climbs into the back of the truck with me and the other paramedic.

"Let's roll," he shouts, shutting the back door.

"No. Wait." I attempt to sit up, but the straps aren't having any of it.

"It's okay. It's okay," smiling brown eyes tells me. "We're getting you to the hospital now to get you checked out. You lost a lot of blood, but you're going to pull through this." He takes my hand and replaces the oxygen mask over my face.

A second later the ambulance pulls away from the curb.

But I didn't get to talk to Profit. More tears swell behind my eyes. Will Profit follow the ambulance to the hospital or will he go riding shotgun with his brother to retaliate against the Gangster Disciples?

God help us. This war will never end.

11

Hydeya

Ruby Cove

If I keep telling myself that my ass is sober, then maybe it'll be true. Now that my initial shock from reading Momma Peaches' letter is over, that Jack Daniel's I guzzled down earlier has returned to slosh through my veins. I'm going to block out the fact that I was nearly T-boned running through a traffic light during my race over here. The second I turn onto Ruby Cove, the whole area is lit up like the Fourth of July.

"What in the world?" It looks like every emergency vehicle from every law enforcement agency is here—and so is every news van in the tri-state area. *I'm definitely going to need to be sober for this.*

I find a place to park on the curb, then have to walk several houses down to get to the crime scene. I take special note that it's the house directly across from the Barretts. The last time I paid a visit there it was to arrest Qiana Barrett for the murders of Yolanda Terry and Tyneisha Gibson. We haven't been able to figure out the motive or how Qiana, a Vice Lord Flower, even knew Ms. Terry, but the department successfully matched her vehicle to tire tracks at the scene of the crime. The only problem was that by the time we were able to get a warrant and roll down here, the girl was in the wind with the baby we believe she stole from Ms. Terry's corpse.

No matter. We'll find her—eventually.

"Captain Hawkins! Thank heavens you finally made it down here."

I glance down at my watch and pretend to read it. "Chief, I came down right after I got the call." I don't like the way she makes it sound like my ass took too long or something. *She was the one who placed me on some bullshit administrative leave.*

Chief Yvette Brown huffs out her chest and glares up at me. "Any word from Lieutenant Fowler?"

Frowning, I shake my head. "Should I have heard from him?"

She rolls her eyes and shakes her head. "I'm going to kill him," she hisses under her breath before landing her hard gaze back onto me. While she studies, I become extremely self-conscious. *Are my eyes bloodshot? Am I standing up straight? Can she smell the alcohol seeping from my pores?*

When her nose twitches, I'm sure her ass is about to bust me. However, her current options trump her decision-making. Chief Brown expels a long breath and mumbles, "Follow me."

Once the chief spins around to march back toward the house, I allow myself to smirk at the back of her head. Chief Brown has thrown one monkey wrench after another into my investigation of the city's previous supercop, Captain Melvin Johnson. In her words, *We're not interested in the money, weapons . . . O'Malley's murder—or anything else that you've stumbled upon. The public wants to know that we've solved the murder of their local hero. Period.*

As I approach the house, the first thing that leaps out is the number of bullet holes the place has sustained. The front window has been destroyed and it's being patched over with yellow crime tape.

"Excuse us. Coming through," a paramedic announces as he pushes a gurney.

Police officers and state agents quickly scramble out of the way.

As the gurney passes, I take a good look at the bleeding woman laid out on it. Actually, she looks more like a little girl than a woman. *Hey. Don't I know her?* The way that she's looking around, I suspect she's in shock. "Is she talking?" I ask the chief.

"Not much. She was one of the first to call 9-1-1. We'll do our best to talk to her later at the hospital. She's been hit bad, but I think that she's going to pull through just fine." The chief disappears into the house while I watch as the paramedics rush her toward an awaiting ambulance. That's when I notice all the black body bags being loaded up in the city morgue van.

"How many are dead?" I ask no one in particular.

"Twenty-six and counting," Officer Reid answers.

When I glance over at him, I note that he looks as tired as I feel. Actually, everyone looks as though they're tired of being the cleanup crew for the city's growing gang wars. Ruby Cove is the Vice Lords' stronghold, but tonight their enemies punched a big-ass hole in their security.

I know who's my lead suspect in the case. The crates of weapons I discovered at Isaac's earlier tonight flash nonstop inside my head. The irony of the chief and mayor wanting me to stop digging in their backyard so that I can concentrate on digging in my own has not escaped me.

"Lucifer!" a man shouts.

"Sir, you can't go in there." Officers block the entrance.

I spot Mason Lewis pushing his way into the ambulance. The older paramedic or EMT looks apoplectic.

"Captain?" Officer Reid's inquiry pulls me back. "Are you all right?"

I force on a smile. "Yes. Of course. I'm fine."

I march back off the porch to head toward the ambulance.

Now I remember where and how I know the younger man's face. Raymond Lewis. And the girl on the stretcher is Ta'Shara Murphy. I met them both at the hospital after Momma Peaches saved Barbara Lewis's life—by killing Momma Peaches's youngest sister, Alice. Raymond aka Profit had been grateful for everyone's assistance. Ta'Shara had been the silent and shy girlfriend, clinging on his arm.

"Is there a problem over here?" I ask as the paramedics are finally able to move the two men back so that they can close the ambulance doors.

Both Mason and Profit swing their contemptuous gazes in my direction.

I flinch at Mason's charred face, but then recalibrate and remain professional. "Is this your place?" I ask, nodding toward the house.

"Who's asking?"

For the craziest moment, I reach into my pocket so I can pull out my badge, but then remember that the chief hasn't given it back to me yet.

"This is Captain Hawkins," Profit tells his brother. "We've met before."

Mason's singular black gaze rakes me over; his other eye is covered with an eye patch. "So are you the lead cop on this investigation?" he asks.

"I am."

He squares around toward me. "So where is my girl at?" he barks.

I'm taken aback. "Excuse me?"

"My *girl*! *Willow Washington*. The muthafuckas who blasted their way into our crib snatched her. What are you muthafuckas going to do about that shit? Huh?"

"Mr. Carver, I'm gonna need you to calm down."

Fat Ace explodes. "Carver! Bitch, are you confused or some shit? The last name is Lewis!"

Shit. I've done shoved my foot into my mouth already. "Mr.

Lewis, I'm sorry. You're right. My mistake." Both he and his younger brother look at me as if I've just sprouted a second head. Why, oh why, did I walk my ass over here without getting the basic facts of the case? I have no information about a missing person and will have to wing this shit. "My team and I are going to work diligently to find, uh . . ."

"Willow Washington," Profit reminds me.

Behind them, the ambulance pulls away from the curb.

Profit gets antsy. "We got to follow them to the hospital," he tells his brother.

Fat Ace overrules that decision with a hiss. "No. We need to get at the muthafuckas who hit us. We find them and we find Willow."

"I certainly hope that doesn't mean what I think it means," I say, reminding him that he's talking reckless in front of an officer of the law.

Fat Ace's look transmits that he doesn't give a damn about who I am. He doesn't think that I can do a damn thing to stop him.

"You think you know who did this?" I ask, because I need to say something to break the tension between us.

"If *you* don't know who is responsible for this shit then your case is already fucked."

He moves past me, but I jump to block his path. "Where were *you* tonight?"

He stops and glares. "Out."

Smart ass. I cross my arms and make it clear that I'm not budging until he answers my questions.

"My brother and I weren't here when this shit went down. Trust me. There would have been a different result had we been here."

"That wasn't my question," I say. "*Where* were you?" When it looks like he's not going to answer my question, I continue. "You're going to have to forgive me for my insistence because the last I heard, you were dead." I unfold my arms so that I can reach out and touch his shoulder. When my finger touches flesh, I add, "No. You're clearly not a ghost."

"Sorry to disappoint you," he says, his hard expression un-changing.

"Where were you?" I insist.

"Tonight I was at work. I own a funeral home not too far from here. Besides that, I've been back for a couple of months. As you can tell by my face, I was in a serious car accident. I don't remember much about the details of the accident, but I was fortunate to survive."

"Yeah. The whole city saw it play out on the evening news. You were believed to be in the same car as Terrell Carver."

A muscle twitches along the side of his face. "Like I said, I don't remember much."

"Yeah. I caught that." Our gazes lock for a few uncomfort-able seconds before I try to discern any features that we may share from our father. So far, all I can tell is that he has one hell of a poker face.

"Hawkins!" The chief shouts across the yard like she was raised in a barn.

"Looks like you're needed inside." Mason smirks. "Don't let me keep you from doing your job."

I clench my jaw tight to keep from saying shit that I'd probably regret later. "We'll find Ms. Washington, and in the interim, you should make a point to come visit me downtown. There are a lot of questions I have pertaining to this and *other* cases. Say for example, Officer Melanie Johnson's case."

A second muscle pulses on the opposite side of his face.

"Hawkins!"

I ignore the chief. "Tomorrow—any time after lunch."

He rakes his gaze over me again. "Fine. I'll see if I can squeeze you into my schedule."

Triumphant, I wink and backpedal my way toward the house.

Mason looks as if he's growling inside of his head.

Don't think we are starting off on the right foot. I spin around and then jog into the house, where Chief Brown greets me.

"I'm glad that you can finally join us."

"I was interviewing one of the residents."

She frowns as if she doesn't know who I'm talking about.

"Mason Car . . . Lewis." I thrust my thumb over my shoulder. "He said that he lives here." They look clueless so I fill them in. "He said that his girlfriend, Willow Washington, is missing."

"Ms. Washington is the name on the deed to the house. I wasn't aware that someone else lived here." The chief marches back to the front door as all hell breaks out between angry Vice Lords and the police.

12

Mack

"**S**hit is really about to hit the fan now," I tell my girl Romil.

Judging by the way Romil is twitching and pacing, she's thinking the same damn thing. "What the fuck are we going to do?" she asks every other minute, like clockwork.

Each time her voice gets a little louder.

"Shhhh." I look around. "Keep your voice down."

Romil ain't hearing me though. She's geeked as fuck. "This shit is all on us."

A couple of heads in the crowd turn in our direction and I snatch Romil by the arm and pull her aside.

"What the fuck are we going to do?" Romil shouts.

I smack her hard across the face.

When her head snaps back, a few gasps from the crowd let me know that we've drawn the kind of attention I wanted to avoid. "What the fuck are y'all looking at?" I stare down a few eyeballs until they look the other way. Afterward, I address Romil, who's holding her cheek like a child on the brink of tears.

"Are you good now?" I ask.

She flinches when I step closer.

"Calm down. I'm not going to hit you again, but we have to stay calm."

"Hey! Isn't that the new captain of police?" someone asks from behind me.

I turn toward an attractive woman in painted-on black jeans, blue top, and a black leather jacket as she marches her way through a swarm of news cameras.

"She's smaller than she looks on TV," Romil comments.

"Nah. Nah. That's the police chief."

"Somebody needs to tell her that she's wearing the wrong damn colors on this side of town," Lola, a Flower who lives next door to Tombstone and his father, Nookie, comments.

"Fat Ace!" someone shouts, and the crowd lurches forward.

Romil and I remain rooted where we stand as we watch Fat Ace and his younger brother, Profit, attempt to bum-rush their way into Lucifer's house.

"Lucifer!" Fat Ace shouts as police officers line up to form an impenetrable wall to block him.

"Get your hands off of me, muthafucka! Lucifer!" Fat Ace's roar makes goose bumps pimple my arms.

He races over and climbs into the back of the ambulance where they've taken Ta'Shara. I have no doubts that he wants to hear what happened to Lucifer from her mouth.

The punk-ass EMTs grab a cop to help get Fat Ace out of the back of the ambulance. Soon Fat Ace and Profit climb out. Fat Ace is pulled aside by the new captain of police and they stay huddled up for a moment. However, minutes after she goes into the house, the cops keep giving him shit and a fight breaks out between cops and Vice Lords. The surviving soldiers jump into the mix to show that they have our leader's back.

The cops are not prepared for the chaos. A full-out brawl ensues. News reporters and cameramen rush forward to get the melee captured on tape.

Shit gets crazier when the rest of the crowd then attacks a few of the camera crew. One muthafucka's camera gets snatched off his shoulder and is smashed to the ground and stomped on.

The cameraman finds his inner thug and launches his own attack.

I can't believe what I'm seeing. The only real thing to happen next is the sound of gunfire.

Pow! Pow! Pow!

I leap back and snatch Romil with me.

The police are taking a calculated risk firing up in the air with this crowd. It's not like they're the only ones with weapons out here.

When I see one cop clock a Flower right in her face, I drop Romil's arm. "Fuck it! Let's go!"

We spring forward and join the mayhem.

13

Ta'Shara

*P*rofit. *I want Profit.*

Not until the paramedics slam the ambulance's door do I realize how scared I am. The adrenaline that I've been running on all night has waned. All that's left banging around inside of me is fear and ghosts. LeShelle's bloodcurdling screams echo in my head. I recall the smell of burning flesh and crackling hair. I'm never going to get these images out of my head. *Ever.*

Fat tears roll as LeShelle's screams grow louder and then transform into a high-pitched cackle. It's as if the bitch is laughing at me from beyond the grave. A chill comes over me. Soon after, I'm freezing and the air rushing through this oxygen mask is coming in too fast and strong.

How much longer will it be before we get to the hospital? It doesn't seem as if we're going all that fast. The seconds tick by like minutes and the minutes like hours. I'll bleed out by the time we get to the hospital. I can't die. Not like this.

The idea of being another statistic of the city's street violence fills me with disappointment. After everything—to fall victim of the life that I told myself I would never be a part of is pathetic.

My tears quicken as every mistake I've made in the past two years replays in my head. The fervent wish to go back and do everything all over balloons in my heart, even as I know that I'm wishing for the impossible.

The ambulance's back doors fly open, disorienting me as people hustle and bustle around. They keep talking and asking questions that I can't comprehend.

But then they shout for me to nod if I understand what they are saying. I nod even though I don't understand them, because I want the shouting to stop.

Next, I'm bathed in a bright white light. Needles are stuck in me, my eyelids are lifted and a ballpoint flashlight blinds me. There's an argument about which surgery room is available. A man says something about giving me something to relax me, but instead of asking whether I understand, something ice-cold is injected into my veins.

LeShelle's screams and cackles fade away and the chill disappears. Actually, I feel . . . good. Damn good.

I smack my lips because I swear I can taste Profit's spearmint kisses on my lips. I can feel his strong arms wrapped around me . . .

"Shhh. You don't want us to wake your parents," Profit whispered as he daddy-long-strokes in between my legs.

We were back in my pink princess room at the Douglases'. As he did most nights, Profit had climbed up the lattice and through my window. We loved making love under my foster parents' noses.

Our love was still young. Innocent—or naïve.

No one in either of our warring families knew that we were dating yet. No one had been killed. We foolishly believed that we could continue our love on the down low. Ignorance truly was bliss.

This was the moment that I wished would last forever . . .

14

Lucifer

Déjà vu.

It's the second time in six months that I've awakened in an upside down SUV with the heavy stench of gasoline burning my nose. The word *pain* is too mild a word to describe what my body is enduring, and it's impossible to block the shit out of my mind and do what I know must be done: *Get the hell out of here.* I twist my head this way and that way, sending a wave of broken glass cascading out of my hair.

Beside me, Python's ugly ass is knocked the hell out. He's also sporting a huge gash on his forehead, where blood streams and then drips all over my leg. At the sight of that foul shit, I struggle to move my leg. I don't care that they seize and cramp. I don't want this muthafucka touching me.

When I'm able to get my leg free, I look for the gun I snatched from Python and used to blow the back of the driver's head off. To my surprise, I'm still holding it. *Why can't I feel my hand?* I stare at my right arm as if it's a foreign appendage. The shit is swelling up right before my eyes.

"Ugh . . ." King Isaac's woeful moan from the front seat steals my attention.

I have to get the fuck out of here. I look around to the windowless door and crawl toward it, when my inner gangster demands I take care of business first. I aim at Python's head despite my swollen hand. *Ain't nobody going to miss this muthafucka, least of all my ass.* I tap the trigger.

Click

What the fuck? I tap it again.

Click. Click.

The muthafucka is empty.

Click. Click. Click.

Python's eyes fly open.

Oh shit. I drop the gun, turn, and bolt for the window. I only get the upper part of my body through the door before Python's gorilla hands wrap around my ankle. *No! No!*

"Where the fuck do you think you're going?" With a hard yank, I'm pulled a few inches back into the car, but I use my other foot to stomp the shit out of him. The shit is just as painful for me is it is for him, considering my feet are bare. However, I get a few good kicks in at his already cracked head, and he loses his grip on my foot. That's all I need to jet back out of the missing window.

"Fuck!" Python thunders.

I don't dare look back. My survival instincts are on full blast as I tumble onto soft, damp earth. Apparently the vehicle has tumbled down into a thickly wooded area.

"Hey, that bitch is escaping," a voice shouts.

I can only guess that it is more of King Isaac's minions. When shots ring out, I duck and dodge but keep hustling through the woods while expecting a bullet to hit and finish me off. As soon as the gunfire starts, it stops. My curiosity is too strong for me to resist a glance over my shoulder. I see nothing and no one. I've disappeared out of their line of fire.

An overwhelming rush of relief causes me to stumble, and before I know it my knees hit the ground. *Don't stop.* The voice in my head is so loud that I'm convinced that another person is shouting in my ear. I'm back on my feet in no time. Running like my life depends on it because—my life and my child's life really do depend on it.

As the woods get thicker and darker, the ground becomes a blanket of sharp rocks, broken tree branches, and other sharp objects. I slow down and tell myself that I don't think that King Isaac or his goons are following me.

No. Don't stop. This time the voice isn't as strong or as powerful. My gait slows down even more.

Don't stop.

I move above a light jog.

Don't stop.

A fast walk.

Don't stop.

A slow walk—until I find myself leaning my weight against a tree. "I just need a couple of seconds to catch my breath," I tell myself. However, the deep breaths bring my attention back to the pain radiating throughout my body. That's when I feel more blood trickling down my leg.

My baby. Head bowed, I drop down onto my knees. I can't explain it, but an overpowering sense of loss overwhelms me. I don't know how I know, but I just know that little Mason Junior couldn't have survived this hellish night—and it's my fault. If I had not been out avenging my brother's, Bishop, death like a madwoman against Shariffa's raggedy crew, she would never have ended up in my bedroom tonight, set on murdering me. Had I not been in the condition I was in, maybe I'd have been able to take Python and Isaac out when they came crashing through my door. I think about Ta'Shara lying in that pool of blood. She saved my life; that wisp of a girl. I never thought her more than a nuisance and maybe a bit of a pain in the neck. She never belonged in our world, but was dragged in kicking and screaming the night her sister had her gang raped.

I felt nothing when Ta'Shara landed in the mental hospital. But I took out her attackers solely because those same men were also responsible for putting Profit in the hospital with seventeen bullets in his chest. I had to make it clear to the Gangster Disciples that they couldn't come after the Vice Lords' prince and get away with it. When Profit first brought Ta'Shara home to Ruby Cove, she looked and behaved like an abandoned puppy that Profit found on the side of the road. That is until the kiss. I still don't know where the fuck that shit came from, but Profit kissed me and his girl saw it. Her change toward me was a complete one-eighty. It was the first time that I saw her potential to be a real Vice Lord Flower. Then I was the one who needed saving and she was right there. I feel shitty for how I treated the girl—and now she's dead. If I survive this night, no doubt Profit will blame me. How could he not? I blame me.

I sigh. The pain in my lower abdomen eases, but my fear for my child remains intact.

A howl whines through the woods. My head snaps up as I guess the direction that it's coming from.

A twig snaps.

My heart leaps but I climb to my feet. Leaves rustle and the night air dips several degrees. *You need a weapon.* I glance around, looking for something—anything to arm myself with, but all I see are branches that are either too large to pick up and wield or too small. Even the rocks are either embedded in earth or are sharp pebbles that wouldn't do much damage to a fly, let alone cause any sort of damage to a potential predator.

Crouched, I strain my eyes into the dark woods, waiting to see what will appear to attack and finish the job that King Isaac and Python failed to do.

The leaves rustle louder. The temperature plunges lower. The hairs on my arms and the back of my neck stand up straight. No matter what happens, I tell myself, I'll meet death like a soldier. Minutes passes and I remain tense and prepared for anything.

The rustling grows even louder—closer.

When a small head rounds a large tree in my direct line of vision, I'm shocked—and then disappointed. *Why disappointed?* I ask myself. My best answer is that I may have been eager for the torturous night to end. The small four-legged animal isn't the ferocious beast that I had expected, but the thin, malnourished dog sizes me up. My best guess is that it's a yellow Labrador, but I'm not sure. I've never been too keen on dogs and don't know one breed from another. One thing for sure, he's more afraid of me than I am of him.

Relief floods out my disappointment, and once again I'm back on my knees, not to cry or even pray, but to laugh. I've gone mad.

This also must've relaxed the dog a great deal because his pink, stinky tongue licks the side of my face as the laughter bubbles out of me.

Then the pain returns, stealing my breath and my laughter.

The dog steps back, watches. When I moan he howls as if in solidarity. My contractions intensify and it isn't too long before I'm sweaty and shivering in the cool night breeze and then prepare for the worst.

15

Cleo

Club Diesel

Tonight is a big night, but unfortunately I've fucked up every lead-in to every song through both sets on stage. However, I manage to pull it all together for a strong finish. As I walk offstage, I apologize to the band. They all give me the *pull your shit together* stare before marching backstage.

I wish I could—but it's been nearly two weeks since anybody has seen my ex-fiancé-slash-business-manager, Kalief. We're officially over, but it doesn't mean that we've cut emotional ties. Yes, he's a dog that loves pussy way too fucking much. Yes, he has lied, cheated, and stolen from me more times than I care to count, but our love story is . . . complicated.

Among other things, Kalief is an addict. He'll sniff, smoke, and inject about anything. On top of that, he drinks like a fucking fish and gambles away money that his ass doesn't have. Despite the circus of monkeys on his back, I still love him. I love him even though he entangled my ass with this club's owner, Diesel Carver.

One of the club's scantily clad waitresses taps my shoulder as I come offstage.

"The boss wants you."

Cool as a cucumber, I give the girl a small nod to let her know I heard her, but inside my stomach twists into knots while my heart claws its way through my throat. I don't trust Diesel—though he's tried hard to win me over with his fake charm. I almost fell for it. A couple of weeks back, the powerful thug pressured Kalief with an indecent proposal: I go out with Diesel and, in exchange, he wipes out Kalief's debts. The kicker: Kalief agreed. Ain't that some shit? To tell your girl that she has to go out on a date with another nigga to erase your gambling debts? Sure, Kalief dressed it up as a business date, dangling the carrot that Diesel Carver, with his deep connections in the music industry, was supposed to be our knight in shining armor—our ticket to stardom.

I went on the damn date. And yes, Diesel put on quite the show. First, a one-of-a-kind Givenchy beaded gold gown was delivered to the house and then a ride in a classed-out, top-of-the-line limousine through one of the roughest hoods in the city. Nearly every banger in a three-mile radius came and watched me do a red-carpet type walk before climbing into the backseat. Since then that's all it's taken for folks to wag their tongues about my ass being Diesel's new woman.

I'm not.

The limo ride took us to a small airstrip, where Diesel and I boarded a private jet that flew us to Atlanta. In the air, I was given a breathtaking diamond-and-platinum necklace, where I admit a few of my defenses were lowered. Then there was the kiss. The one that I sometimes still feel and taste. Where was my head to let him kiss me like that?

But it was . . . nice.

That shit is painful to admit—even to myself. From there Diesel took me on a night out on the town. Fine food, introduction to plenty of celebrities, and all the while, Diesel gassed me up about how he's going to make me a star. I fell for the shit and signed a contract making him my new manager. Another mistake in a long lifetime of mistakes.

My biggest one was not being around to protect my sister Essence. It's *my* fault that she's dead. *I. Let. It. Happen.* I should have kept her away from LeShelle's evil ass. I've always known that the bitch wasn't right. She's the latest wifey Python plucked off the pole at his old strip joint, the Pink Monkey. Essence was best friends with LeShelle's sister, Ta'Shara. And when a whole bunch of avoidable shit went down between the Murphy sisters, Essence was smack dab in the middle.

LeShelle pulled rank and ordered Essence to snoop around Ta'Shara's Vice Lord boyfriend's hospital bed—the bed that LeShelle had put him in by dumping a full clip in him on the teenagers' prom night. Essence was murdered for her efforts.

LeShelle told everyone who'd listen that Lucifer was behind the hit job. Like a fool, I believed her. I swore that I would avenge Essence's death, but the night that my path crossed Lucifer's, in the middle of a cemetery of all places, she was the one to get the drop on me. By the time I heard her and thought to go for my weapon, Lucifer made it clear that such a move was suicide—and I believed that too.

Lucifer is not like any other bitch in the game. Danger rolls off of her in waves. I didn't have the balls to go toe-to-toe with her. Which is why I believed her when she said that she didn't have anything to do with my sister's death. She had no reason to lie. I posed no threat to her that night. But LeShelle? If that bitch's mouth is moving, she is lying.

I never told the rest of my family. I never will. What's the point? Python has since married LeShelle's trifling ass, which makes her untouchable. He wouldn't give a single fuck about what LeShelle did to Essence. I told Lucifer that night where she could find LeShelle and Python, in hopes that the ruthless gangster would take the bitch out. But bullets bounced off them when the Vice Lords performed a drive-by outside the church where Python and LeShelle got married.

"Boss man wants to see you." Beast, one of Diesel's right-hand men from Atlanta, appears at my side before I make it to my box-size changing room.

"I know. I know." I take a nervous breath.

"Don't worry. You sounded good," Beast adds smiling. He *never* smiles.

Diesel, the six-foot-four, honey-brown gangster with striking greenish blue eyes has turned plenty of women's heads since he's moved to Memphis from Atlanta. People bump their gums about how he's taken with me and I've had more than my share of jealous glares—from the Queen Gs on the block as well as the women who work here.

Frankly, they can have his ass. Now that I've shaken off his charm offensive, I can add up all the shady shit that isn't sitting right. Like my seeing him fleeing from the Power of Prayer Baptist Church the morning I discovered Momma Peaches lying dead on the church's floor. And what about that envelope stuffed with cash that I saw him hand to his boy Beast on the day Momma Peaches's funeral was shot up? *Everyone* pinned that drive-by on the Vice Lords.

I have my doubts.

I don't pay attention to the whole blow-by-blow of who's up and who's down in the street wars. I'm a Queen G, but I've never done more than petty shit when I was a kid. At the end of the day, I ain't about that life—never have been and never will. Shit ain't been right since Diesel Carver rolled into this city. I should be distancing myself from this man, but instead I'm contractually bound to him.

With butterflies in my stomach I stroll over, with the best smile that I can manage, to Diesel's reserved table. Seated are Nefertiti, the club's general manager and omnipresent Amazon, and R & B legend and music-star maker Kenneth "K-Bone"

Wallis, who grins at me and looks more moneyed than any rich white man walking around the entire city of Memphis.

"Ms. Blackmon. Ms. Blackmon." K-Bone stands from the table, clapping. "I gotta shake your hand." He takes my hand and pumps it as if he's jacking up a car. "When Diesel told me that he has found the next Whitney Houston and Mariah Carey combined, I thought he was blowing smoke up my ass. But after that powerhouse performance, I'm a true believer."

The flattery and his exuberance make me light-headed.

"Why, thank you," is all I can think to say.

"Please. Please. Sit down." K-Bone rushes around the table and assists me into the U-shaped booth. It may be my imagination, but I swear on a stack of Bibles that the man brushes his soft, manicured fingers over the back of my hand like a caress.

By the time he and Diesel settle into their seats, there are two sets of lustful gazes staring back at me. I'm not surprised. The music industry is filled with horny hoes who prey on female artists.

Without Kalief, for the first time I'm navigating through these shark-infested waters by myself.

A bottle of Cristal is delivered to the table.

K-Bone asks, "Tell me your life story and why I haven't heard about you until now."

I came prepared, and rattle off an edited version of the truth.

K-Bone nods and laughs in the right spots, but I know that he's only half listening. Whether he's figuring out my commercial appeal or what it will take to get in between my legs, I'm not too sure.

I smile and make my chess moves, hoping that a real deal is actually on the table. One thing for sure, Diesel has wasted no time coming through, and it has me rethinking some of the bad shit I'd concluded about him. K-Bone is as legit as they come.

"Well . . . I definitely want you at Kingdom Records. We need to set up a time and date for the whole team to meet you."

"Whoa. Whoa. Pump the brakes." Diesel laughs. "We'll need to discuss what you're offering. I have a lot of cats lined up to meet my star here—and save your breath," Diesel adds when K-Bone opens his mouth, "if you're talking about a standard slave contract. Pull that shit on someone who doesn't know any better."

Diesel bossing up at the table takes K-Bone by surprise.

"No. No. I wasn't thinking nothing like that," K-Bone says, after downing a full glass of Cristal. "But let me ask, what are *you* considering in order for me to get you to tell those other cats to take a hike?"

Beast interrupts. "Excuse me, boss." He leans over and whispers in Diesel's ear.

Diesel's affable smile melts off of his face.

K-Bone and I shoot nervous looks at one another.

"Excuse me for a moment," Diesel says and jets up from the table.

What in the hell? My phone vibrates from within my dress's bustier. "Just a sec." I spin in my seat and slyly retrieve my phone. My grandma is at home with two young children, so I answer the call when I see her home number pop up on the screen.

"Where's Kobe?" Grandma shouts before I get *hello* out of my mouth.

"What?" I plug one finger into my right ear so that I can hear better. "Where's what?"

"Where's your brother?" she demands. "Please tell me that his fast behind ain't part of this mess going down at Ruby Cove. It's plastered on all the local channels."

Nothing she's saying is making any sense to me. "What about Ruby Cove? What are you talking about?"

"They're calling it a massacre by the Gangster Disciples and Kobe isn't home. Please tell me he ain't involved in this gang-banging mess."

My heart drops and my grandma's panic becomes a contagion over the line. *Where is Kobe?*

16

Hydeya

Ruby Cove

A half hour later, the police regain control of the crime scene and a slew of Vice Lords, including Mason and Profit, are crammed into paddy wagons and taken downtown. Shortly after, Lieutenant John Fowler finally arrives on the scene.

"I came as soon as I got your message," Lieutenant Fowler explains, jogging up the two steps at the scene of the crime. "What's the situation?"

"The situation is that I'm here now and *I* have everything under control," I tell him, unable to wipe the smirk off my face even if the Lord Almighty sent Jesus back down here to ask me politely.

Fowler doesn't spare me a glance. Instead he focuses his attention on Chief Brown. The look on his face makes it clear that he expects the boss to override what I just said. When the chief doesn't answer, I turn around and stare. *What fucking kind of game is she playing?*

"Hawkins got here first. She has the lead on this one," the chief rules, looking none too pleased about her decision before spinning on her heels to march back inside the house.

Fowler's painted-on smile drops before his eyes creep over

in my direction. "I guess that means that I should be welcoming you back?"

"Contain your excitement." I roll my eyes, turn, and fall in line behind the chief.

Fowler takes up the rear and hisses, "What happened to your administrative leave?"

"I guess since you don't know how to answer your phone when you're on call, it ended."

Chief Brown and another officer give a brief rundown about where tonight's sole survivor of this house's attack was found bleeding out. "Our victim's name is . . ." The officer looks down at his notepad.

"Ta'Shara Murphy," I fill in for him.

Three sets of eyes shift in my direction.

"I met her once at Baptist Memorial a couple of months back. Her and her boyfriend, Raymond Lewis aka Profit." Thrusting up my chin and flashing a smile, I congratulate myself. I may not kiss the ring like they always want me to do, but I know most of my cases like the back of my hand.

"What do you know? We're making progress," the chief quips, and then gestures for the officer to continue the briefing.

"We also have Miss . . . Murphy's 9-1-1 call. She called in and reported that she had shot an intruder. We're assuming that was the body upstairs."

I step back. "I want to take a look."

The chief, Lieutenant Fowler, the officer, and myself turn and head for the staircase. The bullet-riddled living room is nothing compared to the bloody carnage found in the master bedroom. In here, the forensic team has their work cut out for them.

"Holy shit," Fowler swears, arriving last.

"Tell me about it." The chief sighs as her gaze sweeps around the room. "Just when you think that you've seen everything out here in the streets, there's always some sick fuck roaming around to prove you wrong."

I keep my *amen* to myself while I watch the EMTs zip up a woman with half her head missing into a body bag. It's easy to conclude that it's her brain that's shattered into small bits and pieces all over the walls and floor. There are also two weapons lying on the floor: a huge Browning knife and a .38. One of the windows in the room has been demolished. Shards of glass are strewn everywhere.

"What about our kidnap victim? Was she taken from here?" I ask, referring to this Willow person that Fat Ace—or rather Mason—brought up.

"Possibly." The chief turns and shrugs. "You might want to check around with the other officers downstairs."

I nod and make my own notes.

"Anybody have any idea what all of this shit is about?" Fowler asks.

"The same thing that it's *always* about," the chief says. "Power."

"Or revenge," I add cynically.

Brown and Fowler nod in agreement.

"So who is the other chick?" I ask, gesturing to the zipped body bag being carried out of the room.

"Don't know. No ID was found on her."

One forensic team member stops snapping pictures to inject himself into our conversation. "She isn't from around here."

"What makes you say that?" I ask.

The photographer strolls over to our small group. "Here. Look." He holds up the screen on the back of his camera and scrolls through a series of pictures before settling on an image.

"Crip Rider?" I frown.

The photographer nods. "It's the tattoo on our brainless victim's back. The girl is a Crippette."

Fowler bristles. "What is she doing here on this side of the tracks?"

"Sooo . . . this was a Crip hit?" I question, unable to hide my surprise. I was sure that I would be slapping handcuffs back on my jailbird daddy by the end of my shift.

"That would be my first guess," the forensic guy says.

The chief shakes her head. "The gossip on the street says that it was the Gangster Disciples. Of course none of them want to go on record."

All I can think about are those crates of weapons that were in Isaac's living room tonight. I *know* what the truth is. I can feel it in my gut. *Why the fuck would he put me in this goddamn position?*

I shift my gaze to Fowler, who is studiously nodding and scribbling notes. "What are you doing?" I ask. "I already told you that this is my case."

"And since when do you not share?" he asks, perplexed.

Ever since I found out that you're really after my job. "I got this. Why don't you go back to whatever it was that kept you from doing your job tonight?"

Fowler's face twists up as if I'm speaking a foreign language. "Are you serious?"

"Don't I look serious?"

Fowler flips his notepad closed, but before he's able to give me a piece of his mind, the chief breezes her petite frame between us to instruct, "Now you two play nice. There are plenty of dead bodies for you guys to share."

"LET ME IN! THIS IS MY DAUGHTER'S HOUSE!"

Bam! Crash! Boom!

"Let me go! I have to check on my daughter!"

"What in the hell?" The three of us chime together before taking off to see what the latest commotion is about downstairs.

"Ma'am, please. I can't let you inside. This is a crime scene," Officer Wendi Hendrix explains as she struggles to block the woman's access into the house.

Behind the older woman are two other cops, tugging her back.

"What's going on down here?" I ask, taking control of the situation.

"My daughter," the distraught woman wails. "Where's my daughter?"

"And *who* is your daughter?" Fowler questions.

I know the answer before the woman says it.

"Willow . . . Willow Washington. This is her house. Somebody said that they took her away." Her wild eyes mist. "They can't do that. They already killed my other baby. They have to give her back." Whatever strength she is relying on caves, and she doubles over and releases a wail so deep that my own grief from Drake's senseless murder stirs.

Officer Reid consoles her. "Ma'am, we're going to do all we can to find your daughter, but you gotta let us do our jobs."

It's doubtful that the mother hears a single thing that's being said.

Grief counseling isn't the chief's forte, so she meanders off without a sound.

I draw a breath, tap Reid on the shoulder, and tell him, "I got this now."

Reid looks up with hopeful eyes. "Are you sure?"

"Yeah."

"Thanks."

After giving him the *don't mention it* nod, I take over soothing the mother. First, I give her a moment to release the pain that's overtaking her. I lost it, too, when Drake was killed.

Fowler disappears, too, but when he returns, he's holding a glass of water. "Here. Get her to drink this."

I take the glass without thanking him. "Here you go, ma'am. Drink this. It should help you to calm down. Go on. Take it."

The older woman's hands tremble as she reaches for it.

Concerned that she won't be able to maintain her grip, I help her to bring it to her lips. "That's it. There you go." I smile like one might at a newborn baby. When she's drunk half the water, I pull the glass away to make sure that she doesn't choke. "How are you feeling?"

"Better," she answers through quivering lips, but more tears fall. "I just want my daughter back—safe. Where she belongs. I can't lose her too."

"I understand."

"No. You don't." She clutches my arm. "I've already lost too many—and we . . . well. There are so many things that we've never said to each other. I mean, she has always been so angry and distant. Ever since her father was gunned down . . ."

I tense in fear that I'm about to be subjected to a long soap opera about her family. "It's going to be okay," I assure her. "If she's out there, we'll find her."

Her grip on my arm tightens. "P-promise? You promise me?"

"We're going to do all that we can," I tell her, avoiding making the rookie mistake of promising a grieving parent anything. They tend to hold you to it. The look on her face says that she knows *exactly* what I'm doing. Her expression is of true devastation.

"Do you live far from here, Mrs. . . . ?"

"Washington," she mumbles before taking another long gulp of water. "Call me Lucille. I live down the street."

I glance up in the direction she's pointing and see that the crowd of neighbors in the street is still growing behind the yellow crime tape, along with more news vans. They are still waiting to find out how terrified the city's citizens should be tonight. "Is there anybody here who can walk you home?"

Her gaze drifts off.

I turn to Fowler. "I'll be back. I'm going to walk her home and get a statement."

"Do you want me to come with you?"

The look I give him asks *What the hell do you think?*

"I'll stay here and help hold down the fort," he responds.

"*Or* you can take off like I've asked you to several times already." I flash a fake smile.

"Don't I know you?" Mrs. Washington asks, peering up into the lieutenant's face.

"Who? Me?" he asks, pressing a hand against his chest.

Mrs. Washington nods and stares up at him.

Fowler's laughter sounds like it's coming from a busted tailpipe. "No. Not that I recall."

I stare at him until he looks at me oddly.

"What?" he barks.

"Nothing." I shrug but watch his strange behavior until he turns around and goes back into the house. Had I known that was all it took for him to stop shadowing me, I would have stared at him sooner.

"C'mon, Mrs. Washington. I'll walk you home."

Compliant, she turns and walks, still clutching the water glass. Once we get on the other side of the tape, neighbors tell Mrs. Washington to keep her head up. Others give her sympathetic looks. For me, there is nothing but contempt and scorn. The media, however, descend like locusts.

"Captain Hawkins, can you tell us what happened here tonight?"

"Captain, how many bodies have your department found?"

"Captain, should the people of Memphis be worried about the acceleration of gang violence in the city?"

My head hurts. "Excuse us. Please let us through," I say, holding up my hand to block the bright lights on some of their cameras.

Mrs. Washington's home is a few doors down from her daughter and is a near replica of the two-story home. When we enter, it's like I've stepped into a haunted house. The place is dark, unkempt, and cold. In fact, I believe that it's warmer *outside* in the wintry night.

"Excuse the mess," she says. "I haven't cleaned the place up in a while."

"No problem." My gaze darts around. I wouldn't say that she is a hoarder quite yet, but the potential is here.

"Please. Please. Have a seat," she offers, picking up a stack of newspapers and magazines.

"That's okay, ma'am. I don't mind standing." I retrieve my pen and notepad again. "If I can take your statement and perhaps get a picture of your daughter?"

"Oh yeah. A picture." She covers her mouth as she looks around the clutter. "A picture . . . a picture . . ."

My heart goes out to her once again. It's probably a trick of the damn lighting in here, but she appears so lost and fragile.

At last she flashes me a wobbly smile. "You have to forgive me. Willow has never been one for taking pictures. I don't know why, because she's such a pretty girl. When she was little I used to love putting her in cute dresses." She swipes her eyes. "Then after her father Darcell died, she became such a tomboy." She snaps her fingers. "Wait. I know." She crosses to a huge Bombay chest and digs through the drawers. "I know that I have her graduation picture around here somewhere."

While she searches, I ask her questions. "So where were you when the shooting took place tonight?"

"In bed," she says. "The first couple of shots I didn't react. But then it went on and on . . . and on. I didn't know what the hell was happening. There's so much foolishness going on out here in these streets that I try to keep to myself."

"So you didn't actually *see* anything tonight?"

"No. I lay still until it was over. Afterward I took something for my nerves, then tried to go back to sleep. When that didn't work I turned on the news—and that's when I found out." Another tear skips down her face before she resumes her search. "Oh, here it is." She removes a gray shoebox from the bottom drawer. "I know it has to be in here." She shuffles over to the couch.

I follow, wanting to hurry this up. I hang over her shoulder while she thumbs through the box of photographs.

"Here it is." She removes a striking picture of a beautiful

girl in her cap and gown, dark shoulder-length hair, warm chest-nut complexion, and captivating and intense brown eyes.

"She's pretty."

Lucille's smile brightens. "Yes. She is."

"Mind if I keep this?" I ask.

She hesitates.

"I'll make a copy and bring it back to you." Gently I pry the picture from her trembling hand. When it slips free, a fresh wave of tears rushes over her lashes. "I knew from the minute Willow started following her brother, Juvon, and that *boy* around that this day would come. He ain't been nothing but trouble since that white girl brought him around here."

I have no idea what she's talking about. However, another picture lying in the box catches my attention. *Is that who I think it is?* I reach over her shoulder and pluck the photograph out of the box. There's no mistaking the man smiling back at me. "How do *you* know Captain Melvin Johnson?"

17

Hydeya

Bam! Bam! Bam!

Lucille and I jump at the hammering on the front door.

"Oh my. Who is that?" Lucille asks, setting her box of pictures aside and attempting to stand up.

"Don't trouble yourself," I tell her, hanging on to the pictures of Willow Washington *and* Captain Johnson. "I'll get it."

She sighs and gives me a relieved smile. "Thank you. You're too kind."

Bam! Bam! Bam!

I rush to the door, annoyed. I can tell by the persistent knocking that it's one of my guys. When I snatch the door open I am surprised to see Chief Brown instead of a patrol officer.

"We gotta go," she snaps, jutting a thumb over her shoulder. "These muthafuckas are shooting up the whole damn city." With no further explanation, she turns and scrambles off the porch, giving me no time to ask her a follow-up question.

"Who is out there?" Mrs. Washington shouts from the living room.

I race back with a hurried explanation. "Mrs. Washington, we're going to have to continue this conversation later. Something has come up."

I can't tell whether the initial look on her face is of disappointment or relief. But she pushes up a brave smile and clambers to her feet. "I'll appreciate whatever you can do to bring my baby back home."

"Yes, ma'am. We'll certainly do all we can." I wish I could *promise* her that everything will work out, but I want to keep my bullshit to the absolute minimum.

After Mrs. Washington and I say our goodbyes, I slip the two photographs into my pocket and jog back up to my vehicle where Chief Brown is pacing like a caged tiger. The crowd has thinned and the media vans are gone. All in all, it doesn't look good.

"What's up? What's going on?"

"Some kind of shooting and an overturned SUV matching the description of the one fleeing here have been reported off I-55." She hops into her car. "I'll meet you over there."

Oh shit. Isaac. Obscenities flow through my head as I hop behind the wheel of my car. I struggle to push my emotions to the side as I follow the chief and a convoy of news vans to the crash site.

I arrive at the scene within minutes and with half the city's news crews in tow. Riding in my own personal vehicle, I'm missing the police chatter over the radio. It doesn't matter, because I already know what everyone is thinking: that we may finally have our guys. One of them may very well be my father.

I exit my vehicle prepared for anything. It's crazy how my emotions are all over the place for a man that I profess to not be able to stand. Family ties are crazy. They can hurt you without trying.

"What do we have here?" I ask the first officer that I come across, ignoring the throng of reporters shouting questions.

I rush over to the cliff, where the vehicle has tumbled off the road. As I look down the dark embankment, a thin sheet of rain drizzles against my skin. I remove my shades and use my hand to hood my eyes. I have trouble making out anything.

A few officers make their way down the cliff, skidding, tumbling, and busting their asses on the way down. Drawing another deep breath, I take my first step; the soft earth gives way beneath my feet. A dramatic and ungraceful windmilling of my arms ensues as I attempt to keep my balance, but in the end it fails, and I, too, skid, tumble, and fall the rest of the way down.

At the bottom of the cliff, I have nothing more than a busted ass and sore limbs and a bruised ego. I sweep the red earth from my clothes and wobble my way to the SUV.

Empty.

Relief whooshes through my system—so much so that I have to lean against the vehicle. There is no doubt in my mind that this is one of the SUVs involved in the massacre on Ruby Cove; it's littered with bullet holes. There's no license plate and the VIN number has been scratched off. But what gets my heart pumping is the amount of blood that's splashed within the interior. *Isaac could've been in this car.*

I exhale a long breath. I knew that his release from prison would complicate my life. I was right. I just didn't think it would happen this fast. The rest of the forensic crime team makes it down the embankment and immediately marks off and secures the area.

I draw in another cleansing breath and envision tomorrow's headlines. No doubt the reporters will be relentless. The endless comparison to the late, great Captain Johnson will no doubt go on, everyone forgetting that this hell started under him before he was struck down by the very violence that he was charged to end. Despite hitting the ground running, I've yet to put any *wins* on the board for the city. I have to get *something* on the scoreboard.

Deep in thought, I circle around the perimeter. As I pass by one of the numerous trees, something catches my eye. I lean in close. I place my hand against its trunk. *A bullet.* I lean back and glance around.

"SOMEONE GET ME A FLASHLIGHT!"

The officers scramble to hand one over. I click the flashlight on and direct the bright beam up another tree trunk.

"We need to expand the perimeter," I shout, successfully jerking everyone's attention in my direction. I then set about swinging the flashlight beam from one random tree to the next, taking me farther and farther into the woods. Once I run out of bullet-riddled trees, I move the light to the rocky ground. Another oddity catches my attention.

"What you got?" Chief Brown asks, huffing up behind me.

I hadn't even noticed that she had joined the search. Before answering, I kneel onto one knee and make a closer inspection of the dead leaves and pine needles. "Blood. A person or an animal has been recently wounded out here." Once again, my father springs into mind. My hearts trips over a few beats. It has taken me years to master my emotions about that man, and in one night, my discipline has been shot to hell.

I quickly make out the direction of the bloody trail. Deeper and deeper we go into the woods. The entire way my heart hammers, my hands sweat, and I brace for the worst.

Suddenly, as if he'd just spat out of the earth itself, a yellow dog appears in front of us.

Woof! Woof! Woof!

Everyone's guns come out of their holsters.

"Wait," I shout before some reckless officer fires.

Silence.

I kneel down again. "Hey, boy. Now where did you come from?" I stretch out my hand, letting him know that I'm cool.

The dog sniffs, turns, and trots off. When he sees that no one follows, he stops and turns back around. *Woof! Woof! Woof!* "I think Lassie here is trying to tell us something." I climb back up onto my feet and lead the team in following the dog.

"There's something up ahead." At least a dozen flashlights sweep up.

"Oh shit." There, up ahead, isn't the big, muscular frame of my father, but one of a sweaty woman, huffing and puffing the cool night air. One look at the woman's face and I recognize her from her mother's picture: *Willow Washington.*

18

Cleo

Bolting out of my seat, I rush backstage to the dressing room to grab my duffel bag, clutch, and car keys. Before I head out the back door I catch members of my band huddled together.

"I'm telling you, King Isaac smoked those fools," Gabe, our drummer, brags. "The game has officially been changed. The Gangster Disciples has a real fucking leader again." That announcement is followed by hoops, dabs, and shoulder bumps before they return their attention to their smartphone screens.

"Can I see?" I ask, throwing myself into the mix.

Robbie, the bass player, turns his high-wattage smile in my direction. "Don't tell me your nigga ain't told you the dealy-yo!"

"Who, Kalief?"

"No. Not that bum-nigga. Your new man—Diesel. I *know* he's in on this shit too, 'cause his ass is in *everything* since he got here."

Head shaking, I reach for Joel's smartphone, and then tap the screen to replay the news clip. With all the noise that's going on backstage I can't hear what the young reporter is saying, but I'm transfixed by all the chaos behind her. There's no doubt about it, that is Ruby Cove behind her, along with what looks like the city's entire emergency response team with their lights flashing. Beneath the reporter, the words *Breaking News* appear in huge block letters.

"I don't understand. What happened?" I lean in close and catch a few words. Only *massacre* and *gang wars* stick out.

"King Isaac is what happened," Gabe says with a smile stretched from ear to ear. Every member of the band has gang ties. We're out here doing our legit hustle, but what happens in the street still affects us. "That shit is payback for that bullshit that happened at Momma Peaches's funeral. Those foul mutha-fuckas are shooting up churches and now burial sites? Niggas nowadays ain't got no fucking chill button. The disrespect has been going on for far too long, if you ask me."

"Mm-hmm." Every one of the guys bobs his head in agreement.

Encouraged, Gabe jumps on a soapbox. "And if you ask any real nigga on the street, Python's ass has been slipping for real. Ever since he rose up off Shotgun Row, the Vice Lords have had a clear path running these streets. Fuck. The only people who have even done anything to keep them in check is a group of purple bitches who took out that she-devil's brother at Da Club."

"The Crippettes," I fill in for him as I hand him back his phone.

"Yeah. Yeah. Python's ex-old lady, Shariffa. That bitch changed fucking flags and then bought a whole new set of brass balls. I ain't mad at her."

Jase laughs. "What the fuck are you talking about? That bitch is the last muthafucka you wanna be right now." At our rapt attention, he continues. "Word is that each one of those bitches that were involved in that hit at Da Club are either MIA or have been chopped up like chop suey. You think that a bitch like Lucifer is going to let niggas keep breathing when you go gunning for her fam? If you do, I have a bridge in Brooklyn that I'd like to sell your monkey ass."

The image of Lucifer in that cemetery creeps back to mind and I have to agree with my bandmate. I wouldn't want to be anywhere near the infamous gangster's shit list. I know that I'm sick of the street drama. Lord knows that bullets are never going to stop.

"I gotta go," I tell them, exiting the conversation. "I gotta find Kobe. I hope he ain't involved in this nonsense."

"Good luck," a few of them mumble, avoiding my gaze. I rush out the back door and hop into my old Toyota. Only my car refuses to turn over. "Please. Please. Don't do this," I beg. But my car isn't listening to me. I grab my phone again and dial Kobe's cell. "C'mon. C'mon. Answer the phone." The line rings in my ears. In my head, I see the news reporter breathlessly talking about the escalation of the city's gang warfare. Several witnesses named the Gangster Disciples as this night's terrorists, but none of them wanted to make such claims on camera.

This morning Kobe and his friends were excited about something that they were supposed to be getting into tonight. I dismissed their conspiratorial looks and whispers as their usual Saturday night plans with the latest teenage thots that twerk for drinks down at the hottest clubs. Now I have a sinking feeling that I misread the whole situation.

Kobe was excited about the return of King Isaac to Shotgun Row. He bragged that shit was going to change and that Python's leadership was in serious jeopardy. Kobe never did real gang-banging shit, just a few petty crimes, nothing too serious. He's mainly a jokester with a weed and PlayStation addiction. On second thought, maybe I'm overreacting.

My call goes to voicemail. The knot in my stomach tightens. Still. I have to remind myself that doesn't mean anything.

"Kobe. It's Cleo. Call me as soon as you get this message." I turn over the car again and still nothing.

I look up in time to see Diesel exit out the back of the club with Beast, Madd, Matrix, and Bullet. I grab my shit and hop back out of the car. "Hey! Diesel. Wait up." I race as fast as my pinched-toe silver pumps will allow.

Diesel, with his phone still tucked between his ear and shoulder, slows up.

"I need a ride. Any chance that you can swing by my place?"

He spears me with a singular look. "Hop in."

Bullet opens the back door.

"Thanks," I say, relieved.

Beast climbs in behind the wheel and Diesel climbs in from the other side. I only vaguely wonder about K-Bone, who we left stranded in VIP with Nefertiti.

Beast rolls out of the parking lot while Diesel punches another number into his phone. When his attempts are unsuccessful, his large hand tightens around the smartphone and the muthafucka warps instantly. He's pissed.

They didn't tell him.

Python and King Isaac, the only two men who could have leveled tonight's attack, hadn't clued Diesel in on their plans. All the GD soldiers and Queen Gs have been gossiping for the longest time about Diesel's ascension in the Memphis game. After all, he's been running shit and keeping muthafuckas fed since Python was forced underground.

Like Kobe said this morning, King Isaac's return changes everything. Diesel is no longer successor to the throne. The expansion of his Southern empire is officially on hold.

An unexpected smile flutters to my face. This shit couldn't have happened to a more deserving smug son-of-a-bitch.

With the radio off and the men blowing steam through their noses, the car ride is the most awkward one I've ever experienced in my life. I can't help but curse every red traffic light that lengthens the ride. More than once, my gaze sneaks its way back to Diesel. I can't help but be fascinated by his whole change in demeanor from just minutes ago in VIP.

Someone's cell phone goes off and we all scramble to look at our screens to see which of our people are trying to get in contact with us.

"Python," Diesel answers, sounding both overexcited *and* pissed off at the same time. The tension that was already in the car now rises to the level of being unbearable. The ache in my chest is either from my stomach looping into a giant knot or from my heart hammering against my rib cage. It only gets worse as the silence stretches while Diesel presses his ear to his phone and listens to his caller.

Beast's curiosity has him daring glances to the back of the car through the rearview mirror.

I wonder if he's any better at reading his boss's expression than I am.

"A doctor?" Diesel says as if asking for clarification. "Where are you?"

Another long pause.

Car horns blare and I look in time to see that Beast must've shot through a red light and nearly caused a traffic accident. The car has also picked up speed as if he gives zero fucks about being pulled over by police.

I grope around my ass for the seat belt. Just because Beast doesn't care whether his ass sees tomorrow doesn't mean I'm ready to meet our Maker with him.

"All right. We're on our way," Diesel announces and then ends the call. Before Beast can spit out a question, Diesel announces, "Change in plans. We need to head out to Frayser."

"Frayser?" I ask, twisting up my face. "You're dropping me off at my place first, right?"

"Later," Diesel says, already dialing another number into his phone.

"But—"

Diesel presses a finger against my lips to shut me up while he makes his call. For a second I'm too stunned to remove his hand from my mouth, but then when my pride and dignity kick back into gear, I brush his hand away and glare at him like he's lost his mind. I shouldn't have bothered, because his attention is on his call.

"I'm cashing in a chip," he tells the other person on the line. "Where are you?"

I fold my arms and glare.

"Be ready in five minutes," Diesel adds and then disconnects that call. "Beast. You remember where Dr. Ngozi stays?"

Beast shakes his head.

Diesel reviews a business card from the black billfold he keeps in his suit's breast pocket and then leans forward to pass it up to Beast in the front seat.

Beast hangs a sharp right at the next light and I'm forced into the uncomfortable position of bringing the subject back to me.

"I need to get home," I say rather weakly.

"And we will get you home—later. There is something more important I have to take care of first." His tone makes it clear that he wants no further argument from me.

I ignore it. "You can just drop me off up at the next corner. I'm sure that I can make my way home."

Beast's hard gaze shifts over to me in the rearview mirror.

Diesel's mouth flattens into a firm, flat line. "Later."

My heart shoots up into my throat, blocking any other response from spilling out of my mouth. Whatever the fuck that's about to go down, I'm going to be a part of it whether I like it or not. Sullen, I shut the fuck up and sit in my seat while Beast chauffeurs us through the city at nearly eighty miles an hour.

When we pull up into a huge house in Germantown, a short, squat man rushes out with an old-fashioned doctor's bag that I've only seen on television with doctors who run around making house calls.

Diesel climbs out of the backseat and rushes to greet the doctor, who I'm certain is African. There's a brief shaking of hands and a number of words that I can't make out through my rolled-up window.

Hopping out of the car here doesn't even occur to me until after the square-shaped doctor has piled into the backseat with Diesel and me. Bullet and Beast remain in the front.

Dr. Ngozi smiles and pushes up his thick, black-rimmed glasses. I can't get myself to smile back. With tension in the car being what it is, the last thing my system can take is the doctor's cloying cologne. He must've taken a bath in the shit. I hit the button for the window but the child lock is engaged. "Can I *please* get some air?"

Beast takes a second from his NASCAR driving to unlock the window.

The first gush of air that streams into the car feels like heaven. My performance tonight already feels as if it was years ago. Kobe, please. Please. Don't be entangled with this mess. I try again to call him, but the call goes to voicemail. I tell myself that I'm overreacting, but my anxiety refuses to abate.

Beast pulls up to a busted-looking warehouse out in the middle of Frayser. If I didn't know any better, I'd think that the place was haunted. Beast kills the engine and the men jet out of the car as if someone shot off a starter pistol. I'm stunned by how I've been forgotten. I consider staying my ass right here in the back of this expensive-ass car—until I spot about a half dozen crackheads in the general vicinity, creeping and shaking. I make the immediate decision to get my bougie-looking ass up into the scary-looking building with the brothahs with

guns, rather than hang back in here with nothing but a .22 and
a pair of stilettos against an army of crackheads.

I'm strong.

Not stupid.

I hightail it out of the back of the car and then race to the
heavy metal door, but I'm totally unprepared for the bloody
mess that is King Isaac and Python.

19

Lucifer

I'm hallucinating again—I must be. There's no other way to explain the team of police officers that have magically appeared in these woods.

"I NEED A PARAMEDIC!" a woman shouts before storming to my side. The mangy dog that had been whining and fretting by my side for the past half hour returns and runs its funky tongue along the side of my head.

"Aaaargh!" I bear down as another contraction hits with the force of a Mack truck. Sweat pours out of places on my body that I would've never thought possible. Nothing in my life has prepared me for this. I'm seriously having visions of taking a knife and cutting this kid out myself. The pain can't possibly get any worse.

"Willow? You're Willow Washington, right?" the wide-eyed cop asks, brushing back my wet hair.

I attempt to answer, but at the next small break between the contractions, I puff air in and out of my cheeks like a child's imitation of a locomotive.

"It's okay. It's okay, Willow," the female cop assures, but she looks and sounds as panicked as I am. "Help is on the way. We're going to get you to the hospital, where you can deliver this baby. Okay?"

"Aaaargh!" My body locks up again and I bear down, pushing with everything I've got. I don't have the strength to tell this woman that my child is ten weeks early . . . that there is zero chance of him surviving after the night that I've been through.

That harsh reality unleashes a lifetime's worth of tears. I'm unabashedly caught up in my feelings and there's not a damn thing that I can do about it. Why didn't I take more precautions? How did I allow Shariffa and then the Gangster Disciples to catch me sleeping? The questions and the pain inch me closer to insanity.

After a while I can't make sense of anything this cop is saying. The frenetic scramble of activity doesn't seem like it's happening to me but to someone who looks like me while I hover above myself.

I'm not going to make it.

Death doesn't faze me. Sure, I'll miss the love of my life and the unborn child that I have yet to lay eyes on, but there is something incredibly seductive about leaving the troubles of this world behind. No more banging. No more death and dead bodies. And no more trying to be hard twenty-four/seven and being afraid of showing my soft side to anyone but Mason. I hadn't been able to show him until the night he knocked me up. Before then, I conveyed my love by showing him how loyal a soldier I could be. Wherever he and Bishop went, I wanted to be by their sides in the thick of things. Nothing scared me off—not even witnessing my father, Dough Man, gunned down in our front yard.

As I give my body over to the unrelenting pain, my mind tumbles back through time. The good and bad times sharpen into focus. It's easy now to spot all the mistakes that I've made, some I would do over and others I cherish for the lessons that I learned.

"It's not your time," a voice as clear as a bell says to me. When I look around, it's not any of the emergency responders who are scrambling to get me into an ambulance that catch my attention.

It's the unsettling image of my brother, Bishop. The gunshot wound to his head is still visible. I'm bothered *and* happy to see him again. When I last saw him alive we weren't on the best of terms.

The Vice Lords had believed Mason was dead, and instead of the leadership automatically falling to me, his right hand, Bishop made it clear that my having a pussy should be a disqualifier. Our having never squashed our beef is painful, because I know that we eventually would have.

"It's not your time," he repeats.

But I don't believe him. I'm not too sure that I want to.

"You gotta go back," Bishop insists. His eyes are kinder than I remember, maybe because he senses how much I want to stay with him—at least for a while. With him, I am no longer seized by the never-ending contractions and Mason Junior's dead body refusing to leave mine. Suddenly there are a million questions I want to ask, but none crest my lips and Bishop doesn't say anything else. There's that loving look of forgiveness and the expectancy for me to do the right thing.

Suddenly, my soul is sucked back like a super magnet. I'm slammed back into my body when I take in a huge breath of air.

"We have a heartbeat," a man shouts.

I'm confused about my whereabouts even as my gaze dances around the cramped space. My exhausted body is still wringing with pain.

"Ms. Washington, can you hear me?" the young man asks. His grim face tells me that he doesn't have too much hope of my surviving this nightmare either.

Tears pour from my rarely used tear ducts. Bishop's disappearance feels like betrayal. It's not logical, but emotions rarely are. I figure out that I'm in the back of an ambulance and redouble my efforts to concentrate on what the EMT is telling me, but the man may as well be talking in Greek. I'm only able to capture a few words.

Hospital. Baby. Push.

The back door of the ambulance explodes open and few more frantic EMTs jump inside. They lift me and carry me out.

The hospital. I *hate* hospitals. And just because it's my turn being rushed through double-wide doors with a team of faces around me that I've never seen before, I'm not about to change my opinion anytime soon. Where is Mason? Where is that female cop from the woods? Hell. I'll even take that foul-smelling, mangy dog as source of reassurance.

I don't know what to expect. I should kick my own ass for not being better prepared. After all, I've known about my pregnancy since literally weeks after it happened.

Finally, I'm wheeled into a bright room where a red-faced white man rushes through an introduction while the nurse's cold hands cram my legs into stirrups.

"Epi . . . epidural," I beg. Pride be damned.

"Sorry. We're too far along for that," the doctor says, not sounding too damn sorry at all. I don't understand why they can't give me *something*. Don't I look like I'm in sufficient pain?

My head hurts—badly. Images swim all around me.

The doctor rattles off something else, but I'm way past the point of understanding a word that he's saying. All I can do is pray that the end is near.

But once again, God isn't answering any of my prayers. Hours later, I hear the word *C-section*. At this point, I don't care what the hell he does. I want this baby cut out of me. *Now!*

I hear the words *spinal tap*. At long last, relief from my body's pain, but not my head's. In fact, my head feels as if it's about to explode wide open. Though I can't quite feel my lower extremities, there's an extreme amount of pressure and then nothing. Is it all over?

I lift my heavy head. Beads of sweat roll all over my body. Everyone's faces have lost their color, even the only black nurse in the room. I know before anyone tells me. "It's dead, isn't it?" I can't get the pronoun *he* past my lips. I'm already re-treating from acknowledging its humanity. If I do, I may lose what's left of my sanity.

The doctor doesn't answer. The doctor and nurses begin a rash of frantic activities.

"Doctor?"

To my amazement, he turns his back on me. The room blurs behind a wave of tears. *Don't ask him again. Don't.* "Doctor, please. Tell me. Is it . . . ?" A boulder of emotions lodges in my throat, and despair clutches my heart, despite my lame attempts to stop it.

He's dead. He's dead. He's dead.

A strangled cry pierces the silence. Startled, my despair transforms to joy. "I'm a mother. I'm really a mother." I laugh and then reach for the baby, but a small glass casing—an incubator—is wheeled into the room while nurses wash and wrap the baby with quick efficiency.

"Wait. I want . . . I want . . ." The pain in my head detonates. A white light flashes before my eyes. I gasp and then collapse into total darkness.

20

Cleo

The Frayser warehouse

"**C**heck out my boy first," King Isaac tells Dr. Ngozi, shrugging him away even though he looks the worse of the two.

The nervous doctor questions whether Isaac is sure, but at Isaac's decisive nod, he turns to Python, who puts up the same protests.

"No. No. Do him first," Python insists. "I'm good. I'm good."

The doctor's frustration eclipses his nervousness after a solid minute of their back and forth.

Python is examined first. He pulls off his black, tight-fitting T-shirt and reveals an incredible muscular body and heavily tatted chest. I have always known that Python was an incredibly fit guy, but there's no denying how physically cut he is. He's not handsome by any means, but throw a paper bag over his head and there isn't a sister alive who wouldn't work that body. While I assess Python, I become aware of being watched.

I cut my gaze from Python over to Diesel. His hard expression is of constrained anger. *The fuck?* It's not like he's my man or some shit.

"Thanks for finding us a doc," King Isaac tells Diesel.

Diesel returns his attention to King Isaac. "Not a problem."

Silence stretches between the men before Diesel asks, "So does anybody care to fill me in on what the hell went down tonight? The streets are on fire and y'all got me standing up here holding my dick, not knowing shit."

"We were taking care of some family business," King Isaac says with a shrug. "I think that we got our point across tonight. What do you think, Python?"

Python winces as the doctor punctures his shoulder with a needle and thread. "We *definitely* got our point across. I hate that that bitch Lucifer got away. If we'd kept hold of her, we could've brought that damn Fat Ace to his fucking knees tonight. Squash this shit once and for all."

Lucifer? I stiffen.

"You are the one who took your eye off of her and she blew the back of Slim's head off and nearly killed us in the process," King Isaac reminds him, disappointed.

"Yeah. That shit was a fucking rookie mistake, but the bitch is like a fucking terminator. You can't put her ass down. Pregnant or not."

"Don't worry. Fat Ace will come gunning for us soon. When he does, we're going to bring the hammer down on that ass for blasting up Peaches's funeral. Disrespectful muthafuckas." King Isaac shakes his head. "Y'all young niggas ain't got no fucking kind of home training. Unwritten rule has always been that you let muthafuckas bury their dead."

A soft murmur of agreement floats around the room among the Gangster Disciples. I, on the other hand, return my hard gaze back to Diesel at the memory of him handing Beast a bundle of wrapped cash the afternoon of the shooting at Momma Peaches's funeral. I have no proof what the money was for, but I haven't been able to shake the feeling that somehow he was involved. Just as I haven't been able to shake the feeling that he also had something to do with his aunt's death.

My problem is that I haven't been able to work out *why* he would do it.

Diesel smiles. "Still. I wish you guys'd clued me in on what was up. I could've helped out, you know?"

King Isaac doesn't seem too charmed by his nephew by marriage. "We didn't need your help."

The growing tension makes it difficult to breathe.

"Is there a problem here that I'm not aware of?" Diesel asks, cocking his head and then swinging his gaze back and forth between Python and Isaac.

There's definitely a power play going on.

"There's no problem that I'm aware of," Isaac says. "Should there be a problem?"

Diesel's green eyes cool to an artic blue.

"Let's get something straight here, Diesel," Isaac says, chuckling and shaking his head. "Your . . . help has been much appreciated. But I don't have to run shit by no muthafuckin' body, especially an opportunist from Atlanta, looking to expand his territory."

Damn.

"An opportunist?" Diesel glances around, uncomfortable having this conversation in front of so many foot soldiers. "You got a few things twisted, *Uncle* Isaac. I didn't just pop up. I was called here—as a favor for a family member." He stabs Python with a look. "I didn't push for cuz here to pack his shit up and run to Mexico. That shit was his fucking plan—at least until shit died down, is what he told me. I came through. And I continued to come through even when Python changed his mind and decided to ride this heat out. So don't come at me like you're doing and think I'm going to stand for it. You got a nigga twisted if you think that's how this shit is going to play out."

King Isaac steps forward.

Diesel matches his step and lifts his chin, even though he's a good three inches taller than his uncle.

I don't know what to do or prepare for. Surely, Diesel understands math and knows that his ass is outnumbered.

Python speaks up. "C'mon, you two. This is not the time or the place for this shit. We're family. Squash this shit *now!*"

King Isaac and Diesel stare each other down. I know that I'm not the only one wondering what's going to happen if they decide to ignore Python.

"You're right, Terrell," Isaac says, pulling back. "This is not the time or place for family disagreements."

Python nods, satisfied. "Good. It's time to celebrate. Seven-four!"

The soldiers shout back, "Till the world blow!"

Hours later, I arrive home. "Kobe!" I'm shocked to find him home, chillin' in his favorite spot on the couch with his friends, playing video games.

"Yeah?"

"You're here," I say, sounding crazy even to my own ears.

Kobe chuckles without pulling his eyes up from the screen. "Where else would I be?"

"Oh. I don't know. Maybe riding shotgun with King Isaac and Python while they lay siege on Ruby Cove?"

He pauses the game and he and his excited friends hop up. "You heard about that? That shit was tight, wasn't it? King Isaac ain't playing. He's here to change the game."

"So you *were* there?"

Kobe leans forward to look down the hallway toward Grandma's closed bedroom door. "Cleo, that shit was fuckin' major! You don't even know." He hops up and acts out the night's adventure. "You should have seen it. We mowed those roaches down like the shit was nothing."

I rush over and smack him on the back of his head. "Are you crazy?" I glance around and his friends drop their heads. "You could have been killed. And for what?"

"For what?" he echoes. "For standing up for our turf. Those slob niggas came at us first. We can't just let them keep disrespecting us. We've been standing on the sidelines with our dicks in our hands for far too long. It's time to check niggas and let them know what time it is."

"What the fuck is all this *we* shit? Since when are you a banger, huh?"

Kobe laughs and puffs out his chest. "Chill, Cleo. You don't need to be all up in my business. I don't tell you *everything* I do. I'm grown."

"Oh? You're grown, huh? So Granny knows that you were part of that mess while she was blowing up my phone stressing about where the hell you were?"

Kobe's *grown* butt takes another quick glance down the hall and he lowers his voice.

"No. And she doesn't need to know. I handle my business. That's all that matters." He pauses and looks me up and down. "Where the hell have you been? That shit went down hours ago."

"Out looking for your big knucklehead." I smack him again, but not as hard.

He smiles. "With King Isaac back, things are changing around here, Cleo. Watch and see."

Grief

21

Mack

The worst part about getting arrested in the middle of the weekend is that you have to wait until Monday morning for your arraignment. The fight between the Vice Lords and the police department ended up having those who hadn't been gunned down during the massacre packed into paddy wagons, and now we're jammed into these holding cells like a bunch of sardines. It's been almost twenty-four hours in this bitch, more than a handful of us need some soap and water to hit our asses. As usual, my aunt Lizzie gives me nothing but lip when I call her to come bail me out.

When am I going to grow up? When am I going to get my ass up out of these damn streets? On and on it goes before she promises me that she'll call Henry, the bail bondsman.

Though the men and women are housed in different cells, we do have a pretty good view of all the things that are going on with the brawling Vice Lord soldiers across the hall. The men have pretty much given our chief and Profit a pretty broad space to pace out their frustrations and anxieties.

The two Gangster Disciples who had the misfortune to be locked up in the cell with them on this night, were fucked up on sight. Cops raced in and stopped a double homicide in progress. The bleeding Gangster Disciples were transported to the nearest hospital. More charges will be added to our soldiers who participated in the brawl, which was captured on surveillance cameras.

Fat Ace and Profit didn't look the least bit interested in those skinny niggas. Their minds are wrapped up on the other thing. One would have to be stupid as shit not to know who it involves.

"You think Ta'Shara is gonna pull through?" Romil asks.

"She's a tough girl," I tell her, not blowing smoke up her ass. "I'm sure that she's gonna be all right."

Romil glances across the way to the men's cell, and I can guess what's she's thinking. Profit doesn't look like he has too much faith about his girl pulling through, but then again, he could be thinking about the status of their relationship. After all, Ta'Shara called because she was ready to leave his ass again.

Mack, keep your nose out of other people's business. I bob my head at my own advice. Shit. It doesn't make any sense for me to be so concerned about other bitches' men when I don't even have one my damn self. All I can do is hope for the best for my girl Ta'Shara, and then keep it pushing.

"Mason Lewis." The bailiff shouts Fat Ace's government name.

Fat Ace shoots him an angry look.

"We need to ask you a few questions," the bailiff tells him, twisting his jangling keys in the lock.

Fat Ace remains rooted on the metal bench. His irritation at this disrespectful jailor is written on his face.

Both jail cells fall silent as we wait and watch to see what he's going to do. The bailiff's frustration matches our brooding chief's. "Look. You can either come along nice and easy or I can get a couple of fellows and we can drag you out."

The gauntlet has been tossed down.

Fat Ace allows several beats of silence to pass, as if waiting for the cop to go and gather the appropriate number of homies he'll need to take his ass down. But the city's new captain of police sashays her thick ass back here to give Fat Ace the news he's been waiting for.

"We've found Willow Washington. Come along."

Fat Ace stands, but his mask of worry remains.

"Is she . . . ?"

The captain takes pity on him. "She's alive."

The two large public cells erupt into spontaneous cheers. Myself included.

Lucifer is a bad bitch and her reputation will now, no doubt, be cemented in Memphis's mean streets.

Fat Ace's bruised, battered, and burned face manages to reflect his relief. And as a reward to the captain for this news, he strolls out from behind the iron bars without so much as acknowledging the still heated face of the bailiff.

The Vice Lords' celebration continues after the cops lock up and disappear.

My nosy ass may be grinning, but I wonder how the cops found Lucifer. Does that mean she killed her kidnappers to get away? Did the police save her? Have the Gangster Disciples suffered a major blow? What?

While the questions loop inside of my mind, my gaze falls back on Profit's glum expression. For him, the torture of not knowing continues.

22

Hydeya

That Jack Daniel's I guzzled down less than twenty-four hours ago seems more like some distant dream. The lack of food in my system is the number-one contributing factor to the pounding migraine that's threatening to push my left eyeball out of its socket. Add to that there is an ungodly amount of caffeine also pumping through my system.

For the last hour, I have been ignoring the weird sounds emitting from my stomach. Instead, I march one foot in front of the other. I find myself taking special note of the familiar lines and contours of Mason's body. He has Isaac's dark complexion—and even his high cheekbones, but that's about all. If I was to guess, I would say that he was a solid inch to an inch-and-a-half taller, but given the extensive burns, bruises, and tattoos, I can't make out any other similarities . . . except Isaac and Mason have the same walk. I watch his slow swag as he moves toward the interrogation room and I wonder if my mind is playing tricks on me—or maybe I'm forcing myself to see things that aren't really there. Could Momma Peaches have been wrong? I remember her letter that's still jammed in my pocket. Her claim that this man is my brother is fucking with me more than it should.

When Mason arrives at the interrogation room I nearly crash into his back and have to mumble a quick apology before reaching out and unlocking the door. "Go in. Have a seat." From my right pocket, I remove the key to his handcuffs. He stands patiently as I unlock one hand and then cuff the free bracelet into a hook on the table. "Have a seat," I tell him again.

After staring at his cuffed wrist and then at me, Mason folds his large frame and settles into the metal chair next to the table. After that, he stares up at me, wary and grim faced.

My throat squeezes tight, making it difficult to push words out. "Can I get you anything to drink? Water or a soda?"

He ignores the question to ask two of his own. "How is Willow? How's my kid?"

I cough to clear my throat, but it doesn't work. My answers come out sounding like a hoarse bullfrog. "We . . . were able to locate her. She'd been in a car accident with her kidnappers. Somehow she managed to get out of the car and seek shelter in the surrounding woods. When we found her, she was in early labor. We did manage to get her to the hospital in time to deliver the baby."

Mason exhales a long breath, allowing his large shoulders to droop a few inches.

"How about some coffee?" I offer, not ready to delve into the bad news.

"I'd rather have a beer," he says.

I chuckle. "Sorry. We're fresh out."

"Then I'll take a bottled water."

"You got it." I turn and exit out of the room, perhaps too fast because by the time I pull the door closed behind me I'm light-headed and out of breath.

"Are you all right, Captain?"

I look up into Officer Hendrix's concerned face.

"Yeah. I'm good."

She glances around and then strolls over to me as if she doesn't want to take my word for it. "Are you sure? You look . . ." She struggles for the right word.

"I'm fine. I'm fine," I insist. My dizzy spell is over and I push away from the door. "Excuse me." I move past Officer Hendrix and head to the break room to get that bottled water.

"Looks like you reeled in the big fish," Lieutenant Fowler says, wrangling my attention.

"What?"

Fowler scoops coffee into a filter at the counter. "Fat Ace," he says, smacking the brew button. "I saw you taking him into one of the interrogation rooms."

"Oh. Yeah." I open the refrigerator and grab a bottled water.

"So. What's his story?"

"Nothing. We haven't started talking yet." Silence and then, "Thank you."

"For what?"

I shrug. "I guess for being *incompetent*. Thanks to you, my administrative leave will go down in the department's history as the shortest one on record."

He laughs, but anger flushes his face. "Incompetence? You're putting it on a bit thick, aren't you?"

"Hmm, no. Not really. I mean, c'mon. You *turned off* your phone?"

"I *lost* my phone," he clarifies.

"Yeah. That sounds worse." The tension jacks the temperature in the room.

"You're still angry with me."

"You've been plotting to steal my job."

"I *never* plotted to steal your job."

"Right." I roll my eyes. "But for the record, I'm not angry. I'm *pissed*."

Fowler sighs.

"Going forward, let's keep it simple. We're not friends, buddies, or pals. We're colleagues. You play on your side of the fence and I'll play on mine."

"I'm not the enemy," he says.

I push my eyebrows up high at that bullshit. "If you're not *for* me, then you're against me."

"Who says that I'm not for you? Why are you the only one allowed to have any ambition in this relationship? In order for us to be friends—you have to be the boss?"

"Get the fuck on with that shit. You're not going to flip the script on me. What you did was wrong and it was dirty. End of story. You pretended to have my back while the whole time scheming to steal my promotion."

"It wasn't anything like that."

"Uh, huh." I exit out of the break room.

"Hydeya. Hydeya, wait!"

I ignore his ass and march back to the interrogation room. "One bottled water," I announce and then set it in front of Mason.

"Did you have to go to Alabama to get it?" he asks, snatching it up and twisting off the cap.

"Almost."

He grins, or at least I think he does. His features are hard to read without getting distracted by not only his burns and scars, but also by his eye patch. He chugs down the water without thanking me or even appearing grateful.

I pull out my own chair. The metal legs screech before I settle into my seat and meet his singular black gaze. I regret not grabbing a bottled water for myself.

Tired of waiting, Mason launches the interrogation. "How is she?"

"How is who? Oh." I shake my head for my forgetfulness

and then brace to lay out the bad news. "Your girlfriend, Willow . . . I'm sorry . . . but soon after she delivered her baby, she suffered . . . a brain aneurysm."

"What?"

"For the moment, she's stable. The doctors did have to place her into a medically induced coma and are actively trying to reduce the swelling."

Silence.

"I'm sorry," I add.

"Willow is in a coma?" he asks as the words sink in.

"Yes."

"And the baby?"

"He is . . . quite small—but he's in the neonatal intensive care unit at Baptist Memorial. My understanding is that his lungs are underdeveloped, but the doctors believe that he'll pull through."

Mason's anguish seizes his face, and he pounds a fist down onto the table. It and myself jump. "Those dirty muthafuckas!" He tugs in a breath, but it fails to calm him down. He hammers his fist on the table again, while his nostrils flare.

His emotional reaction is hard to watch. *Isaac did this . . . to his own son.* I shake my head, not sure how to fix this, if it *can* be fixed. After a full minute, I push a stupid question out of my mouth. "Are you going to be all right?"

He glares at me. "What the fuck do you think?"

"I think that . . . you and your girlfriend . . . and your son *will* pull through this. But you'll have to remain strong."

Mason unclenches his fists and eases back in his chair. "So . . . you're the new captain of police as well as the new Dr. Phil now?"

"No. I'm encouraging you. I don't have to tell you that things could have gone in a different direction. Right now, I need for you to calm down and answer some questions."

"Calm down? How the fuck does someone *calm down* from this shit? How the fuck would you react if this was happening to *your* family?"

"It is happening to my family," I say before thinking. Drake's lifeless body flashes before my eyes and I drop my gaze before a rush of tears embarrasses my ass.

Mason twists up his face.

"My husband was killed the other day while we attended Momma Peaches's funeral. A smaller massacre, but people are saying that you and your Vice Lords are responsible for that."

"That's bullshit. We didn't have shit to do with that hit."

"I was there."

"I don't give a fuck. I'm telling you what's real. It wasn't me or my people."

Dubious, I shake my head.

"Look. I heard the rumors, but somebody tryna set us up—make it look like it was us—but it wasn't us."

I sigh and then glance over to the side window and see that we have gathered an audience. *Nosy asses.* I stand and move to the window and close the blinds. A few of them give me the *what the fuck* look, but I ignore them.

Momma Peaches's letter burns a hole in my inner jacket pocket. I could hand it to him and let him read it. I reach into my pocket and pull it out, but instead of handing it over, I stare at it.

"Is there something else?" Mason asks after a long silence.

Give him the letter.

Mason's gaze falls onto the letter while his expression collapses into confusion. "What's that?"

I pull another deep breath. "A letter."

"Okay."

"I found it last night . . . before I was called out to Ruby Cove. I found it in Momma Peaches's Bible."

Mason stiffens.

"She was expecting to see you that day, wasn't she?"

"I'm through talking now," he informs me. "I'd like to go back to the holding cell, if you don't mind."

"I'm going to take that answer as a yes." I return to my seat. When I do, his eyes follow the letter. "Aren't you going to ask me what it says?"

"I don't give a fuck what it says," he lies.

"Should I read it to you? Or would you like to read it?"

Knock! Knock! I look up as the door springs open and Fowler juts his head inside. "Chief Brown wants to see us."

I sigh. I'd hoped to avoid an ass–chewing on a Sunday. "All right. I'll be right there."

"She said *now.*"

I sharpen my narrow gaze. "I said I'd be right there."

Instead of nodding and walking out, Fowler lingers.

My patience snaps. "Are you fucking hard of hearing or something?"

He opens his mouth to say something else, but common sense kicks in. He nods, glances at Mason, and then backs out before closing the door.

What the fuck? I glance back at Mason, who's now avoiding my gaze. *Do these two know each other?* I climb to my feet and stuff the letter back into my jacket, but then think better of it. "I'll be right back. Why don't you give this a read while I'm gone and then we can discuss it when I return?"

I place the letter with his name scrawled across the top of the envelope in front of him. "It really is an interesting read." I turn and leave.

Fowler is two feet away from the door, leaning against a desk with his arms crossed, talking to Officer Hendrix. The strange thing is that Officer Hendrix looks like a hot mess. *Something is up with these two.*

Fowler looks up and pushes way from the desk. "Are you ready, Captain?"

"I didn't realize that I needed an escort," I bitch. "I know my way around."

Fowler allows my sarcasm to roll off of his back as we march together in angry silence to the chief's office.

23

Yvette

Shit has hit every fan in Memphis. The *Commercial Appeal* openly questions whether it's time for the mayor to replace me as the chief of police with this morning's headline: "What Has Brown Done for Us Lately?"

I've been a cop for a long time and I have thick skin, but I'd be lying if I said I wasn't sweating under the bright spotlight of the national media. Even CNN is asking every hour on the hour whether Memphis has become another South Chicago or Detroit. I watch James pace in my office. He too, is feeling the heat. The next set of poll numbers are set to come out in two days.

"I know I've said this before," James starts. "But I miss that dirty bastard Captain Johnson."

"You and me both," I tell him, rummaging around in the top drawer of my desk for my blood-pressure medicine. I have a sinking feeling that I might have forgotten to refill the prescription again.

"First a massacre out at that biker club, then the one at that cemetery, and now this. We have nearly a *hundred* bodies from those three incidents alone. How the hell are my team and I going to spin that shit into something positive?"

"I don't know, James," I parrot, like I've been doing for the past half hour.

He stops pacing and looks up. "How in the fuck can you be this calm?"

"I don't know—practice."

Even my joke is taken as a personal affront. "You trying to be funny?"

"No, James." I slam my desk drawer. "I'm not."

"Good. Because I don't want to have to remind you that it's not just my job on the line here. If I lose—you lose."

My anger simmers. "You think that I don't know that? You and the whole city keep reminding me of that every damn time I turn around," I shout, grabbing the newspaper from my desk and hurling it at him. The picture printed beneath the headline isn't of me but of him, looking grim faced, and of his *wife* clinging to his arm for moral support.

James and I glare at one another, our eyes saying everything that our lips wouldn't dare. At last, he bends a knee and swipes the newspaper up from the floor, strolls to my desk, and smacks the paper down. "Pull yourself together. Side chick behavior is unbecoming for an officer of your rank."

"Fuck you," I hiss. As our heated glares set off sparks, I'm aware that my ass is actually turned on.

A rap on my door crashes us back down to earth and James and I step back to give each other much-needed breathing room before I bark, "Enter."

Deputy Chief Richard Collins breezes into the office. My blood pressure ticks upwards.

"If you came in here to deliver bad news, I swear I'll shoot you myself," I warn him.

Richard, who is long used to my sarcasm, responds with a dry chuckle. "Then I hope that you take no news as good news. All is calm on the streets for the moment, but I can't say the same for the media. They are raking us over the coals. We've got to get a handle on this shit and fast."

"No shit," I mumble. "If you come up with any ideas on *how* we do that, feel free to fill out a card for the suggestion box."

"Is it too late to state for the record that I miss that son-of-a-bitch Johnson?"

I cut a look over to James, who smiles at having his words echoed back at him.

"We *all* miss Captain Johnson," I say, casting my own vote. "But we have to deal with the here and now."

Knock! Knock!

"Enter!" I brace myself as Lieutenant Fowler pokes his head into the office.

"You wanted to see us, Chief?"

Despite him hogging the doorframe, I spot the other pair of legs standing behind him.

"Yes. C'mon in." I give James a *here we go* look.

Fowler relinquishes the doorknob and enters the office with his chin up. After Hawkins clears the threshold, I instruct her to close the door.

She follows the order and then both officers move to stand in the center of the room. I don't need to be a mind reader to know that she's still salty about my placing her on administrative leave. It's written all over her face. Apparently my having to call her back to duty isn't enough crow for me to eat. She can forget it.

"Take a seat," I tell them.

Fowler rushes toward one of the chairs, but Hawkins doesn't move.

"If you don't mind, I'd prefer to stand."

"But I *do* mind," I tell her. "Take. A. Seat."

Hawkins's jawline hardens. I assume that a long stream of obscenities is rushing through her head, but she forces one leg in front of the other until she plants her ass in the chair next to Fowler. *Why does everything have to be a battle with this bitch?*

There is a lot to admire about Captain Hawkins. Her work ethic and dedication to the job is something much appreciated by the powers that be, but her stubbornness and tenaciousness are a constant pain in my ass. From time to time, she can be petulant and moody. It's a surprising trait for someone who served time in the military, where one learns the importance of working as a team.

"Do we still have a problem, Captain Hawkins?"

A few strained beats of silence pass before she answers. "No, Chief."

"So we *don't* have a problem?" I press.

Another beat. "No, Chief."

It may be my imagination, but my office is a sauna. I can't afford to have this trouble escalate any further than it has. Hawkins has hit the ground running since I called her back to duty. My faith in her second hand, Lieutenant Fowler, was misplaced. Regretfully, I'm the first one to break eye contact. I open up my bottom desk drawer and pull out her badge and service weapon.

"In any case, I believe that you'll be needing these," I tell her.

Her stern face softens when her gaze lowers to her badge. Hydeya stands and moves toward the desk. "Thank you, Chief." She holsters her weapon and slides her badge into her jacket.

"You're welcome." I watch her as she creeps back to her seat. "Now that's been taken care of," I say, switching my attention to Fowler.

He launches into his excuses for last night. "Chief, before you start, I want to apologize for my screwup last night."

"Okay." I lean back in my chair. "Go ahead."

Fowler blinks as if surprised that his opening statement wasn't a sufficient apology. "I'm sorry. I—I'm not sure what happened. My cell must've slipped out somewhere. I'm not sure where. But I promise you that something like that will never, ever happen again."

"You can promise that without knowing what happened?" I ask, dubious.

"Y-yes, ma'am." He swallows hard.

"Uh-huh." I cast a look over at James, who's unimpressed.

"I have to admit that I was expecting something a little more colorful, but I guess that sorry excuse is going to have to do for now, isn't it?"

Fowler squirms in his seat while his jaw hardens. *Two for two.* "Regardless, you will be written up for your *lost* phone incident. I look forward to further discussions between you and your union representative. Meanwhile, you'll go back to answering to Captain Hawkins. I'd prefer it if she'd keep you on the Ruby Cove case." I look back to Hawkins to receive yet another slow head nod. "Good. A press conference will be arranged for ten tomorrow morning. Be prepared for another ass-chewing from the media and our concerned constituents. I'm hoping that you and your team will give us *something* before we have to stand before the national media."

Hawkins sighs. Her hatred for all things media has been made clear on more than one occasion.

"So what do we know so far?" I ask. "Is either of the two women at the hospital talking?"

Hawkins shakes her head. "Ta'Shara Murphy has given a statement to one of our officers, but I haven't visited her myself yet. I will. It's definitely on my to-do list. As for Ms. Washington, after she delivered her baby, she suffered a brain aneurysm and is, as far as I know, still in a medically induced coma."

I nod, not surprised by more roadblocks placed before this department. "Ms. Murphy wasn't exactly talkative last night."

"And judging by the report I read this morning, she's not saying too much now either."

"Another *fuck the police* card-carrying member, huh?" I shake my head. "I swear that *these people* will cut off their noses to spite their faces."

Hawkins nods. "However, the word on the street is that this was a Gangster Disciple hit job. We all know that the GD and VL in this city are the largest and deadliest gangs spilling all of this blood lately."

"Did anyone see a face? Know a name? Something? The cold case files are *not* an option. I need a perp-walk for those cameras. If not by tomorrow, no later than Tuesday. Hell, as far as I'm concerned, that big ape you have in holding will do just fine."

"But it was his place that was attacked last night. He and Willow Washington live together."

"And where was *he* at the time of the attack?"

Fowler shifts in his seat.

"I don't know," Hawkins says. "When he returned home, he got into a scuffle with the police securing the area for not letting him into his own house. That's the only reason he and the others were booked. Our slapping cuffs on the victims probably won't play well."

"What? Are you his fucking lawyer now?"

"I'm just pointing out the facts, Chief."

"Then get me somebody. Get me the chief of the Gangster Disciples. I'm sure that we have whoever it is on record."

"We've been trying to get ahold of him. It's Terrell Carver."

"Terrell Carver? Isn't he deceased?"

"According to the news, yes. But I saw him with my own eyes in that police chase a month back."

"Then maybe you were mistaken?"

Hawkins shakes her head like she's above making mistakes. "I know what I saw. Terrell Carver is very much alive."

It's my turn to harden my jaw and glare back. "Then *get* him or bring in whoever is second in command, his flunky—I don't give a damn."

"I'm not sure that we know who's been in charge since Terrell was driven underground."

"Actually"—Fowler speaks up—"King Isaac was recently released from prison. Two of the three massacres have happened since his release."

Captain Hawkins's head snaps in his direction, her anger laser-focused on the side of Fowler's head.

He shrugs. "I mean. It can't be a coincidence, right? It was his wife's funeral where the last massacre occurred." Fowler turns to Hawkins and gives her a flat smile. "I know it's a touchy subject with you. I mean, you losing your husband and all."

"You don't have any proof that Isaac Goodson is behind the Ruby Cove situation," Hawkins snaps.

"Ruby Cove is more than just a situation," I tell her.

"We still don't have any proof."

"Tell me, Captain. Are you running a gangster defense fund that I don't know about? Get their asses in here and let the courts work out who did what."

"I'm just saying—"

Fowler cuts her off. "And I'm saying that it's one hell of a coincidence."

"Coincidence does not make a case."

"You let the district attorney worry about that. I need perp-walks and *a lot* of them. Do you have a problem with that?" I have a hard time reading the emotions splayed across Hawkins's face, especially when she looks at Fowler. If I were to guess, I'd say that it resembles betrayal. "Bring King Isaac in—at least for questioning. Surely you don't have a problem doing your due diligence?"

"Yes, Chief."

"Today."

"Yes, Chief. Is there anything else?" Hawkins pops up out of her seat.

There's that petulance again. I lean back in my chair and allow the heated silence to stretch between us. Hawkins has a habit of bouncing her ass out of that chair before I'm finished talking, but I'm going to let the shit go. "Yes. That is all, Captain."

Hawkins cuts another evil look toward Fowler and marches out of the office. The door slams behind her.

"What the fuck is her damn problem?" I ask, returning my attention to Fowler.

Fowler holds his tongue.

"Well?"

"He's her father."

"What? Who?" His words are gibberish.

"King Isaac," he clarifies. "He's Captain Hawkins's father."

James takes a seat. "Say that shit again."

"Sorry, Mayor Wharton, but it's true."

I explode. "Why the fuck is this the first time I'm hearing about this shit?"

"There's never been a reason to bring it up. He's been locked down for the last ten years. Before she became a cop here at this department. Hell, according to her, he's not even listed on her birth certificate. I guess it's one of those family secrets."

"But *you* knew?"

"She confessed it to me once years ago when we grabbed some drinks together. But hell, she's hardly the only cop in this place who has a few embarrassing branches on the family tree."

He's right about that. "Is there something *else* I should know?"

Fowler glances over to James, but then finally shakes his head. "No. That's about it."

24

Hydeya

That dirty muthafucka! I can't believe that he just did that shit. All because he needed to save face, he took something I told him in private and used it for his own benefit. More and more I realize how much I really don't know my ex-partner. *What the fuck?* How in the hell have I been so wrong about him all this time?

Heat fuses into my body, my hands clench and unclench as I march across the department. I don't have the luxury of being caught up in my own feelings for long. A huge ruckus catches my attention.

Bam! Boom! Crash!

Now what? My marching strides turn into a quick jog. When I realize that the noise is coming from the interrogation room where I left Mason, my heart jumps so high that it gets caught in my throat. I arrive on the scene and there are at least six police officers crammed into the room with Mason while he demolishes the desk that he'd been handcuffed to.

"FUCK THIS SHIT! GET THE HELL OFF ME, MUTHAFUCKA!"

Mason looks like a black incredible Hulk, tossing cops off of him as if they weigh nothing.

"Get him! Get him!" an officer barks.

Half the officers in the room reach for their holsters.

I panic. "Taser him. Don't shoot him."

A few startled looks slice my way.

Officer Hernandez makes the mistake of being distracted for too long and Mason's huge fist sends him reeling back against the wall. That shit pisses off even more of the officers.

Against my better judgment, I jump into the fray. The moment I latch on to one of Mason's muscular arms, I'm treated much like a rodeo clown on the back of a bucking bull. The shit is crazy. It gets worse when two of the officers get their hands on their Tasers.

Mason's muscles tense, and then I'm slung left to right and then up and down. *Shit. Is that shit making him stronger?*

"Get down on the ground! *Now*," the officers shout.

More voltage is shot into Mason and still his ass refuses to go down. More cops jump into the mix. It's hard to tell what the hell is going on, but we get Mason on the floor.

A second set of handcuffs is latched onto his wrists.

I roll off of him, battered and bruised. I hear something rustle beneath me. I glance down and see Momma Peaches's rumpled letter. I grab it and shove it into my back pocket. Guilt twists my stomach into a tight knot.

The other officers struggle to wrangle Mason back onto his feet. More than a few really want to have a go at him and don't bother hiding their contempt. Everyone turns their attention toward me, their faces asking what I want them to do with Mason now.

Mason's eye patch is missing, and his milky white eye and his black one glare back at me. Rage rolls off of him in waves.

"Take him back to holding," I tell them. I glance down and spot his eye patch. "Wait." I go and retrieve it and then shove the patch into his jeans pocket. His chest heaves as he gulps air after his recent exertion. I don't want to think about what he'd actually do to me if he wasn't handcuffed and subdued right now. *You shouldn't have given him the letter.* "Now you can take him."

The men jerk Mason forward toward the door.

I remain behind to survey the damage of the broken table and chairs. So much for handcuffing a suspect to an unbolted object.

"Are you all right?"

I glance back up at the door to Fowler's inquisitive face. In a snap, Mason is forgotten and Fowler's betrayal is back to the forefront of my mind. "Don't," I warn.

Playing dumb, he scrunches up his face as if confused.

"I'm not in the mood for your mind games right now. You need to find yourself something else to do and get out of my face," I tell him.

Fowler chugs in a deep breath. "Please, don't take what I said back in Chief Brown's office personally."

"Not take it personally? Have you fallen and bumped your muthafuckin' . . ." I stop myself and count to ten. The shit doesn't work, so I march over to the door, grab him by the collar, and jerk him into the room and slam the door. "How in the fuck do I not take your trying to pin all this shit on my father *personally*?"

"Your father?" he asks. "You're claiming him now?"

"What?"

"Exactly," he snaps back. "All the years that I've known you, Isaac Goodson was nothing more than a sperm donor. You told me plenty of times that you despised the man. And whether you like it or not, he *is* and should be the department's prime suspect. He has the perfect motive to blast Ruby Cove off the fuckin' map and you damn well know it. But because he's your father, I'm supposed to sit on my hands and not say shit—do I understand that right?"

"You're supposed to let me handle it."

"Why is that? King Isaac is a known gang leader. His wife—and your *husband*—were killed by the Vice Lords."

"We don't know that."

"There were plenty of witnesses who claimed the gangsters were flagging black and gold. So Ruby Cove, a well-known Vice Lord territory, is then leveled by people, albeit off the record, are saying their attackers flagged Gangster Disciple colors, and shouting, 'six poppin', five droppin',' and you still don't think we should drag your father in here? Did *you* fall and bump *your* head? Whether we're friends or colleagues, I'm still expected to do a job here."

"No. You were brown-nosing your way back onto the chief's good side. You want to impress people with your job skills? Try learning to keep up with your phone."

Fowler's shoulders slump. There is no point in arguing with me and he knows it. "Got it, Captain."

"Good." Desperate to get away from this muthafucka before I catch a damn case myself, I snatch open the door and march out of the room.

25

Ta'Shara

Baptist Memorial Hospital

All too soon, someone calls my name and tells me that it's time for me to wake up. I groan at the voice, hoping that whoever it is will take the hint and go away.

They don't.

Once again my eyelids are peeled open and another prick of light is shone into my eyes. Logic says that it is a small flashlight, but my current mental state has no problem believing that the light is attached to a runaway train.

Pain explodes inside my head. I whine and whimper.

A voice apologizes and then turns off the light. I ask a few questions, but I'm too annoyed to answer. One thing for sure, my mouth is as dry as the desert. "W-water," I croak.

"I can give you a couple of ice chips, but that's it for right now. Okay?"

I nod and drop my mouth open but the few chips he sprinkles on my tongue evaporate almost as soon as they land. "M-more."

He hesitates, but then sprinkles a few more into my mouth.

It's not enough, but I'm grateful.

I drift back off to my cherished princess room where I'm greeted by more spearmint kisses, soft caresses, and tender lovemaking. The next time my name is called, the voice is familiar.

"T, baby? Can you hear me?" Profit's warm breath drifts across the shell of my ear.

I smile without opening my eyes. The sound of his voice is like home.

"Ta'Shara, honey. It's me, Profit. If you can hear me, squeeze my hand."

His hand? Am I holding his hand? I attempt to find out, but my limbs are heavy as hell. Alarmed, I pull in a breath and try again.

"Good. That's my girl."

Did I do it? I didn't think that I did. I attempt to open my eyes, but I'll be damned if they don't feel as if they've been superglued shut.

After great effort I get them open, but my vision is cloudy.

"Hey, baby." Profit's blurry face cracks a sad smile.

"H-hey." The one word sends me into a coughing fit, causing bright spots to form in front of my eyes. Shifting into caregiver mode, Profit produces a plastic cup with water. The instant relief to my inflamed throat makes me greedy for more. I down too much too fast. Before I know it, I'm choking and spilling it all over my chest.

"Careful, baby. Careful." Profit pulls away the cup and then leans me forward so that I don't drown. Once the coughing ends, he settles me back and smiles. "Better?"

I nod and smile. After that, silence stretches between us. A laundry list of things I want to say scrolls too fast in my head that I can't get the words out.

He appears to have the same issue.

"I can't tell you how scared I was the other night," he begins.

The other night? I glance to the right and notice the bright sunlight, pooling into the room. *How many nights has it been?*

"When I saw you lying on that gurney bleeding like that, I thought . . ." He drops his head and takes a few seconds to gather himself. "It terrified me, especially after how we left things between us. The things that we said to each other." He shakes his head and thumbs away something from his eyes before I get a chance to see what it is.

"I know that I hurt you. I'll spend the rest of my life being sorry for that. I'm just hoping, praying that you can find some way within your heart to forgive, and give *us* another chance. I promise that I'll do whatever it takes to make you happy again." Another hand squeeze. I can feel the strength and warmth of his touch radiate through me.

However, before I can open my mouth, a sound jars me awake. Confused, I blink several times.

I force open my eyes again but this time I see that I'm not alone in the room. "Tracee." I whisper the name even though I know what I'm saying isn't possible. Tracee, my foster mother, is dead—killed by my evil sister, LeShelle.

"How are you feeling, Ta'Shara?"

Warm tears crest and blur the kind, smiling face. It's not Tracee, but Tracee's mother, Olivia. She was always kind to me. The dull ache in my shoulder fades, but the one in my heart grows.

Profit was never here. It was just a dream.

Still smiling, Olivia brushes hair away from my face. "When the police called and told the family that you were here, we were scared to death. We have been looking all over for you."

We?

My gaze drifts over her shoulder to the ring of older, familiar faces of the Douglases and the Sullivans. They are my foster grandparents, Reggie's and Tracee's parents.

"Are you comfortable, sweetheart? Is there anything that we can do or get for you?"

More tears leak from the corners of my eyes while her soft hands caress my face.

"I'm so sorry," I whisper.

"You have nothing to be sorry for, sweetie. We know that you had nothing to do with Tracee and Reggie's death. We've talked to the police and they've told us that they are dropping the charges."

But I am responsible. They are dead because of me. If I had simply followed the rules of the street, I'd be in high school, probably prepping for college. Essence and I would still be best friends. Reggie and Tracee would have gone through with the adoption to become my real parents. The enormity of it all crushes me. The sobs that rack my body draw everyone in the room closer to the bed.

Soon there is more than one set of arms looping around my neck. My tears must be contagious because there isn't a dry eye in the room.

We cry for a long time. It's hard to believe that they are treating me like I'm still a member of their family. It's more than I deserve.

"Okay," Olivia says. "Enough crying. What's important now is that we have you back. We are going to help you get through this, then you are more than welcome to come and live with me in Houston."

Houston?

"That's *only* if you want to," she amends, as if picking up on my surprise.

"Or you're more than welcome to live with us here," Reggie Douglas Senior cuts in. "We'd also be happy to have you." Everyone's sincerity makes me cry harder.

One thing I know for sure is that it can't go on this way. I don't want to be one of those girls with a rap sheet that is as thick as the Lord of the Rings tomes. I don't want to be married to the streets and play the game where I collect as many bullet scars as possible without dying. Though I love him with every beat of my heart, I don't want to be Profit's ride-or-die chick. I deserve more than what the streets offer.

My hospital room door opens.

"Well now. Look who is awake today." A doctor beams an unnatural smile. "How are you feeling?"

"Sore."

"That's to be expected." She nods and smiles as if I haven't voiced a compliant.

"Can you give her something for the pain?" Olivia asks as if reading my mind.

"Sure. Sure. I'll put in an order for that. But let's see if we can at least isolate where you're feeling the pain."

I watch her as she approaches the bed. A series of flashing lights as she performs random tests are more of a nuisance than anything. However, I catch the looks passed between the Douglases and the Sullivans, and that nips at my curiosity.

There's something that they're not telling me.

"Now Ta'Shara, tell me if you feel this," the doctor says, pulling back the sheet on the bed and placing her pen against the bottom of my foot. I only know that it's there because I'm watching her. But when she moves the pen up and down, I don't feel anything.

"How about this?" She moves the pen to the top of my leg and rubs it up and down.

Nothing.

"Why don't I feel that?" My confusion gives way to panic.

The doctor gives me another smile. "Don't worry. There's a chance that it's just temporary."

Soft whimpering cries sneak out around me while I get my brain to accept the thing that the doctor is not saying.

"Tell me the truth. Am I paralyzed?"

She hesitates. "For the moment, from the waist down, that may be the case. I'm sorry."

26

Hydeya

Another day, and another dead body has been discovered in one of the murder capitals of America. I just don't understand why I'm getting the call. There are plenty of detectives who are more than capable of handling a simple murder case. But then the name Qiana Barrett clears my mental fog and I'm climbing out of bed and rushing into some clean-ish clothes before jetting out of the house. I don't bother heading to the Mississippi River where the body was discovered, but instead catch up with the body down at the city morgue.

The medical examiner is expecting me and leads me to the body in question. The bloated body in no way, shape, or form looks like the mouthy teenager I met months ago. But despite the bloat and the massive burns to the body, the two jagged scars on each side of her face tell me that this is indeed Qiana Barrett.

Despite my having been once eager to slap handcuffs on this teenager for the murder of Yolanda Terry and Tyneisha Gibson, I'm disturbed about how this girl's short life ended. After all, I was once her: lost and confused, thinking that I could find validation in the streets, too dumb to know that the street can never and will never love anyone. Its power is seductive, but it's an illusion. A powerful illusion, but still *just* an illusion. The Terry-Gibson case is officially closed, but now Qiana's name will be added to a growing pile of cases that will likely never be solved.

When I return home, I don't bother climbing back into my cold and empty California king-size bed. Instead, I crash for a couple of minutes on the pleather couch that I've always hated. Drake bought the piece of cheap furniture at a flea market without checking with me, and then refused to get rid of it. He always loved the art of getting a good deal. I smile warmly and shake my head at how bitterly we fought over this damn thing.

And now . . . I love it because I loved him. I feel guilty about there not being a funeral for him, but Drake told me and the rest of his family that he never wanted us to go through a pointless and ridiculous sad ceremony just to say goodbye. How ironic that he ended up dying at someone else's burial.

Hours glide by in a few blinks of the eye, and I remain sitting in the middle of this sofa chugging one beer after another and staring at the large silver urn sitting over the living room's fireplace. I loved my husband, but I feel some type of way about his ashes remaining in the house like this.

By the time I arrive back to the station, it's considered the booty-crack of dawn and it feels as if my ass just left this place. On the murder board there are more names scribbled underneath Qiana Barrett: Georgina Smith, Avonte Chambers, Myeisha Bach, Erika Waters and . . . LeShelle Murphy?

I stop cold and stare at the last name.

When Officer Wendi Hendrix strolls by me, I grab her by the arm. "When—where did this happen?"

Hendrix looks up at the name I'm pointing to. "I'm not sure. I think Officer Reid picked up those cases."

I spin and go in search of Officer Reid. Along the way, I see Fowler strutting through the doors. I ignore him. We've been through a lot over the years, but I doubt I'll ever be able to forgive him for that stunt that he pulled with Chief Brown so that he could get back in her good graces.

"Hawkins!" Fowler shouts.

I find Reid, a seventeen-year veteran on the force, at his desk. He looks away from the mug shots on his computer screen and pulls the phone away from his ear. "Hey, boss. What can I do for you?"

"LeShelle Murphy—tell me about it."

Surprise colors his dull brown face as he returns the phone to its cradle. "She was on your radar?"

"Oh yeah. She happens to be Terrell Carver's wife or wifey, depending on who you ask in the streets." I fold my arms and lean against the cubicle.

"Her body was recovered from a shallow grave out off Mudville Road. Whoever dumped it there gave zero fucks. At first the coroner couldn't tell whether the body was male or female, but the dental records came back as a match about an hour ago. It's her."

"You got dental records back that fast?"

A smile creeps across Reid's face. "I have a few people who owe me a number of favors."

"I bet you do." I give him a conspiratorial wink. "Any suspects?"

"I'll take a wild guess and say it could be any one of a number of rival gang members, including the Vice Lords."

I straighten up. "You have a time of death?"

"That's proving to be more difficult. I should have an answer in a couple of hours. I do know that smoke inhalation indicates that she was alive at the time she was set on fire and that the accelerant was gasoline."

"Set on fire?" *The same way as Qiana Barrett.*

"That's what it looks like," Officer Reid confirms and then pulls in a weary breath. He appears to have aged ten years since our conversation started. "You know, you can never get used to this bullshit going on out here. It's like these young folks don't give a damn about nothing and nobody."

"They're responding to a system that's designed to keep them in iron cages. If you have nothing to live for—no buy-in to the American dream . . ." I shrug.

Reid leans back in his chair and reassesses me. "You're talking from experience?"

"Aren't we all?"

He nods and we share looks that say there is so much that we will never reveal about ourselves—and how high the gang violence really is in this city. According to the Tennessee Gang Investigators Associates, there are over ninety-one hundred documented gang members and one hundred and seventy documented gangs and subsets in the area. That shit doesn't count the *undocumented* members. There's no way that we'll ever win the war on drugs, the main driver behind the gang violence, and it looks like we'll never reach the number of kids that we need to to prove to them that there is a better way out here for them. The fast money, girls, and cars are too seductive for people who have never had much. Add in the human need to connect to something or someone and it makes joining a gang to be a part of a family—any family—irresistible. We cops out here are fighting something that we have no chance of winning.

"Keep me posted on any updates," I tell Reid before exiting his cubicle so he can get back to work.

Fowler catches up to me immediately.

"Don't tell me that I'm going to have to slap a restraining order on your ass for stalking."

"I would hardly call what I—"

"What do you want?" I ask, rounding on him in hopes that he will cut to the chase.

"I—I just wanted to see if you needed me to tag along when you go and interview your father on the Ruby Cove massacre."

"Ruby Cove massacre." I roll my eyes and resume walking.

"That's what they are calling it on the news," Fowler informs me. "Plus, the chief made it clear that she wants him brought in."

"And *I* will bring him in," I snap.

"When?"

I face him again at my office door. "Sometime *after* you get your shit out of *my* office."

That shuts his ass up. In fact, we get locked into a staring contest that there's no fucking way he's going to win.

Finally he enters the office and starts removing his things. I stand, perhaps like a petulant child, until he retrieves every bit of it.

"You know, things don't have to be like this. What do you say that after work, we go down to Alex's and grab a couple of drinks and talk things out?"

"I say that there's not a snowball's chance in hell that's happening. Now take your shit and get out of my face."

27

Ta'Shara

The Douglases and the Sullivans are being so good to me. The fact that my foster parents, Tracee and Reggie, saw to include me in their wills has opened up a wide range of options. They left me five hundred thousand dollars, payable on my eighteenth birthday. But it's the idea of my walking away from Profit permanently that has a knot still lodged in the center of my throat.

I've lived on or near Ruby Cove for three months, and in that time, I've already bodied about five people—or was it six? This wasn't supposed to be me. While I was striving to *not* be like LeShelle, I ran headlong into the street trap. If I don't get out now, the state has a set of iron bars, if not a lethal injection, with my name on it. Why is this even a question with me? I *have* to get out now—at least while I still can.

Besides, it's not fair to burden Profit with the probability of my permanent paralysis. Why would he want a cripple to take care of for the rest of his life?

I turn my gaze toward the lone window. The Memphis landscape is cast in gray. It's as if the entire city is in mourning. Every day that the gang wars escalate is another day that it loses another bit of its soul.

In my room, there's a chilly silence. In the hallway, I can

hear the hustle and bustle of the hospital. My mind drifts to what time the doctor will sign my release forms. One thing that I've learned about hospitals is that they believe in taking their sweet time.

Knock. Knock. Knock.

Speak of the devil. I sit up straighter in the bed before a head pokes inside of the room. But it's not Dr. Nelson's head—nor is it any of the nurses.

"Ta'Shara Murphy?" she asks.

Captain Hawkins. My defenses rise as I watch her creep into the room.

"I don't know if you remember me, but I'm Captain Hydeya Hawkins with the Memphis Police Department. We met a few months back when . . . your boyfriend's mother, Barbara Lewis was here in the hospital."

And now she's dead, too. "Yes. I remember you."

She nods and assesses me. "How are you feeling?"

"Like I've been shot a few times," I answer without a smile.

"Well, I know what that feels like." She chuckles and then manages not to look offended when I don't join in. "I came to see if you're ready to talk more about what happened the other night."

"I already gave my statement," I tell her.

"Yes. I did take a peek at that." She leans against the bed and crosses her arms. "I guess what I'm asking is whether you want to add anything else to it. You have had more time to think about that night. Sometimes trauma can make us forget important details. Like, did you happen to see the people who stormed into the house and grabbed your friend Willow?"

"Humph. She's hardly a friend of mine." The moment the words are out of my mouth, I regret them. What goes on in a family should stay in the family. As a Vice Lord Flower, Lucifer and I are a part of the same family.

Captain Hawkins nods, absorbing my words. "Regardless of what happened, it is fortunate that you and Ms. Washington

survived the ordeal. A lot of other people weren't so lucky."
She pauses for emphasis. "I'm afraid that my coming over here
isn't solely about what happened to you in that house, but . . .
I need to tell you about some bad news."

I tense as my imagination flies. "Is it about Profit?"

"Profit? Oh. You mean your boyfriend, Raymond? No.
Last I heard he posted bail this morning. This is . . . uh, about
your sister, LeShelle. I'm sorry to have to be the one to tell
you, but . . . her body was discovered early this morning."

I drop my gaze and then become self-conscious about how
I should act. Should I gasp? Cry? I doubt that I even have
water in my tear ducts to fake cry for that evil bitch, so instead,
I allow the room to get incredibly quiet while I show no reaction at all.

"Are you all right?" the captain asks, her face scrunching
like she already finds my behavior odd.

"Yes. I'm fine."

When a full minute of silence passes, Hawkins hits me
with, "Don't you want to know what happened?"

I don't trust myself to speak, so I simply shake my head.

Hawkins presses forward. "I know about what happened at
the Memphis Mental Health hospital. A few months back, you
attacked your sister with a pair of knitting needles, if I recall.
So I understand that there may still be some bad blood between the two of you, but I just thought that you should know
what happened to her."

Silence.

Captain Hawkins exhales a long breath. "Ms. Murphy, I'm
going to go out on a limb here. I talked to the Sullivans and
Douglases out in the lobby and they told me about your in-
heritance and their offer for you to move down to Houston."

My gaze creeps back up to her face.

"Look. Once upon a time, I used to be just like you."

"Humph!" I shake my head in disbelief.

"No. It's true. I came up rough on the wrong side of the

tracks in South Chicago. My own juvenile record was expunged when I turned eighteen and I joined the military. I want you to know that there *is* better out there. I see the road that you're going down . . . and if someone is offering you a chance to get out of the game before the game drags you down or takes you out, grab hold of it and run like hell."

Apparently, my tear ducts aren't as dry as I thought because the room swims and the knot in my throat becomes painful.

"Just think about it." With her hip, Captain Hawkins pushes herself away from the bed and heads toward the door.

"Thank you," I whisper before she slips out, not knowing whether she can hear me.

"You're welcome."

28

Lucille

"Wake up, sweet baby. Please wake up."

There's no response, but I know Willow can hear me. That may be irrational or illogical, but it's the only thing I have to hold on to. I've suffered so many losses that it's hard not to believe that God hates me. What other excuse could there be?

I am grateful that somehow Mason Junior survived the trauma of his early birth. He's not going to be without his own health challenges in the future. But he *will* live.

Willow? It's not looking too good. I can't even understand most of the medical terminology that the doctors keep throwing around. How can someone so young, who has never had any major health issues, just up and have a brain aneurysm? From the way that it was explained to me, Willow must've suffered a traumatic brain injury during the car crash. A clot formed and then steadily built while she went into labor. Then it exploded. It all sounds crazy, but I just want them to fix my baby.

Through fat tears, I rub Willow's hand, disturbed by how cold and clammy her skin feels.

"Wake up, baby. Wake up."

Beep! Beep! Beep!

I close my eyes against the sound of the heart monitor. As

frustrating as it is to listen to it, it's still better than the alternative: a flat line.

"C'mon, Willow. You know you have to wake up so that you can meet and hold that beautiful baby. He's going to need you. There's nothing that can take the place of a child's mother," I tell her. "I know that maybe we haven't always seen things eye to eye. But you got to know that I've always tried to do right by you and your brother. Even after Darcell left us, I mean. There are a lot of things that I should've been more honest about. Things were easier when you were younger. When you grew older, you were so angry." I stop and pull myself together. "I'm not trying to lay all the blame on you. None of it was your fault. It's me. It's *my* fault; but I pray that you really do know that I love you. You are my baby girl. Forever and always."

Tears rush like a waterfall. There's no way for me to stop them so I let it all out.

Beep! Beep! Beep!

29

Hydeya

As I exit out of Ta'Shara's cold and somber hospital room, I already regret not saying more to the young teenager. Despite all the internal alarms going off regarding the girl's reaction to the news of her sister's death, there is something delicate if not vulnerable about the wide-eyed teenager that makes me want to protect her rather than persecute her. *Did Ta'Shara have something to do with her sister's death?*

I sigh as I glance down the crowded hallway and spot Raymond Lewis, or rather Profit, striding toward Ta'Shara's room. I take special note of his downcast head and his tense body language. I hate to admit it, but he reminds me of my own forbidden teenage love for a boy named Cash. Looking back, our love was doomed from the moment we laid eyes on each—but you couldn't tell us that.

Cash was a product of the system. He loved those South Chicago streets as much as he proclaimed to love me. Slinging drugs and gang-banging gave him an adrenaline rush that left him as addicted to the game as his customers were addicted to his product. To a young girl with daddy issues, I was attracted to him like a moth to a flame. I didn't give a shit whether I ever got burned or blew up in flames. I wanted to be with him—no matter the cost.

Finally, Profit notices me a full second before walking right into my ass. He starts to say something before recognition flashes into his puppy-dog brown eyes.

I push up a smile. "We meet again."

"What are you doing here?" His lips curl with a snarl as his downtrodden body language becomes more defensive than what is warranted.

"Is that a real question?"

He backs up a step. "Look. I don't have anything to say to you unless you're here to tell me that you put down the mutha-fuckas that pumped bullets into my girl and destroyed my neighborhood."

"How do you expect us to do that when everyone involved is evoking the no-snitch rule?"

Raymond shrugs. "I can't tell you how to do your job, but if it were me, I'd round up the entire Gangster Disciple crew and put the heat on them until they crack. Harassing the *victims* is not going to get you anywhere."

"The last time I saw you, you were thanking the department for helping your mother."

"Well, she's dead now so . . ." He looks away from me when my head cocks in surprise.

"Dead? How? When?"

"Look. I don't want to talk about it right now. I want to see my girl, so if you'll excuse me." Raymond reaches for Ta'Shara's door, but I block his exit from our conversation.

"Don't let the rules of the street cloud your judgment here. I'm *not* the enemy."

He laughs. "C'mon, lady." He takes another step back. "How long have you been in the game?" he asks, but doesn't wait for my answer. "You didn't make captain without knowing how all of this shit works. You are most *definitely* the enemy. All you want to do is lock up as many niggas as humanly possible. You don't give a shit about us or what we have to do to survive out here—so run this game on another player who hasn't bothered to read the playbook. Okay? I have nothing further to say to you. Now please, step out of my way."

In order not to bring myself down to his level, I clamp my jaws tight and then force myself to sidestep to the left.

"Thank you." His fist slams open the door before he storms into his girlfriend's hospital room.

I'm left to stand in the hallway, stewing that I have to let a punk like him curse me out. The knowledge that he'll soon learn one day that I'm right and that he should have accepted the olive branch that I'm offering him doesn't tamp down my anger.

I need a cigarette. It's a wild thought since I don't smoke. Turning, I walk away from Ta'Shara's room with the intent of leaving the hospital to make the long-dreaded pit stop at Shotgun Row, but instead I walk to the hospital's intensive care unit. I enter Willow Washington's room, where I find her mother, sobbing and begging her daughter to wake up.

The only answer she gets is the steady *beep* from the heart monitor, the steady hiss from the breathing machine, and a stream of air that blows through the small tube in her daughter's nose. It's a scene that has me backpedaling as fast as I entered.

"The baby is doing well," Lucille whispers to her motionless daughter. "He's a strong one, just like his mother."

Gone is her daughter's long hair. Her complexion is now a dull brown and her full lips look as though they are chapping. As if she heard my thoughts, Lucille reaches into her black purse and removes a tube of ChapStick. I watch through watering eyes how she lovingly takes care of Willow. Even pulling out a tube of cocoa butter to moisturize her hands.

I think of my own mother and how she and my militant stepfather have only seen fit to fill my voicemail with concerned messages rather than hop on a plane to Memphis to see personally how I'm holding up. While it's true that my stepfather saved me from the streets, he never accepted a white man as my husband. They love me, I know, in their way, and I shouldn't compare them, or even King Isaac, to this loving mother, but at this moment, I can't help it.

Exiting Washington's room, I make my way down to the neonatal intensive care unit. It's a nursery that provides around-the-clock care for ill or premature newborns. After flashing my badge, I quietly search around until I find Mason Lewis Junior. When I spot him, I'm momentarily amazed by how small yet perfect his tiny body appears in the incubator. There are a few tubes attached to his nose and arms, but he appears to be sleeping soundly.

While watching him, a genuine smile forms on my face. I repeat to myself over and over again that he's going to make it. Inevitably, my mind tumbles over memories of the constant arguments with Drake about when I was going to come off the pill and start our own family. I hemmed and hawed for years, thinking that we had plenty of time. Foolish statements and arguments float through my mind. What I wouldn't do or give to have a child with Drake's kind eyes and dimpled cheeks.

A kind-faced nurse walks over to Mason Junior's small incubator and then lovingly stretches her hands inside to give him a few minutes of encouraging human touch. When she looks over at me, my eyes are swimming in an ocean of tears. I turn and leave before making a complete fool of myself. Outside the unit, I stop next to a long window that displays the darkening gray cityscape. The image reflects my mood. I'm dreading my trip out to Shotgun Row and subjecting myself to whatever lies my father is going to sling my way.

I know that he and his guys are responsible for the Ruby Cove massacre, as Fowler called it, so how do I go about proceeding with this mess without implicating myself? After all, I saw the weapons when he and his goon squad locked me in a bedroom, and I have yet to mention those facts to anyone. On the surface it makes me look complicit or like I'm aiding and abetting my father's crimes. Hell. That's exactly what it is. It's exactly the kind of thing that the chief would use to snatch my badge again, and this time I may never get it back again, despite Fowler's major fuckup for not responding to the department's calls and texts.

My sigh is long and heavy. The very thing I feared happening when King Isaac was released took less than a month to actually come to pass. My gaze drifts away from the skyline and down toward the multilevel parking lot, where a scene playing out has me thinking that my eyes are playing tricks on me. Squinting, I zero in on the two guys and one female, huddled together and talking while constantly glancing over their shoulders. It's not a trick. It's Fowler, Hendrix, and Mason Carver-Lewis.

What in the hell are they up to?

30

Ta'Shara

Still mulling over Captain Hawkins's words, I'm unprepared when Profit enters my room. But the moment I see him a smile eases onto my face and tears rush to my eyes. "Profit."

The worry lines that were grooved into his forehead smooth away as he looks at my face and sees that I'm okay. "Shara, baby." He strolls over to the bed and gathers me into his arms. I cling to his strength and warmth while my love for him overwhelms me. After everything, this man still holds the key to my heart. It doesn't matter that he's no good for me or that thus far our love has only brought pain and destruction to so many lives. All that matters is right here and right now.

Profit pulls back and breaks the temporary spell. "How are you feeling, baby?" He kisses the center of my forehead and then peppers kisses across my cheeks, nose, and lips. "You have no fucking idea how worried I was about you."

"I'm fine," I tell him with tears streaking from my eyes. "You heard about . . . ?" I can't even get myself to say her name. What if I see more than just a brotherly concern for Lucifer in his eyes? Will I be able to handle it? Will that damn kiss always stand between us?

Profit drops his head. "Yeah. I heard. Mason is tore up over it. I'm still having a hard time believing that shit even happened."

"Yeah. I know what you mean." A slow panic creeps over me. I don't want him to notice my non-moving legs.

"Do you remember any of it? Can you tell me what happened?"

I close my eyes and press my forehead against his. Just the idea of going over that nightmare again exhausts me.

"You don't have to if you don't want to. I swear, all that matters to me right now is that you're still here, because that means that there's still a chance to fix this mess I've made of our lives. That's if you'll let me."

I've prepared for this moment. I've gone around and around on what to say.

"Shara?" Profit whispers, drawing my gaze to meet his watery one. "You *will* give me another chance to fix this, won't you?"

"Profit. I love you. God knows I do, but . . . there's so much that has happened and I've lost so much that . . ."

He pulls away from me, wrenching my heart out of my chest. I already regret the few words that I've spoken. Yet I refuse to take them back.

"Surely after all that happened you . . . I mean, how many times do I have to apologize?" he asks.

"It's not that, Profit. Really. I accept your apology. I believe you when you say that you're not in love with Willow."

"Then why . . . ?"

"Because nothing good can come from this—from our being together. I don't belong in your world. I've already lost so much of myself. The things that I've done in the last couple of months will haunt me for the rest of my life. I don't want to be a Vice Lord Flower. I don't want to be someone's ride-or-die chick or just some wifey to the throne."

"Then we'll get married," Profit says. "Now. Today."

My heart soars at the proposal, but the battle within me

rages on. "And then what?" I ask, hating myself for throwing the question out there. "Our lives won't change. We'll still be in the thick of a gang war that's getting worse every day. I can't go through another night like the other night. I don't have it in me."

"And you won't have to. Baby, I swear. I'll keep you safe."

"You can't guarantee that. Look at . . . Willow. There isn't a badder chick in the game and look where she is. Hell. Look where her brother is. My sister. My best friend. It's not going to stop until I'm standing over your grave or you're standing over mine. Is that what you want?"

"Don't be ridiculous." Frustrated, Profit bounds up from the bed.

"How can you say that I'm being ridiculous? Are you not paying attention to what's going on around us?"

"Of course I'm paying attention. Those muthafuckas took out a lot of my friends the other night. And they're not going to get away with this shit either!" He's as angry as I've ever seen him. His face and neck have darkened and he has visible veins pulsing along his temples.

"Listen to yourself. You're talking about more bloodshed. Don't you see? It's never going to end."

"Are you saying that they should get away with killing our soldiers in *our* neighborhood? You know, your girl Dime was one of them."

"What?"

"Yeah. I didn't think you knew about that. This shit is fucking personal, Shara. This wasn't a smack on the hand, and we can't let the shit slide. If we do, who knows what the next two-dollar gang will try to flex on us."

"Profit. You're proving my point," I tell him, certain that he can hear the frustration in my voice. "I love you, but I can't go back to that life. I can't."

Profit clamps his jaw tight and glares at me. "You want me to beg."

"No." I shake my head. "I've made up my mind."

"So nothing has changed?"

"That's not true. I'm not angry with you. I'm not angry with anyone. I just want to do what's best and . . . I want to go back to school. I want to go to college and medical school. I want to be that doctor that I've always wanted to be."

Profit rolls his eyes. "That bullshit again."

"Bullshit? You think my wanting to be a doctor is bullshit?"

Profit backtracks. "I didn't mean it like that."

"How in the hell other way could you have meant it?" The pain in my heart surpasses the pain from the bullets that I took the other night. I'm staring at the man I love without the rose-colored glasses, and I'm not sure that I like who I see.

"Ta'Shara, of course, I think that you can be anything that you want to be. I'm trying to figure out why you don't want to be with *me* anymore. You love me, but you won't marry me. You forgive me, but you won't come back home. Help me understand this shit."

"Then understand that it's not always about *you*. How come being with you means that *I* have to give up everything *I* want? When the hell do your sacrifices kick in? What have you given up?"

"Are you kidding me? I lost my mother—"

"You mean the mother who didn't want you to get mixed up in this gang life in the first place? The mother who didn't want you to move up here from Atlanta in the first place?"

"If I'd never moved back to Memphis then *we* would've never met."

I press my lips together and the room fills with a heavy silence.

"Oh." He steps back, screwing up his face. "Is *that* your point? You wish that we never met?"

"I didn't say that."

"But do you deny it?"

I hesitate a beat too long and Profit tosses up his hands. "Fuck it." He heads toward the door. "You wish that you never met me, then let me help you rectify that situation. Good luck to you, *Ms.* Murphy. You don't ever have to worry about seeing my ass again."

"Wait. Profit . . ."

He doesn't stop. In fact, he leaves out the door with a final, "Fuck you, Ta'Shara."

31

Wendi

"What?""You just want to waltz up to him in a hospital parking lot in broad daylight?" I ask Fowler, flabbergasted. "That doesn't sound too damn smart to me."

Fowler huffs out a breath. "Will you please chill the fuck out?"

I glare at him. "Who the fuck do you think you're talking to?" I snap back. "I have just as much shit on the line as you do, and I have an equal interest in making sure that you don't fuck it up."

Fowler inhales, closes his eyes, and I assume counts to ten. "You're right. I'm sorry. But we got to know whether to fill that order. The Vice Lords lost a lot of soldiers during that GD assault. If I arrange that shipment and Fat Ace can't pay, that'll be a headache none of us can afford."

He's right, but I can't shake the feeling that this shit is all wrong. I bite my lower lip.

"Right?" he presses.

This time before I can answer, Fat Ace climbs out of the driver's seat of a black Escalade.

"Hold that thought," Fowler tells me. "It's showtime." He bolts out of the car.

I make the sign of the cross and then rush after him.

"Yo, my man," Fowler booms.

Fat Ace pivots around to see who the hell is yelling across the open parking deck. When he recognizes Fowler he does a double take to make sure there're no other cops about to spring up like jack-in-the-boxes. "What the fuck do you want?"

"Just a few minutes to holler at you." Fowler grins and then removes his mirrored sunglasses in order to look the intimidating gangster in the eye.

My heart pounds so hard it's a wonder I haven't dropped dead. This is risky. This is reckless. This is insane.

"What? You came to bust me again?" Fat Ace asks. "I just bonded out an hour ago."

"Nah. I ain't got shit to do with that. I'm checking to make sure you still want that order before I put it in. My supplier don't work on credit or issue refunds."

Fat Ace's one black eye bounces between Fowler and me. "Are you fuckin' serious?"

"Yeah. I just—"

"Nigga, is you wired or some shit?"

"Nah. Nah. It's nothing like that." Fowler laughs. "I know that your set has been hit with a big tragedy and all. I'm just saying that *if* you need more time, we can push off the next delivery until you're ready."

"Man, I don't know what the fuck you're talking about and I don't appreciate you rolling up on me like this when I'm here to see about my fiancée and my son."

"All right. All right. Calm down." Fowler holds up both hands. "I didn't mean to upset you. I was just checking. I'll let you go do what you gotta do. Everything is good."

Fat Ace glares at Fowler as if he can't believe the man came at him the way he did. Hell, I don't even fucking believe it. We look like two fucking amateur idiots. Of course Fat Ace is thinking we're trying to entrap his ass.

"Hey. Forget I said anything," Fowler says, trying to make up for his error.

Fat Ace steps back, shaking his head.

I fidget and keep glancing around. I know that doesn't help the situation, but I can't help it. I'm nervous.

Fowler steps back, too. "Just give me a call if you have a change of plans. I completely understand given the circumstance."

Fat Ace shakes his head again, spins, and then marches off toward the hospital.

I exhale, not even realizing that I'd been holding my breath. "I told you that was a bad idea."

Fowler ignores me.

"What if he now *cancels* the order because he doesn't trust us anymore? Did you ever think of that?"

Silence.

I stomp my foot. "Fowler! You hear me talking to you!"

Fowler shields his eyes as he looks up at the hospital building.

"What the hell are you looking at?" I mimic his stance to see what has caught his attention.

"Not what. Who," Fowler corrects me.

Then I see her. "Captain Hawkins."

32

Hydeya

Glued next to the hospital window, I watch the suspicious huddle between Mason, Fowler, and Hendrix, and try to make sense of what I'm seeing. Sure, it could be any number of things that my colleagues could be discussing with the notorious gangster—but my Spidey senses are going off like a muthafucka. Hendrix is a dead giveaway. Her jittering ass looks guilty as hell—but guilty of what?

Mason, appearing angry and frustrated, breaks away from the two officers and heads into the hospital.

My gaze follows his long strides into the building and then swings back to Fowler, who is now looking up toward my window. Has he spotted me? I'm up on the tenth floor, so I doubt it, but I'm not sure. Not until Hendrix also looks up am I certain that I have been spotted—but I'll be damned if I'll be the first one to walk away. After a full minute of our standoff, Hendrix tugs on Fowler's arm and pulls him away.

I move away from the window and instead of leaving the hospital as I intended, I wait until I see Mason arrive on Ms. Washington's floor. When he steps out of the elevator, other patients, nurses, and doctors scurry out of his way from the mere look of him. With his huge physical frame and grotesque burns and eye-patch, he looks like a monster from a children's horror story. I even see a few kids in one of the waiting areas point and erupt into hysterics.

Mason is oblivious to it all. He's focused on reaching his girlfriend's hospital room. Even when he passes me, I'm certain that he isn't ignoring me. He simply doesn't see me. He stops a nurse, who jumps back when she sees him, and asks where his girlfriend's room is.

The nurse points him in the right direction and he continues on his way. I know that I should leave him alone—allow him some personal time with Willow—but knowing that he's my brother casts an almost trancelike spell over me.

He enters Willow's room, and a few minutes later, a somber doctor with a resolute-looking nurse also enters the room. It isn't much longer after that when Lucille's mournful wails pierce through the room's door.

More bad news.

My heart plummets to my knees as I imagine the worst. My mind skips back to when we discovered the wild-eyed woman, drenched in sweat, squatting in the woods like a wild thing. The woman had to have been made of some stern stuff to survive two attacks and a car crash to deliver her baby, but it'll likely take a miracle for her to survive these latest developments.

A minute later, the somber doctor and nurse exit the room with their heads hanging lower than when they entered. The nurse gives the doctor a comforting rub on the back. Once they step away, I head back toward Ms. Washington's door. I ignore the voice in my head telling me not to enter, and push through the door anyway.

Lucille is on her feet with her face planted in the center of Mason's chest, sobbing as if her world has ended. "Whhhhyy? Whhhhyy?"

Mason has his muscular arms wrapped around the older

woman, but he is staring down at Willow while tears slide down his face. He doesn't look like he's capable of saying anything, and then, "This is all my fault."

The declaration quiets Lucille's wails.

Mason's thick, emotional voice continues. "I should have been there. They wouldn't have gotten her out of that house. She should have been with me, picking up that shipment from that Fowler cat. She has always gone with me. Always."

To be honest, I'm not sure I heard what was said after the name Fowler. I mean . . . I couldn't have heard that correctly. Could I? I don't know what I did to have drawn attention to myself, but Lucille's accusatory voice snaps me out of my reverie.

"What are you doing in here?"

Mason's big head swivels in my direction, and with naked rage he drops his arms from around Lucille and storms toward me.

In my lifetime, I've been in street and in war combat. My reflexes have never failed—until this moment. I freeze, I'm jarred out of my temporary paralysis when Mason's enormous hands lock around my upper arms and propel me out into the hallway.

"You've got some goddamn nerve," Mason growls, throwing me up against a wall. "You have no right to invade our privacy like this!"

"Get your damn hands off of me," I hiss back.

Curious heads jerk in our direction, but Mason's grip on my arms only tightens.

"If I have to tell you again, I *will* throw you so deep back into a cell, you'll forget what sunlight feels like." I make sure my game face remains fixed on his stony features. Little by little, the grip on my arms loosens. At last I'm allowed to slip down the wall to stand back on my own two feet, but I have to keep my head thrown back to meet his lone visible eye, unblinkingly.

"Stay away from me and my family," he says coldly. "This is your one and only warning."

"Careful," I say. "That sounds like a threat. Threatening a police officer is still against the law the last time I checked."

The corners of his lips hike. "I don't make threats, *Captain* Hawkins. I make promises. Stay. Away."

He walks off, but I'm not through with him yet. "What shipment were you talking about involving Lieutenant Fowler?"

Mason stops in the middle of the hall. He takes his time glancing over his shoulder with an icy silence.

"It was *Lieutenant* Fowler who you were referring to, wasn't it?"

"I don't know what you're talking about," he lies smoothly.

"I'm sure you don't." *But I'll find out.* Turning, I stroll down the hallway with my chin up and my mind rewinding to the night of the Ruby Cove massacre. *Fowler was unreachable that night—and Mason wasn't home.* Suddenly that little huddle outside takes on a whole other meaning. By the time I reach my car in the parking garage, I'm rethinking a whole lot of other shit, especially the Captain Johnson case and Fowler and *Chief* Brown's insistence that I close the case. All of that hoopla about the fallout from all the local politicians who had hitched their wagon to the myth of Memphis's famous supercop. The amount of money and weapons stashed in his residence was astounding. There was no way that he wasn't dirty. But the man couldn't have been an island unto himself. He had to have had help—but I never dreamed that it could be a man I've trusted time after time with my life. The sneaky maneuvers to steal my job are one thing, but to be a dirty cop entangled in a gang war is another thing entirely.

Sinking in behind the driver's seat, I contemplate my next move. Like Captain Johnson, Fowler can't be acting alone in this. Who else is involved? Hendrix, clearly. Her jittery ass is a dead giveaway, but who else? How far up the chain? *Chief Brown?* How about her secret lover, whom she thinks nobody else knows about, Mayor James Wharton? The depth of this rabbit hole overwhelms me. How in the fuck do they put me in the impossible position to clean up a mess that their illegal activities are creating? I'm damned if I do and damned if I don't.

This bullshit is what I sacrificed my marriage for? I chuckle under my breath and then I laugh. Hard. Hysterically. *I'm fucked.* I know it and surely they know it, too. I start the car. At times like these, a girl needs to have a long talk with her father.

33

Mack

The survivors of the Ruby Cove massacre are on pins and needles. We're all waiting for the call from either Fat Ace or Profit on what our next moves are going to be. People attended funerals and wakes in waves. Everyone wants to pay respects; that includes to GG and Qiana.

Romil and I remain quiet when members of our crew spread rumors that the Gangster Disciples are also to blame for their deaths. Tombstone took the shit hard. I've never seen that brothah lose his shit the way he has. His rage narrowly focused on Diesel Carver. Apparently, Tombstone had the man all up in his house once. This convinces Tombstone that Diesel had played Qiana's ass to get information on the Vice Lords. He's telling everyone who'll stand still long enough that the slick muthafucka used Qiana to pump information out about Ruby Cove.

Other soldiers and Flowers agree.

Guilt trips all through me, but what choice do my girl and me really have in keeping our mouths shut? Confessing that we had a hand in Qiana and GG's murders would just turn our own against us. In a way, LeShelle Murphy *is* responsible for Qiana and GG. Her and Qiana's treasonous deal is what led to both of their deaths, so fuck it.

The thing is, when Profit makes the call, I'm not too sure he'll reach out to Romil and me. Whatever is going on with him and Ta'Shara is a done deal. He's let it be known that he doesn't want anyone to mention her name. The fact that she was so cool with us now has him looking at us sideways. A reminder as to why it's important to stay out of muthafuckas's relationships. The second that shit goes left, people choose sides.

I'm pulling out of Dime's funeral with Romil when Tombstone's number pops up on my screen. "Hello."

"It's going down tonight," he rumbles over the line. "You in?"

Finally. "You know it."

"Be at my crib, three o'clock. Three o'clock. Don't be late." He disconnects the call.

"Got it," I say though he's already gone. I glance at Romil. She reads my excitement. "What? Was that the call?"

I nod.

"Good. This fucking sitting and waiting is for the birds. The whole damn city talks like we fell off. We're not the only ones who've sustained a hit." After Shariffa's body was inexplicably found in Lucifer's crib, the police then discovered her husband, Lynch, the chief of the Grape Street Crips, decapitated out in Tupelo. When LeShelle Murphy's body made the news, cheers went up on Ruby Cove, but hours later, people worried about retaliation.

Romil and I follow Profit's lead. Since he's quiet about LeShelle's murder, our lips are sealed, despite the fact that we would've been treated like celebrities. Will the Gangster Disciples come gunning for us again? Some are split on whether it was her death that set everything off in the first place.

Romil and I return to my place. Our mood goes from excitement to somber reflection. So much has happened so fast and our clique is now so small. It's only natural to wonder about shit going left.

By two, we're dressed for combat. We're more than forty-five minutes early, but there's already a crowd mobbin' around the house. Everyone got their game faces on, heads nodding, repeating, "All is well" every other sentence.

At two thirty, Profit emerges from his house, mean mugging and exchanging dabs. There's certainly a change about him. There's no trace of the wide-eyed teenager who moved up here over a year ago, wanting to hang with his older brother Fat Ace. But most know that the newest change has more to do with his breakup with Ta'Shara than any of the battle scars he has earned from the streets.

When he approaches, I'm disheartened that he doesn't acknowledge us.

At exactly three o'clock, Tombstone exits his house. To be honest, he and Profit are competing on who can hide their pain better.

"Let's ride out."

34

Hydeya

It's never a good idea to roll into gang territory without backup, especially when you're a cop and everyone knows your face. However, I'm in an *I don't give a shit* kind of mood and decide to take my chances. The second I cruise down Shotgun Row, I feel several sets of angry eyes on me. When I climb out of my car and bound up the steps to Momma Peaches' old place, those same curious neighbors mill around their houses to get a better view of what is about to go down.

I hammer on the door, step back, place my hand on my holstered weapon, and wait.

No answer.

I repeat the process, but bang on the door harder.

No answer.

"Maybe he's not home," a smirking woman on the porch next door suggests.

I ignore her and the crying baby, who is wearing Pampers that look to be carrying a mighty load. Instead, I move over to the window and peer inside. I can't see shit, but my gut tells me that my old man is in there, hiding from me. "Ain't this some shit?"

"If you want," the smug neighbor says, "I can tell him that you came by when I see him again."

I cut my gaze in her direction and wonder if the slim cigarette is what I think it is. "Really?" I ask. "You're gonna smoke
that shit right in front of me?"

The woman looks at the blunt, her slow mind kicks into
gear, and she drops the muthafucka like she's shocked to see
the weed in her hand.

I roll my eyes. I swear these muthafuckas out here get
dumber with each passing day. After a couple of calming breaths,
I turn my attention back to Momma Peaches's closed door. I tell
myself that I should leave and come back later, but the other
part of me, the angry and frustrated part, whips out my service
weapon, aims it at the door, and fires.

Pow! Pow! Pow!

"Holy shit!" The neighbor jumps and grabs her screaming
baby while I send a solid kick to the door. It bangs opens and
I proceed inside.

"What the fuck? You can't do that shit," the neighbor
shouts.

"She's right, you know," Isaac says, appearing in the hallway. He looks me up and down and then crosses his arms as if
holding down his territory. "I hate to be the one to tell *you* the
laws that you're supposedly sworn to uphold, but shooting
your way into a private residence without a warrant is against
the law."

"Funny." I smirk, holster my weapon, and back-kick the
door closed. "We need to talk."

"Humph." He looks me up and down. "Are you here to
talk as my chip-on-the-shoulder daughter or as the pain-in-
my-ass cop?"

"Both." I stroll farther into the house and make myself
comfortable in one of the chairs in the living room.

Isaac's gaze follows my movements, but he doesn't budge
from the hallway. "What do you want, Hydeya?"

"Hydeya? What? I'm not your little princess anymore?"

His chin comes up as he struggles with how to play out the

current situation. "Of course you'll always be my little princess. Now. What the hell do you want?"

I laugh. "So we're going to play stupid this afternoon. All right. I'm game. We both know that it was you and your folks that leveled Ruby Cove. I saw the crates of weapons that night, remember?"

"I wouldn't bank too much on your memory of that night. I recall you being highly intoxicated when you came over here." Isaac moves out of the hall and strolls into the living room, where he eases into a chair across from me.

It doesn't get by me that his movements are slow and stiff.

I watch him and shake my head. "Un-fucking-believable." My blood pressure shoots through the roof. I'm just surrounded by frauds, cheats, and con artists. "What the fuck am I supposed to do now?" I ask him. "Pretend that I don't know what I know? You killed thirty-seven people that night. They were people's sons and daughters. You looked me dead in my eyes and told me that you were out of the game, that you were going to stay on the up-and-up." My voice rises. "Am I going crazy? Did I imagine this conversation? All your pathetic letters over the last ten years were bullshit, right? Your *word* is bullshit. It always has been."

Isaac remains calm while I lose it.

"Now your *bullshit* may cost me the very job I've worked hard to get. A job, by the way, that I take great pride in. I told you that this was my fucking city. That the bullshit you do puts my shit on the line. But I know, like I've always known, that my life, my shit, is a non-muthafuckin' factor to you."

"That's not true," he says tactically, subtle remorse rippling across his features.

"Don't lie." I close my eyes and keep the begging out of my voice as I add, "Please. I can't take it if another muthafucka lies to my face."

"Princess—"

"I'm not your fucking princess. Let's at least get that shit straight," I say, shaking. "It's taking everything I have not to put a bullet in the center of your forehead and claim self-defense. We both know that nobody would blink an eye if I did."

Amusement hugs the corners of Isaac's lips. It's a tell that his ass doesn't believe for one second that I'd do it.

Maybe it's his smugness that has me going for my weapon and firing off a shot that narrowly misses his head.

"THE FUCK?" Isaac is out of his seat and magically palming his weapon.

"Ah. Ah. Ah," I warn. "You don't want to do that."

My father looks at me with new eyes, but he lowers the gun.

"You do know that as a felon you're not to own or possess a firearm, right? I mean, with you being so up on what is and isn't against the law. Surely, you know that."

"So what's the play here?" Isaac asks, wanting to cut through the BS. "You came down here to shoot me or arrest me. Which is it?"

"I haven't made up my mind yet," I tell him honestly. "Tell me what you know or remember about Captain Melvin Johnson."

His outrage changes to confusion. "Why the hell do you want to know about that dirty muthafucka for? His ass is dead and gone. Good riddance."

"Yeah. I know that he was dirty. My question is how dirty? My investigation into his corruption has hit a brick wall."

Isaac laughs. "I'm not surprised. Y'all muthafuckin' cops are the worst of the worst out here. But y'all get y'all's rocks off locking brothahs like me up while guaranteeing the bloodshed continues as long as y'all pigs get your share of the profits."

"Not all cops are dirty," I tell him.

His laughter deepens. "I stand corrected."

"Tell me what you know."

"What's not to know? Every nigga out here knew Captain Johnson was as dirty as they come. He made his whole career by keeping his foot on the necks of the Gangster Disciples while propping up the Vice Lords. Probably because his brother was a Vice Lord pimp. Nigga by the name of Smokestack. He's still in the joint, still preaching that black power bullshit."

"Wait. Sooo . . . Captain Johnson was a Vice Lord?"

"Is that so hard to believe? You're the new captain and I bet you still got that six-pointed star on your back."

Heat rushes up my neck. I start to protest that Captain Johnson and I are in no way alike, but then I think about how I'm protecting Isaac right now by not hauling his ass to jail, and I keep my mouth shut.

"So yeah. Captain Johnson did their bidding. He supplied the Vice Lords with arms and gave protection when their drugs shipped in. Those muthafuckas couldn't have gotten a sweeter deal if they fuckin' tried. But their superman is gone. I bet their asses don't feel so invincible now." Isaac stares at me as I take it all in. "C'mon. You can't tell me that you didn't know at least half of this shit."

"I've been able to put a few pieces of the puzzle together," I confess. "My main concern is how far up the Johnson corruption goes."

"I'd imagine pretty damn far. No way he could get away with his shit for as long as he did without some fuckin' cover. I'm sure as long as they kept the money flowing to the right people, everything was just copacetic."

"What about Lieutenant John Fowler?" I ask. "Have you ever heard anything about him?"

Isaac shakes his head. "I can't say that the name is familiar. Then again, I have been locked down for a dime, remember?"

"But you can ask around, right? Run the name by Terrell?"

Isaac tenses. "Maybe."

I nod, appreciating him not playing me crazy.

"Speaking of Terrell—" I pause, trying to figure out a way to transition into a more delicate subject.

"Yeah?"

"LeShelle Murphy—her body was found in a shallow grave off of Mudville early this morning. Know anything about it?"

One look into his shocked face and I have my answer. "Well, I hate to be the bearer of bad news."

"She's dead?" he asks.

"Afraid so."

"Shit." Isaac hangs his head while the house fills with an uncomfortable silence. After a moment, he looks at me. "Now what?"

"Now I don't know. I'm getting a lot of heat about that stunt you pulled."

"Stunt?" Isaac repeats. His dark eyes level with mine. "Those Vice Lords killed my wife. Did you forget that shit? The very damn day I get out of the joint. To make matters even worse, they have the audacity to blast up her funeral and kill my baby girl's husband right in front of her face."

"Oh. So now *I'm* the reason you went all terminator on that block? Please. Miss me with that bullshit. You didn't even fucking know Drake, and I could tell that you didn't like him when you met him."

Isaac's gaze remains locked on me. "I didn't have to fucking like him. You loved him, and that was enough. Do you have any fucking idea what it was like to hear you scream the way you did out in that cemetery, or watch the way you hugged and cradled his body? Those muthafuckas did that to *my* baby, my princess, and there wasn't a damn thing that I could do about it. What kind of man do you think I am? Did you really think that I was just going to dust my shoulders off and chalk it up to the game? They declared war on *me*. And now you're up in here, putting bullets in walls because I did what you couldn't do? You're right. I don't give a fuck about that badge that you covet so much, but I *do* give a fuck about *you* and about what those assholes did to you. And you're sorely mistaken if you think that I'm going to apologize for any of it."

I lower my weapon, touched beyond words by what he has confessed. Before I know it, I'm being gathered in his embrace, wetting up his chest with tears that I've been trying to suppress ever since Drake's urn was delivered to the house by UPS. I don't know how long we stand in the living room with our arms locked around each other, but when we break away, I've made a decision to slap handcuffs on his wrists.

"What the fuck?"

"Sorry, Dad. But you're under arrest."

35

Wendi

"What do you think he means by 'take her out'?" I ask John as he disconnects the call with the mayor.

"What the hell do you think?" he asks, giving me a hard, impatient look before sighing. At least it's a sign that he's having a problem with possibly taking out a fellow cop.

I like Captain Hawkins. I actually do believe that she's really one of the good ones; the ones who believe in the good fight, and in our ability to make a difference out here in these streets. I used to believe in those things. It was why I joined the force myself. But it doesn't take long before you realize the kind of cesspool we're dealing with out here. The hours are often long, the respect is nonexistent, and there is absolutely no money in the job.

The money. That's what it all boils down to: I need the money. There's no way for me to take care of my mother's medical needs without it. An unbelievable amount of shame sweeps through me, but it's a shame that I'm forced to live with because I don't have any other options.

"Are you cool?" Fowler asks, his gaze hard and assessing.

"Yeah." I shrug. "You?"

John doesn't answer. He sits sullenly behind the wheel until we spot Captain Hawkins exit the hospital.

We watch in silence as Hawkins makes her way to her vehicle. I struggle to read her body language. Hawkins is a cool customer. She carries herself with such confidence that she's one of the most difficult people to read. I know if I had a husband who was just gunned down in front of me, I'd still be curled up in the fetal position somewhere. Captain Hawkins doesn't have an off switch.

It's unfortunate that it might be the very thing that'll get her killed.

The moment that Captain Hawkins pulls out of the parking deck, Fowler starts up the car and follows. While we tail our own captain, my stomach loops into a tighter and harder knot.

"Where is she going?" I ask when I notice that we're not following her back to the station.

"She must be going to see her father."

Her father. I'd almost forgotten about Fowler's revelation about Hawkins's biological father actually being one of Memphis's most notorious gang leaders. I've lived here all my life, unlike Fowler and Hawkins, and I remember what it was like back in the day when King Isaac dominated the streets. He was brutal to his enemies and a saint to his friends. And he did it all without the amount of bloodshed we see out here now on a daily basis. New York, Compton, Detroit, and Chicago were the problem cities. Nobody ever dreamed Memphis would ever get as bad as it has.

Aren't you contributing to the problem?

I lower my gaze as I look out the window to the pothole-littered streets. The guns were to prop up the Vice Lords over the Gangster Disciples because Captain Johnson claimed that we needed to back the lesser of the two evils. That was how it was presented. Well, that and the money. I keep circling back to the money.

When Captain Hawkins corners onto Shotgun Row, Fowler

doesn't follow. For good reason, I'd imagine. The street isn't that long, and Hawkins would undoubtedly pick us out, if she hasn't already. Instead, Fowler circles around onto East Trigg Avenue so that we're now *behind* King Isaac's place.

I look around the neighborhood, disgusted by how folks on this block don't take any pride in their neighborhood. Dead or dying lawns, trash littered everywhere, and old cars propped up on cement blocks. These people have long stopped giving any kind of fuck about anything.

"PIG!" somebody shouts.

I take another glance around, and the number of people loitering about has tripled in less than a minute. Their hard, curious gazes are locked on us. The few older women I saw rocking on their porches have climbed to their feet and are going into their houses.

"Are you sure that it's safe for us to be out here without backup?"

Fowler hardly spared the gathering crowd a look. "Relax. We're fine. They aren't going to do anything."

I remain cool on the outside, but my mind is rioting on the inside. I don't put nothing past anyone, and if these dangerous kids are behind the massacre of Ruby Cove, what the hell is taking out two nosy cops to them?

"Hey. Someone is going out the back door of Momma Peaches's crib," he says, leaning across my seat to squint between the houses and into the backyards of Shotgun Row.

I squint to see who he's looking at.

"Right there. There he goes," Fowler says, pointing.

I make out the fleeing figure. "Is that who I think it is?" I squint harder. "Terrell Carver."

Fowler smiles. "Hawkins was right. Damn her." He reaches for his door.

"Wait." I grab his hand. "What do you think you're doing?"

"I'm going after him." He goes for the door again.

My grip tightens as I point out the growing mob. "*They* are not going to let you just race after one of their leaders when it's clear that our asses don't have backup." I can't believe that I have to tell him this, but he's so gung ho to get back on Chief Brown's good side that his sloppiness might get us both killed.

Pop! Pop! Pop!

Rat-a-tat-tat-tat

Rat-a-tat-tat-tat

We flinch and duck. "What the fuck?"

36

Mack

Shotgun Row

Any minute, I expect the Gangster Disciples' corner boys to sound off the alarm, but we get damn deep into their territory before the gunfire erupts. Instantly, my heart speeds up, and when the adrenaline kicks in, it's on and poppin'.

"FORKS UP!" Big Boy shouts, hitting the power button.

The dark tinted windows roll down and everyone props their weapons on the sill, takes aim, and then taps the triggers at the first muthafuckin' thing we see.

Rat-a-tat-tat-tat

Rat-a-tat-tat-tat

I hate that I didn't think to bring earplugs. With all of our weapons being so close together, my eardrums are taking a pounding. It's hard not to get excited at seeing these mutha-fuckas running and taking cover. I give no fucks at seeing them, young or old, male or female. As far as I'm concerned, these muthafuckas deserve what's coming to them.

I get one bitch-ass gangster as he runs out of the house firing two automatic weapons at the same damn time. I cut his ass in half with the simple sweep of my AK. The GD soldier goes down, still screaming but firing up in the air. He's replaced by another fool who pounds his chest like King Kong, daring our asses to take him out. Nappy-headed boy got to be on that molly because he looks confused when he's lying on his back and choking on his own blood.

In a way, it's like we're all playing in one big-ass video game. The blue flags are our enemies and the random crack-heads are zombie extras. The shit is feeling so good to me that I start laughing. Every bullet is for my girls: Dime, Lucifer, and Ta'Shara. I want these muthafuckas to pay for the destruction they did to our family. The only thing that would make this shit sweeter is to get both King Isaac and Python in our crosshairs. If we take those two out, then it's a wrap. Game over. The Vice Lords win.

Our murder train rolls on. However, when we do corner onto Shotgun, we finally hit some real resistance. Bullets fly everywhere. Romil and I duck to the floorboard.

"Shit!" Big Boy roars.

I climb back up to my seat to see that he's been hit. But shit doesn't stop this gangster. He sprays more bullets and talks more shit, as if to prove that these paper gangsters ain't got shit on him. Inspired, I return to my window with my weapon, determined to hang in the fight for as long as I can.

37

Hydeya

"**I** can't believe you're arresting your own father," Isaac grumbles with amusement. When he laughs, his entire body quakes.

"I can't believe you put me in this situation," I respond, shoving him through the front door. "If I don't do my job, then it'll make me no better than Johnson. I can't have that."

Isaac smirks. "I'm proud of you. My little princess has integrity."

"Yeah. I must have inherited it from *Mom's* side of the family." I shove him toward the porch steps.

"All hell. You done arrested King Isaac again," the neighbor whines. "Damn. He just got home. Can't you cut a brother some slack?"

"Damn. Does that chick ever mind her own business?" I mumble under my breath.

"Not that I'm aware of," Isaac mumbles back before addressing his neighbor. "It's all right, Chantel. We're just going downtown for a more intimate chat." He hits her with one of his winsome smiles that gets the young girl twirling her hair around her finger.

I roll my eyes, guessing that daddy dearest here has already fucked his neighbor. No sooner do Isaac and I move off the front porch steps than gunfire snatches our attention.

Pop! Pop! Pop!
Rat-a-tat-tat-tat
Rat-a-tat-tat-tat

"The hell?" I reach for my weapon. Less than a second later, a train of black SUVs corners onto Shotgun Row, tires screeching, while another burst of gunfire erupts.

Chantel screams. Her baby cries.

Rat-a-tat-tat-tat
Rat-a-tat-tat-tat

"Shit!" Isaac pivots one-eighty and does a full-blown tackle, knocking my ass down. Before I even hit the ground, hot lead whizzes by my head and body. The air is knocked out of my lungs and the back of my head smacks against something hard. The pain is instant and I have trouble making sense of blue sky and white clouds swirling above.

Rat-a-tat-tat-tat
Rat-a-tat-tat-tat

Gangster Disciple soldiers pour out of their houses with their weapons drawn like they've been waiting for this moment.

I roll over and attempt to get up.

"Stay down," Isaac shouts, covering me.

Déjà vu. This is how Drake died, protecting me. "Get off! Get off!" I shout while looking around for my weapon. It was knocked out of my hand and now I can't find it.

"The key!"

"What?"

"Where is the fucking key? I gotta get out of these handcuffs," he shouts.

Rat-a-tat-tat-tat
Rat-a-tat-tat-tat

I shake my head no and search the ground for my weapon.

"Goddamn, Hydeya. This is no time for your bullshit. Give me the key!"

"No!"

A bullet slams into the back of Isaac's shoulder, spinning him around.

"Dad!" This shit can't be happening. Not again. "Dad! Dad! Are you all right?" I scramble back to his side, oblivious to my own safety.

He grunts and groans as he crawls around the corner of the house.

I follow, and along the way retrieve my gun from a bush. Unclicking the safety, I return fire along with the other Folk Nation. The murder train mows down a number of people, but their first three vehicles take on heavy return fire. Shattered windshields, punctured bodywork, and still they keep rolling through.

Once my clip is empty, I take cover behind my own car. A fast clip change and then I go right back at it.

A car peels onto Shotgun Row, spitting more gunfire. I take one look and recognize Fowler. *How in the hell did he get here so fast?* The second I ask the question the answer appears obvious. *He followed me.* That shit gets my blood boiling—but at the moment, I do appreciate having *some* backup.

The gunplay takes me back to my military days, and a particular battle where my unit was hemmed in by enemy fire comes to mind. An incredible calmness comes over you when you're in life-and-death situations. Your thinking gets clearer.

The event doesn't last long before the train is spinning around at the end of the road, running up on curbs, sideswiping cars—including mine. The initial hit to the car knocks me forward, but it's not enough to knock me out. But I am at an angle to see more bloodied bodies hit the concrete.

Police sirens fill the air as the glow of the taillights of the last SUV in the murder train disappears from Shotgun Row. Those of us still standing fire at the retreating cars, but we take no more casualties. When it's all over, everyone does a stunned assessment of the carnage.

"Captain Hawkins," Officer Hendrix shouts, jumping from Fowler's car and racing toward me. "Are you all right?"

The bitch is a hell of an actress because she genuinely looks concerned.

"Yeah. I'm fine." I give her my back before she can reach out and touch me. The sudden screaming cries of mothers, wives, and girlfriends fill up the street as the women pour out of their houses and race to their wounded men.

I stroll back to the side of Momma Peaches's house where I left Isaac. He sits leaning against the house, his blood visible through his black T-shirt.

As I approach, he smiles and nods. "You handled yourself pretty good out there."

The compliment actually makes me blush. The complexity of our relationship grows. "How is your shoulder?" I ask.

Isaac grins and shrugs. "I'm sure it's a scratch. What doesn't kill me makes me stronger. You should know that by now."

I nod. "Now *that* I inherited from your side of the family."

"Wait," Hendrix says, staring from my right. "You're bleeding, Captain."

"What?" I turn to my right and feel a stinging sensation. I press my fingers to my right temple. When I pull them away they are covered with bright blood. "Damn." Then I do something I've never done: faint.

38

Hydeya

The Med

"I'm fine. How many times do I have to keep telling you that?" I attempt to hop off the doctor's exam table, but Fowler isn't hearing it and presses his large hand against my shoulder to prevent my escape.

"How about we let the doctor tell us how fine you are?"

"Oh please." I roll my eyes. "Angling for me to get a medical leave now? Can you be a little *less* transparent?"

"Can you be a little less paranoid?" he argues. "Damn. Why is it hard for you to believe that I'm concerned?"

I fold my arms and give him a look. I'm not buying the bullshit he's peddling.

Fowler tosses up his hands and acts as if I'm the crazy one. "Fine. Hate me if you want, but sooner or later you're going to realize that we're on the same team."

"I doubt that."

"Okay. Here we go," Dr. Logan says, entering the room with his nurse trailing behind. "It looks like everything is in order. You suffered a flesh wound, like you thought."

"See? I told you." I sneer at Fowler before I hop off the table.

Fowler's pinched expression looks comical.

Dr. Logan continues. "I do recommend that you engage in *less* police shooting. You don't need a doctor to tell you they aren't helpful for a woman in your condition."

"My condition?"

The doctor nods and then notices my confusion. "For the baby," he says, as if that clarifies things.

"Baby? What baby?" He isn't making sense.

"I'm sorry." Dr. Logan backs up. "I assumed that you knew that you are expecting."

Speechless, I stare for a long moment and then decide that I didn't hear him right. "Can you run that by me again?"

Dr. Logan's gaze swings between Fowler and me. "I take it that this isn't good news for you two?"

"Me?" Fowler shakes his head. "Leave me out of it. I'm definitely not the father."

"I'm . . . pregnant," I say, letting the words sink in. In my head, I replay the last heartfelt conversation I had with Drake on the matter . . .

"I married you because I wanted to have more sex with you, not less. C'mon. Did you forget that we're supposed to be starting a family this year? What? Did you change the plans again without consulting me?" Drake asked, hurt.

"No. It's nothing like that," I lied. However, the problem with being with someone for so long is that they learn how to read you like a book.

"Aww, Hydeya. Don't do this." He sprang up from the bed.

Don't do what?" I asked defensively. "You know how much this new promotion means to me. And now I have the chief threatening to take it away."

"Maybe that's not such a bad idea. Maybe you are in over your head."

"What? I set my coffee aside on the nightstand and climbed out of bed. "What are you saying?"

"Look, Hydeya. I know you love your job. I respect that. But what about me? What about us? I'm supposed to be getting something out of this marriage, too."

And what? I'm supposed to quit my job and let you pump me full of babies? Is that it? How the fuck is that fair?"

"Why in the hell do you think people get married? We're supposed to be creating little people who look like us. I'm not ashamed to admit that I'm looking forward to being a father. All my friends have two or three of them. Even my parents are asking me when we're going to make them grandparents, like every other day."

The more he talked, the more I felt like I'd been cast in a horror movie.

"What?" He caught my expression.

"Nothing."

"Damn it, Hydeya. Don't make me feel like the bad guy. We made plans together. We had a plan."

"Plans change sometimes."

"For how long?"

"I don't know. I just know that I'm not ready to juggle all of that right now. I want to do my job, and I want to do it well. We still have plenty of time for kids."

Drake clamped his jaw and shook his head.

Guilt rattled through me, but I couldn't help how I felt. Yet, at the same time, I didn't want to signal that I wanted to bail on the relationship. I drew a breath and softened my approach as I slid my hands around his neck. "I'm not saying that I'm bailing on the family plan completely. I just want to postpone it for a little while. That's all."

"For how long?" he pressed.

"I don't know. Another year—or two." Or three.

"A year," he said, latching on to the lowest number. "You promise?"

"I can't promise, but—"

"Damn it, Hydeya!" He broke away. "Quit jerking me around."

"Then you quit being selfish and unreasonable. If the shoe was on the other foot and your career was taking off, I'd understand and adjust our plans."

"What the hell is that supposed to mean? What the hell is wrong with my career? The guys and I have booked that audition down at that new club. It'll be a long-term local gig. I thought that's what you wanted after our last summer tour."

"I did. I do. That's great, but that's not what I mean. I just . . ." I sighed. "I don't want to argue. Not today. I'm stressed out enough as it is. The job. Isaac."

"Then go," he said, equally upset. "Go to the funeral. Go babysit King Isaac. That's what you really want to do anyway."

"Don't be like that."

"Be like what? Isn't that the real reason you want to go to the funeral—to verify whether or not your father is really out of the game?"

He had me on that one.

"One year," I told him.

Drake stopped pacing. "What?"

"One year from today and I promise that we can start seriously trying for a baby."

He searched for the truth in my eyes. When he saw that I was on the up-and-up, his smile returned. "Deal."

"How far along?" I ask.

"I'm not sure," Dr. Logan says. "You'll need to get to your ob-gyn and schedule a sonogram. Do you remember the date of your last period?"

I take a deep breath, but draw a blank. "Um, no. I'll have to get back to you on that."

Dr. Logan nods. "Well. Either way, take it easy and make that appointment with your doctor."

I nod and exit the room in a trance. A baby. I'm going to have Drake's baby.

"Well. At least now we know why your mood has been swinging all over the place," Fowler says, smiling. "You're about to be a proud new momma." He slaps me on the back. "Congrats."

"Go to hell." I shrug off his dirty touch.

"Hey!"

I spin and jam my finger in the center of his chest. "Don't *hey* me. I'm on to you—and your flunky Hendrix."

"What the hell are you talking about?" Fowler backs up and then looks around to see if anyone is paying any attention to our conversation.

"Just know that I'm on to you—so you can cut all the bullshit and the phony concern. I'm not here for it."

"If I were you," he hisses, "I'd take a moment to calm the fuck down and really reassess what it is you're talking about."

"We both know what I'm talking about." I move in closer and stab him harder with my finger. "I know about the shipment and where you really were the night of the Ruby Cove massacre. Really, you think that you're going to continue arms dealing under *my* nose? You must have lost your fucking mind."

39

Yvette

"If it isn't the mighty King Isaac," I say, entering the small hospital room. "Funny seeing you again."

Isaac takes a long look at me while a slow smile hugs his lips. "Well, if it isn't Lieutenant Yvette Brown—oops. I'm sorry. It's Chief Brown these days, isn't it?"

"You've been keeping up with my career. Good to know."

Isaac tosses back his head and laughs. "Don't flatter yourself, Chief. I don't have nearly enough time to diagram all the pig dicks you had to suck to get your brand-new position—but if I had to guess, it was probably a whole train of those muthafuckas. For a bonus guess, I'd say you're fucking Mayor Wharton."

"What?"

Isaac's smile spreads. "Yeah. I've seen those secretive smiles y'all be giving each other in those press conferences. Y'all ain't fooling nobody."

"Fuck you." In case he's hard of hearing I give him the finger, too.

"Ha. Not even with an industrial-strength condom would I ever put my dick anywhere near that pussy—if you can still call it that. Tell me, does that shit still have any walls left to it?"

"You're not fooling anybody. You're just dying to find out."
I stretch a flat smile. "You didn't waste any time jumping back
into trouble. Thirty-seven bodies—that's gotta be enough for
them to give you the needle this time."

"I'm sure that I don't have any idea what you're talking
about."

"Ruby Cove ringing a bell? You massacred those people for
shooting up your wife's funeral. Not smart."

"That sounds like an interesting theory. Too bad it's not
true."

"Yeah, yeah. Tell it to the judge. All I need is your coming
perp-walk in front of the camera and then I don't care what
kind of hell they toss you into."

"Tired of your incompetence being splashed in the headlines every day? I don't blame you."

That shit strikes a nerve. "You're a regular comedian,
aren't you?"

"It doesn't take a comedian to recognize that you and your
department are a joke."

"Does that include your daughter?"

He glares.

I grin for having found his kryptonite. "Ah. You probably
didn't think I knew about that."

"She told you?"

"Nope. I have my sources."

"If it makes any difference, Hydeya doesn't claim me. She
kind of views me as just being a sperm donor."

"Please spare me the family drama details. I really don't
have the energy to pretend that I give a shit."

"Always was the cop with a heart of gold."

"And you're the dick that always has to fuck every chick in
a fifty mile radius. You being a sperm donor doesn't surprise
me. God knows how many damn kids you got running around
the whole country."

"Another interesting theory that still doesn't explain why I've never fucked you—no matter how hard you tried back in the day."

"You're delusional. All I'm thinking about is slapping your ass back in jail."

"Your only problem is my alibi."

There is something about the way he's gloating right now that makes me pause. "What alibi?"

"I have an alibi. I'm surprised my daughter hasn't told you, but I was with *her* at the time of the Ruby Cove massacre."

"What?"

"She came to my house pretty upset about you having put her on administrative leave. She may not want to say this, but she was pretty lit that night. I was surprised that she jumped up and went running to the crime scene after you called. But then again, that's my girl—dedicated to that bullshit badge."

My heart stops. "You were *with* Captain Hawkins that night?"

My hastiness in calling for a new press conference for King Isaac's perp-walk is now biting me on the ass. I even called James so that he could be there to claim credit for the department's progress. We are hoping that it will stop his slide in the polls.

"What's the matter, Chief? You don't look too good."

"Fuck you." I spin on my heels and march out. I can barely see straight as I march back out into the ER in search of Captain Hawkins. I could strangle that woman with my bare hands. When I burst into the room that Captain Hawkins was in a few minutes ago, I'm stunned to find the room empty. "The fuck?" I turn and run smack into a nurse who is leading another patient to the room. "Where is she?" I snap.

"Who?" the nurse asks, confused.

"Captain Hawkins. She was just in here."

"Oh. She left."

"I can see that. Never mind." I stomp around her and then

spot Fowler and Hendrix hugged up near the entrance. "Where the fuck is she?" I demand.

Fowler coolly looks up and then jerks almost to attention when he recognizes me. "I'm sorry, Chief. Where is who?"

"Who else? Captain Hawkins. I have a bone to pick with her."

"She left, Chief."

Deep breath. "I gathered that. Did she say where she's going?"

Fowler shakes his head. "Knowing the captain, she's probably on her way back to the office, despite getting some rather interesting news."

Another deep breath. "What interesting news?" I ask.

"According to the doc, Captain Hawkins is expecting a little bambino."

"She's pregnant?"

Fowler nods, grinning.

I swear, men are the worst gossipers.

"Good for her. But tell me"—I change up the subject—"did Captain Hawkins happen to mention that *she* is King Isaac's alibi for the night of the Ruby Cove massacre?"

Fowler's smile drops. "What?"

"So it's a surprise to you, too?" I cross my arms in hopes that it will prevent me from hitting something. "This shit is developing into one big mess, and by God I want some damn answers." I march off to the parking deck, and to my surprise I find Hawkins there. "Hawkins!"

The captain's head snaps up, and when she spots me she doesn't bother to hide her annoyance. Her disrespect annoys me, but yet at the same time, Hawkins always being who she is, is something to be admired—but not today.

"What is this shit I hear from your *daddy* that he was with you at the time of the Ruby Cove massacre?" I challenge her head-on.

"What?"

"That's what he just told me—and what he'll tell the cameras if we arrest him. Is that shit true? And if so, when the fuck were you going to tell me? Before or *after* I embarrass myself on national television?"

"I . . . I can't deal with this right now." She shakes her head and then attempts to turn away from the conversation.

I do something that I've never done and grab her shoulder and spin her back around. "You better *make* time for this. We have a city fucking falling down all around us and my fucking captain of police is the fucking daughter of the city's most notorious gangster. How the fuck do you think that's going to play when it gets out?"

"Ha." She rolls her eyes. "Did Fowler tell you that, too?"

"Don't worry about what the fuck he told me. Is the shit true?"

"The truth is complicated," she says, as if that's an answer.

"It's not that fucking complicated. Either you have half of his DNA or not! Plus, he's telling me that you were drunk that night. Is *that* true? Did you show up at my crime scene drunk?"

"Are you fucking kidding me? You called—I showed up and did my fucking job."

"Drunk?"

"I was *not* drunk," she insists.

For the first time, I don't believe her.

Hawkins sighs and tries again. "I was drinking that night before you called. I did go to Isaac's house that night. Yes. He was home when I got there, but then he locked me in a room and left." She takes a deeper breath. "There were weapons in the house when I got there and they were gone when I left."

"So Isaac could very well be our suspect?"

Hawkins hesitates but then nods.

My blood pressure lowers. "So it's your word against his," I say, nodding. "Okay. I think I can deal with that. I need a few minutes to think of what our next play is going to be."

"Are you charging him?" she asks.

"You're damn right, I'm charging him. No offense—but your daddy is an asshole."

Hawkins shrugs. "He has his moments."

I reach into my pocket and remove a cigarette. I need it badly. Once I plop one into my mouth, I offer the packet to Hawkins. She waves it off. "Oh yeah. I forgot. You're pregnant. Congrats."

"Damn. Whatever happened to doctor/patient confidentiality?"

"Fowler told me." I light my cigarette and tug in my first drag.

"Jeez. That man really can't hold water."

I have to agree with her on that. "Yeah. He's an . . . odd one." I spin around to lean my butt against the hood of Hawkins's car. When I do, I catch Fowler again. This time by the hospital's entrance, huddled up with James, and I have a bad feeling in my gut. *What the fuck are they up to now?*

Decisions

40

Ta'Shara

The room is so quiet that I can hear a fly land on the wall. It's been seven days and nothing has changed. Olivia keeps a death grip on my hand while she sobs during the doctor's running list of hypotheses of why I still can't feel my legs. My hysteria has long passed, though my grief remains profound. I'm working on acceptance. *I'll never walk again.*

I look down at my legs with a sense of betrayal. Think again: Why should they be any different? The closest people to me have betrayed me, so why not my own body?

"I'm sorry, Ms. Murphy," the doctor finishes. "I wish that I could give you better news, but I want you to know that there are a lot of excellent rehab facilities here in Memphis. I don't mind telling you that I've seen a lot of miracles in my time. There's a chance that this is all temporary."

"I understand, Doctor." I flash him a smile to make *him* feel better. I know that delivering this kind of news is equally hard on the professionals. With nothing else to add, he pats me on the shoulder and wishes me well.

Reggie Senior offers handkerchiefs to his wife, Mary, and Olivia. The old-fashioned kind. The ones with his initial embroidered at the bottom. His son used to carry those things around too.

"We'll get you the best doctors and physical therapists, no matter where you decide to go," he assures me.

Sniffling, Olivia bobs her head. "That's right, baby. This isn't a death sentence. There are plenty of paraplegics who live *very* full lives. This is *not* a roadblock."

I nod and smile. She means well. "Can one of you still take me to go see Lucifer?"

"Of course. Of course." Reggie scrambles around for the hospital wheelchair he'd rolled in here earlier and brings it over to the bed. Once the wheels are locked, he scoops me up.

While I'm still suspended in his arms, the door bursts open and Mack and Romil strut inside with bundles of cheap carnations.

"WHERE IS OUR GIRL AT? Oh." Mack pulls up short when she notices Reggie and Olivia. "Sorry. We didn't know that you had company."

A smile balloons across my face at seeing my friends. I didn't realize how much I missed and needed to see them until this very moment. "Hey, Mack, Romil. Y'all finally came to see me, huh?"

My girls ignore my question, but stare at the way Reggie is settling me into the wheelchair. "Oh. You two haven't met. Um . . ." *What the hell do I call them?*

"Hi," Reggie says, straightening back up. "I'm Reggie. Ta'Shara's grandfather."

Grandfather? My heart melts. I hadn't expected him to do that.

"And I'm Olivia. Her grandmother . . . on her mother's side." She walks over to the girls and offers them her hand.

"Uh-huh. It's nice to meet you, ma'am," Mack says, rustling the flowers around in her arm in order to accept Olivia's hand. "Mackenzie. My friends call me Mack."

"Mackenzie. What a lovely name." Olivia smiles, her red eyes lightening. She turns her attention to Romil and the girl stumbles all over her tongue.

"H-hey, um. Romil."

"Romil?" Olivia repeats to make sure that she got it right.

"Yes, ma'am."

"Well. That's a lovely name, too. I'm pleased to meet you young ladies. Are you friends of Ta'Shara's from school?"

The three of us laugh and the adults exchange confused smiles.

"No . . . Grandma. Um. Mack and Romil here are just friends of mine from around the way over off Ruby Cove."

"Yes. That's right," Mack agrees. "I've been out of high school for a little while."

"Oh." Olivia lowers her hand as her smile fades. "Are you two in a gang?"

Mack's and Romil's eyes buck, even though she asked politely.

"C'mon, Olivia. What kind of question is that?" I ask, rescuing my friends.

"A simple one," Olivia says. Her voice has lost its previous warmth. "And, I may add, it's a yes-or-no question." She stares at my girls, waiting for an answer.

"Why. Yes, ma'am. We are. We're proud Vice Lord Flowers. All *three* of us."

Aww, shit. My entire face burns as Reggie, Mary, and Olivia's shocked and disappointed gazes zoom to me. "Um, can you please give us a few minutes alone?" I ask my *grandparents.*

The looks on their faces say *hell no,* but somehow they manage to get their mouths to say, "Sure. Of course."

"Actually, I could use some coffee," Olivia adds, grabbing her purse from the chair next to my bed.

"We'll be back in a few minutes," Reggie says with a sigh before escorting Olivia and Mary past Mack and Romil. Once they leave the room, Romil rolls her eyes and Mack jabs a fist onto the side of her waist.

"So how far are those sticks rammed up their asses?"

"Mack, be cool. That's not fuckin' called for," I say.

"Not called for? She's the one who started it," Mack spits out. " 'Are you two in a gang?' " she says, mimicking Olivia's haughtiness perfectly. "Really? She's lucky her old ass is your grandma or she would've gotten cursed the fuck out."

"Mack," I snap.

"What?"

"I said chill out on that shit. Don't you have any damn home training?"

I know she wants to clap back, but apparently she realizes that she is, in fact, in the wrong.

"All right, girl. Whatever." She plops her wrapped carnations down next to the vase of roses that Reggie brought me. "What I want to know is how are you holding up?"

"I, uh, fine," I lie, tugging at the blanket wrapped around my legs. "I'm just taking shit one day at a time."

Mack bobs her head in understanding, but her laserlike gaze zooms in on how I'm tugging at the blanket.

I stop.

Romil steps forward and crosses her arms. "They aren't your *real* grandparents, are they?"

I shake my head. "No. There were my foster parents' parents. I guess since Tracee and Reggie told everyone that they planned to adopt me that . . . I don't know. They still view me as being part of the family."

"Aww. That's sweet." Mack's voice drips with sarcasm. "I guess that means that you're no longer our little orphan Annie?"

I frown. "You're in a foul mood."

She shrugs. "There's a lot of foul shit going around. But that doesn't mean that I'm not thrilled to see you up and about. You lost a lot of damn blood that night . . . and of course, we lost Dime."

"Yeah. I heard." I drop my gaze again; pull at a loose string in the blanket. "Dime was a cool chick."

We fall silent. None of us really wants to relive the night of that massacre.

"Have you gone to visit Lucifer yet?" Romil asks. "We were thinking about swinging by her room after we visit you."

"No. But I was actually about to do that when you guys turned up."

"Well then, let's all go together. Who knows? Maybe our positive vibes will get her to wake up."

"Is that what you think you're emitting? Positive vibes?" I ask.

Mack laughs. "All right. I deserved that one. I'll be better by the time we get to her room." She rushes to my wheelchair and unlocks the wheels. "Are you ready to roll, speed racer?" She doesn't bother to wait for an answer before she takes off and I have to grip the arms in fear of her crashing me into something.

Once I'm out of my room, Mack terrorizes the halls by racing me around doctors, nurses, other patients, and roaming visitors. By the time we reach Willow's floor, I'm smiling and laughing at Mack's antics.

The mood dissipates when we push our way to into Willow's room.

My gaze takes in Willow's shaved and bandaged head and even her murky skin color. If I were to be honest with myself, I'd say that Lucifer looks like she already has one foot in the grave. No doubt the two people at her side notice this, too. She no longer looks like the woman I spent the last couple of months hating, the woman who threatened my and Profit's relationship. She's just Willow Washington, clinging to life.

A woman who looks like an older and stockier version of Lucifer, turns and smiles. "Oh, look, Willow. Some more friends of yours have come to see you."

From the other side of the bed, Fat Ace moans and then slowly lifts his head from Willow's lap.

My gut churns at seeing his hideous condition. He was never a handsome man, but his scarred and burned face makes him look demonic. At the same time, my heart goes out to him. He has to be taking all of this incredibly hard.

"Ta'Shara," he says when his one good eye focuses in on me.

He releases Willow's hand, climbs out of his seat, and strolls straight over to me. "I can't thank you enough for doing all that you did to save Willow *and* my son from that crazy bitch Shariffa." He reaches down and takes my hand. "If there's anything that I can do for you, and I mean *anything*, don't hesitate to let me know. You got that?"

"I got it," I say as my eyes fill with tears.

Fat Ace releases my hand and then pulls his tall frame up. "Don't worry. Willow is going to pull through this," he assures me. "The doctors did an occlusion. That means they stopped the blood flow leading to the brain aneurysm and then they, um, did this bypass by grafting some blood vessels from her leg so that it feeds the damaged artery."

I nod, listening. He sounds like he's knowledgeable about all the procedures. But I wonder how much sleep he's had, and how much Lucifer's mother has had. Neither of them looks like they're faring much better than the patient.

Everyone is quiet for a few seconds. Our eyes are on Lucifer.

"Have you seen the baby yet?" Lucifer's mother asks suddenly.

"No, ma'am," I tell her. "But I will."

"He's a precious little thing. A miracle, really," she adds. "Isn't he, Mason?"

Fat Ace nods, though he looks as if he's barely keeping his shit together.

I do more smiling and nodding.

"Excuse me," Fat Ace says, maneuvering around me. "I'm going to step out for a minute." He jets for the door before a tear falls in front of us.

We watch him leave.

"I swear, I never realized how much he loves her before all of this," Lucifer's mom says, sniffling. "But I understand what he's going through. I lost Willow's father up in this hospital. Then a few months ago, we lost her brother and . . . well, someone very close and dear to my heart." She shakes her head while she's clearly lost in her own memories. "This world is so cruel. It doesn't give a damn about anybody . . . and I've never been a strong woman." Her own tears crawl down her tired face.

She jerks herself out of her reverie. "Anyway. Thank God, Willow never took after me. She's definitely more like her father. She's tough—and she's going to pull through this with flying colors. You'll see. The doctors say that the swelling hasn't gone down that much, but it will." She sniffs. "I'm sorry. I didn't mean to ramble on. I'll leave you girls alone with Willow for a few minutes. It's good to talk to her. There's a good chance that she can still hear us, you know."

"Okay." I sniff and wipe my eyes. "We will."

"Good." She pats me on the shoulder and then exchanges smiles with Mack and Romil and heads out of the room.

I look at Mack and Romil. Their long faces look like they're attending a funeral. Suddenly I'm aware that we have no business in this room. Lucifer and I are hardly friends. We are just two women in love with two brothers.

"Should we say something?" Romil whispers, creeping closer to the bed. "You know, in case she really can hear us?"

Mack and I say nothing while Romil starts with, "Heeey, Lucifer. Um, Romil here. I just want to let you know that the Flowers are all rooting for you. We know that you're going to come through this with no problem."

"Yeah," Mack adds, and then falls mute. She's clearly more uncomfortable than I am. She's more of a warrior than a nurturer, and sadly, it shows.

"You know, I think I'm ready to go back to my room now," I say, spinning my wheels around to head out.

"Hold up. I'll take you back." Mack races to take up the handlebars on the back of my wheelchair.

"Wait. Uh, I'm coming too," Romil announces, bolting from Willow's side to take up the rear.

None of us says anything during the journey back to my room. That is until I make the mistake of saying that I need to go to the bathroom.

"Oh. I'll roll you over there," Mack offers.

"No. That's all right. I'll go later," I say.

"Later? Why? It's just right over here." She rolls me to the door of the adjoining bathroom and then locks the wheels. "Here you go." She waits for me to get up.

"I said that I'll wait," I tell her.

"What? You need some help getting up?" she asks, ignoring me. "I'll help you stand up." Before I know it, her arms dig underneath my armpits and she starts pulling me up. "Geez, girl. You're heavy."

"Mack, please. Stop."

She grunts. "C'mon, girl. Push yourself up. I can't do all the work."

"MACK. STOP!"

Reggie's thunderous voice startles us. "What the hell is going on in here?"

Mack drops me, and the wheelchair's wheels must not have been locked in place after all, because it rolls backwards and I hit the hard linoleum floor like a brick.

Olivia screeches. "Dear God, she's trying to kill her."

Despite the pain shooting up from my elbows, I announce to everyone, "It's okay. I'm fine."

Reggie scoops me up from the floor. "I got you."

I catch Mack and Romil's confusion.

Olivia digs in. "What's the matter with you? She's paralyzed. What were you trying to do?"

"Paralyzed?" Mack repeats, looking at my dangling feet and then back up at me.

"Please," I say beseechingly, "don't tell Profit. Please. Don't tell anyone."

When Olivia realizes that I hadn't told my friends, she purses her lips angrily.

"You got to promise me," I plead to Mack. "Promise me that you won't tell."

Romil bobs her head. "We won't tell."

"Mack?" I ask.

She snaps out of her shock. "Yeah. Of course. We won't say a word."

41

Cleo

Kingdom Records

My hand is trembling when I sign my name on the dotted line. Everyone in the room is grinning and probably congratulating themselves for their part in making this happen. Hell, I can't believe that it's happening.

"That's it! You're officially a part of the Kingdom Records family," K-Bone declares, throwing open his big arms. "Congratulations!"

More shouts of congratulations and well wishes go up all around me.

I don't have time to say thanks before I'm being wrapped and squeezed in his arms. And it lasts a bit too long, too.

I push away the second I feel K-Bone *junior* bump against my leg. However, I am released from one set of arms only to be wrapped in another until I am passed around the entire room.

Diesel stands gloating like a panther who already knows what he's having for dinner. "I told you that I'd make all your dreams come true, didn't I?" he asks, once he's broken away from his ever present Amazon, Nefertiti.

"That you did," I say, bracing myself for when he pulls me

into his arms. I haven't forgotten how my body reacted to him during our Atlanta trip. I've only had one lover in my entire life, and I was both shocked and disgusted by the way my body melted beneath his touch. Actually, the disgust came after I had time to think about it. In the moment, I allowed myself to be swept away by the Cinderella fantasy date.

Diesel's arms wrap around my shoulders as he murmurs, "Congrats, Cleo. This is just the beginning."

I know I'm not crazy in hearing the double meaning in his words, but I put up a big smile because I really am happy as shit that this day is happening. "Thank you. This wouldn't be happening if it wasn't for you."

"I'm sure we can think of a few ways that you can show your appreciation."

That one was straight and to the point. I keep a big smile on my face and allow my family, all dressed in their Sunday clothes, to sweep me up and congratulate me.

"Lord, baby. I knew that one day your dreams would come true," Grandma gushes, her eyes swimming in tears. "I'm so happy. I wish that your parents could be here to see this day."

"They are here, Granny. I know that they are smiling down on us today. I can feel them." We exchange a long hug and pepper kisses on each other's cheeks.

Kobe's the only one whose grin is bigger than mine. "You did good, sis." He playfully taps me on the shoulder with a light punch.

"Thanks." I punch him back—harder.

The small signing party rolls on. The latest hits from Kingdom Records boom from the surrounding speakers. There is cake, hors d'oeuvres, champagne, and even some good weed circulating. Everyone appears to be having a good time—there's just one person missing.

Kalief.

I close my eyes and draw in a deep breath. I told myself

that I wasn't going to do this mess tonight. If Kalief wants to keep on ignoring me, fine. He'll come around eventually. He'll need money or drugs or both sooner rather than later.

"You're not smiling," Diesel says, sliding back to my side and handing me a flute of champagne. "Aren't you happy?"

"Of course. I'm thrilled. You know that." I sip my champagne and make it a point to avoid making eye contact.

"Oh. Are we going back to playing shy?" he asks, amused.

"I'm far from shy," I tell him, and then mentally curse myself for allowing him to bait me into looking at him.

"No. I didn't think so. But it's a nice act." He downs his own champagne in one gulp while his gaze caresses my face. Instead of playing this game, I break everything down for him. "It's never going to happen."

"Catch me up. What exactly is *it*?" he asks, grinning.

"You know what it is," I volley, not buying into his wide-eyed innocent act. "We—you and me—are strictly business."

"For now," he says, unfazed.

"Forever."

A waiter waltzes by and he exchanges his empty flute for a full one. "Let me guess. You're still pining away for your old manager."

"I'm not going to discuss Kalief with you."

His smile grows. "Wow. Such loyalty, though it's sorely misplaced. I can't think of a worse nigga to deserve such loyalty."

"Again. We are *not* having this conversation."

"Why? Are you afraid to admit that I'm right?"

"I'm not afraid of anything—or *anyone*." Our eyes lock and once again my body does that slow melting thing it does under his intense stare.

"It *will* happen between us," he says. "I promise you that, but lucky for you I'm willing to wait as long as it takes for you to get over your childhood-love thing." He moves closer, and I will myself to hold my ground. "And when you do, I'll open up a whole new world for you."

I hold his gaze. Not trusting myself to speak—but my panties are fucking drenched.

Diesel chuckles, leans forward, and kisses my right temple. "I understand. I can't wait either."

42

Mack

The streets are silent. That's a bad sign.

Ever since LeShelle Murphy's death hit the newspapers, everyone has been walking around on eggshells wondering what the hell it all means. Some speculate that it was the reason for the Gangster Disciples' hit on Ruby Cove.

Romil, Profit, and I keep our lips sealed about what happened that night out in Hack's Crossing. Privately, Romil and I worry about the real retaliation that's coming.

Surely Python will be able to put two and two together and figure LeShelle's death had something to do with the Vice Lords for the simple reason that her sister Ta'Shara is one of us. Romil argues that it isn't necessarily the case. LeShelle had plenty of enemies that crossed a number of color lines. Anyone could've knocked her off.

It's a good argument, but I have a bad feeling. Whoever Python suspects of having a hand in her death will feel his wrath. Today, a handful of soldiers are meeting up in the warehouse of Lewis & Sons Funeral Home. Profit is laying out his plan to smoke Python out of hiding. He wants to take this fight to the head chief while he's in control. Fat Ace is onboard. He even left Willow's side for a couple of hours to sit in on Profit's meeting. It's good to see him, but he looks like hell.

Profit's next proposed hit: Club Diesel. We know now that the brothah running that joint is Python's cousin, Diesel Carver, by way of Atlanta. Hell. There are so many Carver descendants in the South, I doubt the federal census can keep track of them all.

Romil and I keep our mouths shut about that shit, too. Fuck. I'm walking around with so many secrets that I should apply for a job at the State Department.

Our meeting ends early. A few of us hang back to discuss the Shotgun Row hit, but later, as we're leaving the warehouse, Captain Hawkins strolls through the front door.

"What the hell are you doing here?" Mason barks, spotting her.

Captain Hawkins smiles. "Actually, I came to speak with you. Lucille Washington told me that I could find you here. Do you have a few minutes?"

"No." He marches past her out the door.

Romil and I exchange looks and follow behind when the captain chases after him.

"Look. It won't take up too much of your time. I—I just want to share some information with you."

"More information?" he asks, shaking his head. "What? Have you now mapped out my whole family tree on Ancestry-dot-com?"

"Not exactly."

We keep walking behind them, mainly because my new car is parked next to Mason's ride.

"Look, Hawkins. I don't know how I can make this any plainer, but I don't care for what you have to say. I'm not interested in meeting any new family members. I'm quite satisfied with the family I have. So please—stop trying to help."

He snatches open his car door but then jumps back when three fucking snakes fall out, hissing.

"What the fuck?"

Romil and I scramble back as well.

Captain Hawkins, smooth as you please, whips out her gun and fires three rounds. The snakes' heads explode open. The crisis averted.

"The hell?" Romil wonders, clutching the shit out of my arm.

I lean over and take a long look at the snakes. "Pythons."

BOOM!

Lewis & Sons Funeral Home explodes.

The blast is so strong that I'm aware of being literally airborne as well as feeling an intense heat at my back. When I land, my face nearly kisses concrete and my knees take a pounding.

The second explosion isn't as strong but it finishes whatever job the first explosion didn't complete.

We all stare back at the balls of fire in shock. Seconds ago there was a building and now there's not.

One thing for sure, we know who's responsible because he left one hell of a calling card: *Python.*

43

Hydeya

*H*oly *Shit!*

The war has escalated to explosions. Even as I pick myself up off the concrete and stare at the huge orange balls of fire, I can't believe what I'm seeing. "Is everyone okay?" I check around.

Mason, Profit, and a few other people are picking themselves up. They look as shocked as I feel. What if we hadn't walked out when we did? What if I had talked Mason into speaking to me in his office? I would be dead right now.

I'm prepared to face life-or-death situations every day as a cop, but something like this is hard for anybody to wrap their head around.

Python.

There's no sense in laying the blame anywhere else.

"How many people were in the building?" I ask the Lewis brothers.

They have no idea, but they seem fairly certain that it couldn't have been too many. I scramble to my car and call for emergency responders.

Hours later, I'm still shaken up. I can't have a drink because of the pregnancy, but I could *really* use one.

Until the fire can be investigated, the incident plays out on the evening news as maybe a gas-line leak. That is preferable to telling the citizens of Memphis that the gang wars have reached Isis status. All that's missing now are suicide bombers and beheadings.

I reach out to daddy dearest, but he's feeling salty about my having arrested him. You'd think he'd get over it since he had no trouble posting bond.

The magnitude of the problem I'm dealing with hits me. For the first time in my career, I contemplate early retirement.

44

Cleo

Club Diesel

I have a record deal with Kingdom Records. Even as I take the stage for my second set, I can hardly believe it. With so much going on, I haven't been able to celebrate. The one person that I do want to reach out to is still not returning my calls. This is possibly the longest that we have ever gone not talking to one another. It strange, given that I'm the one who ended things. It's for the best that we are no longer a couple, but I never intended for us to be completely out of each other's lives.

I brush that aside and give a performance. By the time I hit the last note, the crowd is putty in my hands. Backstage, the band high-fives and pumps up my ego.

"I hope that you don't forget about us when you hit the big time, superstar," Stephen says, cheesing.

"How could I ever forget you guys? If I ever go on tour, trust and believe I'm taking you guys with me."

"We're going to hold you to that shit." Milo laughs and swings his arms around me for a congratulatory hug.

"I gotta find Kalief so that I can share the good news," I say. The band groans.

"What the hell is that supposed to mean?" I ask, looking around.

Everyone gets sheepish and avoids making eye contact.

"What?"

"Nothing," Stephen says, hugging his guitar. "I don't understand why you're looking for him so hard. It's not like he's ever done anything for you anyway."

"Yeah. He snatches our money and makes us chase him around town before he pays us—and half the time, he pays us with excuses as to why he ain't got it. You let him go; let him stay gone."

"Well, damn. Why don't you tell me how you *really* feel?" I blast, crossing my arms.

Milo comes back at me. "That's what I'm doing." His courage grows as the rest of the band looks like they're backing him up. "We've been sick of Kalief's bullshit for a long time. We've only been putting up with his ass for you. You love his crazy ass and we tried to love him—but enough is enough."

The band nods with their wide eyes glued on me. The fact is that I know he's speaking the gospel truth about my ex. It hurts to hear it.

Rat-a-tat-tat-tat

Rat-a-tat-tat-tat

I jump as a wave of terrified shouts and screams erupt from the front of the club. Everyone is in a frenzy to get out of the way.

"What's going on?" I shout, moving with the crowd.

Rat-a-tat-tat-tat

Rat-a-tat-tat-tat

No one answers me because they are running too. There's not that much space for everyone to hide. The logical move is to head for the back exits. As the frantic crowd nears the doors, they burst open and a gang of men with gold flags over their mouths rushes inside.

"Where in the fuck do you muthafuckas think y'all going?" a voice thunders before spraying bullets straight up into the air.

Rat-a-tat-tat-tat

Rat-a-tat-tat-tat

I join in on the screaming as I duck and cover my head. Once the initial shock is over, I clamp my mouth shut and pull myself together.

"If everybody would calm their asses down, this shit will be quick and painless," the leader warns.

I glare up at the imposing man to discern whether I can make out his face. Memphis is a big city, but for the playas in this street game, everyone knows the big dogs.

A waitress pipes up. "What do you want?"

"Glad you asked," the leader says, swinging his weapon in her direction.

This causes more screams from the crowd.

"We're looking for the owner, Diesel Carver. If one of you could simply tell us where that big muthafucka is hiding right now, we can wrap this shit up and let you good folks go on your way."

Nobody says shit.

More gunfire erupts from the front of the club. At the ensuing screams, we're all stuck imagining what's going on in there.

"What? None of you muthafuckas got shit to say? We know that nigga got to be here somewhere. C'mon. Cough his ass up."

These muthafuckas can't be serious. No nigga, I don't care whether he's from the streets or not, is going to voluntarily snitch in front of all these people. My ass included. Diesel isn't here, so these grimy Vice Lords aren't going to find what they're looking for. The real question is why are they looking for him? I don't have to think about it for long before Ruby Cove pops back up in my head.

"All of you get up and move your asses to the front of the club."

Everyone looks around, too terrified to move.

Rat-a-tat-tat-tat

We scream.

"Move it!"

We jump to our feet and herd ourselves back to the main floor with the other club participants. There, more Vice Lords with their gold kerchiefs around their mouths are carrying assault weapons.

"Everyone keep calm." Another Vice Lord steps forward and appears in control of the crowd. "Follow directions and nobody will be hurt."

"Profit," somebody whispers close to me. I turn to see that it's Milo. "That's Fat Ace's little brother."

I know the name. This is the boy who was at the center of my sister's death. I glare at the tall figure and wish I had some type of weapon that would take his head off.

"He's not here," someone yells.

"Wait. Who said that?" The leader scans the crowd until one guy attempts to stand.

"You say he's not here. Where is he then?"

The man shrugs. "Don't know. I don't think he came in tonight."

The soldier snatches off his gold kerchief.

I recognize Lucifer's driver, Tombstone.

"You got to be shitting me." He looks back at the men ringed around him.

The janitor's gaze swings around. No one else is cosigning what he's saying. No one would dare. "No. No I'm not." His voice shakes.

"Search this place. This muthafucka comes in every night. He's gotta be hiding in here somewhere."

The crew breaks up and combs the entire club. The crowd remains terrified, on pins and needles while they pull every brother with the slightest resemblance to Diesel to check him out.

Profit marches cool as you please back and forth. Somebody screwed up, and clearly Profit is trying to figure out what to do about it.

"Ain't this some shit," Tombstone swears, looking ready to take his frustrations out on somebody. "Well, we're delivering a message. Tell that illegal gangster that the Vice Lords are looking for his ass. If he knows what's good for him he'll pack his shit up and get the fuck out of our town before we catch up with him."

Rat-a-tat-tat-tat

Rat-a-tat-tat-tat

We scream and duck. The janitor dives to the floor and then trembles like a leaf.

Profit turns to his crew. "Head out."

The men under his command waste no time turning tail and rushing back out the exit doors. However, Profit looks like he's not finished with us.

"Deliver our message to Mr. Carver. Tell him he's on notice."

45

Nefertiti

Diesel's crib

"Oh, bitch. That's my spot." I toss my hair over my left shoulder so I can look at the white bitch pounding my pussy from behind with a Mandingo-size dildo strap-on. This Barbie look-alike growls like she's on the edge of busting a real nut all over my back.

"You like my black cock, momma?" Barbie's seriousness brings a smile to my face.

"Go deeper," I tell her as I reach between my legs and stroke my dripping wet pussy. I'm not saying that this shit is as good as the real thing, but it's damn close. I might have to keep this bitch on standby the next time my ass goes through another dry spell.

"Spread her ass wider," Diesel instructs from across the room in a dark corner.

I don't know about Ms. Barbie here, but I'd forgotten about Diesel being in the room, watching. I flip my hair to the other side and peep him out while Barbie, following instructions, opens my thick booty wide. Air swooshes inside between strokes, causing my pussy to sound like it's blowing raspberries.

Diesel sits in the corner, puffing on a cigar and stroking the top of his Doberman pinscher's head.

"Why don't you come join us?" I ask, and then jump when Barbie slaps my ass with a nice stinging blow. Pleased with herself, she delivers another one on the opposite cheek.

"Maybe later," Diesel responds in his usual cool baritone. "I don't want to disturb the nice flow that you two have going right now."

I poke out my bottom lip to let him know how disappointed I am. In addition to being *GQ* fine with a thug swag, Diesel possesses the sweetest dick that I have ever had. When he slings that monster around, he could straighten a chick with scoliosis back out.

"Are you sure?"

"I'm good, ma. Do you."

We share a smile. In the next second, my mind is snatched into another world. "FUUUUUCK!" I drop my head and come so hard that I can barely stay on my knees.

Barbie is saying some fucking shit that I can't understand while crouching over my back and rubbing on my titties. Her small hands pull me out of the game. I tolerate her pawing me because she really can hook a sister up.

Diesel chuckles and then climbs to his feet. "Does this mean that you approve of our latest product?"

"Oh fuck, yeah." I laugh.

Barbie pulls the Mandingo out of my pussy and I instantly miss my new friend. "Oooh." I drop onto my stomach and roll over.

Barbie's eyes light up at the sight of the black bush between my legs. The girl is a fucking pussy monster.

"Whatcha looking at?" I tease, arching my back and cupping my breasts so that they sit straight up in the air.

Diesel sits down on the edge of the bed and watches Barbie salivate. Solomon, the dog, pads his way over. The moment I hear his panting, I snap out of the moment.

"Get that muthafucka away from me."

Diesel ignores me and reaches over to see how wet I am. The moment he touches me I flush and tingle all over. "Damn. You're soaking wet," he praises.

"Does that mean that you're going to hook me up next?" I squirm as he plunges three fingers in deep.

Instead of answering, Diesel watches my reaction as he finger fucks me. The shit feels so good that my legs inch farther apart while my eyes droop low.

"You like that, don't you?"

"Mm-hmmm."

"You're a nasty bitch. You know that?"

I look him dead in his eyes and remind him, "You *love* nasty bitches."

He chuckles for the first time since his latest obsession, Cleo, left him with blue balls at the signing party.

Solomon whimpers and licks his chops.

"No," I snap, and grab Diesel's arm. "Don't you fucking do it."

He grins. "Do what?"

"Nigga, don't play dumb. Don't forget that I know your freaky ass better than anyone."

Solomon whimpers, moans, and whines louder.

"You should have never got that dog used to licking pussy," I tell him, shaking my head. "I ain't *that* damn nasty."

Diesel and I maintain a long stare-down before he commands Solomon to leave the room. "Out, boy."

Crushed, Solomon drops his head and pads out of the room.

"Satisfied?" he asks.

"Play those games with those other bitches. That shit ain't me," I tell him.

"How do you know? You've never tried it."

"And I never will." I'm pissed. The mood has been ruined.

"Calm down, momma. I didn't mean to throw you off." He glances up at Barbie. "Come here and taste this."

In a flash, she scrambles over to suck my cum off his fingers.

"Mmmm," the greedy bitch moans before glancing back over at me. No lie, she's looking like she could devour my ass.

"I think that it's time for you to let Trixie here show how she knocked Superhead off her throne."

"Superhead, huh?"

Trixie bobs her head as she reaches over to caress my legs.

Once again her small hands leave me cold, but if the bitch can work her mouth even half as good as she can work that damn dildo, my ass is here for it. "All right. Let's see what you got."

Trixie moves like a child waking on Christmas morning. My first shock is when her tongue runs down the crack of my ass. "Oh." I blink my surprise.

Diesel's handsome face splits into a wide grin. "Nice, huh?"

I can't respond. Trixie's tongue goes straight through my back door while two fingers go through the front. My head becomes a jumbled mess. The white bitch here is an ass-girl for sure. I fire off two orgasms in quick succession.

Trixie sops up my cum like it was the best damn meal she's done had in years.

My pussy churns honey by the pound and grows sensitive as shit. I hang in there, but I have trouble breathing.

"Wait. Wait. Stop." I inch up the bed.

Pussy monster ain't having that shit. Her fingers and mouth switch positions and my ass damn near shoots up the wall.

My third and fourth orgasms pop off while I beg her for a break.

Diesel watches and strokes his cock through his silk boxers.

In all the years that I have known him, I have never been able to tell whether he gets more pleasure watching or fucking.

While he watches us, I watch him—or rather I stare at his huge dick until my mouth waters.

"What are you staring at?" he asks. "Huh?"

With Trixie's mouth on my clit, I can't control my breathing long enough to respond.

Diesel stands up from the bed, his silk robe falling open so that his cock stands fully erect. "Come get this sugar, ladies."

Trixie and I spring up at the command. I almost shove her off the bed in order to wrap my hand around his cock first. Instead of shouldering me back, Trixie concentrates on taking care of Diesel's balls. Together we service Diesel with the best blow job of his life.

Diesel folds his hands behind his head and hums. It takes a while to recognize the tune: "Ebony and Ivory."

The phone rings.

Diesel stops humming.

No. No. No. I double up my efforts in the wild hope that he'll let whoever it is go to voicemail. But he never lets it go to voicemail.

"Hold up, ladies. I gotta get that." He waits for us to turn him loose so that he can pick up the portable sitting on the nightstand.

"Hello."

I sit back on folded knees and give him a look to hurry up. To my left, Trixie copies my sitting position but looks comical with the fake black dick still strapped on. When she sees me looking at her, she pushes up a smile. "I love your pussy."

"Thanks."

"I've never had black pussy before." She giggles. "Maybe we can do it again sometime?"

"Uh, well. We'll see."

"Say that shit again?" Diesel snaps his fingers in our direction, telling us to shut the fuck up.

"What the fuck? Yeah, man. I'm on my way!"

My heart sinks. Our private party is over.

Diesel slams the phone down and releases a stream of obscenities. "Those Vice Lord muthafuckas just shot up my damn club."

"What?"

He turns on the lights and snatches up his clothes. "That bullshit King Isaac pulled on Ruby Cove blew back on *my* ass. This shit is more muthafuckin' money out of my damn pocket. I knew that old cat was going to be nothing but trouble when he got out of the joint. Shit! Fuck!"

He looks up and gestures for us to leave the room.

Like a trained puppy, Trixie hops off the bed and scrambles for her clothes on the floor before marching into the adjoining bathroom to get dressed.

I untuck my legs and lean back against the bed. "*Now* will you listen to me? You need to cut your losses and let these backward country negroes have this fucked-up city. Atlanta is where your throne sits."

"I'm not going to talk about that right now."

"When *are* you going to talk about it? Your *cuz* has reneged on the original agreement. They are hardly in the position to pay back what you've already invested, so what else are you going to do?"

"Titi, I said not now."

"Whatever." I toss up my hands and then fold them across my chest. "*But* you know that I'm right."

"Yes. Yes. I know. You're *always* right." He stops and draws in a deep breath while he thinks on things. "I don't like not finishing what I start," he confesses. "But, yeah. This whole thing is one big disaster. But there still may be one way to fix everything."

Suddenly I'm connected to his thoughts. "You want to take out King Isaac."

A sly smile slopes unevenly across his full slips. "You really do know me so well."

46

Hydeya

The scene down on Beale Street is eerily similar to the scene on Ruby Cove. The same reporters shout the same hysterical questions as I make my way into Club Diesel. Inside the huge tri-level club, the police team is doing their best to keep a rattled crowd calm. There are overturned tables and broken glass strewn about, but at least I don't see any white chalk or body bags lying around.

"So somebody catch me up to speed. What do we have here?"

Officer Jones reads from his notes to give me a rundown. His voice gets shaky when the chief enters the building and stops to listen.

"How do we know that they were gang members?" the chief asks.

Officer Jones leans down and picks up a gold flag. "They were all wearing these—what little information we could get is that they wore the colors of the Vice Lords—nobody willing to speak on the record, of course. Hardly anyone is talking at all. You know the drill."

The chief and I bob our heads. We know all too well. But I'm choosing to look at the lack of dead bodies as a gift. I glance up and note the damage to the ceiling. "It's going to be a lot of fun, digging those out." I scan the corners and spot all the cameras. "Bingo."

The chief looks up. "Hot damn. Someone please tell me that those things are working."

I turn my attention to Officer Jones, who is also looking up. "Where's Diesel Carver—the owner?"

"That's the sixty-four thousand dollar question. We're locating him now. We placed calls to his cell—no answer. So we're pulling the license to get a home address. After that we'll send a patrol car over so that he can at least know what's happened down here at his club."

I nod along, remembering my last encounter with the man. Besides being a handsome devil, Diesel is a puzzle that intrigues the hell out of me. "When we get the address, I'll make the visit."

"You will?" the chief asks.

"Is that a problem?"

The chief sucks in a breath, but keeps any commentary to herself.

My hackles rise. "Excuse us for a moment," I tell Officer Jones.

He sighs and scrambles off before I face the chief. "Is this going to be a new arrangement?" I ask her head-on.

"What arrangement is that, Captain?"

"You micromanaging me. I know how to do my job."

"I never said that you didn't." She crosses her arms and leaves it at that, but clearly there's plenty that she's *not* saying.

"So . . . we're on the same page?" I ask for clarification. "You're stepping back and letting me work?"

"I'll let you do your job." The stepping-back part was left out, and her message has been received. My job is hanging by a thread; her ass can't wait for the slightest sign of my ass fucking up before she snips that muthafucka. That, of course, has me thinking about Isaac again. Everything circles back to him.

Chief Brown drifts off to circulate around the club and I'm

off to do the same thing when my gaze snags onto a familiar face.

What's her name? I scroll through a Rolodex of names in my head, but I can't come up with it. I know she's the club's singer, and lately she seems to pop up when I least expect it. I snap my fingers when her name comes to me. "Cleo . . . Cleo Blackmon." I move around overturned furniture and step across broken glass to make my way over to the distraught singer. The last time I saw her, it was at Momma Peaches's funeral. The time before that, Fowler brought her downtown for questioning after the shooting at the Power of Prayer Baptist Church.

"How are things holding up?" I ask, drawing her attention away from one of my detectives.

She shifts her head in my direction and I'm struck, once again, by the woman's undeniable beauty. "Okay. I guess." Her gaze sweeps over me. "I know you. You're that new police captain, right?"

"Yes. And you're Club Diesel's hottest attraction."

Her brows climb.

"The singer," I clarify.

Cleo seems surprised. "Yeah. How did you know that?"

"I've seen you perform a couple of times," I tell her.

Her full lips split into a smile. "Oh yeah?"

"Yeah. You're really talented. I'm sure that you're going to go far in the business."

"From your lips to God's ears."

We laugh before she asks, "Do you know how much longer we are going to have to stay here? I'm really beat and have to be in the studio early tomorrow morning."

"Have you finished giving your statement?" I look over at the officer standing next to her.

He gives me a look that tells me even before he shows his sparse notes that Ms. Blackmon hasn't given him anything. "Honestly, there's not much to tell. Everything happened so fast. I really didn't see much." Past experience has shown me that anytime someone uses the word *honestly* in a sentence, they are full of shit.

"Is that right?" I ask as if I believe her. "And where were you when everything went down?"

"I was backstage—getting ready to leave."

"Did you get a good look at any of the shooters?"

"No." She spits out the answer before I finished asking the question. It's another reason for me to doubt her *honesty*.

"Notice anything odd about them?"

"No."

"No special colors, tats, or strange accents?"

"No."

"Did they say anything—take anything?"

"No—well. They said a few things, but *honestly* I didn't pay any attention to it. I was focused on making myself as small as possible."

I frown.

"You know, so I wouldn't draw any attention to myself. I didn't want to get shot."

"Uh-huh." A few awkward seconds lapse. I want her to know that I'm not buying everything.

"You've been to a fair number of shootings lately, haven't you?"

Her smile craters. "What do you mean?"

"What do I mean?" I laugh. "Are you serious?"

She shifts on her feet while agitation causes a few muscles to twitch. "Look, Captain. I don't know what you're implying, but I'm from the hood. Shootings are a part of life. Keeping the streets safe is *your* job."

"Stay calm, Ms. Blackmon. I wasn't implying anything. I'm just asking questions."

"Uh-huh." She folds her arms and lifts her chin. Our camaraderie is over.

"You're free to go, Ms. Blackmon."

That perks her up. "I am?"

"Sure. But, uh"—I fiddle around in my pocket until I locate a card—"if you remember anything that you think will help, please give us a call."

Cleo hesitates. "Sure. Why not." She takes the card. "I'm free to go?"

"Yes, ma'am. Have a good night."

She flashes another smile, leaves.

Officer Clemmons steps up beside me. "Do you believe her?"

"Not a single fucking word." I return my attention to the destruction around me.

Clemmons asks another question. "Do you think this was retaliation for the Ruby Cove massacre? They didn't leave a graveyard of bodies, but they made it clear that they were looking for the owner. Could he be involved?"

I nod. "Of course he's involved. The Gangster Disciples and the Vice Lords are turned all the way up. The question is whether we can smash this beef before they drag the whole damn city down to hell with them."

The answer at the moment is no.

47

Nefertiti

Diesel is pissed. It's not the first time that I've seen him this way. He usually takes his hits cool and reserved. But every once in a while a dumb muthafucka presses the wrong damn buttons and sets shit off to the wrong muthafuckin' level. I'm woman enough to admit that I've been more than afraid of him when he gets like this. Mercy isn't a dish that he serves often, if ever.

The moment that we arrive at Club Diesel, along with the multitude of news reporters and cameras, I witness the change in Diesel's demeanor. Bouncers G–Mill and B–Locc spot their boss as he strides toward the yellow tape in front of his club and give him an apologetic look while the paramedics attend to their bloody wounds.

A cop races after Diesel when he breaches the crime scene. "Sir! Sir! I can't let you through here."

"This is *my* joint." Diesel challenges him.

Instinctively, the height-disadvantaged cop steps back before remembering that he is the one with the badge and the authority to keep Diesel from contaminating the scene.

"Sir, don't make me have to tell you again." The cop places his hand on his holstered weapon. "Step back behind the yellow tape. This is an official crime scene." The added bass in his voice catches a few of his fellow officers' attention and they come to their colleague's aid.

"Is there a problem?" An African-American cop with a waist size that suggests he's no danger to any criminal that he would have to chase, waddles in between Diesel and the other cop.

"The only problem I have is this asshole who's not letting me into my own property," Diesel says menacingly—and yet coolly.

I reach out and touch Diesel's arm, hoping to defuse a situation before it actually becomes one. "D, let's just go back behind the line."

He's not hearing that shit though. He pulls his arm away and confronts the officers in front of him.

I don't take it personally. I know that it's not the current situation that has him hot. He's struggling from the verbal spanking and blatant disrespect that he suffered from King Isaac, and he's ready to take it out on the first muthafuckas to challenge him.

"Terrance, I got this." A woman, likely another cop, emerges from the club and squashes the beef.

Diesel turns his attention toward the woman, and if anything his defenses rise even higher. "Captain Hawkins."

"Diesel Carver." She tugs in a breath. "Our paths keep crossing."

"I'm noticing that myself."

Silence stretches between the two of them, which gets me wondering if there's something more than what meets the eye here. The prospect of yet another woman vying for Diesel's affection has me all up in my feelings. These bitches always come out of the woodwork.

"So. Do you want to tell me what the fuck is going on here?" Diesel asks, checking his attitude.

"My best guess is that someone is sending you a message." Captain Hawkins's gaze trains on him. "Do you have any idea who that might be?"

"None," Diesel lies. "I'm new to this town, remember?"

Hawkins lifts a single brow while an amused smile tugs her lips. She knows that this is a dance. The question is, which one of them is going to take the lead?

Grudgingly, I develop a kernel of respect for the cop.

"New or not, it appears that you've pissed *somebody* off. One of the gunmen made it clear that they were looking for you. Mentioned you by name—and even insinuated that you had something to do with the Ruby Cove massacre."

"That's fucking ridiculous," Diesel barks.

"Because you're not a gangbanger like your cousin Terrell?" Hawkins challenges without missing a beat.

"Exactly." Diesel smiles, not taking the bait. "I'm a businessman. You should know that one can't help who their family members are."

I don't know what he means by that, but it certainly wipes the smugness off of the captain's face.

"Where were you the night of the Ruby Cove massacre?"

"Right here. Entertaining a record executive for my newest artist. I can pull the security tapes—once you let me into my own establishment—and prove it to you. Hell, I can even pull them for your investigation tonight, if you ask nicely."

"That would be much appreciated," Hawkins says tightly. She then steps back and gestures for him to take the lead into his own nightclub. Her gaze falls on me, and when it does, Diesel cuts her off before she even gets started on some bullshit.

"She's with me."

That's not enough to get me through.

"And you are?"

When Hawkins levels her hard gaze on me, I'll admit that I'm intimidated—and I'm not a woman who is easily intimidated. "Nefertiti, the club's general manager."

"Nefertiti?" she repeats with the same amused smugness I've received most of my life when people learn my name, but then she tosses out an unexpected compliment. "Beautiful name."

"Thank you."

The captain steps back, allowing me to enter with Diesel. The craziness outside is nothing compared to the wrecked disaster that is inside. With the house lights turned up, we see the overturned chairs, broken tables, and shattered glasses, and I can't help but start calculating the total damage. I can tell that Diesel is doing the same thing. All the money he's invested in propping up the Gangster Disciples and now this club, he could've just set those stacks of benjamins on fire. At least that way he would've enjoyed the heat. Angry men and hysterical women recount their stories to various officers spread throughout the club.

And when Diesel spots a shaken Cleo, he veers off course to his office to go check on his precious songbird. I'm stunned. Out of all the girls that filter in and out of our lives, this one is really giving me pause. When Diesel first moved down here, I had to hold my tongue while he head-fucked that stupid teenage Flower, Qiana. I dismissed her, even though the bitch shot at me. But Cleo; she has a different kind of hold on my man and I'm not feeling it.

I hang back with the captain and watch as Diesel tosses all his personal rules out the window to comfort this bitch.

"I take it that you don't care for her," Hawkins says after reading me like an open book.

"I have no opinion," I lie.

"Riiiight."

My respect for the astute cop goes up in smoke. I don't know this bitch and I don't appreciate her ass acting as if she knows me.

Hawkins gives Diesel and Cleo about a minute alone before she waltzes over and reminds him about the security footage.

Minutes later, we enter Diesel's office and he cues up the time frame Captain Hawkins gives him.

There's no question that the men who charged in here tonight were Vice Lord soldiers. Their black and gold flags hung proudly from their back pockets and around their mouths.

"Can you zero in on any of their faces?" Hawkins asks.

Without answering, Diesel types commands into the computer and the camera zooms in on two who appear to do most of the talking.

"Well, I'll be damned," Captain Hawkins mutters. "I know that guy."

Diesel nods, letting me know that he, too, recognizes the man's face.

"Charlie 'Tombstone' Barrett," the cop says. "I got you, you asshole."

48

Cleo

It's late and cold as shit by the time I pile into my car. My damn heater died like two winters ago. I pull out of the employees' parking lot and note that the streets are like the Club Diesel right now: dead. As luck would have it, every traffic light is green as I breeze away from Beale Street.

During the twenty-minute drive out to Kalief's crib, the band's lecture about letting Kalief go plays in my mind. Every word they said was true. In fact, it wasn't anything that I haven't said myself. There's so much to hate about my ex and our relationship: the drugs, the drinking, the gambling, the cheating, the stealing, and the lying. However, like so many other times, after the dust settles from one of our blowups, there's a bond still linking us together.

I'm not a dumb bitch—but I keep doing dumb shit when it comes to Kalief. Maybe it's because at the end of the day, we're truly soul mates. We've been riding together since high school. Back when girls giggled about how much he looked like the actor Morris Chestnut and about him having a knot of cash in his pocket. I made his ass sweat for a long time before I agreed to go out with him. When we finally went out, we discovered that we shared a love for music. We would spend hours listening to old-school albums that my grandmother kept up in the attic. Back then, falling in love was easy.

He was everything that he isn't now.

A tear skips down my face. I miss the good ol' days. I wish that he could be the rock that I've needed since Essence's death, but the truth is he doesn't have what it takes.

My heart sinks when I pull up into the driveway. Kalief's car isn't here. *Where the fuck is he?* I park while this bad feeling creeps into the pit of my stomach. No matter how many times I tell myself to calm down or even remind myself that Kalief has disappeared plenty of times before, I can't help but feel that *this* time, it's different.

Shutting off the engine, I stare at the dark, brick ranch home while reviewing my options. Stay or go home. I mean, eventually he'll show up. *Right?*

The cold helps me make my decision. "Fuck. I'm already here. May as well go inside and wait." I climb out of the car and rush up to the house. It would be great if I still had a key to the place, but a couple of years ago during another heated argument, I'd thrown the key at him. We made up, but Kalief never gave it back. Doesn't matter. A locked door don't mean shit to a Queen G. I'm inside the house in less than a minute, but once I'm in, the bad feeling spreads.

"What's that smell?" I don't know why I bothered to ask the question because I *know* that smell. On cue my eyes water and my legs threaten to drop me where I stand. *I have to know.* Somehow, I get my legs to move. It's at a slow creep, but I follow my nose through the dark house, not bothering to hit a light switch. However, at the closed master bedroom door, I hesitate. *Maybe I shouldn't go inside. If I don't go in then I won't know . . . and I'm not sure I'm ready to know.*

More tears spring from my eyes while I stand there a full minute with my hand on the doorknob. Things like *you're being silly* and *he's probably fine* don't ring true in my gut. Then with one burst of courage, I open the door.

Oh, Kalief, no.

I crumble to the floor in the doorway with my eyes glued to the distended body lying across the bloody white sheets. With the shimmering moonlight splashed across Kalief's bloated face, the macabre scene looks like something out of a horror film. Whatever happened here was ugly and violent.

I remain on the floor until my shock dissolves into grief, but when it happens, the hole in my heart grows so big that it swallows me whole. Kalief's face blurs behind my tears. *How long has he been like this?* I don't want to believe that it's been the entire time since I last heard from him. That would be too cruel.

I want to scream and throw things, but that would require energy that I don't have—and what would it solve? Hell. I don't even have enough energy to pick myself up off this floor. I'll have to do it eventually, but what is the rush? At the moment, I need to get this cry out of my system. So I have at it. But it isn't long before questions tumble through my mind. *Why? Who? When?*

With Kalief, the why could have been for any number of reasons. Kalief had accrued more enemies than friends. That was because he always had some hustle going on that required him to rob Peter to pay Paul. He had the robbing part down to a science, but that *paying* part didn't happen too often. The when? Clearly it's been at least a few days, if not the entire two weeks since I last spoke to him.

The who—my mind circles back to that enemies list. There's only one name and one face that keeps cropping up: *Diesel Carver.*

"No. No. No." I drop my head into my hands and scrub those thoughts out of my mind. I went out on that date. It erased Kalief's debt. Why would he kill him? *Would a man like Diesel really wipe out a six-figure debt for a date?* There's no point in my answering that question because anybody with the slightest lick of sense *knows* the answer.

"That lying, sneaky son of a bitch," I hiss under my breath. I should kick my own ass for not realizing this shit sooner. That bastard played me—played us. The longer I sit here on this floor thinking about it, the angrier I get. It's the anger that gives me the energy to climb up off the floor and storm out of the house.

49

Hydeya

A train of police cars races across the city. My heart hammers inside of my chest. We're going to put something on the scoreboard for the good guys. While we can't identify everyone on the club's surveillance tape, I'm hoping against hope that once I get Charles "Tombstone" Barrett into the interrogation room, I can get the names of his crew. The odds are slim. But there's a chance.

I press the accelerator all the way to the floorboard, but it seems I'm not going fast enough. "C'mon. C'mon." I jerk in and out of lanes, drum my fingers on the steering wheel. By the time we blaze onto Ruby Cove, my car's clock tells me the long haul only took eight minutes.

A sea of blue and white lights surrounds the Barretts' residence, and to our surprise, Tombstone is already outside mobbin' twenty deep.

"Charles Barrett, put your hands up."

Tombstone's shock dissolves. Steely determination is reflected in his eyes and stiff jawline. I'm not surprised when he whips out a gun.

Bad move.

All officers go into combat mode.

I grab the megaphone. "Drop the weapon!"

"Fuck you!" Tombstone puffs his chest. "Y'all niggas want a piece of me? Then come and get me, you fuckin' pigs!"

"This is your last warning," I yell. "You don't have to do this!"

Tombstone cocks his head. "I know you! You're that fucking pig that was out here looking for my sister." He coughs up a sad laugh. "Well, bitch. If you're still looking for her, she's down at the cemetery. She's down there with my girl GG. But you probably had a hand in that shit!"

I shake my head. He's wrong. I'm more concerned about the number of cell phones being held up to capture this unraveling fiasco. The last thing this department needs is a potential fuckup to go viral.

"Charles, you don't want to do this! Lower the weapon, and we can take you in and talk about whatever questions you may have about your sister."

"And what about GG? Huh? I was gonna marry that girl." He bites his lower lip and sticks his chin up even higher.

I draw a blank at the name. There's no doubt about the naked hurt etched in his face. "We can talk about whatever you want to talk about," I assure him, "but you're going to have to put the weapon down!"

More people creep out from their homes to bear witness to what happens next. The night's chill numbs my face and hands while I calculate the odds of our bringing Charles Barrett in alive—let alone getting the names of his accomplices.

Every cop's weapon is drawn on Tombstone. We're sitting on top of a lit powder keg.

"Lower your weapon," I plead. I don't want to send another body to the morgue.

"I'll see all y'all asses in hell!" Tombstone gives no fucks. With a smile, he lifts his weapon.

Every cop surrounding him fires.

"Noooo!" I shout, lowering the megaphone. But there's nothing that I can do other than watch the young thug as he's swept up and back a good three feet before collapsing to the ground, his blood painting the street.

So much for getting a win tonight.

"Holy shit. Did y'all just see that?" someone to my right yells. I glance at the growing anger on everyone's face. "Oh shit." This may be a problem.

"Muthafuckas shot that nigga cold."

"Secure the area," I order and then call in the shooting and request a body extraction.

To my left, I catch sight of another familiar face: Raymond aka Profit. He looks different. He's hard. Distracted. Detached. *Could he be one of the Club Diesel shooters?*

Profit's gaze cuts away from Tombstone's body over to me. *If looks could kill, the forensic team would be white-chalking my ass right next to Tombstone's.*

50

Nefertiti

Diesel takes a final look around at the damage to his club. The night's shaken crowd is gone and the police are bullshitting in front of the news cameras.

I'm biting the shit out of my tongue in order to stop myself from singing *I told you so* at the top of my voice. By now, Diesel knows that he needs to get out of this raggedy-ass city. Ain't shit popping but country niggas with poor eyesight tryna toe-tag everybody that looks at them wrong. It ain't like Atlanta where brothahs boss up and show the fuck out. That's where a chick like me makes serious gold coins sexing niggas with more cash than brains.

Diesel came up here to expand his empire, but it's got to be painfully clear that his cousin Python played his ass for a fool. He got Diesel to pump money into his thinning crew, and then the moment his uncle Isaac springs out of jail, all deals are off.

"So what's your next move?"

Diesel refuses to look at me when he responds. "Obviously somebody's ass got to pay for this shit."

I nod. "No doubt. But who? The Vice Lords think you had a hand in that massacre that your uncle launched, and this is payback. So do you go after them or do you go after your uncle?"

He stops and looks at me. "Both."

Minutes later, we're back in his ride and headed out to that creepy-ass warehouse in Frayser. I keep glancing around, unable to shake the feeling that we're being watched, but also unable to prove it.

"What the hell is wrong with you?" Diesel asks after watching me twitching in my seat for twenty minutes.

"Nothing. I'm being cautious," I tell him.

Diesel checks around and then asks his driver, Beast, "Are you spotting anyone following us?"

"No, boss."

Diesel glances at me, but tells Beast, "Keep an eye out."

"Yes, boss."

Another ten minutes and we arrive at the dilapidated warehouse. The place is as creepy as it was the last time we were here. I'm all for fixer-uppers, but this is damn ridiculous.

Diesel hammers on the door three times before entering, then shouts, "Python! I know your ass is in here!"

There's a long silence.

"Python!"

A rusty door creaks open from somewhere in this bitch before a steady thump of heavy, booted feet pounds the cement floor. When Python materializes at a railing on the floor above us, I have to say the muthafucka looks awful. He doesn't look like he's slept a wink since his burnt-up wife was reported dead on the news.

"Why the fuck are you making so much noise?" he thunders.

"We need to talk," Diesel says, cutting to the chase.

"About what?"

"What the fuck you think? Those Vice Lord muthafuckas shot up my club in retaliation for shit that you and your damn uncle did behind my back!"

"Behind your back?" Python thunders. "Since when the fuck do we have to clear our business with you?"

"Since you dragged my ass into your business. Let's not get

amnesia and shit. It's my money and my supply that is *still* keeping your asses afloat. All this reneging shit you done ain't flying with my ass no more. I help your ungrateful ass out and you can't give me the proper *respect* of a damn heads-up?"

Python clamps his jaw tight. His ass is hot to death, and I don't think that too many people talk to him like Diesel.

"I'm catching fallout over some shit that you and Isaac conspired on. One of you muthafuckas is going to have to pay up."

Python rolls his eyes. "Cuz, get on with that, I got bigger problems to deal with right now."

"Bigger problems? Nigga, do you know how much shit this is gonna cost me—on top of the fucking money that I already lost in propping up your bullshit crew?"

"Bullshit crew?" Python's face twists up, making him uglier—if that's possible.

"Yeah, muthafucka. You heard me. I don't stutter and your ears don't flap." Diesel focuses his gaze like a laser on Python. "You played me from Jump Street, and now instead of letting me and my crew take over for the Folks Nation up here, like you *promised*, you're handing the whole deal back over to your uncle."

"You don't know what you're talking about. And he's your uncle, too."

"I don't know that nigga and he don't know me. But what I *do* know is that *we* had a deal."

"We talked about my change in plans months ago, remember?"

"Yeah, but that didn't include you making other fucking arrangements. Now we have ourselves a situation where I'm being dicked over. In case you haven't heard, *nobody* dicks me over. *Nobody.*"

The men's gazes lock.

"Are you threatening me?"

"Call it what you want, but you better get me my stacks. There ain't going to be any more of my ass chalking shit up to the game. From now on, we're strictly business. No more fucking family favors. No cash? No more bricks, weapons—nothing. Let's see your King Isaac get your money up."

"Yeah. We had another deal, too. The one where you promised me that you'd stay with Aunt Peaches until the cops came, but from what I hear, your ass was MIA when the cops arrived and pronounced her dead."

"She died. I fail to see how my sticking around would've helped the situation."

"You promised," Python thundered.

"So sue me." Diesel shrugs. "Maybe I should've let your ass hang around for the cops to lock up. Is that your fucking point?"

Python clamps his jaw.

"Yeah. That's what I thought." Diesel turns but then stops when he realizes he's not through. "Now back to my muthafuckin' money. Either you or your precious uncle need to unass all the fuckin' dollars that's due to me. That includes the itemized bill I'm going to hand you for Club Diesel. Once you receive it, you got thirty days to get me my fuckin' cash or *we* are going to have a serious fuckin' problem."

"Thirty days?"

"I'm still not stuttering," he says. "Business is business."

This shit is uncomfortable to watch.

When it's clear that Python doesn't have anything else to add, Diesel signals me to follow. But as we near the door, Diesel pulls up one more time.

"Oh, and by the way, my condolences on that LeShelle situation. According to the news, it sounds like someone really fucked her over. If you ask me, it probably had something to do with that Flower bitch she hired to cut your baby out of that high yellow bitch you were fucking around with."

"What?"

"C'mon, cuz. You *really* didn't put that shit together?" Diesel shakes his head as if disappointed in his cousin's intellectual prowess. "Thirty days!"

We exit the warehouse, leaving Python looking like he's stuck on stupid. As we settle into the car, I get that sense of being watched again. I glance around the car but fail to see anything. "Well, that escalated quickly," I say, breaking the ice.

Diesel grins. "You haven't seen nothing yet."

51

Cleo

My car doesn't turn over. When I beg and promise my four-wheel baby that I'll take him in for a tune-up on my next payday, the engine roars to life. I coast out to Diesel's place, pulling my thoughts together on exactly what I'm going to say or do. I can't come right out and accuse him of killing Kalief, can I? What are the chances of him copping to the truth? *Zero.* Then what?

My mind draws a blank. Halfway to Diesel's crib, I ease my foot off the accelerator. The hardest part though is coming out of my feelings to reassess the situation. All the stories that I've heard about Diesel and how he runs shit down in the ATL flood my memory. Add to that my own questions about Diesel's involvement with Momma Peaches' murder and the shooting at her funeral, and suddenly I'm not sure what my storming over to his place to demand answers is going to accomplish.

I want to see whether he will lie to my face. Of course he'll lie, I argue back.

Then what?

By the time I arrive at Diesel's place I still haven't come up with an answer on what I'm going to do. I just know that I have to do something. It's only my second time to Diesel's home. He's setting himself apart from the other hood rich negroes in the city. His willingness to flaunt his money showcases that he has all the right people on payroll.

Who am I to go up against the Diesel machine?

I pull up behind a line of cars in the driveway and then shut off the engine. I can't believe that I drove all the way over here only to have second thoughts about confronting the man. Yet, the thought of turning around and going home with my tail tucked between my legs doesn't sit right with me either. I did nothing after Essence's murder—even after I discovered who her real killer was. Am I about to do the same thing for Kalief's killer?

I reach over to the glove compartment and pull out the .38 that my grandma bought me for protection years ago. It's probably best if I don't think about what I'm about to do and let the situation develop on its own.

I climb out of the car, tuck my weapon into my jeans, and proceed toward the front door. A dog somewhere in the house barks its head off.

"STOP RIGHT THERE," a voice commands from out of the darkness.

Stunned, I do exactly what I'm told.

"Put your hands up where I can see them," the voice orders.

Again, I comply. My heart pounds wildly.

A man steps out of the darkness and I recognize him instantly: *Bullet.*

"What are you doing here, songbird?" he asks, cocking his head to the side. "Are you lost?"

"What? No. I . . ." I lower my hands.

"Ah. Ah. Ah. Keep them up," he commands, stepping into my personal space.

Up they go. My second heart attack comes when Bullet pats me down.

"Well, well. What do we have here?" He removes my weapon and holds it up in front of me.

"What? You know a girl ain't safe out here without her own personal protection."

"Uh-huh." He steps back but holds on to my weapon. "And you're here because of what?"

"I came to talk to Diesel."

"He's not there. Would you like to leave a message?"

"Where is he?"

"None of your business." He gestures toward my car. "Go home. I'll tell Diesel that you stopped by."

The look on his face and his body language tell me that this is the end of the discussion. It's just as well. I can't think of anything that I can say that's going to get me into that house. "Well, can I get my gun back?"

He stares at me for a long moment and then finally hands over my weapon. "You stay safe now."

I pluck the weapon from his fingertips and then turn and head back to my car. In my head I'm calling Bullet every muthafucka under the sky.

Headlights swing up the drive. I turn and see Diesel's Mercedes roll up to the house. My anger returns in full force. I race toward the car before it stops.

Diesel climbs out from the backseat when Bullet wraps his arms around my waist and pulls me back.

"Let me go!"

"What the hell is going on here?"

I put everything I have into stomping down with my stiletto heels onto Bullet's foot.

"Ow!" He loosens his hold enough for me to break free and swing on Diesel. Unfortunately, Diesel ducks and catches my wrists. "What the fuck?"

"Let me go, you fuckin' murderer. You killed him! I know you did." I struggle to free my hands, but Diesel's grip is like steel—so I kick and tear those knees and ankles up.

"Cleo! Stop it! Calm the fuck down!"

"Murderer!" *Kick! Kick! Stomp!*

"Cleo! Goddamn it, Cleo. Stop!" He struggles to keep hold until his hand slips on one of my wrists and I claw my nails down the right side of his face. His reaction is swift. He backhands my ass and stars explode behind my eyes. I fall, but Bullet catches me before I hit the ground.

"Damn, Diesel." Titi climbs out of the car.

"Don't start," he barks. "You see her. She's hysterical."

I recover, bolt from Bullet, and land more blows. My violent squirming frustrates Diesel, but he doesn't let me go.

"You need any help, boss?" Beast asks.

"Just get the fucking front door so we can get her into the house," Diesel barks as Bullet plucks me off Diesel again.

"NO!" I'm not going in that house.

"Yes, boss." Beast rushes off.

"Let me go! You murderer. I'll kill you!"

Diesel's laughter throws me for a loop as Bullet struggles to carry me across the threshold and into the house.

"All right. Calm down," Diesel rumbles in a low, menacing voice. "Titi, make her a drink so she can calm her nerves and she can tell us who exactly it is she thinks I killed."

Titi turns toward the bar.

"Don't play me stupid." I sneer. "You know good and damn well that you killed Kalief." Saying his name again, I break down. It's my fault that he's dead. It's my fault.

"Cleo, calm down," Diesel insists. "I did *not* kill your damn boyfriend. Sorry to disappoint you, but Kalief is hardly worth the effort."

The boredom in his voice sends doubt into my head. My wild wrestling with Bullet stops as I assess whether or not he's telling the truth.

"Here, honey. Drink this." Titi offers me a glass with brown liquor. I shake my head but she insists.

"You *really* need to drink this," Titi presses.

I snatch the glass. Maybe I do need to calm down in order to get to the bottom of this. I take sip of the strong whiskey. It burns my throat. I place a hand against my chest and hope that the shit doesn't put hair on my chest.

"Feel better?" Diesel asks, taking a drink from Titi and downing a healthy gulp.

I don't respond.

"Start from the beginning and tell me what the hell all of this is about?"

The bastard looks sincere, fucking up my theory of what happened to Kalief.

"Well?" Diesel sets his glass down on the coffee table and leans back in his seat to give me his full attention. I glance over at Titi and she's waiting for my story as well.

"Kalief is dead."

Diesel and Titi glance at each other. "Yeah. We pieced that much together. Get to the part where you concluded that *I* had something to do with it."

I shake my head, telling myself not to believe his lies. "I know about you," I tell him. "I know that you had something to do with this. You thought by getting Kalief out of the way that somehow I was going to fall into your bed, but you're mistaken. That shit will *never* happen."

There's a long silence before Diesel pushes up a smile.

"So now I kill useless niggas in order to get women to sleep with me? That's your theory? I mean, yeah. I've made it no secret about how I feel for you, but I was thinking more along the lines of wining and dining; maybe some jewelry, haute couture dresses—but murder?"

I shake my head. "Stop talking to me like I'm crazy." I stand and get light-headed. "Whoa." I plop back down onto the couch.

"What is it?" Titi asks from the bar, looking concerned.

"Nothing. I just . . . stood up too fast."

"Or you've worked yourself up for no reason," Diesel injects. "I hate to disappoint you, but I didn't kill your boyfriend."

"Kind of how . . . how you didn't kill Momma Peaches, too?" I challenge recklessly. Why is my tongue so thick?

"What did you say?" Diesel's amusement fades.

"I-I saw . . ." My head spins and then I struggle to remember what it was I was about to say.

"You saw what?" Diesel asks.

I look into his intense green eyes. "I saw you speed away from the church that morning. I know that you had something to do with her death."

He doesn't answer. The room swims around me.

"Cleo, are you all right?" Titi asks, coming toward me.

"Yeah. I'm fine. I . . ." I attempt to stand—at least I think I do. "Whoa. It's hot in here." I tug at my top and then hand-fan myself. "Don't you have air-conditioning? Why is it so hot in here?"

Diesel stares.

I look to Titi. "Aren't you hot?"

She shakes her head.

"Then I guess it's just . . ." My gaze falls onto my drink. *Something's wrong.* Before I can figure out what, I close my eyes and can't open them again.

52

Nefertiti

"Thank God she finally shut up." I pick up one of Cleo's limp arms and then allow it to plop back down.

"How much did you give her?" Diesel asks, standing.

I shrug. "I don't know. Enough to shut her up." I take a look at his face and wince. "Damn, D. You're really losing your touch with the ladies."

Diesel shrugs off my touch only to stare longingly at his precious songbird. "I just wanted you to give her enough to relax her—not knock her out."

"Oops. Maybe next time we should sync up our drugging codes."

He doesn't pick up on my sarcasm. He's too busy staring. "She really is a beautiful woman."

I take another look. "She is pretty." Though she has none of the brick-house curves that he normally goes for. Her breasts are B cups, but she does have a nice onion ass that I can get into. After another minute passes and he doesn't peel his eyes away from her, I ask, "So did you do it?"

"Do what?"

"Whack the boyfriend."

Diesel shrugs. "He was an annoying piece of shit."

"Humph." I shake my head. "You fucked up. She's never going to forgive you."

"There's nothing to forgive. What she doesn't know won't hurt her." He sits down next to her and then brushes her hair from her face.

I fold my arms while jealousy creeps over me. "She's not a doll, you know."

Diesel doesn't respond. Instead his fingers glide from her hair down the side of her face, over her collarbone, and then to the V-shape of her neckline. That's where his fingers linger, stroking her creamy breasts. "She's so . . . perfect," he murmurs, and then pinches a nipple. To my surprise both those bitches get harder.

Diesel chuckles. "She's attracted to me even though she'll never admit it."

I watch him watching her. The whole thing is weird. She's the one knocked out and he's in a trance.

"I bet she's a hellcat in the bed."

"If the scratches on your face are any indication, then I'm going to have to agree with you."

He peels back the shoulders of her dress and then works the material down until her pink and black lace bra is exposed. When he unsnaps the center clasp, I ask, "Are you really about to do this?"

His pulling open both cups is my answer.

My assessment of her B-cups is upgraded when I see how perky those bitches naturally are. When Diesel lowers his head and sucks her nipples, I'm turned on. In fact, my clit pumps so much honey that my panties are drenched.

Diesel moans as if she's the best thing that he's tasted in years. In no time, he has both of her brown orbs glistening with his saliva. Gently, he shifts her body over so that she can lie flat against the leather sofa.

Diesel pulls off his shirt and T-shirt. When he goes to unbuckle his pants, I ease into an armchair and sip on my own vodka and tonic.

Diesel's cock bursts through the slot of his silk boxers, so he goes ahead and removes those as well. Returning to the sofa, he lifts the hem of her dress to above her waist. Next, Diesel takes his time rolling down her panties. When he spreads her legs, I spread mine and play with myself while Diesel rapes his beautiful songbird.

53

Ta'Shara

Baptist Memorial Hospital

I'm numb.

I've finally succeeded in pushing Profit away. *So why aren't I happy?* Maybe happy is the wrong word. Even when I was the one leaving, I was never going to be happy. The real question is whether I still feel as if it was the *right* decision.

Sadly—I do.

My door bursts open and a smiling Reggie Senior pushes an empty wheelchair into the room. "I know you gotta be ready to get out of here. Checkout time!"

Reggie's broad smile proves to be infectious. I wipe my eyes and beam back. Two weeks in this drab place with the bad food and limited cable channels is more than enough.

"Are you ready to go?" he asks.

"About as ready as I'll ever get."

"Did the doctor come by and sign the discharge papers?"

"Got them right here." I hold up the papers and wave them.

"Hot dog. Then let's blow this joint." He winks and then comes over to the bed to pick me up. I haven't gotten used to being treated like a doll, but Reggie does it with such ease that

I don't think he minds at all. It's the same when he's fastening me in the passenger seat of his blue Cadillac, too.

After that, we're on the road to Germantown to his and Mary's nice two-story colonial home. He's quick to explain how he and his wife bought the home. It was when his son was still in high school. Reggie and Mary had scrimped and saved their way into the middle class. There were stories of him and Junior tossing the football around in the yard, the many barbecues in the backyard, and, of course, when he and his wife first met Tracee as a surprise dinner guest during one of Junior's spring breaks in college.

It took no time at all to deduce that Reggie Senior is still grieving for his wonderful son.

After parking in the drive, Reggie hops out of the van and gets me settled back into the wheelchair in almost Superman speed. It isn't too long before guilt finds a permanent home in my soul. It isn't right that he and his wife are taking care of a foster kid that their son hadn't legally adopted, but all signs point to Reggie being happy to do it. And when I enter the house to the distinct smell of some good ol'-fashioned soul food cooking, I know that Mary is also thrilled that I will be staying with them, temporarily.

Olivia Sullivan, Tracee's mom, is still bidding for me to move to Houston. She's called daily at the hospital to talk to me about one rehab facility after another that she's found on-line. Everyone remains so positive that I'll be able to walk again.

I'm not so sure.

My paralysis is a fitting punishment for my crimes. I'd rather this than being on death row or six feet under, which was clearly the road I was traveling down.

"I got you a surprise," Reggie announces, excited.

Mary clasps her hands together and grins.

The whole black *Leave It to Beaver* scene is making me uncomfortable.

"Okay. What is it?" I ask.

Reggie rolls me over to the set of stairs. I panic, until Reggie gestures dramatically to the contraption on the wall. "Ta-dah!"

I keep the plastic smile carved on my face, but I have no idea what the heck I'm looking at, yet they are waiting for me to say something. "Oh, yeah! Um. What is it?"

"It's a stair lift," Reggie explains. "You roll your chair over here like this." He takes me over to the wall. "Back up until you hear this series of clicks." Sure enough, three short clicks sound from behind me. "And then you press this button." He points to an LCD-lit button. "Go ahead. Press it."

With the Douglases grinning around me, I follow instructions and push the button. A mechanical winding noise starts and the next thing I know I'm being lifted up the staircase at a snail's pace.

"Oh wow," I exclaim.

"Pretty cool, huh?" Reggie asks with his chest puffed out.

It's so silly that I struggle not to laugh. "Yes. It's great." Except that it takes three whole minutes to reach the top when it only takes Reggie and Mary three *seconds* to jog after me. Still proud as he can be, he shows me how to detach from the electronic unit and then wheels me to my new room. At first sight of the pink room, I break down in tears.

"Oh, Ta'Shara. I'm sorry," Mary frets from behind me. "You don't like it."

"No." *Sniff.* "No. It's not that. In fact, I love it. It looks so much like my old room."

Mary beams. "We prayed that you'd like it. We really want you to feel that this is your new home."

I get it now. There seems to be some kind of bidding war

going on between the Douglases and the Sullivans. Both families want me to pick them to be my new parents or guardians. It's incredibly touching to even be wanted, given my disability.

"We know the place will need some more of your personal touches, so if you'd like, I could go to your last place of residence and pick up your belongings."

I choke. The idea of sending the Douglases anywhere near Ruby Cove is crazy and dangerous. "That's okay. I'll text my address to my friend Mack and she can bring my stuff."

"Oh. Okay." Reggie nods, relieved.

"Well, if you want to wash up, dinner should be ready in a few minutes," Mary says, smiling.

"Okay. Great."

The doorbell rings.

"Ah. That should be Olivia," Mary says. "Right on time."

Two hours later, I'm participating in a strange play where everyone is being overly nice and accommodating, but each is working my nerves.

Eventually, the discussion turns to my plans for the future. They agree that there's no point in my returning to school until the fall. The idea of having to repeat the tenth grade, then being two years behind my original class, sends my spirits spiraling.

The Douglases assure me that there is no shame in having to repeat a grade, especially after all that I've been through the last year. However, Olivia comes up with the perfect solution. "I say the hell with it. Take the GED and then enroll in a community college, then transfer to the university of your choice. Simple."

I smile. "I like that idea."

Olivia beams.

Reggie and Mary exchange looks for having lost a round.

Mary clears her throat. "That's an option that you can do here in Memphis, too."

"But Houston has better facilities for the type of rehab that you'll need," Olivia adds.

"That's not true," Mary snaps, pounding her fist on the table.

"All right, ladies. Calm down," Reggie advises. "There is no need for everyone to get upset. We don't want to overwhelm Ta'Shara. After all, the decision is hers to make."

Three sets of eyeballs shift to me.

"Uh. I—I haven't had time to think it all through," I tell them, hoping that is a satisfactory answer.

Reggie nods while Olivia and Mary exchange warring glares.

After dinner, I'm full and tired. I ask to be excused and resist Reggie's offer of help working the staircase lift. However, once on the second floor, I need help getting into the special bathtub that Reggie installed. By the time I'm washed and tucked into bed I'm exhausted *and* humiliated. The number of things that I'll have to relearn in order to take care of my basic needs is overwhelming.

Despite my exhaustion, sleep eludes me, and the walls of my new pink princess room close in on me. Sometime past midnight, I click on the side-table lamp and drag myself backwards so I can lean against the headboard. I glance around the room. I'm no longer anyone's pink princess. That li'l naïve girl is long gone, and I have no idea how to reach her again. Tears skip down my face. I mourn the girl I used to be and wish that there were some way I could get back to her.

On the nightstand are a few paperbacks that the Douglases thought I'd enjoy reading. The family has always been big on reading. I pick up a couple of them, but there is nothing that I want to read. I check out what else is in the nightstand, and I'm surprised to come across a pack of matches. Picking them up, my heart trips inside my chest. With trembling fingers, I strike one match and stare, fascinated, at the small orange glow.

LeShelle's screams replay in my head, but I no longer feel tortured by it. In fact, I'm pleased by it. The flame touches my hand and I extinguish it with a casual wave. I strike another—and then another. I marvel at how each flame is more beautiful than the last.

Destruction

54

Mack

While Fat Ace and a handful of soldiers remain by Lucifer's side at the hospital, Profit has stepped up and made his presence known. The talk about when and how to hit the Gangster Disciples is heating up, and Profit is all over the shit. I'm impressed. Until recently, the young blood has had limited experience. But now he's the man with the plan, and our shell-shocked soldiers are eager to follow someone.

The Shotgun Row and Club Diesel hits were major successes. The shit with Tombstone was fucked up though, but Profit promises the next hit will be just as big. Tonight we celebrate. Ruby Cove gathers together for an impromptu block party. It's better than another night of exchanging sad stories about the people we've lost. We're all on a good high, bragging about the number of bodies we dropped and hating that we haven't toe-tagged Python or King Isaac.

I'm glad to see Profit being elevated, but not all the changes I'm seeing are good. Sure, it's important for him to be hard and fearless, but I don't think that he's taking his breakup with Ta'Shara too well at all. For one, he's drinking like a fish, and before when the thots and hoes tried their best to throw pussy his way, he ignored them. Tonight that's not the case. While the music bumps and our people keep the alcohol flowing, Profit is receptive to the females and he's grinding on a few of them a bit too hard. I know the shit ain't none of my business, but he's really pissing me off.

Romil hasn't said much, but I can tell by the few looks she's cut my way that she feels the same way I do. As the night drones on, my promise to Ta'Shara eats me up. If Profit knew that his girl was now a paraplegic, he wouldn't be out here, rubbing on bitches' asses like a fuckin' jerk.

The shit got so dire that I put word in circulation that if I see a single Flower go inside to break Profit off some pussy, they'll have to answer to me. There are a few odd looks, but everyone sees that my ass ain't playing. Profit can drink all the liquor he wants, but pussy is off the fucking menu.

I've known Ta'Shara for a short time, but she's good people. There's something about her that makes you want to protect her, even though she has proven that she's more than capable of taking care of herself. At midnight, a good hunk of us gather around to pour beer for the lost soldiers. We say their names, one by one. Next come the ones who were wounded but survived. There's an uncomfortable silence when we get to Ta'Shara's and Lucifer's names; especially Lucifer's.

There are already rumors floating that the most dangerous chick in the game is brain dead and that our leader, Fat Ace, is having a hard time accepting that shit as fact. So far, he's refusing to leave her side. He and Lucifer's mother hold vigil day and night. Sooner or later, a decision on whether to pull the plug will have to be made.

But for now, none of us feels comfortable pouring beer out in her name.

A drunken Profit nibbles on Amira's ear and tugs her in the direction of his crib. She giggles like a teenybopper and allows him to pull her away. I glare at her ass, waiting for her to look in my direction. At the door, Amira looks at me, but then gives my ass a Kanye shrug and goes inside.

"That fucking bitch." I slam my beer bottle to the ground

and take off toward Profit's house with Romil close behind. I
don't even think twice about kicking in the door.

Bam!

Profit's head snaps up. "What the fuck?" His hand goes to
his weapon.

"Slow your roll, cuz. It's just me," I tell him while I march
straight toward Amira's trifling ass.

Her eyes grow big as fuck when I latch on to her fresh
sew-in weave and snatch her.

"Heeey!" she screams.

"Shut up!" I crash the butt of my weapon across her jaw.

Blood sprays across the floor.

"Whoa. Whoa." Profit attempts to stop my next blow, but
I'm too quick and Amira drops like a stone. "What the fuck
you doing?"

"This is Flower business," I tell him. "Don't you worry
about it."

"Don't worry?"

I shout at Amira, "You still here? What the fuck are you
waiting on?"

Amira glances up at Profit.

Pissed, I kick the bitch in the gut to get her to move. "What
the fuck is you looking at him for? Get up outta here!" I deliver
another kick.

Amira scrambles across the floor, but the second she moves
past me, Romil slams her Timberland into the back of her ass,
just so she can brag that she helped two-piece her ass.

Once the bitch is gone, Profit is confused about what the
fuck happened.

"So what's this? You're into random bitches now?" I ask.

Profit glances around. "You talking to me?"

"You're standing there, ain't you?"

"No. You can't be talking to me out the side of your neck
up in *my* crib."

"This ain't no side nothing. I'm coming to you direct because Ta'Shara is my girl and I'm not the type of friend to allow any disrespect for my fuckin' friend."

"Humph. News flash: Your girl and I broke up. I'm a free muthafuckin' agent and I don't need your permission to bring another shorty up in here if that's what I choose to do."

"Nigga, who you foolin'? Your ass ain't nowhere near being over Ta'Shara. You're just hurt because she's making shit hard for you right now. You should be happy that she is, because that shows that she ain't like these other bitches who are trying to fuck you for status. You need to figure out how in the fuck you're going to win Ta'Shara's ass back. You two belong together like peanut butter and jelly. You're not going to find a better bitch, especially out here."

"You don't know what you're talking about," he says, taking a drink of beer. "Ta'Shara made it clear that she doesn't want to have any more to do with me."

"I doubt that Ta'Shara knows what the fuck she wants right now. The bitch has been through more shit in a year than my ass has the entire twenty years I've been in the game. You got to be patient with her. I mean, *if* you really do love her."

"Of course I love her." He clamps his jaw tight after confessing that much. He drains the last of his beer before continuing. "Look. I get what you two are doing, but at the end of the day, I can't make Ta'Shara love me when she's too busy regretting the day that she ever met me."

"She said that?"

He hesitates. "Pretty much."

"And your dumb ass believed her?"

Profit frowns. "Yes. I believed her. She was looking me dead in my eye when she said that shit at the hospital."

Romil and I glance at each other. "You saw her at the hospital?"

He walks over to his couch and plops down as if carrying the world on his shoulders has worn him out. "Yeah. Of course.

I went up there the day I got released—much good that shit did me."

"And . . . you didn't notice anything different?"

Profit frowns. "Different? Different how?"

Romil and I exchange another look. I fuckin' hate secrets.

"What the fuck?" Profit says with a combination of frustration and irritation.

"Look. I got a voicemail from Ta'Shara asking that I bring her stuff to her new address out in Germantown." I eye him. "I think maybe you should be the one to take her stuff to her tomorrow."

55

Cleo

Kalief and I are making love. I've forgotten how good we are together. This time however, we are a little hotter. He knows where to put his hands and mouth before I even know I want them there.

Moaning, I lower my hand between my legs and place them against the side of Kalief's head.

Kalief's head game has never been better. My mind spins as I struggle to breathe. When my orgasm hits, I toss around with abandon, but when Kalief crawls up my body, his scent is different. He's not wearing my favorite cologne, Polo Black.

Everything is different.

Kalief is heavier, his shoulders and back bigger.

I run my hands along his sinewy muscles, swept up in the moment. I struggle to open my eyes, but they weigh a ton.

Kalief lifts my legs and I obligingly wrap them around his waist. Only—his waist is wider—taut. Everything goes all fuzzy again. I feel . . . wonderful and strange at the same time. It goes on and on until I wake with sunlight warm against my face. I moan, stretch, and even smile before I successfully open my eyes. However, I'm confused when I don't recognize anything around me. I sit up and gasp at the unfamiliar bold décor and silk sheets. I scramble to remember the previous night, but keep hitting a brick wall. The more I hit it, the more frustrated I become. Seconds before my head explodes, I whip back the sheets.

I'm naked. *Fuck! What did I do? What happened?*

I pound my fist on the side of my head. I jar a few images loose. *The club. The shooting. The police. Kalief.*

I gasp at the bloody images. I fly out from my nest of silk sheets, then drop like a stone when my rubbery legs refuse to hold me up. When I hit the hardwood floor, my knees, elbows, and chin explode with pain.

When I hear padding feet, I push myself into a sitting position and snatch the top sheet from off the bed. I manage to get it around me before a smiling Nefertiti breezes into the bedroom.

"Oh. You're up. That's good." She marches over to the nearest window and opens the blinds all the way.

The thin slices of light are now each a full laser beam, penetrating my skull and rendering me insane with pain. "Close it! Close it! Please!"

Nefertiti closes the blinds again and the pain goes away. "My goodness, girl. Are you all right?" She appears at my side and places her cold hands against my shoulder to help me up.

"Yes. I think so." On my feet, I lean against her, not trusting my own strength. "What time is it?"

"It's past noon," she answers.

"Jeez. I slept the whole morning away."

Nefertiti stops walking.

"What?"

"Actually, you slept all day yesterday and this morning."

"What?" I pull away from her, but my wobbly legs threaten to drop me. I hold on to her for dear life. "That's impossible. I just . . . what the hell happened to me?" I float the question before I become aware of a strange soreness and wetness between my legs.

"I'm not sure," Titi says, smiling. "You showed up quite upset, ranting and raving about some boyfriend." She stops and gives me a hard look. "You made some horrible accusations that I hope now, in the light of day, you are ashamed of. You need to apologize to Diesel."

I frown at being scolded like a child. Then the memory of my drive to Diesel's house plays in my mind. I attacked, wrestled with him, and even scratched his face.

"Then what happened?" I ask.

Titi shrugs and flashes that weird smile again. "We tried to calm you down but you had worked yourself up into such a state that you got sick and started throwing up everywhere."

"I did?"

Nefertiti nods. "Don't worry. Diesel carried you up here, but I was the one to strip you out of your clothes and clean you up. I sent your dress to the cleaners yesterday. I'll run out and pick it up in a few minutes." We make it to the door of the adjoining bathroom and push it open.

I don't know what to say, so I just say the first thing that comes to mind. "Thank you."

Titi's smile widens. "Don't mention it."

I'm embarrassed that she has to help me all the way to the toilet, but once I'm sitting on the porcelain throne I tell her, "I can handle it from here."

Titi takes her time pointing out where I can find everything—towels and toiletries—before backing out of the bathroom and shutting the door. When I'm alone again, I speed through the recovered memories of the previous night.

Have I really been here that long?

It doesn't seem possible.

I run through everything two or three times while I piss like a racehorse. Clearly, they made sure my ass stayed hydrated. I wipe, then look down at the toilet paper and frown at the mucus-like substance. Why the fuck does it look like . . . *No.* I toss the toilet paper into the bowl and flush. When I stand up, bracing myself against the wall, my attention focuses again on the dull ache between my legs.

My tears are instant despite my brain trying to reject my suspicions. It didn't happen. It couldn't have.

Lastly, the memory of making love to Kalief replays in my head, but I know that couldn't have happened. Kalief is dead. He's been dead. The image of Kalief is replaced by one of Diesel. The muscular shoulders, the broad chest. The powerful ass . . . and the larger dick.

"Oh my God." I spin around and throw up into the toilet bowl. Only I don't have that much food in my stomach, so it isn't long before I'm dry heaving and cramping.

Knock! Knock! Knock!

"Are you all right in there?" Titi calls.

I slap my hand over my mouth as horror creeps over me. "Cleo?"

The doorknob turns and I'm able to say, "I'm fine. Everything is fine!"

The door doesn't open, but there is a long pause. "Are you sure?"

"Yes!" I flush the toilet and hurry over to the shower to turn it on. "I'll be out in a few minutes," I shout above the water spray.

"Okay. I placed some clothes on the bed. I'll go down and make you something to eat before you go. You must be starving."

"Yeah. Great!" I cover my mouth with my hand again to stop a sob from bursting out. I wait a minute until I'm sure that she has moved away from the door before rushing over and locking it.

Now what?

I catch my reflection in the vanity mirror and am completely horrified by what I see. My thick mass of natural curls are standing straight up on my head, as if I placed my hand into an electric socket. My three-day-old mascara makes me look like I have two black eyes. I'm pale and my lips appear abnormally swollen.

Again. Horrifying.

Despite my ass wanting to bolt out of here, I'm also overwhelmed by the need to scrub my body clean. That's exactly what I do once I jump into the glass-walled shower. I set the water as hot as I can get it and I scour every inch of my body until I am in pain.

Somehow I push the trauma of my rape aside, shut off the shower, and towel off. I twist two plaits in my hair, unlock the bathroom door, peek around the corner, and dash to the clothes lying on the bed.

I've never dressed so fast in my life. I'm still sliding into a pair of tennis shoes as I rush out of the bedroom and fly down the stairs. The scent of brewing coffee and frying bacon is enough to make my stomach lurch. But when I get ready to bolt out of door, I don't have my clutch, my gun, or my car keys.

More tears pool in my eyes when it dawns on me that I'll have to ask Nefertiti for my shit. I don't know if I can handle facing that smiling bitch again. She's gotta know what had happened to me. Was she in on it?

While I'm contemplating what to do, the front door bursts open and Beast steps into the house with a large Doberman pinscher. He takes one look at me and drops his gaze. "Hello, Cleo."

"My purse and keys," I say simply.

"They are in the study on the coffee table."

I turn and race to the room where Diesel carried me the other night. When I rush inside, I remember lying on the sofa and Titi handing me a drink.

My stomach clenches. I slap my hand back over my mouth

and wait for the wave of nausea to pass. Once it does, Beast is standing before me and handing me my purse.

"Are you able to drive?" he asks, looking sorry for me.

I snatch my purse from him. "All of you can go to hell!" I spin and run out of the house. The drive speeds by in a blur— a watery blur. Once the tears start, I am helpless to stop them. I cry the whole way to the police station.

56

Hydeya

"I'm pregnant," I tell my reflection for the thousandth time. Still, neither it nor myself believes the words that are coming out of my mouth. But the doctor and the dozen home pregnancy tests I've used are all telling me the same damn thing. "I'm pregnant."

How in the hell am I going to raise a kid all by myself?

The idea of wrangling up a babysitter or finding a decent day care short-circuits my brain. But then, I have a part of Drake growing inside of me. In about seven and a half months, I'll see his eyes and smile again, in our child's face.

There. That flutter of excitement again. I smile at my reflection. As I dress for work, I start humming. I opt for hot tea instead of coffee and take time to make oatmeal and cut up some fruit for breakfast. Eating three balanced meals a day has never been my thing, but that will be the first in a long series of changes.

I'm uncharacteristically late when I arrive at the department, but nobody else notices or cares. Another name is added to the murder board: Kalief Cummings.

When is the tide going to turn?

"Your dad posted bail this morning," Fowler informs me, popping up at my door.

"Good for him," I say without looking up.

"Happy? Sad?"

"I don't give a damn," I say. "Don't you have cases to work?"

Silence.

I look up and he's looking at me strangely. He seems to be torn between answering and cursing me out.

I lift one eyebrow in amusement. "Is that a yes or a no?"

"It's a yes." Fowler pushes himself away from my door to find something that will keep him out of my hair. But once he's gone, his sidekick Hendrix arrives. "A Pastor Hayes came by looking for you. He waited but then left ten minutes ago," she informs me.

"Pastor Hayes?" I remember him from the Power of Prayer Baptist Church. "I wonder what he wanted."

"He didn't say."

"Okay. Thanks." I look up as Hendrix backpedals out of my office.

I got them spooked. Good. Once she's gone, I shake my head and wonder how I'm going to root out the bad cops who were in on Captain Johnson's criminal network. On top of a modern urban city burning down around me, daddy issues, and preparing to be a single mom, it will take a Herculean effort on my part.

I toss down my pen and pinch the bridge of my nose. The beginning of another headache is coming on. I whip open my top drawer and retrieve my bottle of Excedrin—but then stop. Am I allowed to even be taking these?

I stare at the bottle, unsure. I don't even want to think about the damage I may have caused before I knew that I was knocked up. I toss the bottle back into the drawer and pick up the phone. Of course I ignore the red flashing light that's alerting me that I have messages, because I know that ninety-eight percent of them are from the media. Everyone wants a quote or progress report about what the city is going to do to stop Memphis's fast descent into chaos.

Since I can't tell everyone that there is nothing that can be done as long as the drug and gun laws are what they are, I'd rather avoid putting myself into situations where I'm forced to lie to the tax-paying public.

Now completely frustrated, I pick up an envelope on my desk and remove the disc inside it. It's a surveillance video from a store where the owner was murdered. I pop it into my computer. I'm only half paying attention when I look up and recognize a familiar face.

The singer. *Cleo Blackmon.* I stand up from my chair to get a better look through my glass walls. *Yeah. That's her.* I wonder if there's something else that she's recalled from the Club Diesel shooting the other night and rush out of my office to greet her.

"Ms. Blackmon," I call out.

When Cleo faces me, I'm taken aback by her morose expression. I drop my smile and reach for her. "Is everything all right?"

Ms. Blackmon's eyes well up and her bottom lip trembles uncontrollably.

"Come with me," I instruct, then lead her toward my office. I open my top-drawer pharmacy and remove a travel-size pack of tissues.

Cleo snatches out a few sheets, wipes her eyes and blows her nose.

I wait until I she has reasonable control. "What can I help you with?"

Big mistake. Another wave of gut-wrenching sobs racks the young girl's body.

"It's okay. Take your time." I rub her back and hand her more tissues. Ten minutes later, she's springing up out of the seat and mumbling, "I can't do this. This is a mistake."

"What?"

Cleo rushes toward the door.

"Wait." I race after her, and before she clears the threshold I latch on to her wrist. "If you know anything more about the club shooting—"

"No. This is a mistake. You can't help me." She snatches her hand from my grip and sprints across the department as if her life depends on it.

"Damn."

57

Cleo

"**W**ell, look who's decided to bring her ass home." Granny lights into me the moment I enter the house. "I know that you're moving up to the big time, but while you're staying in *my* house, you will abide by *my* rules. And the number one rule around here for you *grown* kids is to call and let somebody know if you ain't resting your head here at night."

I drop my head and close the door behind me. "Sorry, Granny."

"I don't care about you being sorry. I care about you not doing it no damn more."

"Yes, ma'am." I'm rooted next to the door, fighting the urge to race to take another shower.

Granny looks at me. "What's wrong with you? You look pale. Have you had anything to eat?"

I shake my head, tears slide down my face.

"Oh, baby. What's the matter?" She rushes over. By the time she wraps her arms around me, I'm a sobbing mess.

"Granny, why is Cleo crying?" six-year-old Kay asks.

"Don't y'all worry about that right now. You and Jamie go and play in your rooms."

"But—"

"G'on now!"

My li'l cousins drop their heads and shuffle off toward their rooms. "Yes, ma'am."

Granny tucks me under her wing and pulls me into the living room. "Now you c'mon in here and tell me what's wrong. Did you and Kalief get into another fight?"

I cry harder.

"Aww. Now. Hush, baby. Everything is going to be all right."

"No. It isn't, Granny. He's dead!" My thoughts twist and turn, laying Kalief's death at my feet. My head knows that what my heart is saying is bullshit, but in this moment, it feels true.

I can hardly believe I could've saved Kalief from Diesel when I couldn't protect myself from him. The tears flow faster, harder.

"Oh, my baby." Granny sits next to me on the couch and proceeds to rock me back and forth. "You go ahead and let it all out. I know how much you loved that boy."

Yes. Most of the tears are for Kalief, but a fair amount of them are for me, too.

"What's going on?" Kobe asks, entering the living room. Behind him is his usual clique. No doubt they were coming to play their video games like they do most afternoons.

"Kalief has apparently passed away," Granny informs him, still rocking me. "Y'all go in and play somewhere else." She shoos them away much like the cousins, but Kobe doesn't move.

"Are you going to be all right, Cleo?" he asks.

Silence.

Kobe turns to his friends. "Look. I'm gonna catch up with y'all later."

"Yeah. Sure. No doubt," one of them says before they all exchange dabs and then bounce.

Once they are out the door, Kobe joins me and Granny on the couch. "What happened?"

Sniffing, I pull away from Granny to level my tear-brimmed

gaze on him. "I'm not sure. I went to his place after the club shooting."

Granny clutches my arms. "So. You *were* there that night? Lawd have mercy."

"Were you hurt?" Kobe asks, his face more serious than I've seen it since Essence's passing.

"No. I wasn't hurt—then." Damn. That feels like a lifetime ago. He frowns.

"Since Kalief's been ignoring my calls and texts, I went over there to talk to him. I let myself in and then . . . I found him in the bedroom. There was blood everywhere." I turn back to the comfort of Granny's arms and sob.

"G'on, fix her some chamomile tea," she tells Kobe. "That should calm her down."

Kobe hesitates, but then bounces up to go do what he's told.

The tea helps. By the time I work my way halfway through the cup, I've calmed down.

Kobe speaks. "I heard about Kalief's death yesterday. I had no idea that you were the one who found him. Did the cops keep you for questioning?"

I shake my head. "I didn't call the cops."

Both he and Granny look confused.

How much of the story do I tell them? Lord knows I don't want to upset Granny. She isn't exactly in the best of health, but I've kept a lot of shit from them regarding Essence's true murderer; and now possibly hiding my own rape.

Kobe is in full investigative mode. "If you weren't down at the police station for the past two days, where have you been?"

Silence.

I have to make a decision. "I went to see Diesel."

Kobe withdraws. His dislike for Diesel Carver has been clear from the jump. "Why the fuck would you run to that muthafucka? Are you finally fuckin' him?"

Slap!

Granny waves her finger. "Kobe, you apologize to your sister!"

He rubs his smarting face. He's stunned by how fast she'd launched toward him.

"There's no need for that kind of talk. You see that she's upset."

Kobe grinds his back molars before he spits out, "Sorry."

His apology swings my emotions in the opposite direction. "Oh, Kobe. You were right. Diesel is a monster! What the hell am I going to do?"

"Wait? What?" Kobe tenses. He has never liked it when females get too emotional. When my grip tightens around his neck, he awkwardly pats me on the back. "There, there. It's okay. Everything is going to be okay."

I shake my head. "No, it's not. It's never going to be okay."

"Oh, my poor baby," Granny says, closing in on both Kobe and me to do a three-person hug. "We're gonna get you through this, baby."

"Why did you call him a monster?" Kobe asks, suspicion seeping into his voice. "Did Diesel have something to do with Kalief's death?"

"I—I think so."

"Damn." He pulls me back and cups my face so that he can look me dead in my eyes when he asks his next question. "Did Diesel hurt you in any way?"

Don't tell him. You can't tell him.

"Cleo?" Kobe's eyes harden to black diamonds. "Tell me the truth. Did that nigga hurt you?"

I nod and shame sweeps over me. "He raped me."

58

Ta'Shara

My first day in physical therapy at the Regional One Health hospital whipped my ass. The simplest exercise had me sweating like a damn hog. The amount of upper body strength that I'll have to develop is a monumental task that has me lying awake in bed yet another night. No matter how many times I fell flat on my face or ass, the therapist and my competitive foster grandparents cheered me on.

I smiled and tried my best not to let my frustration show. But now, while no eyes are watching me, I'm having serious doubts about whether I can do this—on top of preparing for the GED and pursuing all the dreams that I once had. In the back of my head, I realize my disability doesn't mean that I can't do them. There are plenty of doctors in the country with a wide range of disabilities. *Even now I'm still giving myself a pep talk that I don't feel.*

I click on the nightstand lamp again and pull my body up against the headboard. Everyone is asleep and the house is quiet. When will this place feel like home?

I miss Profit. I only admit it to myself in the middle of the night, though it's true every minute of the day. It's been too long since we've lain next to each other, feeling his breath against the back of my neck or his arm draped over my hip as we snuggle in our favorite spoon position. I close my eyes and recall his scent and his spearmint kisses. I'm convinced that I'll ache for him for the rest of my life.

I did the right thing. I'm doing the right thing. Tears streak down my face, but there's nothing that I can do about the pain. I'm hoping what everyone says about time healing all wounds is true. I open the drawer in the nightstand and pull out my box of matches. After a dozen small flames, my concentration is interrupted.

Tap! Tap! Tap!

What in the hell? I snap open my eyes and my attention is drawn to the bedroom window.

Tap! Tap! Tap!

I lean forward to make sure I'm really making out a face on the other side of the windowpane. "Profit?" *Am I hallucinating?*

My visitor gets tired of waiting and pulls up on the window. It's unlocked. Profit climbs through, holding my duffel bag.

"What are you doing here?" I flip the blanket over to cover my legs and glare at him. I try to glare. He really is a sight for sore eyes. He's still working out and I'm feeling the sexy stubble he has growing in.

"Mack said that you needed your things." He plops the duffel bag in the center of the floor and then glances around my new room. "So you're the pink princess again, huh?"

I ignore his question to ask a question of my own. "*Mack* told you to bring my stuff?"

"Yeah. Her and your girl Romil are waiting outside," he adds. "They are of the opinion that we belong together."

Silence.

Profit shrugs. "I agree with them."

Silence.

"You don't have *anything* to say?" he asks, shoving his hands into his pockets.

I have a lot to say, but there's no way I'm going to say it.

"Humph. Un-fucking-believable." He tilts his head back to gaze up at the ceiling. "So once again, I've made a fool of myself, thinking that there's some kind of hope for us?"

"Profit. It's not like that." I lower my head.

"No?"

"This . . . decision . . . isn't easy for me. I don't want you to think that it is."

"What's that smell?" he asks, sniffing the air. "Is something burning?"

I take a whiff and catch the scent of burning plastic. *Shit.* I glance down at the wastebasket and see flames lick up the sides of a plastic container. "Fuck. Fuck." I search around for something to extinguish the flames.

"Here. I'll do it." Profit moves forward as I stretch too far over for the bottled water I left on the other side of the nightstand before retiring for the night. My ass pitches forward and falls out of bed. I hit the floor like a stone. My breath is knocked out of my lungs, my head bangs against the leg of the nightstand, and the wastebasket tips over and lights my nightgown on fire.

"Shit!" Profit exclaims.

I gasp but don't scream. I can't. I'm fascinated by how fast the fire spreads. Since I can't feel my legs, I'm more enraptured by the dancing flames than the damage it's causing.

Profit snatches off his jacket and beats the fire—and me—until it dies.

"Ta'Shara. Are you all right?" Profit grabs me by my shoulders and shakes me out of my trance.

The bedroom door bursts open and Reggie Senior rushes inside, tying his bathrobe. "Ta'Shara, honey. Are you—who the hell are you?"

Profit glances up, no doubt experiencing déjà vu from the time the other Reggie busted us in my bedroom. At least this time we have clothes on.

"Mary!"

"Yo. Yo. It's okay," Profit says. "I'm a friend. I brought Ta'Shara her things." He gestures to the duffel bag.

Reggie sniffs the air. "What's burning?" He spots the smoldering basket. "The hell?" He races to the wastebasket, grabs it and races back out. A couple of seconds later we hear the shower in the hall bathroom come on.

Profit tries a joke. "Damn. We're losing our touch. Second time we've been caught."

Instead of laughing, I struggle to sit up.

"Here. Are you burned?" Profit reaches for my burned gown to try to take a look at my legs.

I swipe his hand away. "I'm fine. I'm fine."

"Are you sure?" He attempts to look again.

"I said I was fine. I don't need your damn help!"

Profit pulls back, staring as if I've sprouted two heads. "What the fuck?"

"I'm just saying that I don't need your help." *Reggie, hurry back.*

"Well, fine. Fuck. At least let me help you off of the floor." I swat his hands away. "Stop. I don't need your help."

"Jesus. When the hell did you become such a bitch?" He jumps to his feet. "I can't do anything right as far as you're concerned. I come flying over here, yet again, to pour my heart out to you and this is how you treat me?"

Tears burn my eyes. "You should go."

Reggie and Mary rush back to my bedroom.

"Son, I don't know how you got in here. But you have one minute to get out of the house before we call the police."

Profit stands, chuckling. "Who are you fooling? You already called the police."

The Douglases exchange guilty looks.

"Whatever." Profit looks down at me. "I'll go out the front door. I'm getting too old to be climbing in and out of windows." He heads for the door.

My heart tangles into knots as I watch his straight back walk toward the door, out of my life yet again.

Reggie springs into action again. "Oh, Ta'Shara. Let me help you up. Let me take a look at your legs. Are you burned?" He takes a look at my legs, too. "Maybe we should get you to the hospital to check out those burns. You probably can't feel it, huh? Do you want to get into bed or your wheelchair?"

Busted.

Profit stops, turns.

Reggie scoops me off the floor. For a brief moment, I bury my head in the crook of his shoulder, as if it would make me invisible.

Reggie sets me back in bed. Profit watches the whole procedure with laser focus.

"What's wrong with her legs?" he asks.

Mary finds her voice and steps to Profit's imposing figure. "Young man, you need to leave this house right now. We know who you are. You don't scare us."

Profit ignores her and asks his question louder. "What the hell is wrong with her?"

All eyes are on me. I can't look at Profit and I can't force anything out of my mouth. Profit looks around the room and spots the wheelchair. On the floor is one of the brochures that I attempted to put the fire out with. He walks over and picks it up.

"Profit, please. Leave," I beg. Guilt and shame riot within me.

He glances up, eyes glistening.

We have hurt each other plenty of times in the past, but

the look on his face is pure devastation. I should say something. Anything.

Someone hammers on the front door downstairs.

"That should be the police," Mary says, relieved.

"Don't worry," Profit tells her. "I'm leaving." Our eyes connect. "For good this time."

59

Wendi

The Drop

"He's not coming," I say, keeping my eye on the clock as we wait in the truck. I knew you fucked this shit up. I knew it."

John glowers. "Will you shut the fuck up?"

"No. Not this time, John. Do you know how much I need this money? Do you have any idea how much it costs to keep a parent in a nursing home? I'm drowning in medical bills and two mortgages because the housing market is shit in this town and a house that my parents lived in for over fifty years is now considered to be in a bad area. Of course the shit wouldn't be so bad if they had never taken out a second and third mortgage to pay *his* medical bills before he died."

"Are you done?" he asks.

I ball my hands and glare at his know-it-all face. "This is your fault. You spooked Fat Ace. He thinks that we're a bunch of narcs. I don't blame him."

"Wendi, chill the fuck out. I'll fix it."

"How? Are you going to just call him up and say 'Hey. We got those illegal guns you ordered. When can you pick them up?' "

John huffs out a breath, but he knows that he fucked up. "I said that I'd fix it. I'll fix it."

I shake my head. "This is a bad omen. Maybe we should just cut our losses. What if Hawkins said something to Fat Ace? You saw how hard she was grilling him a couple of weeks ago. For all our team knows, we could be under surveillance right now. She told you that she'd take us down. Maybe it's time to take her at her word." Paranoia has taken hold of me. For the millionth time tonight I wonder why I ignored my instincts about joining this run tonight. The money. It's always the money.

"It's been two hours," I tell John. "Let's just go."

John sits behind the wheel, chewing his bottom lip. "I *can* fix this, but first we need to seriously address our main problem."

"Oh? And what is that?"

"Not what. Who."

I sigh. The last thing I want to talk about is knocking off a fellow officer, let alone the city's new captain. "Count me out," I tell him. "This shit is not worth it."

"So how are you going to come up with the money to take care of your mom?"

"I'll figure something out." Though I have no idea what.

"Look. This shit will be simple. With Hawkins out of the picture, I'm sure that Chief Brown will promote me to captain. Once that happens, we're back in business.

"You have no guarantee you'll get that position. You said that she was pretty hot about your not responding to the department's calls and texts during the Ruby Cove massacre."

"She was. But don't forget the ace in our corner."

"Mayor Wharton," I say, nodding. "But what happens if he loses the election?"

"He won't lose."

"How do you know? Haven't you seen his slide in the polls?"

"Forget the fucking polls. We got to get this ball rolling again. You're not the only one feeling the financial heat around here."

John is heated, but I wonder how he can casually contemplate murdering someone he was partners with for years. Could he get rid of *me* with the same callousness? We're good fuck-buddies, but that's no guarantee of anything if I come in between his money. This shit is so fucked up.

"So what do you say?" John asks.

"What do I say to what?"

He faces me and holds my gaze so that he can read my reaction head-on. "What do you say about our eliminating Captain Hawkins?"

60

Lucille

"I think it's time to consider pulling her off the machine," I whisper.

Mason's anguished face snaps up. "What?"

I take a deep breath, swallow, but the lump in my throat refuses to bulge. "I know. I can't believe I'm saying this myself." Tears crest my eyes. "But I know my daughter, and there's no way that she would want to spend *years* on a respirator as a vegetable."

"Willow is not a goddamn vegetable," he barks, jumping to his feet as if it'll intimidate me. "We're *not* pulling the plug. She's going to wake up."

"Maybe." At least I hope so.

Mason stares as if I'm a traitor. "We're *not* giving up on her."

"I'm not giving up. There's a chance if we take her off the machines that she'll wake up."

A small chance. I don't add the last line, but it echoes in the space between us as if I had.

"No." He shakes his head.

"Sorry. But it's not up to you." I force myself to meet his angry black eye. "I'm her next of kin. The decision is *mine* to make."

"She's *my* fiancée. She's the mother of my child!" he yells.

"And she's *my* daughter."

"Give me a fucking break. You don't know shit about her," Mason thunders out, hurt and angry. "She couldn't stand you. You shouldn't be the one making the decision."

I lower my eyes and allow the tears to fall.

"Willow . . . doesn't understand the choices that I made. That's because she has always viewed me through the eyes of a child, but regardless of her resentment, I reject any notion that my daughter—my flesh and blood—hates me."

His nostrils flare in anger, Mason clenches and unclenches his fists. "You can't do this. I won't let you."

"I haven't made up my mind. I simply said that it's time to *consider* it."

We stare at each other while Willow's heart monitor beeps between us.

Then finally, "I swear, Lucille, if you do this, I'll make sure that you never have a moment of peace."

I laugh sadly. "I don't know peace now. If you haven't noticed, my family has been wiped out. My husband, my son—my daughter."

"And your lover?"

I gasp. His disrespect knows no bounds. "My relationship with Melvin was long, complicated, and *none* of your fucking business."

"Is that why you never told Lucifer that he was her father?"

I gasp again. I'm on the brink of a heart attack. "How did you know? Who told you?"

Mason laughs. "It wasn't that hard to guess." He sucks in a breath. "This is the type of shit that I've always wanted to avoid. Men like Melvin Johnson—aka Cousin Skeet—and my own damn father, running around town fucking everything that isn't nailed down. There are so many muthafuckas around here that are related and don't know it, it's ridiculous."

I lower my head in shame. Again, we're left to listen to Willow's beeping heart monitor.

"Were you *ever* going to tell her?"

I shake my head. "What would've been the point?"

"To get her to understand. She idolized Dough Man and hated Cousin Skeet, even though *he* was her real father." He laughs. "That's actually something else that we have in common. I just found out that a man I spent a lifetime hating is . . ." He sighs. "My head is all fucked up and I can't deal with that right now." He clasps Willow's hand. "All I want is for Willow to open her eyes. She and my son are all the family I need."

"If you pull the plug," he adds, "I'll make sure that you never have a place in your grandson's life."

His threat is a good one, a real solid punch to my heart and gut. "You wouldn't."

"C'mon, Lucille. You know me about as well as you know your own daughter. Am I the type of man who makes idle threats?"

No. My eyes burn at the thought of being cut out of my grandbaby's life. I may legally be Willow's next of kin—but as Mason Junior's father, Mason will be able to fulfill his threat to keep me away.

"I haven't made a decision," I whisper.

"Then I suggest that you seriously rethink pulling that plug." He moves away from the bed and heads for the door. "I need some air."

I hold it together as best I can until I hear the door close behind him. Then I bend over at the waist, sobbing. Of course I don't want to give up on my tough-as-nails baby, but I'm *not* wrong. Willow would not want to lie up in this bed forever while a machine keeps her technically alive. I'll give it some more time. But how much time? I move closer to the bed.

"Willow, sweetheart. I want to do right by you," I tell her. "I hope that you understand and believe that."

I grip her hand and will her to open those big brown eyes. "I could use a sign right about now."

Beep! Beep! Beep!

Crestfallen, I leave the room and search for Mason. I pass the Vice Lord soldiers keeping watch outside Willow's room and make a beeline to NICU. It's the only other place we split our time. But I don't see Mason. The floor is quiet; two nurses are stroking the backs of babies in the incubators.

"Are you looking for Mason's daddy?" a nurse inquires, approaching me.

"Yes. Is he around?"

"You just missed him. Said that he was going out to take a walk. He seemed a bit distracted."

He's mad. He's done this a couple of times in the past two weeks. "Thanks," I tell the nurse, and then go downstairs in search of my daughter's fiancé.

The moment I exit out of the hospital doors and into the cool night air, I see an SUV speeding toward Mason's back.

"Mason! Look out!"

The vehicle's revved engine must've caught his attention. Mason spins but doesn't dodge out of the way in time.

I scream as Mason is knocked back a good five feet, where he crashes into a parked car.

I rush forward as three big men jump out of the SUV and race to grab Mason.

"Hey! What are you doing?" I sprint, but my knees are bad. "Help!"

Regardless, the three suit-wearing thugs punch Mason, drag him to the Mercedes SUV, and toss him in.

I'm able to make it to within ten feet of the SUV before they pile back in and peel off.

"Stop! Wait!"

Tires squeal and the engine is gunned. Before I know it, the SUV is gone.

61

Cleo

I can't get my mind right. I'm a tough girl. I've always been tough, but something happens to you when a man violates you as if your humanity is of no consequence. It makes you feel so low that you want to crawl under a rock. *What am I going to do? Who is going to believe me? How am I going to get out of my contract with Diesel Carver?*

My family has been wonderful. Even my little cousins Jamie and Kay are in on the comfort train, bringing me hot tea and Granny's delicious pecan pie. In between those treats, I'm in the shower scrubbing myself raw but never getting clean.

Kobe is angry. Angrier than I have ever seen him. Yesterday, he paced around the house like a caged tiger. I have no doubt that if my rapist had been a random brothah on the street, Kobe would've murked the guy without a second thought—but Diesel isn't some random. Depending on who you ask, he's the third most powerful man in the set here in Memphis, not to mention the resources he controls from Atlanta. Toss in that he's also the man holding the golden ticket to take my career to the next level, and we're stuck between a rock and a hard place.

Diesel doesn't give a damn. He called my cell phone several

times earlier today. In each message he stated how he's only checking up on me and asked me to call him back. Does the muthafucka really believe that I don't remember what he and his Amazonian bitch did to me? Did Bullet and Beast also get in on the act?

I block that thought from taking root in my mind.

I haven't seen Kobe today. Maybe he's tired of watching my ass mope around this house without being able to do anything. *I shouldn't have told him.* It's another regret that I'll add to the list of regrets in my life. In addition to dealing with the rape, I'm still weeping for Kalief. I'm confident that his life was snuffed out because of me. Of all the vices he had, I'm the reason that he's no longer drawing breath.

Sleeping in fits, I wake up late and find Granny in the living room, stressed out.

"What are *you* still doing up?"

Granny sighs and turns away from the window. "Kobe isn't back."

"Where did he go?" I ask, continuing on to the kitchen to check whether we have any ice cream. There's a half gallon carton of butter pecan left, and instead of grabbing a bowl and scoop, I select the largest spoon in the dish holder and dig right in. When I return to the living room with my soul-soothing ice cream in tow, I realize that Granny hasn't answered my question. "Granny, where is Kobe?"

She avoids my gaze as she settles into her La-Z-Boy.

Alarm bells go off. "Please tell me that he hasn't gone and done something stupid."

She shrugs.

"Granny!"

Her gaze snaps up. "He's simply being the man of this house and protecting those who live under this roof."

"Oh my God." I stumble backward.

Granny refuses to look cowed.

"What have y'all done? Do you *know* who Diesel Carver is? Do you know what he can do to Kobe without hardly lift-ing a finger?"

"I don't give a damn who he is. Nobody comes after ours. We take care of our own. What happened to Essence will *not* happen again."

I shake my head, wondering how I'd forgotten that my granny has a strong thug streak in her. Kobe going after Diesel could be as much her idea as his.

"Oh my God." I spin around and drop the carton of ice cream in the kitchen sink before racing to my bedroom to throw on some clothes.

"What are you doing?" Granny asks, reaching my bedroom with remarkable speed.

"What do you think? I'm going to stop my brother from committing suicide." Jeans on, shirt on, I drop to the floor and search under the bed for my sneakers.

"You're going to do no such thing," she snaps back. "You let your brother do what he has to do."

"My brother doesn't need to *die* for me. That would make this a whole lot worse. Can't you see that?" I cram my feet into my sneaks and try to race past her.

"No!" Granny latches on to my wrist with surprising strength. "You stay here. I mean it."

It pains me, but I rip my arm out of her grasp and keep head-ing toward the front door. I sprint past the sleepy faces of Jamie and Kay, who've awakened to the sounds of my and Granny's arguing.

Granny, on her bad knees, hobbles after me out the front door. All the while, she demands that I get back in the house. For once the car starts right up, but as I peel away from the curb, I have no idea where I should go. The club? Diesel's house?

I have the option to call Diesel just to find out where he is, but realize that doesn't solve our main problem. We need help. We need power. There is only one place where I can get both of those things: *King Isaac.*

62

Nefertiti

In the SUV

Listening to Diesel and Beast land one punch after another on this Fat Ace character has my stomach rolling. It's bone crushing bone, and wet sounds signal that our victim is bleeding all over the backseat.

Fuck. Fuck. Fuck.

How do I let Diesel talk me into these illegal capers? But after a solid five minutes of this, I figure I have to remind them. "Don't kill him yet." That translates in my head to mean *don't kill him around me.* If they are going to make another mutha-fucka disappear, I'd prefer to know close to nothing about it. At least my reminder gets the punches to slow down. Hell, I'd be surprised if the man is even conscious. I didn't intend to hit Fat Ace with the car, but Diesel reached over, took control of the wheel, and pressed his foot on the accelerator.

"Y'all muthafuckas have picked the wrong brothah to mess with," Diesel sneers. "Where's that other little nigga at? Your brother Profit," he shouts.

Fat Ace grunts.

There's another hard punch across his jaw.

"We can do this shit all muthafuckin' night if you want to.

Y'all niggas thought it was fuckin' cool to roll y'all's asses down to my club and take money out of my pocket? Y'all sloppy muthafuckas don't know who the fuck you're messing with."

There are a few more punches, but I keep my eyes on the road.

Twenty minutes later, I pull behind Club Diesel. Before I can even shut off the engine, Diesel and Beast are dragging Fat Ace's big ass out of the vehicle.

I remain in my seat.

When the men reach the back door, Diesel turns around and hollers, "You comin'?"

It didn't really sound that much like a question—more like an order to get my ass in the building. As always, I pop out of my seat and rush to the door.

Once we get into the building, Madd and Matrix join in and the interrogation begins. "Just tell me where he is," Diesel repeats. "I understand that you don't want to rat out on fam. I understand your dilemma, but I know that nigga was here—I recognized him and your boy Tombstone on the tape. Tombstone did my ass a favor in committing suicide by cop. But your li'l bro's ass got to go, too. Bet that shit."

Silence.

Diesel whips out his .45 and blasts a hole into Fat Ace's left foot.

Pow!

Fat Ace's body jerks but he doesn't make a fuckin' sound. The second bullet blows open a kneecap.

Pow!

"Grrrrr!"

"Oh. Do I now have your fucking attention?" Diesel asks, nostrils flaring. Nobody expects this man to talk, so I can only guess that Diesel has only one real plan here: murder.

63

Cleo

Shotgun Row

My heart is in my throat when I knock on Momma Peaches's old home. It's strange to be over here when she's no longer here to hold down the fort. Memories of the block parties and barbecues that I've attended over the years flash in my head, but I remain focused on the current problem.

"Heeey, Cleo," Chantel greets, waving from her front porch. "Whatcha doing over here?"

Nosy ass. "I need to speak with Isaac."

Chantel looks me up and down. "Making a play for the crown?"

"What?"

She waves me off. "I don't blame you. Every bitch on the block is throwing their hat into the ring."

I roll my eyes and bang on the door. The idea of the neighbor keeping tabs on King Isaac's supposed booty calls is more than sad. After the banging grows desperate, a shirtless Isaac snatches open the door.

"What the fu . . ." He looks me up and down and a grin hugs his lips. "Li'l Ms. Cleo. What brings you to my door?"

My heart bobs in the center of my throat.

He lifts a curious brow when I remain mute. "Well, I don't believe in keeping a beautiful woman out in the cold. Care to come in?" He steps back.

Despite Chantel staring a hole in the side of my head, and my sudden terror at being around such a large and imposing figure, I step inside.

King Isaac's smile spreads as he closes the door. "I have to admit that I'm surprised to see you. Can I get you a beer?"

I shake my head. It'll probably be a long time before I accept a drink that I haven't poured or bottled myself.

"All right. Mind if I grab one?"

Again, I shake my head.

"It's a good thing that you can sing well. You're not much of a talker, are you?"

I flash a nervous smile. "Sorry."

"No problem." He strolls toward the kitchen, and though I've sworn off men, I note the impressive prison muscles and smooth swagger of the OG. Momma Peaches was a lucky woman.

Seconds later Isaac returns, taking a drink of his chilled bottled beer and staring at me.

I look around, nervous about how to go about this.

"Soooo . . . ," Isaac begins. "Would you like to join me in the living room? I'm in the middle of binge watching *Game of Thrones.*"

"I . . . I . . ." My throat squeezes shut. I march into the living room and plop down on the sofa.

Isaac eyeballs me. "Oookay." He strolls behind me. "You're going to have to help me out. How am I supposed to play a nervous, beautiful woman knocking on my door at this time of night?"

"I . . . I have a problem that I need your help with, and I don't know how to ask."

Silence.

I glance up. Isaac is still sipping and staring. "Is this favor money or . . . ?"

"It's my brother. He's about to do something really stupid, and I need your help to stop him."

Isaac laughs. "Can you be a little less vague?"

I swallow and go for it. "Kobe is going to try and kill your nephew Diesel."

Silence.

"Kobe . . . is no match for Diesel. I'm hoping that you could step in?"

"And why would I do that?" Isaac takes another drink. "I say good luck to him."

Stunned, I blink. "I don't think that you understand what I'm saying."

"Surprisingly, it wasn't that difficult to follow." He takes a seat in an armchair.

"You don't understand. Kobe isn't . . . strong. He isn't . . ."

"He's a soldier?"

I nod. "But—"

"Then I'm sure that he can take care of himself."

Tears spring to my eyes.

"Aww. Don't do that. I can't stand it when women cry."

"But you are my last hope. I've already lost a sister. I can't lose my brother, too. It's all my fault. I shouldn't have told him about . . . what Diesel did to me—but I was upset."

"What did he do to you?"

I keep my mouth shut and fight back a tidal wave of tears. "That . . . that isn't the point. I just need someone to stop Kobe. He's no match for Diesel. He's a monster. I mean, I'm sorry. I know he's your nephew."

"By marriage, but frankly I can't stand the son of a bitch. I'll send positive vibes in Kobe's direction. Other than that, I let men settle their own beefs." He tips up his bottle again.

I weigh my next words carefully. "What if I told you that . . . I think that Diesel had something to do with Momma Peaches's death?"

The bottle comes down. "What?"

I swallow hard under Isaac's hard stare. "That day, I found Momma Peaches in the church. Seconds before, I saw Diesel speeding out of the parking lot."

"Oh. That." He returns to his beer. "I know about that. It's not what you think."

Shit. "So you know about him paying his goons to shoot up her burial, too?"

Isaac's face changes. "What?"

"After we attended the funeral, he gave some excuse why we needed to head to the studio to work on my demo instead of going to the burial. But after the shooting, I saw Diesel paying one of his bodyguards a lot of money."

"That doesn't prove anything."

"Beast still had a gold flag hanging from his back pocket," I lie. I hold my poker face while Isaac stares again.

"Why didn't you tell me sooner?"

"I didn't think you'd believe me."

"And you think that I believe you now?"

I fucked up. He's not going to help. Diesel will kill Kobe. And it will be all my fault. *God, I need a miracle.*

Bang! Bang! Bang!

Someone hammers on the door.

Isaac sighs and turns. "I'm popular tonight."

I exhale and berate myself for not having a better plan.

"Well, I'll be damned. Old Ruff Dog! How the hell are you?"

"Good. Good. I hope I'm not disturbing you?"

My head bounces up as I catch the voice of Pastor Hayes.

"No. No. C'mon in." Isaac closes the door. "I know I didn't get a chance to thank you for the lovely service you helped me put together for Peaches. Except for the fireworks at the end, I'd say that everything went well."

Pastor Hayes's nervous laughter drifts in my direction. "Well, Peaches is why I came over," he says. "I got ahold of some disturbing information and I've prayed about what I should do about it. I went down to the police station, but then . . . the old

Ruff Dog came out and told me that I needed to bring this information to you to handle."

"Oh yeah? What kind of information are we talking about?"

"Well. A few months back the church installed new security cameras inside the sanctuary. I didn't know about it at the time. Ms. Josie handled most of the church business and things like that. Since Ms. Josie's passing, a few things have slipped under the radar. When the security company didn't get their last payment, they called me. I looked into it and found out that the cameras are set to record anytime someone comes into the sanctuary. Motion detection. Anyway, they were on the morning Peaches was killed."

I hold my breath as I listen in on the men's conversation.

"Are you fucking with me?" Isaac asks.

Pastor Hayes shakes his head. "Peaches was a good woman. She may have colored outside of the lines a time or two. But she was a good woman. She didn't deserve what happened to her."

The pastor holds up a disc. "I made a copy. You should see this."

Both Isaac and I stare at the silver disc.

Pastor Hayes finally notices me. "Oh. Cleo. I didn't know that you were here." His face darkens.

"It's okay," I say. "I want to see the footage, too."

Isaac takes the disc from the pastor and walks over to the DVD player beneath the large-screen TV. By the end of the recording, we're all left speechless.

64

Hydeya

At home, I step out of the shower to the sound of a ringing phone in the bedroom. I throw a towel around my body and rush to answer the call, just making it before the call goes to voicemail.

"Hello."

"Yes. May I speak to Captain Hawkins, please? It's an emergency," a frantic woman shouts.

"This is Captain Hawkins," I tell her.

"Oh. Thank God. You gotta come. Hurry. They grabbed my son-in-law right here in the parking lot."

"I'm sorry. What? Who grabbed who from where?"

"I'm sorry. This is Lucille Washington. I'm at Baptist Memorial Hospital and I just witnessed my—Mason Lewis—being kidnapped by a group of thugs."

Oh shit. I race over to my chest of drawers and pull out clothes. "Do you know who grabbed him? Were you able to make out any faces?"

"No. No. It all happened so fast."

Shit. "What about the vehicle. Did you catch a license plate or get a good description?"

She cries. "No. Oh my God. They are probably going to kill him, aren't they? Oh God!"

"Mrs. Washington, please. Calm down. You probably know a lot more than you think you know." I hop into a pair of panties and then slap on a bra. "You said thugs grabbed him. Do you remember how many?"

Silence.

"Mrs. Washington, are you still there?"

"Yes. Um. There were three guys who jumped out of the SUV. They were wearing suits. And—"

"Suits?"

"Yes. Suits. But I think it was a woman behind the wheel. I'm not one hundred percent certain, but I'm fairly sure."

"Okay. Okay. Good." I shimmy on a pair of black jeans and grab a white T-shirt. "Now what kind of vehicle were they driving?" I ask because it's a standard question. I already know that the answer will be a black SUV, so I'm stunned when Lucille's answer is a silver Mercedes SUV. I freeze. "I'm sorry. What was that?"

Lucille repeats her answer.

There's only one gangster rolling around in an expensive car like that: *Diesel Carver.*

"Okay, Lucille. I may have a hunch. Let me call you back," I holster my weapon.

"Are you sure? How long will it be before you get here?"

"I'm not sure. I'll call you back." I race out of my bedroom and up the hall. But once I reach the living room my strides slow. *Why is the balcony door open?* A noise behind me has me diving to my left without turning around. Before I hit the floor, I do manage to spin my body around with my weapon in hand.

The dark figure blasts two shots.

I return fire.

"Aargh!" The figure falls back but doesn't drop.

I fire again.

My intruder crashes against the brick wall, his arms flail and knock Drake's urn off the shelf over the fireplace. It tips over and clunks my intruder over the head. He finally hits the floor.

I stare at the figure, stunned.

Then someone else is moving—running—back toward the balcony.

"Freeze!"

The second intruder keeps moving.

Pow! Pow!

"Don't shoot! Don't shoot," a woman screams. I make a move to the light switch. When the lights flick on, I'm stunned shitless to be staring into a face I know. "Officer Hendrix?" With my gun still trained on her, I turn my head toward the motionless form on the floor.

The dead body of Lieutenant John Fowler.

65

Mack

Germantown

"How did it go?" I ask Profit when he climbs back into the car.

"Do you see the patrol car?" he snaps. "How the fuck do you think it went?"

I glance back to the backseat where Romil gives me the *I told you to stay out of it* look.

"What did she say?" I press.

"Just drive," he snaps. "I want to get as far away from this place as possible." Profit slumps down in his seat and turns his solemn face toward the passenger-side window.

"Did you—"

"Drive, goddamn it! Stop asking me so many damn questions. Are you writing a book?"

I'm not accustomed to having muthafuckas yell at me. I reel in my temper. I have to cut the young pup some slack; he's in a lot of pain right now.

Starting the car, I, look up at the house a final time. Ta'Shara is in front of her bedroom window. "Oh. There she is," I point out.

Profit doesn't look. "Drive."

This was a bad idea. It had taken me days to get Profit to

agree to bring Ta'Shara her stuff, and all my work was for nothing.

"Take me to the hospital," Profit says. "I want to check on Mason and Willow before we head home."

I bob my head. Profit makes it a point to check in on his brother every night. Their bond is strong. I'd imagine that it's hard to be strong for other people when you're falling apart yourself. During this time he's trying to show support for Fat Ace's current situation, but who's got him?

"How long have you known?"

"How long have I known what?"

"Kill the dumb act," Profit snaps, turning away from the dark scenery outside of his window. "You know that Ta'Shara is crippled. That's the whole reason you set this shit up. Well, I know now. Happy? That shit doesn't change anything. She treats me like something stuck to her . . . fucking wheelchair. She's doesn't want to have anything to do with me!"

Romil pipes up. "Maybe she's just scared. I know that I would be."

The car falls silent.

Romil continues, "Maybe *we* should talk to her again. See where her head is at?"

"No," Profit snaps. "She's made her decision and how I feel doesn't factor into shit. She wants me out of her life, then good riddance. No more begging from me and no more cock-blocking from you. Are we clear?"

Silence.

"Are we clear?" he thunders.

"Clear," Romil and I answer.

But in my head, the wheels are turning.

66

Lucille

"Please hurry. Hurry." I keep my eyes peeled on the hospital's parking deck for any sign of Captain Hawkins or the police. My heart races like crazy. Somehow I got to keep it together. The other Vice Lords who were strategically placed around the hospital are now all having a shit fit.

The Mason grab happened so fast that none of them were at the right place at the right time.

Two patrol cars turn into the parking lot. I struggle to push myself up out of my chair in the main lobby. The hospital security guard beats me out of the sliding doors and relays my version of events to the police.

A white officer with a bulging belly and skinny legs rolls his eyes before the security guard finishes with his briefing. The cop's partner, an equally fat African American man, shifts his attention to me as I reach the group.

"Are you the witness in this kidnapping, ma'am?"

"Yes. Yes, I am," I tell him. "It all happened so fast."

"We have it on surveillance video," the guard says, cutting me off.

This is the first I hear of any of this being on video.

"Can we take a look?" the white cop asks.

"We got it all cued up and ready to go for you," the guard informs them.

Everyone bobs their heads and proceeds to follow the security guard, myself included, until Profit walks through the door.

The Vice Lord soldiers spot him and gather around him.

"Wait. What?"

I pull up from following the officers just as Mason's men point toward me.

"Ms. Lucille," Profit calls, rushing toward me. "What's this about my brother being snatched out in the parking lot? By who?"

"I don't know," I tell him. "There were four people in a Mercedes and—"

"A Mercedes?" he questions. "What kind of Mercedes?"

"A silver one, but it was like a SUV."

"A GL class?" he asks.

"Oh, baby. I have no idea. I recognized the emblem. The three men were in suits and I believe the driver was a woman." I jut my thumb over my shoulder. "I called that nice captain of police. She said that she was on her way over. But the hospital also called the police and—"

"That's okay. I think I may have an idea who has him." He turns and runs out of the hospital.

67

Hydeya

It's strange to call the police to my own house. It's even stranger to see everyone's expression when they recognize the dead body lying on my living room floor. But the good thing about capturing Officer Hendrix alive is that there is collaborative testimony about her and Fowler breaking into my home. With the department knowing how Fowler and I have been going at it, my word alone might not have been good enough.

However, when Hendrix is pressed to explain their motivation for trying to kill me, she clams up and refuses to speak without her lawyer. It takes everything I have to not bash in this bitch's brains.

"What are you doing with that?" I ask an officer on the forensic team.

He blinks up at me while holding Drake's urn. "I'm packing it. It may be the actual murder weapon."

"It's justified homicide. Self-defense," I remind him.

He swallows hard. He doesn't know how to respond to that. Chief Brown is en route and I keep dialing my father's cell and praying each time for him to pick up.

"Yeah," he answers, agitated.

"Dad!" I turn my back to the forensic team.

"Dad?" he questions. "Who is this? And what have you done to my daughter?"

"Look, Dad. I don't have time to fuck around. I need you to check out a hunch."

"Excuse me? First you arrest me and now you want me to help you with your hunches?"

I ignore the sarcasm. "Fat Ace has been kidnapped."

Silence.

"Dad? Are you still there?" I plug a finger into one ear in hopes I can hear better.

"Really," Isaac follows up. "Couldn't have happened to a better guy. Look, I have another problem—"

"Dad, you got to go over there and help him."

"Now I *know* that you've lost your mind. That muthafucka—"

"Dad." I take a deep breath. "He's your son!"

Silence.

"Dad?"

"What are you talking about, Hydeya? I've already heard some of this nonsense from Python . . . Are you telling me he's right?"

"Mason Lewis is Mason Carver—and according to your wife's letter and the DNA test I had run, he's *your* son. Your blood flows through him as much as it flows through me. I don't need to know all the particulars. It's true. You got to find Diesel and stop him before it's too late."

Silence.

"Dad?"

"Diesel has Mason?"

"Isaac, I wouldn't bullshit about something like this."

"Fuck. I gotta go."

"Go where, Dad? Where would Diesel take him?'

Silence.

"Dad, please!"

Click.

68

Nefertiti

Club Diesel

"I know you're not planning to smoke this fool before I get a go at his ass."

Everyone's head whips around to Python's imposing reptilian figure. He steps forward from his two bodyguards, June Bug and Kane.

"Cuz." Diesel lowers the weapon from Fat Ace's bleeding face. "What are you doing here?"

"You made such a big stink about the hit on your club, I came by to see the damage for myself." He stops and looks around. "You're right. Looks like the Vice Lords fucked your shit up pretty good."

Diesel steps back while Bullet moves forward. I watch this with growing dread. Nothing about this shit feels right.

Python's black gaze locks onto Fat Ace. "I gotta hand it to you, your ass did the impossible and captured this piece of shit gangster."

Diesel lifts his chin. "I was handling some business that has nothing to do with you."

Python nods and then strips off his black T-shirt, cracks his neck and then his knuckles. "I call dibs. I've been wanting to get at this muthafucka for years."

Unbelievably, Fat Ace rolls his bloody head around and laughs. However, it's not a normal laugh. The sound is demonic as hell and gets my skin crawling. I look around to find an escape route.

Diesel appears to be at a loss for words. He wants to handle this shit himself, but doesn't want to step on the wrong toes.

Fat Ace's laughter dies down. He locks his disturbing, mismatched eyes on Python. "Give me all you got."

Python charges. "Aaargh!"

Fat Ace climbs to his feet as Diesel steps out of the way.

Bam!

Python hits Fat Ace with a full body tackle, knocking Fat Ace to the floor. Fists fly as the men send blow after blow upon each other. The soldiers circle around like they are in a Thunderdome cage. Cheers go up for each punch Python lands on the muscular giant.

I duck, flinch, and mumble "Jesus" a few times, but I can't look away. Before long Diesel smiles and joins the cheering crowd.

For a time, Fat Ace rallies, knocking the wind—if not the holy hellfire—out of Python. Frankly, I've never seen a man with fists the size that Fat Ace slings around. Each time those boulders crash against Python's chest, side, or face, I wonder how the fuck Diesel's cousin is even breathing.

"They're going to kill each other," I whisper.

Somehow Python gets the tide to turn back in his favor. Before anyone knows it, he rains punches like a souped-up machine.

Soon, Fat Ace doesn't look like he can take much more. The energy goes out of the man. It's as if he's decided to stop fighting, as if he figures he has nothing to live for.

"C'mon. C'mon. Fight," I urge.

Diesel twists his head in my direction.

I shrug, as if answering his silent question: Why am I rooting for a man he was going to kill himself? The truth is that I really don't know, other than I always tend to root for the underdog.

That is, until another wave of soldiers, all flagging black and gold, burst in with a hail of bullets.

The Vice Lords.

Pow! Pow! Pow!

Rat-a-tat-tat-tat

Alarmed, we look up at the gold-and-black-flagging soldiers spilling into the club. My heart leaps into my throat. I spin around, wanting to get out. There's no chance of that. The exit I'd mentally selected bursts open—more men carrying scary weapons.

"Aww. Shit." I back up into Diesel. "Tell me that you have a plan to get us out of this shit."

He grunts as our own people lock in around us. Had we been in Atlanta, no doubt we would be on solid footing and would stand a better chance going head-to-head with any of these sets.

Within the Thunderdome circle, Fat Ace and Python stop fighting. Both look like hell.

A young man steps forward, a cute young thang.

"Profit," Diesel growls, eyeballing the kid.

"What? Him?" I squint. "Are you sure?"

Diesel's cold gaze follows the kid's every move. I place my hand over his hand that's holding the gun, and shake my head.

"Sorry to interrupt," Profit boasts. "Our invitation must've gotten lost in the mail." He smiles.

He's a cutie.

The Vice Lords outnumber the Gangster Disciples. What's going to happen next?

"Bruh, you all right?" Profit asks.

Fat Ace nods, swiping blood from his mouth. "Yeah." He

struggles to his feet but with an open kneecap, it's damn near impossible. But then he drives a punch across Python's jaw. Blood sprays across the floor.

"Fuck you, nigga!"

Python laughs. "You're a big man now. If your little brother hadn't come to rescue your ass, I'd pound you into the ground. You killed my aunt, asshole. As long as I have breath in my body, I'm coming after you for that shit. Believe that."

Fat Ace laughs.

Diesel whispers, "We have to get the fuck out of here."

"You have a trap door that I don't know about?" I ask.

Fat Ace's laughter titters out. "We've been beefing a *long* time," he starts. "We dropped a lot of bodies over the years; all for different reasons and advantages. I have no problem owning up to the shit that I've done. The one thing that I *didn't* do was kill your precious aunt."

"You mean *our* aunt, don't you?" Python hisses. "You can change your last name if you want, but we both know that we have *some* of the same blood coursing through our veins, bruh."

The club erupts with buzzing whispers. Everyone struggles to keep up with the damn conversation.

Fat Ace's lip twitches. "Yeah, bruh. *Our* aunt." He looks around the room. "You heard that right, guys. The world's worst secret: Terrell—mind if I call you Terrell?" He plows ahead without waiting for a reply. "Terrell and I are brothers. Blood brothers. We were both born to a crack-addicted prostitute who, in my case, didn't know the difference between a baby's bed and an oven. Fuck her. And fuck you. It takes more than blood to make someone family. See that boy over there?" He points to Profit. "He's my *real* brother. We don't share a single strand of DNA between the two of us. You, on the other hand, don't mean shit to me. But I still did not kill our aunt Peaches. She was already shot when I arrived."

"Liar!"

"Why the fuck would I lie? Look around. My soldiers have you surrounded."

A new voice booms into the room. "I wouldn't say *completely* surrounded."

Every head turns as King Isaac and a new wave of Gangster Disciple soldiers pour in from another door.

"Aww shit." I move closer to Diesel, only to find that he's no longer standing there.

Weapons come up and my ass crouches on the floor.

"HOLD YOUR FIRE," King Isaac commands, and both Vice Lords and Gangster Disciples heed his words. Once it's clear that not a single bullet is about to be fired, King Isaac walks down the center of the club, straight toward Fat Ace and Python. Once he's in front of Fat Ace, everyone expects Isaac to take a swing, but instead he takes his time walking around and staring the man up and down.

Fat Ace lifts his head.

"You know already, don't you?" King Isaac asks.

Fat Ace doesn't respond.

"Yeah. You know," Isaac concludes.

"Know what?" Python asks, looking confused.

Isaac draws a deep breath. "That I'm his father."

The whispers start up again.

Shit. "This is some good ass tea," I whisper. It's like watching *All My Children* on a cliffhanger Friday.

"What?" Python twists toward King Isaac. "How the fuck . . . you and my mother?"

King Isaac nods. "And Mason here isn't lying about your aunt Peaches," he adds and looks up to his men. "Bring him in here."

The Gangster Disciples part and a man is escorted down the center of the club. Even Cleo Blackmon is here.

"Everyone knows Pastor Hayes from the Power of Prayer Baptist Church?" King Isaac asks.

"Humph. A pastor," I mumble, wondering what's happening next.

"Pastor Hayes here wasn't always a man of the church. Once upon a time, he was a foot soldier for me back in the day. We called him Ruff Dog."

A few snickers go up.

"Ol' Ruff Dog brought me something mighty interesting tonight." Isaac reaches into his leather jacket and pulls out a disc.

"What's that?" I whisper, swept up in the moment.

"This," Isaac says as if hearing my question, "is a recording of what went on at the Power of Prayer Church the morning Peaches was killed. It shows that Peaches' longtime frenemy and neighbor, Josephine Holmes, shot her that day in the sanctuary."

More whispering ensues.

Python looks confused. "What? But I saw—"

"Mason and another woman arrived minutes later. It looked like they were helping her when you and Diesel showed up."

Silence.

Nobody knows what to say or do after that revelation, my ass included.

"But Josie's bullet isn't what killed my wife. The bullet that killed her came from the very person she never trusted. Your cousin, Diesel Carver."

"Oh shit!" A hand wraps around my mouth. Startled, I attempt to scream, but that option is taken from me when Beast snatches me.

"Shhh. We have to get you out of here," Beast hisses.

"Where the fuck is Diesel Carver?" King Isaac thunders, looking around the crowd. "Bring me that muthafucka. I want his fucking head on a goddamn platter."

"This is bullshit!" Diesel shouts before firing his weapon. He aims his weapon and fires.

Python lunges in front of a confused Fat Ace. The bullet hits Python squarely in the chest. He careens backward into Mason. Chaos breaks out and more bullets rip through the crowd.

Beast, Bullet, Diesel, and I reach a wall and to my surprise the muthafucka swings open and we rush into a secret room. Diesel takes the rear. Madd and Matrix are nowhere in sight. "Move! Move! Move!"

Seconds later, the room leads us to another door that dumps us outside. We scramble to Diesel's Mercedes and take off with gunshots and police sirens sounding off in the background.

69

Cleo

Python has been hit. The Gangster Disciples go for their weapons and the Vice Lords respond in kind. King Isaac stands tall while bullets fly all around him. "Somebody stop that muthafucka!"

I'm in shock. These things always happen faster than anyone's mind can comprehend them. Pastor Hayes pushes forward, shouting for me to help him render aid. It's a weird scene, with Python lying against Fat Ace's large body, struggling to breathe.

"We need a doctor," King Isaac shouts, dropping next to the two men. "Terrell, hang in there."

Mason is confused. "Why the hell did you do that, man? Are you crazy or something?"

Bullets zing around us.

Python stares up at Fat Ace. "It . . . it . . . was all my fault."

"What was all your fault?" Mason asks.

Pastor Hayes jumps in. "I need something to help stop the blood." He looks around. "Try to stay calm, Terrell."

"Mason!" Profit fights through the warring crowd. "Are you hit?"

Fat Ace shakes his head but remains focused on Python. "Help me understand. Why did you take the bullet?"

"I'm sorry. I . . . put you in that oven. Not Alice. It was me."

"What?" Fat Ace's expression hardens.

Python coughs up blood but is determined to get out what he has to say. "I panicked because I dropped you . . . I didn't mean to hurt . . . it was all my fault. You slipped. I panicked."

"Terrell, please. Don't talk," Isaac says.

Pastor Hayes takes off his jacket and adds pressure to the wound. "We've got to get him to a hospital."

The two Vice Lords look at each other. It's a strange situation. Are they going to help a sworn enemy?

"We also got to get these knuckleheads to stop shooting," King Isaac adds.

Python grabs Mason's arms and pleads, "I destroyed so many lives. I should have been a better big brother to you. I should have . . . I should have . . ." He licks his lips while sweat breaks out across his forehead. "I'm sorry. I'm so sorry."

Fat Ace caves. "It's okay, man. Save your breath. It's all good."

"Yeah?" Hope lights within Python's eyes, but then he coughs up more blood. "I wish . . . I wish mom and aunt Peaches was here to see this." When he smiles his teeth are covered in blood.

He's not going to make it.

Fat Ace gives his long lost brother a smile. "I'm sure that they are looking down on us right now."

Python's smile grows as he clutches Fat Ace's hand.

My vision swims as the scene plays out. The shooting behind me fades. The club doors burst open and a swarm of police pour into the scene.

"Freeze! Police!"

The chaos grows as soldiers from both color lines scramble. I turn my head for less than thirty seconds and when I glance back down, Python is dead.

70

Hydeya

Club Diesel

It's hard to make heads or tails of what has taken place here. A good number of gang members from both the Vice Lords and the Gangster Disciples managed to take off through the back of the club, but we also captured a fair number of them, too. However, I was not prepared for the bloody scene surrounding a deceased Terrell Carver.

"Are you okay, Dad?" I ask, touching Isaac's shoulder.

"Dad?" Mason looks up.

I nod. "I've been trying to tell you."

Profit shakes his head. "I can't keep up with this shit."

Pastor Hayes mumbles a prayer over Python and then closes his eyes. "I pray that he finds peace."

Mason shakes his head. "He saved my life after damn near beating me to death. I don't get it."

"Your brother has always had a soft spot for you," Isaac fills in. "All the years that you were gone tore him up inside. I had no idea the extent to which he blamed himself. A lot of us blamed ourselves. The Carvers looked for you for so long . . . I can't believe that you're really that kid—that you're *my* kid."

"Let's hold off on the family reunion," Mason says. "I'm . . . I'm going to need more time to process all of this."

Isaac nods. "I understand."

We exchange awkward looks before Mason adds, "I'm not saying that we can't eventually get there. I'm saying that I need time."

Isaac tries to suppress a smile, but fails. "Absolutely."

I sigh. "Well, I hate to break all of this up, but . . . Dad, I'm going to have to ask you to assume the position."

"What? You're arresting me again?"

"Afraid so."

71

Nefertiti

Beast rockets our asses across Memphis at a breakneck speed. Everyone's adrenaline is at overdose levels, but none of us know what the fuck to say. I attempt to work out what all this means.

"I should've killed that muthafucka when I had the chance," Diesel scolds himself. "If I'd put him down before Python got there, none of this would be happening."

"There still would have been the surveillance tape," I remind him and then turn in my seat. "Really? You killed your own aunt?"

Diesel rolls his eyes. "It was a snap decision. She wanted to get those two lost brothers back together, and I was trying to save my investments."

"And how did that work out?"

"It would have worked out fine if King Isaac's ass was still behind bars. Ever since his release I've been scrambling around plugging one hole after another on a sinking ship."

No shit. "Are you calling up reinforcements?"

"Fuck no. I can't go up against both Vice Lords and Gangster Disciples. King Isaac will come after me with everything that he's got for killing Aunt Peaches *and* trying to kill his son. *His son?* The fuck?"

"Yeah. I wasn't prepared for that curveball either."

We whip into Diesel's estate and then file out as fast as we can.

"Grab the essentials and meet back down here in fifteen minutes," Diesel orders before heading to the safe in his study.

I race up the staircase to the master bedroom. The second I walk through the door, I am stunned shitless to see Solomon, Diesel's beloved Doberman pinscher, slaughtered in the center of the California king-size bed.

Screaming, I backpedal out of the bedroom.

Bullet and Beast appear out of nowhere to see what's going on.

"The fuck?" Beast asks.

"Who would do something like this?" I ask, shaking my head.

Pow!

We jump.

"Boss?" Beast shouts, leading the charge back down the staircase. We hit the brakes when we reach the study, and throw up our hands. Six Gangster Disciples stand there with their blue flags tied over their mouths. On the floor lies Diesel, the side of his face blown open.

"Diesel!" I race forward, but get snatched back by Bullet. "Noo."

"Muthafucka raped my sister," one man hisses before kicking the side of Diesel's head. He raises his weapon toward us. "I bet y'all muthafuckas had something to do with it, too," he shouts.

Beast opens his mouth to say something, but is immediately silenced when the man fires off his weapon.

Pow!

Beast drops to the floor.

Bullet releases me and runs.

Pow!

Warm blood splatters all over me. *This isn't happening. This isn't happening.*

"What about you?" the leader asks. "Are you in on this shit?"

Fuck. I can't get my mouth to work.

"Who are you? Are you involved in this shit?"

I shake my head with no hope that the lie will save my life.

"Who are you?" he demands.

"Ne . . . Nefertiti," I answer, swallowing.

He tugs his flag away so that I can see his whole face. His resemblance to Cleo Blackmon is striking. "What is your relationship to Diesel Carver?"

I hesitate.

"I asked you a fucking question!" He aims at me.

Unable to think, I confess, "I'm . . . I'm his wife."

The man lifts a brow. "Wife? I didn't know this nigga was married." He looks to his guys. "Did y'all know this shit?"

Everyone shakes their head.

"Did you know that you were married to a fuckin' rapist? How do you feel about that shit?" He closes in, his gun pointed at my head.

I sob and shake like a leaf. *He's going to kill me. He's going to kill me.* I close my eyes and wait for the bullet.

It never comes.

I peel open my eyes to stare Diesel's killer in the face.

"You didn't see shit, did you?" he asks.

I shake my head.

"Good. Get your ass out of here before I change my mind."

I spin away and run for my life. Luckily, Beast left the keys in the ignition of the Mercedes. I peel out at top speed and don't let up until Memphis is in my rearview mirror.

Dreams

72

Hydeya

Six months later

"**S**ix Memphis Police Officers Arrested on Corruption Charges"

This morning's headline in the *Commercial Appeal* put a huge smile on my face. Finally, the department is racking up a lot of wins. Of course, some in the department aren't seeing it that way. I am. The city's gang violence has drastically come down in the wake of Mason and Isaac forging a truce between the Gangster Disciples and the Vice Lords. Many don't believe that the truce will last, but I'm betting that it will.

Things aren't looking too good for Mayor Wharton. Internal Affairs took over my investigation into our department. They didn't find enough evidence to back Officer Hendrix's claim that the mayor was involved in the illegal arms dealing, but the accusation is enough to have him down twenty points in the polls a week out from Election Day.

My profile has improved. Mostly because of the recovery of wanted felon Terrell Carver's body and the Vice Lords and Gangster Disciples truce. Exposing the police corruption within weeks of going on maternity leave is a nice feather in my hat and has the national news media burning up my phone line.

I move from my kitchen to the living room and spot Chief Brown on the news, taking as much credit as she can for *my* work. Given the crestfallen looks from the mayor, I gather their secret love affair is over.

Right now, I need to get the house ready. My mother is coming tomorrow. She's staying for a time to help me prepare for the baby. She's also been on my case about quitting the force. Before, that sort of talk would've been out of the question. But as my pregnancy progresses, I think about retiring more every day. My job was on the road to destroying my marriage. I don't want it to come between me and my child. I have a lot of options. I'll take my time weighing each one. But it's good to have a stronger relationship with Isaac. I was able to convince the district attorney not to charge him in the Club Diesel shooting, since I was the reason that he went down there. A few of his flunkies took the hit, but that's street life.

Mason and Profit were also not charged with anything. Mason, in this case, was the kidnap victim after all. So once his foot and knee were reasonably patched up, he was free to return to Willow's bedside, albeit with a cane, where she still lies in a coma. I don't have too much hope that she'll pull through this. The doctors are telling Mason and Lucille almost every day that there's nothing else that they can do for her. A decision on whether to pull the plug will have to be made soon.

73

Mack

Ruby Cove

"Ta'Shara is moving to Houston," I tell Profit when he answers his door. Once again, I'm breaking my own rules about staying out of muthafuckas personal business. I can't help it. These two lovebirds haven't figured out how much they belong together.

Profit blinks for a few seconds. "What?"

"You heard me." I shove him aside and Romil and I storm into the house. The place is a pigsty. It looks as if he has permanently moved into the living room. While the rest of Ruby Cove adjusts to this new truce with the Gangster Disciples, not too many people have seen Profit in daylight. I perform a small spin around the room, careful not to touch anything. "This is so sad."

"Mack, why are you here?" he asks, exasperated.

"I told you. Ta'Shara is moving to Houston to be with her other fake grandma. She got her GED and now she's heading west. So what are you going to do about it?" I settle my hands on my hips.

Profit tosses up his hands. "What the hell *can* I do about it? She doesn't want to have anything to do with me. I'm tired of begging her to take me back. Enough is enough. If she wants to go, then she can go. I don't care."

Nobody in this house believes that.

"Profit, I know that you're hurt, but this may be your last chance. You got to ask yourself, is Ta'Shara rejecting you or is she rejecting our lifestyle? C'mon, you knew from the jump that she didn't belong on Ruby Cove. She's smart and talented and she actually has dreams about being a doctor. How does that fit in over here?"

"So you're making her argument?"

Romil sighs. "What means more to you—Ta'Shara or the Vice Lords? That's the question that she's waiting for you to answer. She can't live in your world. Can you live in hers?"

74

Ta'Shara

Memphis International Airport

Today is the big day. I'm leaving Memphis. I can hardly believe it. I fluctuate from being happy to being sad almost every five minutes, but I'm determined to see this through. I need a new start. It's too difficult to move forward when everywhere I look, my old life and old ghosts haunt me. I'm determined to prove that Reggie and Tracee were right to believe in me. Their attempts to give me a better life will not be in vain.

LeShelle still haunts me, but less today than six months ago. I'm not sorry for killing her. If given the chance, I know that she would've done the same to me. It's sad that our relationship descended the way that it did. Once upon a time, we loved each other, protected each other. The streets changed all of that.

Reggie Senior and Mary took my decision to live with Olivia pretty hard, but deep down I know that they understand why. The compromise: They agreed to visit Houston every year for Christmas.

Overhead, I hear an attendant announce that my flight has been delayed. The waiting passengers at the gate grunt and groan as I whip out my cell and text Olivia the update.

With more time on my hands, I shift the wheelchair toward the large window overlooking the planes and runways. It's always amazing to watch things so big and heavy take off and land. Before long, I'm playing a game of guessing where each plane is either going to or arriving from. Then I think about taking all those dream trips that Profit and I will never share.

"I hate flying."

I tense. *Profit.* When he doesn't say anything else, I wonder if my mind is playing tricks on me. I turn my chair around.

He smiles. "Surprise."

For a long moment, I can't get my mouth to work or get my heart rate to slow down. "What are you doing here?"

"I came to get my girl back," he says simply. "Of course, that's if she'll have me."

"But I . . . I . . ." My gaze falls onto my legs. "I can't stay here."

"I didn't say anything about you staying. I get why you have to leave. I'm not here to force you back into a life that you've never wanted to be a part of."

I blink up at him, surprised. Tall, muscular, and extremely sexy, Profit looks like the perfect GQ thug fantasy. He takes my breath away in his black jeans and black T-shirt. Behind him, I catch other women checking him out.

He kneels down beside me so that our eyes can connect. "It's taken me awhile to hear you. I get it. I'm walking away from all of that. It's not the life I want if you're not a part of it. My life is wherever you are while you become whoever you want to be. So . . . if you're going to Houston, then I want to go with you."

"But . . . your family?"

"Families live in different states all across the country. What I need to know is whether you can love me again—can we build a new and different life together."

"But . . . my legs. I—I may never walk again."

"Maybe not. Then again, maybe you will. Whatever happens, I want to be right there, crossing that bridge with you. And if need be, I'll carry you anywhere you want to go."

"You'd give everything up for me?" I ask, stunned.

He nods. "You damn right I will."

My vision blurs as I cup my hands over my mouth. I can't believe that this is happening.

"So what do you say?" he asks. "Do you think you can love an ex-gangbanger?"

Without hesitation, I throw my arms around his neck and shout, "Yes!"

75

Lucille

This is one of the saddest days of my life. Willow has been on life support for seven months with little to no improvement. Mason Junior is now at a healthy weight and we go every day to the hospital to visit his mother. He's a good-looking kid. I'm proud to say that he got most of his looks from Willow. They have the same eyes and mouth. He has no idea of the hell she went through to deliver him. I doubt that he truly understands that she is his mother.

Today is the day *we* decided to pull the plug. There is no reason for us to delay this any longer. Ever since Mason Junior was cleared to go home, I've worked steadily to help his father carry the heavy burden of being a single father. He's doing great. There's no doubt how much he loves his son. It's probably what pushed him to talk to his own father, Isaac. Time will tell how all of it plays out.

When Mason and I walk into Willow's room, we both have a hard time looking each other in the eye. This was not an easy decision.

Mason walks up to the bed to allow his mini-me to give his mother a farewell kiss before handing the child over to me. Then he pulls up a chair and takes Willow by the hand. "Baby . . ." He takes a deep breath. ". . . I've been searching for the words that I

would say to you today—but there are no words that will con-
vey what we're all feeling at this moment. We love you and
miss you." His voice chokes off. He coughs and begins again.
"Thank you for giving me such a wonderful and precious gift:
Mason Junior. I'll make sure that he grows up to be strong and
smart. With the streets cooling off, who knows? Maybe one
day we'll get rid of the idea of their being a throne to rule out
here in the streets. I'm still getting to know Isaac and my new
sister, Hydeya. It's going to take some time before we all gel,
but . . . I think you'd be proud of us mending bridges. I regret
that my pride got in the way of us doing it sooner. Profit
would be here, but he's moved out west—to Texas, believe it or
not. Him and Ta'Shara are going to make it. I feel it in my
bones. And he's happy. I guess that's all that matters."

I lower my head because I know this rambling speech is
difficult.

Mason continues. "I'm going to miss you, baby—but I want
you to know that it's all right for you to go. It's not fair for me
to keep you lingering like this. I know that you wouldn't want
to stay this way forever. I guess what I'm saying is that I'm
ready to let go. I pray that one day we will see each other
again. Tell Bishop I said hi and that all is well down here." He
stands, and then leans over and presses a kiss against Willow's
lips. "I love you, baby. I'll always love you."

My sobs grow louder and Mason Junior pats my head and
comforts me. I say my goodbyes and then we look over to the
doctor and his nurse and give him the signal to shut off the
machine.

The doctor presses two buttons and then excuses himself
from the room. We've been informed that the process can take
anywhere from minutes to days. It all depends on Willow right
now. Months ago we attempted to pull her out of the coma
and she suffered numerous seizures. This time, we're not re-
versing our decision. We're determined to stay here for as long
as possible.

Mason keeps vigil next to the bed while the baby falls asleep on my lap. We've mastered the art of sleeping in these hard chairs. Hours later, Willow's heartbeat remains strong and no seizure has occurred. I leave only to change the baby's diaper or to grab something to eat in the cafeteria. We doze off at different times, but we wake up when Willow croaks, "Mason?"

Stunned, we spring up to see Willow's confused brown eyes looking around.

"Willow!" I gasp. "My God! You're back!"

Epilogue

Vivian

In the near future

"**A**re you ready?" my girl, Rhonda Barnes, hisses from across the dark room.

Smiling, I open my eyes and toss back the covers. I'm fully dressed for tonight's house party. "Girl, my ass was born ready."

We giggle and pop out of bed, arranging the pillows underneath the covers so that it looks like we are still sleeping. Once that's done, we grab our things and creep to the window, careful not to wake the other girls in the next room. We don't have time to deal with jealous bitches.

My ass isn't going to be here much longer. I'll be eighteen soon, and then I can put this group home in my rearview mirror.

Once our feet hit the ground, we take off running and cover three blocks in Olympic time and find our girls, Cassie and Kay, waiting for us in an old Toyota Camry.

"Hop in, y'all. Our asses are late."

"We're not late," Rhonda argues, snatching open the back door and climbing inside.

I shoo her over to the other side so I can climb in.

"I'm moving. I'm moving." Rhonda laughs.

"Let's roll." I slam the door.

Kay peels away from curb like a rocket while Cassie turns up Dr. Dre's classic "Nuthin' but a 'G' Thang" to full blast.

"Hey. Hey. Turn that shit down," Rhonda barks.

"Fuck that. This is my jam." Cassie plants her blunt between her lips and proceeds to bob and wiggle in her seat.

Excited, I bob and wiggle along with her.

Rhonda doesn't look impressed.

"What's the matter with you? I thought you liked the old-school shit?" I ask.

"I do. It's these whack-ass speakers that I can't stand."

Kay looks back through the rearview mirror. "Look, bitch. I can pull over and your ass can walk."

My giggle is out before I slap a hand over my mouth. When Rhonda's gaze cuts over to me, I shrug. Best friends are supposed to have each other's back, but sometimes Rhonda's quick quips are uncalled for and unnecessary.

"Whatsup? I thought you said that your cousin Cleo was going to buy you a new car. Why are you stuck driving her old clunker if she's such a big star?"

Kay gives Rhonda a look that says my girl is fucking with her high. "*Again.* You can walk."

Rhonda shrugs. "I'm just asking. Seems stingy on those benjis, if you ask me."

"Nobody asked you," Kay reminds her.

I elbow my girl.

"Whaaat?" she snaps instead of picking up on the hint.

"Cut it out," I hiss. "We're trying to have a good time. Why are you fucking it up?"

"I'm not," she whines.

"Y'all want to hit this?" Cassie asks, holding up a blunt.

"Fuck. You know my ass." I grab the joint and take a drag. Instantly, I'm high—thank God. Being in the clouds is so much better than dealing with my fucked-up reality of living in a girl's group home. My ass should be used to the system. Lord knows that I've spent most of my life bouncing from one institution to another. But no one ever gets used to it.

My brothers Amin and Malcolm told me once that we were dumped in foster care because the state declared our mother unfit to take care of us. We were only supposed to be here for a short time—until our mother got herself into a better situation. Malcolm believes that the whole thing was bullshit and that she was never really coming back. The fact that she was savagely murdered on some desolate road in the boondocks hasn't softened his opinion on the matter. Amin doesn't have an opinion. As far as he's concerned, it doesn't matter. It doesn't change anything.

I wish that I could remember her better. I have this one memory of her watching us play in the park. From what I remember, she was tall and beautiful with micro blond braids. She was also very, very pregnant. I asked her for a sister. I remember her laughing and smiling.

The blunt makes another pass my way and I greedily hit it again. As Kay coasts out of midtown and over to the seedier side of town, my mind tumbles backwards to that last day in the park with my mother, Yolanda. Over the years, I've wondered whatever happened to the baby some crazy-ass monster sliced out of her belly. Is it dead or alive? Is it a boy or a girl? He or she could be living in a nice home with loving parents—or he could be like us, floating through the system until that magical eighteenth birthday. I wonder—if we ever walked past one other, would we recognize ourselves in each other? Of course, I'm being silly, but it would be nice if it happened. I still want a sister—but I'll take another brother.

Amin is already nineteen, but instead of taking legal guardianship of Malcolm and me, he enlisted in the army and got the hell out of Memphis. I don't blame him. I'm going to leave, too. I'm thinking California or New York. I could act, sing, or paint. I don't care. As long as it's doing something creative.

Malcolm, well. I don't know what's going to happen to him. He went from foster care to juvenile detention. He's still lucky because the guy he shot when he was fourteen survived his wounds. Had he died, they would have tried Malcolm as an adult and he could've gotten life in prison. Malcolm says he doesn't care what the state does with him. Sometimes I believe him and sometimes I don't. I mean, he has to care about something, right?

Kay turns onto Shotgun Row and we nod to the lookout boys hugging the corners. The moment we hear the bass bumping from the house party, Cassie shuts off Kay's radio. "We're heeeeeere," she announces excitedly.

Rhonda and I go for our purses so that we can check our makeup.

"Are you nervous?" Rhonda asks.

"Nervous? Why would I be nervous?"

She leans over and elbows me. "C'mon. Who are you fooling? The only reason you wanted to come to this party is because your man lives here."

Flushed, I wave her off. "I don't know what you're talking about. He's *not* my man."

"YET," all three girls shout in unison.

I flash them two birds. "Fuck y'all."

They giggle and cackle like hyenas as we climb out of the car.

I feel a rush of nervousness as we trek up to the house. This is my second time out here in Gangster Disciple territory. I'm a bit nervous because shit is always popping off down here and I don't want to be a casualty of a random drive-by.

The party looks dope as shit as the crowd has already spilled out into the yard. Everyone it seems has either a drink or a blunt in their hands.

"Ah, damn, li'l momma. Where have you been all of my life?" Khaled, an old nigga who is at least two or three decades too old to be hanging out with teenagers, says, strutting into my personal space while holding his dick as if he's scared the muthafucka is going to run off.

"Ewww." Kay and Cassie twist up their faces.

When I snicker, it sets Memphis's oldest teenager off.

"What are you ghetto bitches laughing at?" he barks. "You know each one of you would be lucky if I let you hop on this dick and ride."

"Boy, bye." Rhonda loops her arms through mine and tugs me up the two steps.

"Girl, who you talking to?" Khaled follows us.

"Ignore him," Rhonda says.

I try to, but remain aware of him catching up to us.

Then like a knight in shining armor, an older man steps out of the house to aid our escape.

"Khaled, get your old ass away from around here."

Rhonda's grip on my arm tightens. "That's him."

My eyes grow as large as two silver dollars. *King Isaac.* The man is a legend—and so is his deceased old lady, Momma Peaches. On my first visit to my grandmother Betty's house last summer, Momma Peaches was all that she could talk about. Grandma Betty went on about how Momma Peaches was a criminal and how she sliced up a good man that Granny was in love with. She did that instead of explaining why *she* couldn't take in me and my brothers instead of letting us rot in the system. After she did that, she spent a lot of time bad-mouthing my momma, too. Malcolm was right. It was a wasted trip.

"I—I'm leaving," Khaled stutters, backing up and bumping into people.

"Hey! Watch it!" A GD soldier swipes some spilled liquor off of his arm.

"Oh. My bad. My bad," Khaled apologizes.

King Isaac folds his arms and watches Khaled make a fool of himself as he tries to hurry away.

Once he's gone, Isaac turns toward us with a softer expression. "You girls good?"

"Y-Yeah." I nod. "Thanks."

He smiles. "Then y'all come on in and grab yourself something to eat and drink. My boy is around here somewhere." With his tall height, he easily glances around the heads of the crowd. "There he is. Yo, Chris!"

Christopher Carver turns and glances in our direction and Kay quickly grabs my other arm.

"Oh, my God. I'm going to die," she whispers under her breath.

When Christopher's dark gaze shifts toward us, he flutters a brief smile and lifts his plastic cup in greeting before returning his attention to the other popular boys in his posse. As soon as the spotlight is off, Kay's grip eases and the blood in my arm circulates again.

"Oh God. Did you see how he looked at me? You do think that he was looking at me, right? Wait. How do I look?"

I laugh as we move through the dancing crowd. "You look fine," I assure her. Of course, I don't know what the hell she sees in the boy. Christopher Carver is *not* exactly easy on the eyes. In my opinion, he has a face that only a mother could love. His body, on the other hand, isn't all that bad.

"Well, don't laugh," Kay says as we arrive at the table in the kitchen, where all the refreshments are displayed. "But one day, watch, he's going to be mine."

"Well, all right, girl. Mark your territory." Cassie holds up a hand and receives a high five.

I nod along.

"What?" Kay stares pointedly at me.

Confused, I answer her question with my own. "What?"

"What's that look for?" she challenges.

"What look?"

"Girl, stop playing. I know that you don't like Chris. You ain't gotta fake it." Anger and hurt are written all over her face.

"No," I lie again, but she cocks her head. "Okay. I just don't see what you see in him. You can do better."

"Better than the Prince? You know that's what they are calling Christopher. Isaac is grooming him to be the next leader of the Gangster Disciples. If he becomes king, you know what that'll make me."

"Head bitch of the Queen Gs," I say, nodding in understanding.

"That's right. And let me tell you, a lot of these trifling hoes sniffing around him are trying to hop up on the throne—but, baby, that bitch got my name written all on it." Kay lifts her bottle of beer and taps a toast against my own longneck.

"You go, girl." I take a long, hard pull and then we all struggle to make our way back to the heart of the party.

Minutes later, I'm cornered by a guy who's in my math class at Morris High. He throws his best game at me, but the whole time, he doesn't realize how badly his breath stinks. Not even when I cover my mouth and nose with one hand. I sneak a quick look around to see whether my girls can help me out, but different soldier boys have them cornered too, running game.

Then *he* walks in, the new boy at Morris High, the one that I've been crushing on for the past two weeks.

Cassie must have escaped from her admirer, because the next thing I know she's squeezing in between me and stank breath and pulling me away. "He's here," she whispers into my ear.

"I know. I know. I see him." And boy, do I see him. He's about six-four with a nice peanut-butter brown complexion. The body is banging, too. I mean, he must spend the hours he's not in school pumping weights.

In no time, Kay and Rhonda return, both asking whether I

see who came through the door, despite the fact that I can't seem to take my eyes off of him.

"Yeah. I see him."

"Yo, nigga! You came." The Prince laughs, greeting my crush at the door. The new guy is younger than me, but he doesn't look it. And I hear he's smart too. He's skipped two grades and I have been held back one. So he'll graduate just a year after me unless he skips another grade before then.

Kay and I watch both boys slap palms and shoulder bump each other. I don't know why, but our dream boys have become fast friends at the school. It's the main reason I knew that he would come to this party.

As he moves through the room, I mentally beg him to look in my direction. It takes him a whole five minutes to do so. When he does, my hearts skips every other beat.

He excuses himself from the Prince and his boys and strolls toward me.

Oh my God.

"He's coming this way," Rhonda hisses excitedly.

My girls giggle and I shush and tell them to calm down.

"Hello," he says in the smoothest voice that I've ever heard. "You're Vivian, right?"

"Yeah. That's right." I glance to my sides, and my girls have disappeared. When I gaze back up to his eyes, there's a connection that I can't explain. I love everything about him. From the nice curl of his hair to his smoldering eyes and that cute horseshoe-shaped birthmark on his neck. I don't know whether this is what falling in love feels like, but I know that we're meant to be in each other's lives.

"Well, it's nice to meet you, Viv. I'm—"

"I know who you are," I tell him. "You're *Jayson.* Jayson Barrett." His kissable lips spread into a smile that takes my breath away. Deep down, I know that this night is going to be the start of the rest of our lives together.

Dear Reader,

I have to tell you that when I first began I had no idea where this rabbit hole would lead, but I let the characters in my head just lead me around by the nose until the final conclusion. I still can't believe that it's over—or is it? I got a feeling when meeting the Prince (Christopher Carver), Jayson and Vivian (Yolanda's children), as well as Kay Blackwell (Cleo and Essence's cousin), that some things are doomed to repeat themselves. I don't know. We'll see. But thank you again for being a loyal reader of this series. I can't tell you how much your emails and social media postings have sustained and inspired me.

Also, it's important for me to always stress that I do not advocate, condone, or encourage the behavior, lifestyles, and violence my fictitious characters engage in. Though some storylines are inspired by real headlines and personal experiences, along with a good dose of creative liberties, this series is meant for entertainment purposes only—not unlike books about vampires, serial killers, and magical wizards.

I hope that you enjoyed the last installment of the Divas series. I look forward to seeing your responses.

Best of love,

De'nesha Diamond

QUEEN DIVAS

De'nesha Diamond

ABOUT THIS GUIDE

The following questions are intended to enhance your
group's reading of QUEEN DIVAS

Discussion Questions

1. Life never goes the way we plan. It took a street massacre and life-altering handicap to get Ta'Shara to reconsider her life choices. Do you agree with her decision to leave Memphis? Should she have agreed to start her life over with Profit, or should she have made a clean break?

2. Mack had to point out to Profit that it was the lifestyle, and not him, that Ta'Shara objected to. Profit, as the next heir to the Vice Lords throne, walked away for love. When it comes to relationships, how do you know which one of you is supposed to bend? Is it too much to expect men to be ride-or-dies?

3. Lucifer miraculously survived the Ruby Cove massacre, but then sustained a head injury during a car accident, which led to a brain aneurysm right after giving birth to her son. However, when she wakes, she is the last diva standing. Do you agree that she's the queen of the divas, or does she own the title by default?

4. In Python and Mason's third head-to-head matchup, the brothers get bloody, but then the truth is finally discussed and Python makes his confession. Why do you think Python placing his brother in the oven was the *one* thing that he couldn't get over? With his dying breath, he sought forgiveness. Did he deserve it?

5. Cleo got her dream record contract, only to learn that her new manager is a monster. Given Diesel's reach and influence, do you agree with her decision not to take her sexual assault to the police? Have you been, or known of anyone, placed in this situation? How do you think she should have handled it?

6. Hydeya puts the pieces of her family puzzle together and also brings down the police department's corruption. Do you believe that she can still be effective in her job, or should she take early retirement simply because of who her father is in the streets?

DON'T MISS

The Score by Kiki Swinson
Identity-theft mastermind Lauren Kelly and her lover and accomplice, Matt Connors, have always had a taste for the finer things. When their partner, Yancy, stumbles onto a tycoon's multimillion-dollar bank account, Lauren expects everything will go smoothly—until she discovers Yancy and Matt are planning the ultimate betrayal . . . Fortunately, Lauren is one step ahead of Matt. And once she disappears with every last dollar, they'll have no doubt they chose the wrong woman to deceive.

ALSO AVAILABLE

Red Hot Liar by Noire
Mink LaRue is an heiress to an oil dynasty's mega-fortune. But this expert con-mami will have to go beyond the top of her game to win the biggest hustle of all . . .

Her Sweetest Revenge 3 by Saundra
Mya Bedford's hopes for a normal life, free from the hustle, seem more distant than ever when her best friend's fiancé is shot, Mya's husband is thrown back into the game, and a ruthless new crew hits the streets of Detroit. Now, through the most bitter of tears, it's time for her sweetest revenge . . .

31901064305701